HALL
OF
SMOKE

HALL OF SMOKE

H. M. LONG

TITAN BOOKS

Hall of Smoke
Print edition ISBN: 9781789094985
E-book edition ISBN: 9781789094992

Published by Titan Books
A division of Titan Publishing Group Ltd
144 Southwark Street, London SE1 0UP
www.titanbooks.com

First edition: January 2021
10 9 8 7 6 5 4 3 2 1

A CIP catalogue record for this title is available from
the British Library.

Printed and bound by CPI Group Ltd, Croydon CR0 4YY.

To Grandpa Ian, with love

ALGATT, EANGEN, AND THE NORTHERN TERRITORIES OF THE ARPA EMPIRE

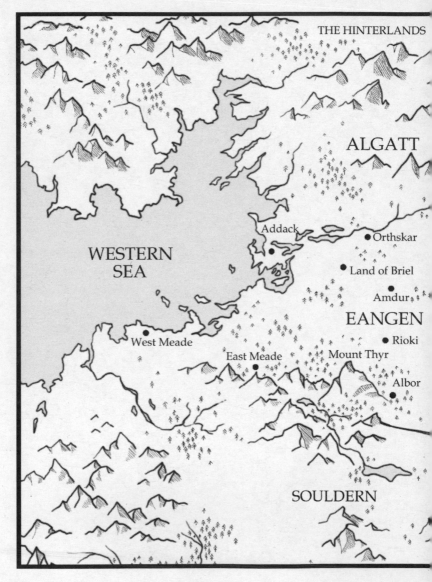

THE HINTERLANDS

ALGATT

WESTERN SEA

Addack

Orthskar

Land of Briel

Amdur

EANGEN

West Meade

East Meade

Mount Thyr

Rioki

Albor

SOULDERN

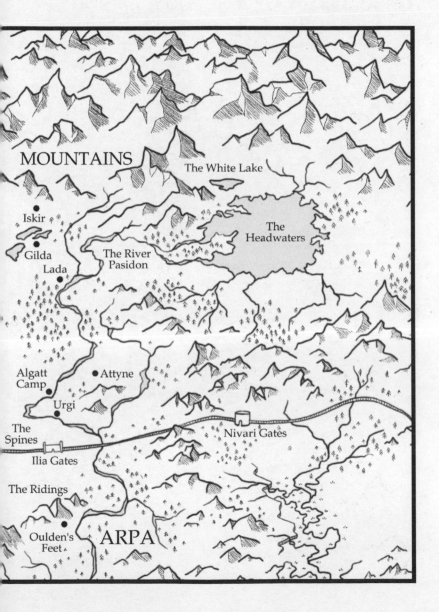

MOUNTAINS

The White Lake

Iskir

The Headwaters

Gilda
Lada

The River
Pasidon

Algatt
Camp

Attyne

Urgi

The
Spines

Nivari Gates

Ilia Gates

The Ridings

Oulden's
Feet

ARPA

ONE

The shrine in the meadow before me was little more than a weathered collection of beams and tiles and stark angles. Poppies were scattered around it, fluttering under the gathering skies, and wood was stacked beside the low stone altar. But there were no ashes in the offering bowl, no scuffs on the earthen floor – only a handful of dangling bones, grey feathers and carved owls.

I was the first to offend the goddess this season.

I pulled warm air into my lungs and sagged against a nearby tree. Higher up the mountain, unyielding evergreens dominated, but here the forest was more varied. I stood under fresh summer leaves and filtered sunlight, each lending me a sense of protection as I willed my legs to stop shaking and eyed the shrine of Eang, Goddess of War. My goddess.

The wind gusted, sending the poppies reeling and pushing me towards the waiting shrine.

I forced myself to move, leaving the shelter of the tree and stepping out into the meadow. The mountaintop came into view on my left, bracketed by looming rainclouds, while forested foothills, streams and small lakes spread in every other direction. A town – a ring wall containing mossy thatch roofs and trails of smoke – lay down there. My family, my people, lay down there. And, if the goddess heard me, I would return to them by nightfall.

I pried my eyes from home, stifled the fear in my chest, and focused on the shrine. Before I passed into its shadow, I eased my worn legs into a kneel.

"Eang, Eang." I whispered the name of my goddess and pressed my palms into the earth. The beaded leather tying my braid fell beside them with a soft thump. "The Brave, the Vengeful, the Swift and the Watchful. I've come to pledge atonement. I…"

My confession stuck on my tongue. The breeze increased and the patter of my heart turned into a torrent. I cracked open my eyes and saw the poppies, blood-red and black-eyed, arching in the corner of my vision.

"Eang, please don't kill me," I whispered. "I didn't know it was him."

My lungs didn't seize. No beast leapt from the forest to justly devour me. The breeze merely departed, and the trills of songbirds took its place.

I crawled into the cool of the shrine and pulled my tinderbox from the pouch at my waist. I didn't stand again until I had lit a fire in the offering bowl, and even then, I kept my head bowed.

Back on my feet, I opened the fine scars on the ends of my fingers and let droplets of blood fall, one by one, into the flames.

The rain began as I stepped outside to finish my prayers. I supposed I deserved that, but I still gritted my teeth as I took up position, straight-backed, head bowed, palms open beside my hips and facing forward. My left hand, the one I had cut, stung fiercely. I deserved that, too.

Inside the shrine, fire danced for the goddess, but I was forbidden from sheltering beneath its roof. So, I stood under the open sky while the rain ran through my hair and soaked my tunic, darkening its pale green into a deeper, clinging shade.

"Eang," I began again. "In your name I sheltered a traveler in the Hall…"

The rain continued, steady and mild. I brushed the back of a salty hand across my mouth and adjusted my stance, the memory of an unassuming smile on a bearded face playing through my mind.

"I didn't know he was an Algatt, Goddess. I didn't realize he was the one until it was too late and then… I was weak. I didn't heed the vision. Please, hear me."

Blood and rain ran down my splayed fingers, converging at the tips in a steady pink drip.

"Let me go. Let me find him." Something blasphemous and bitter coiled inside me in resistance, but I kept speaking. "I'll finish the task you gave me."

The rain increased. I let my hands relax and stared at the fire. It burned brightly against the damp and gloom, but nothing unnatural happened. The High Priestess had assured me that there would be a sign if the goddess accepted my pledge. I had seen those signs before – one didn't grow up in the Hall of Smoke, the seat of Eang's priesthood, without witnessing them.

But nothing happened now. The fire didn't whisper. No owl called from the pines. The smoke didn't twist into a recognizable shape.

I turned full circle, scanning the tree line. Poppies sagged under the rain and thrumming on the roof of the shrine filled my ears.

A minute passed. Then ten. Twenty.

I wrapped my arms across my chest. I couldn't go down the mountain without a reply – I was an exile, and not just from my home, my hearth and my family. There was no salvation for a disgraced priestess of the Goddess of War. No place in the High Halls. If Eang did not speak, my soul would remain in the earth where my forsaken body would eventually fall, exiled and imprisoned until the Unmaking of the World.

The thought made me pale. I shivered and clutched at my arms more tightly, searching the trees again. I couldn't wait here forever, could I? I had no more food. No blanket. No dry clothes. A Climb of Atonement was not intended to be a comfortable experience, even without rainstorms.

I tightened my resolve, ignoring the fear that turned my stomach. Eang was simply making me wait. She would reply. She would accept my pledge. She had to.

Because, if she did not, I could never go home.

~

3

I made myself a second, more modest fire under the shadow of a bent pine on the north edge of the meadow, just enough to lend a little light and protection from the gathering night. Beyond the dripping boughs, the meadow's poppies closed their petals and the half-light of the storm relented to true dark. Eventually, the fire I'd lit in the shrine was all I could see. Then it retreated too, turning into a low, flickering belly of coals.

I closed my eyes. I should have gone back out into the rain, rekindled my offering fire, reopened the painful scabs on the ends of my fingers and prayed again. But my tunic was still wet and the meadow so open, so empty.

I ground my teeth. I was no High Priestess, but I was still a vassal of the Goddess of War, with the scars under my sodden tunic to prove it. One night on a mountain alone should not have made me feel so vulnerable.

But this was more than one night in the rain. This darkness felt like a warning, a glimpse of what the rest of my days – my eternity – would be if the goddess would not hear me.

A stick cracked.

I shot to my feet, smacking my head on a branch and sending a shower of cold rain and pine needles down my scalp and back. Even as I cursed and tried to shake needles from my hair, my hand fell to my belt. No sword. No axe. Just my small ritual knife, barely longer than my thumb, its simple wooden hilt darkened with age.

Another crack.

My heart, already battering against my ribcage, threatened to rupture. My knife was likely useless against whatever was out there – whatever beast Eang was sending to tear me to pieces – but the goddess had given me other methods of defense.

My heel slipped back and I dropped low as a familiar, unnatural fire welled up in the back of my throat. I watched the darkness, steadying myself and letting the heat grow.

The rain pattered and wind rustled the treetops, far above my damp hair. Whatever was in the forest drew closer, edging around trunks and boughs and boulders.

4

My fingers twitched and power seeped onto my tongue.

"Hessa?"

I wilted, half in shock, half in relief. The heat extinguished as a shadow separated from the darkness and stepped into the firelight, pushing back the hood of his cloak. Dark red hair, damp with rain at the brow. Brown eyes, creased with worry that contrasted the soft, unhappy smile tucked into his beard.

A woman came behind him, her lithe form ducking around boughs with all the height and grace that the gods had neglected to give me. Seeing the look on my face, she rounded the fire without a word and embraced me.

In her arms, the cold of the night and the well of anxiety in my stomach lessened. But I didn't have time for consolation.

Before she could speak, I cleared my throat and peeled away. "You shouldn't be here."

"Neither should you. You should have returned before dusk," my cousin Yske retorted, resting one hand on my bare neck before she released me. Her eyes lingered on my throat. "They cut off your collar?"

Compulsively, my own gaze dropped. A bronze ring, little wider than the tip of my smallest finger, rested against the tawny skin at the base of her throat. Firelight caught the ring's fine runes, twined into endless patterns. Brave, vengeful, swift, watchful. They were the qualities of our goddess, the first words of our prayers, and the heart of our identity as warrior-priests – as Eangi.

"Why didn't you come home?" My husband took my cousin's place in front of me. I sidestepped, but the movement was half-hearted and when he pulled me into his chest, I didn't resist. The scent of him – smoke, leather and sweat – disarmed me, thick with memories of a shared childhood, urgent kisses and bloody battlefields. The scent of my husband.

I felt the shape of his own Eangi collar against my temple and pulled back.

"Eidr, stop." The words came too fast. I narrowed my stinging eyes and pointed down the mountain. "This is sacred. You can't be here."

Eidr grabbed the back of my head and kissed my forehead, gently but firmly. "I pledged myself to you," my husband reminded me, holding my face close. "Yske is your blood. You may have been cast out of the Hall of Smoke, but you cannot be cast out from us."

I couldn't hold his gaze, so I looked down at his chest and brushed at the embroidered collar of his tunic. As kind as the words were, they were just that – kind. If Eang refused to shrive me, neither he nor Yske would be able to remain at my side. I wouldn't let them.

"You'll not suffer for my sins, either of you." I separated myself from him again and dragged damp hair from my face. "You need to leave."

"Hasn't she spoken yet?" Yske interjected.

Eidr would not back away, so I did. I put the fire between us and raised my chin, hoping that neither of them could see how badly I wanted them to stay. What if the goddess never spoke and this was the last time I saw them?

Yske spun the clasp of her cloak and pulled it free, revealing a tunic of mild blue, undyed leggings and the knife at her belt. "You're shaking. Wear this, Hessa, please."

"No," I said, proud of the fact that my voice didn't waver. "I ignored a vision from Eang. I broke a vow. I deserve this."

Yske and Eidr exchanged a glance, then Eidr's hand slipped beneath his own cloak. When he withdrew it, he held a hatchet.

"You can't give me that," I snapped.

Eidr gave me a weary look that failed to conceal his concern. "I won't. But Yske and I just climbed a mountain in the rain and I'm cold. If you want to go sit out there and be wet, do it, but I'm going to find some dry wood – somewhere – and build up the fire."

My throat closed. Eidr shouldered off into the night and left me alone with my cousin.

Yske swung her cloak back around her shoulders. "The fire in the shrine is almost out."

I gazed back across the dark meadow. Sure enough, the warm glow of my offering fire was nearly extinguished.

I looked back at her, coaxing my expression into impassivity. "I have to go tend it. By the time I come back, you need to be gone. Both of you."

Yske shrugged and, setting my shoulders, I slipped back out into the rain.

But by the time I had finished rekindling the goddess's fire, watched my blood bubble in the flames and offered my prayers, Yske and Eidr had not left – not that I'd truly expected, or wanted them to. Instead, they had set up a makeshift camp, using Yske's cloak as a shelter, and as I returned Eidr settled himself on a somewhat dry log beneath it. Lifting one side of his own cloak, he nodded to the open space.

"Sit, wife."

I smiled. It was a compulsive, sudden thing that hurt more than my bloody fingers. The title was still novel, only a winter old.

Still, I reasserted, "You shouldn't have come."

His expression hardened, light from the fire he'd built up turning his face into a mixture of warm ridges and familiar hollows. "I'll say it one more time. The High Priestess might have cast you out, but we will not abandon you."

Yet, I added in the quiet of my mind. But it wasn't a matter of abandonment, however he chose to cast it for himself. I was the one at fault, and I was the one that would have to leave forever.

My breath grew shallow at the thought and my resolve, already fragile, weakened. Eidr and Yske were Eangi too, I reminded myself, and unsullied ones. They belonged at this shrine as much, if not more, than I did. Who was I to make them leave?

Yske lifted the other side of Eidr's cloak and wedged herself in without invitation. Resting the back of her head against the man's shoulder, she eyed me. "Who's to say the goddess didn't send us to make sure you don't die of stupidity?"

I raised my brows. "Then she'd hardly send you," I retorted, though the humor felt stale.

All the same, Yske grinned a nose-wrinkling grin and kicked her heels out towards the fire.

"Sit," Eidr broke in. "You made your climb; you made your sacrifice – twice – and there's nothing that forbids you from sheltering at someone else's fire."

I looked back at the shrine. It was well-lit now, my offering set to burn into the morning hours. Perhaps they were right. Perhaps I could sit for an hour at my husband's and cousin's sides, just until my shivering stopped and my clothing began to dry.

"You need to be back before anyone realizes you've left," I said. Then, more soberly, I repeated, "I'll not have you suffer for my sins. Please."

"Fine," Eidr agreed. "Now sit, my arm hurts."

I rounded the fire and sat down.

In the half-light of dawn, Eidr's warm chest left my back and Yske's soft breath, inches from my forehead, moved away. I couldn't bear to say goodbye, so I pretended to sleep on, holding still as Eidr wrapped his cloak around my solitary form and kissed my temple.

I sat up only once their footsteps had been replaced by the trills and lilts of birdsong. The rain had stopped, leaving the world dripping, scented with green and earth and damp. Our campfire had died off, but the one in the shrine burned more brightly than ever. Yske or Eidr must have stoked it.

That gesture alone was enough to make my eyes prickle. Why was I doing this? If Eang hadn't responded by now, did she intend to at all? Yes, the goddess was not everywhere, but she would have heard my prayers. This was her shrine, a place where something of her essence always remained – a place where the fabric between the human, Waking World and the divine High Halls was torn.

Eang knew I was here; there had to be another explanation for her silence. Maybe, I thought, I should go back to town and consult the High Priestess. The idea was a tantalizing one, undergirded with the promise of seeing Eidr and Yske again. Maybe I could still catch up to them.

No. I reined that thought in. The sun was breaking through the canopy, the poppies were unfurling, and my blood was required in the offering bowl.

I crossed to the shrine in the cool of the dawn, pulling my ritual knife and flexing the wounded fingers of my left hand. But as I passed into the shadow of the structure and prepared to slit my thumb for the third time, the sight of dangling feathers and carved owls distracted me. My apprehension turned outward. Upward.

Eang was wildly powerful, ancient and undying, but she was not immortal. Almost no god was – at least, not naturally. What if Eang ignored me because she was in battle? What if she didn't respond because she couldn't? It had happened before.

That thought gave me all the determination I needed. Banished or not, I was an Eangi priestess, and I owed it to my deity to be patient.

I reopened the cuts on my left hand and let the blood drip. I prayed. Then I sat down in the meadow and sunlight, dangled my stinging fingers over my knees, and began my vigil once more.

The morning passed. The sun roosted high above the peak of the mountain, my frizzing black hair burned with heat, and I left my post to drink from a stream. The cool water took the edge off my thirst and the aching hunger in my belly, but only just.

When the rain started again, it was almost a relief. I let Eidr's cloak stay in the shelter of the pine tree while I lay among the poppies and closed my eyes, relishing the droplets of cool water on my face and scalp. Above me, the blue summer sky reverted to the same muted grey as the evening before.

Eidr and Yske would have returned home hours ago. They and the rest of our order would be watching the mountain, waiting for me to join them.

"Eang, Eang," I murmured, willing my words to be heard across distance, time and the division between worlds. "The Brave, the Vengeful, the Swift and the Watchful…"

The rain pattered down on my cheeks, my lips.

"Eang, please."

War horns blasted up the mountainside.

TWO

B ranches. Rain. Mud. Rock. There was no time for aching muscles or precarious footing; instinct propelled me down the same path that had brought me up the mountain the day before – the same path Eidr and Yske had taken back to town that morning.

The horns came again, long, drawn-out wails that ended in two high blasts. Eangen horns. Another bay followed them, this one lower and culminating in a twisting, deep crack. Algatt raiders.

There were raiders at the foot of the mountain, raiders in my home while I spent hours stumbling down a mountainside. Hours during which my people fought and died.

Eidr. Yske. I let out a frustrated, gasping choke and plunged through the forest.

Raids were relatively common. In the south, along the border with the Arpa Empire, farmers battled unsanctioned taxation from rogue legionaries. In the north, the mountains unleashed Algatt raiders once, sometimes twice yearly, initiating weeks of skulking and skirmishing. My own mother, far away in the village of my birth, had been killed in one such raid five years ago – the kind of loss everyone in my world shared.

Scars from fighting off raiders this spring were still fresh and pink under my clothes. But by now, the Algatt should have retreated to their northern mountains until harvest. That was their way. That was how it always was.

Was this my response from Eang? Was this my punishment for

disobedience? The thought crept into the back of my mind, but it was too horrific to hold onto.

Could this raid be my fault?

By the time I sighted the town of Albor, the Eangen horns had long since stopped. I skidded to a halt on an open bluff, staring down into the valley through misty rain and billows of smoke.

My heart dropped. The great timbered Hall smoldered in the center of the town and the circular embankment around the settlement, with its wooden walls and crude towers, was a wreath of flames. The bulk of the fifty homes were still intact, but outlying farmhouses were already ash.

Nothing moved in the town or fields. The only signs of life were riders rounding up flocks on the eastern horizon, sending ewes and husky lambs skittering after the low, spreading bulk of their horde.

My knees threatened to buckle. I was too late. Eidr, Yske, nearly everyone I loved – they were down in that smoking ruin or carried off over the horizon.

I clutched at a sapling and felt myself crumpling towards hysteria. I had been frightened last night at the shrine, but this – this was a feeling I hadn't had in years: the inexorable slide of fear building into a rampant charge. If I let it go, it would tear through my mind like a winter wolf.

But there would be survivors. I blinked, focused on the swaying sapling beneath my hand and the wind on my face. Algatt raiders never killed – or took – everyone.

I dropped off the bluff and landed hard on the forest floor. As I ran, I saw the Hall of Smoke in my mind's eye, whole and vaulted and filled with warmth. Eidr and Yske were there with a hundred other familiar faces, moving around the central hearth, carrying and weaving and sharpening and singing. They wrapped themselves in furs in the winter; in the summer, they returned from the river at dusk, wet-haired and laughing.

The Hall belonged to the Goddess of War and her chosen

warrior-priests, but it was also the heart of our town. The heart of the borderlands. The heart of my people.

Just inside the edge of the forest, the rhythm of hooves shattered my reverie. I ducked into the bushes as three riders barreled up the rise a dozen paces away, following a woodsmen's track. Another came after them more slowly, off the trail on my other side, and then a fifth.

I dropped into a deeper crouch, disjointed prayers clattering through my head. They were Algatt. There was no mistaking them, not with their weathered, pale skin, the cut of their tunics – tapered to a point, just above the knee – fitted trousers, and the blue and yellow paints smudged into their angular fringes.

But why were the Algatt still here? Why would they risk leaving a handful of riders behind? Surely not to hunt down stray villagers. There was no point in that.

The rush of blood in my ears became a thundering river. Even as instinct urged me to run to the village and Eidr, I put out a hand to ground myself. My fingers sank into moss, soft and lush and cool with rain. The feeling steadied me in the midst of my disassembling world.

I waited in the moss, in the shelter of an arch of ferns, until the Algatt moved on.

My muscles complained as I eased out of my crouch, but I kept low, following game trails that I had run for the majority of my life, until the narrow earthen path ended in fields.

There were no fences here, no walls or rises to hide behind, but the wafts of smoke were dense and low. I darted across the open ground and stepped through a smoldering break in the ring wall.

Smoke curled past me. I wanted to call out, but the presence of Algatt in the forest demanded caution. I followed the wall around half of the settlement, gaze flickering between singed wooden walls, grass-covered roofs and small plots of vegetables and herbs, protected by wicker fences. There were no bickering children. No goats stood on their hind legs, trying to crop grass from the eaves. No women knelt at millstones, no men manipulated wood into a new cradle, a new stool. There were only creeping swaths of fire, smoke and an eerie hush.

I stared at fabric fluttering in a window, bold Eangen colors of blue and green and soft greys intertwined in endless patterns. Looking at it, I could almost believe nothing was wrong, that the air did not reek of seared meat. But when I peeked inside the window, the house was overturned and empty, and there was a smear of blood across the floor.

I reached the center of the village and halted, unable to move any further. The Hall rose above me in a lattice of stark, charred beams. My entire body rebelled against looking at it, but the corpses on the ground were worse. The old and the weak lay in piles, as if the Algatt had herded them in front of my home's great, gaping doors to slaughter them in the sight of their goddess.

Then there were the Eangi priests. My people. My family. Some had managed to drag on their armor before the attack, but the rest were in daily working garb. However much warning the watchmen had given them, it had not been enough.

Only the Eangi's narrow collars of bronze declared their status as Eang's warrior-priests – the same collar that Eidr and Yske wore, and that the High Priestess had cut from my throat before I made my climb.

My vision glazed over corpses, shattered doors and churned, bloody mud. I had witnessed slaughter before; there was no one in my world who hadn't, child or adult, priest or farmer. But this was like nothing I had ever seen. This was no raid. This was a massacre.

And in a settlement of this size, I knew everyone. The face of each corpse was familiar to me. I knew their stories, their habits and the obscure ties in our bloodlines.

But Eidr was not there; nor was Yske. Of course they weren't, I told myself. They had escaped. They must have escaped.

Mechanically, trembling, I passed through the sea of bodies, fingering my ritual knife as I went. Every face I saw, every wound, reinforced my growing suspicion that this was more than a raid – an Algatt army had swept through my home, one that even the infamous Eangi of the Hall of Smoke could not stop.

Numbed by this realization, I entered the Hall of Smoke itself. Shafts of light poured through great scorched sections of roof and walls. The flames had died down, but the heat was still close and the air heavy with smoke. I pulled the edge of my tunic over my face and forced my feet forward.

Some detached, emotionless part of me began to give orders. Search the bodies. Find my husband and cousin. Find more weapons than this pitiful knife. Get to East Meade, to the rest of my family.

Give the dead their final rites.

I blinked, wrestling my mind away from flight, and tried to focus on that final task. Exiled or not, if I was the last Eangi standing in Albor, it was my duty to write the runes in the ash and release the spirits of the dead. Only then could they leave the blood-soaked earth and pass on into the High Halls of the Gods.

The High Halls where I could not follow.

Eidr. Yske. Where were they?

My world buckled, cracked and narrowed. Eidr's and my bunk, one of the dozens of Eangi beds clinging to the walls of the hall behind shredded curtains, was a nest of embers. The bearskin that I kept rolled at the back was shriveled and reeked of burned hair. Our dangling bags of belongings were destroyed, childhood talismans spilled into the cinders.

The only salvageable thing was a bone and silver hairpin that Eidr had given to me, carved with birds and the runes for belonging, protection, and eternal promise. I let the collar of my tunic slip from my mouth and, clearing my throat, took up the hairpin. Desperate for some feeling of normality, I tucked its three prongs into my hair and blinked back across the Hall.

My eyes glassed over the bodies again. Somehow, before my gaze found her, I knew Yske was there; a flash of open, staring eyes, all too like a butchered doe. Near her, a flash of red hair. A limp, masculine hand. Eidr.

I did not move. Did not breathe. This was a vision – yes, that must be it. I was lying in a meadow of poppies and this was a vision from Eang, a warning, a…

The hoot of an owl broke into my shock. I thought I saw a grey bird up among the rafters, its feathers sleek and its eyes great, honeyed wells, but as I searched my gaze snagged on the Algatt silhouetted in the doorway.

We stared at one another. I saw a bloodied warrior in mail and decorative leather, eyes rimmed in black and skin streaked with blue and yellow paint. Little older than Eidr, his cheeks were still flushed under blond-lashed eyes and his sun-darkened forearms were laced with scarification – ritual and otherwise.

He, in turn, must have seen a bedraggled young woman in tunic and loose trousers, holding a knife as if it were an empty bucket.

"Come, I won't hurt you," he said. His voice was warm and only mildly accented. "Or you may run. You might even get away."

I blinked sweat and smoke from my eyes. Run? He didn't know I was an Eangi – not in this state, not without my collar. He thought I was just a girl. The offer was a fair gesture on his part, perhaps some acknowledgement that what his people had done here was far beyond heinous, far beyond honorable. Maybe I could even get away, like he'd said.

But the sound of his voice ignited something else in my gut. It was hot. Alive. And it grew.

I made myself look at the bodies strewn across the floor. I named them one by one, forcing the memories into my reluctant, grief-stricken mind to feed the heat – my deadly Eangi Fire.

Yske. There she was, cast over a fallen beam. We had been sent to the Hall together as children, holding hands on the cart for the entire journey. We'd become women together, bled and grown. Trained together. Fought together.

Eidr. His red hair a mass of fraying braids and blood. I'd been twelve when I kissed him and suggested we marry. He'd laughed at me then. But last autumn he had not, and the High Priestess joined our hands at the head of this very Hall.

"*I pledged myself to you*," my husband's words from the night before echoed through the disjointed hum of my mind. "*Yske is your blood. You may have been cast out of the Hall of Smoke, but you cannot be cast out from us.*"

My eyes flicked away. I saw Sixnit, one of my dearest friends, near the central hearth. Sweet and full-breasted, she'd come to the Hall two years ago when she married an Eangi priest. Now her husband lay dead in the hearth itself, and she curled around the silent form of their infant son.

Their son. My dazed eyes fixed on him. The baby was tiny, mere days old – I'd attended his birth, the day before my banishment. Now, the baby's hand twitched on his mother's chest – a chest that, as I watched, rose and fell. She was alive. They were both alive.

The heat finally filled my mouth and burst out in a hiss. The ritual cuts on my fingertips healed, my exhaustion fled, and my mind cleared, clean and sharp as a winter wind.

My fingers slipped into position on the hilt of the knife.

The Algatt barely registered my movement in time. My knife embedded in his forearm, an inch from his face. He turned his cry of pain into an enraged bellow that shook me to the bones. In an instant, his sword was in hand and he charged.

I broke into a forward crouch and screamed. It was low, the undulating, unearthly sound every Eangi was taught. When we lined for battle, when we prepared to leave the forest on a fog-choked morning, we each had our notes. They would clash and blend and rise, sending goosebumps up our own arms, let alone our enemies'.

My cry was alone, but it only made me more furious. I plunged forward, stooping to rip a broken spear from a corpse as I passed.

He never saw the blow. I ducked his sword and drove the spear through his padded tunic, into his gut, with the force only an Eangi could muster. Then I dropped, hauling the shaft down like a lever and opening his intestines with a squelching, sickening crack.

Relief trickled through my fevered thoughts as he toppled. I wiped tears from my eyes with the back of one hand and looked at Sixnit and her barely breathing child, but I didn't try to rouse them yet.

"Eangi?" the Algatt choked from the ember-strewn floor.

I took up his sword and squatted just outside his reach, ignoring the growing stink of his open belly. With every breath I pushed out of my nose, I gathered my grief in tighter and forced my careening heart to steady. I could not look at Eidr.

"Your collar?" He blinked languidly.

"Cut off." I rested the point of his sword in the ash, keeping my eyes fixed on him. "Did the traveler bring you here? Omaskat?"

He stared at me, clutching his welling insides. "Omaskat?"

I rocked my weight into my toes. "The traveler, with the eyes – one gold, one blue. He was here a week ago."

The Algatt said something, but his voice was too low. I leant forward. "Did he bring you here?"

He gave no answer.

I felt a tear bead on my upper lip and swiped it away. "Why are you here so late in the season?"

Even on the edge of death, his fear of the Eangi – and the goddess we called on – was enough to make him speak. "Arpa." His words ended in an agonized croak. "Legionaries. In our mountains. They drove us out... We took the rivers south. Nowhere... nowhere else to go."

Arpa legionaries. Savage, unyielding soldiers of that great empire to the south, on whose rim the Eangen carved out an existence.

"Why would Arpa be so far north?" I slapped his cheek, but he was too far gone. His eyes rolled back and his legs bucked.

Still not looking at Eidr or Yske, I retrieved my knife from the raider's arm and slit his throat in one grim movement. Then I moved to Sixnit's side.

"Six," my voice softened, cajoling and tense with hope. "Six, wake up, please."

She didn't stir, though her chest continued to rise and fall. I couldn't carry her, so I numbly began to disentangle the infant from her arms, trying not to think past that simple step. The child's stillness terrified me more than a thousand Algatt and I checked three times to make sure he was, truly, alive. But breath passed between his tiny parted lips, and his heart fluttered beneath my palm.

Steeling myself, I held him close and began to search the room for something, anything that might help me rouse or carry Sixnit.

But my thoughts refused to stay on task. As soon as the Algatt died, I was left alone again – alone with the corpses of my husband, my people, Sixnit's helplessness and that looming, crippling grief. My eyes darted, faster now, and my breath shallowed. I saw Yske's own, lifeless eyes. The blood in Eidr's hair.

Eidr's hair. Eidr, unmoving, unbreathing. Gone.

My chest threatened to cave in and black sparked across my vision. At the same time, feebleness, a side effect of using Eangi Fire, swept over my limbs. Only a wheezing gasp from the baby in my arms kept me from crumpling. I pushed the knuckle of a trembling hand against one eye and locked my knees. Focus. Just a moment longer.

If the Arpa had gone into the mountains, driving the Algatt into the Eangen lowlands… I had to get us to East Meade, the village of my birth. They had to be warned. I could leave Sixnit and the baby with my sisters—

Warm, slick steel met my throat. "On your knees."

I froze, every muscle still and my breath lodged in my throat. Calculating, hoping, my eyes flew from the infant in my arms to the charred doors of the Hall of Smoke. There, misty daylight fell uninterrupted across the bodies of my people, but the way was clear. I could run with the baby. But not with Sixnit.

More silhouettes appeared in the doorway. More raiders, stalking and spreading out, muttering and eyeing me.

The child let out another fragile, crackling breath. My eyes fell from him to Six, still motionless at my feet, and what little hope I had died. I would risk my own life in a last, desperate play for freedom. But I could not risk theirs.

My throat swelled against the blade as I said, "We surrender."

THREE

Years earlier, under a starry autumn sky, Svala the High Priestess moved through the camp towards me. In the firelight, surrounded by revelers, she might have been our warrior-goddess herself, robed in violence and armored with divine purpose.

There was blood in her crown of braids, spattered where black hair met tawny skin, and a slim ring of bronze glistened above her bloodied tunic. Its runes had worn smooth long ago, but I knew they were clear on my own, only a year old. The Brave. The Vengeful. The Watchful. The Swift. All that Eang was, and all that we must endeavor to be.

Yske and I sat against a boulder on the edge of the celebration, between our comrades and their fires, and the quiet of a far northern night. The trees were sparse here, gnarled and windblown. The expanse of open rock was still warm from the sun and pocketed with shivering clusters of seeding flowers and moss, while above the sky arched toward the distant, shadowed hulk of the Algatt's high mountains.

This was Orthskar, in northern Eangen, where we'd spent the last three weeks hunting down a group of Algatt raiders. Raiders that, today, we'd finally routed and driven back into the mountains under the leadership of the woman who beckoned me now.

"Hessa," the High Priestess held out her hand. "Come with me."

Yske looked up, a cup of honey wine halfway to her lips. When we were children, I might have seen a flash of jealousy in her eyes at the High Priestess coming for me instead of her, but there was none of that now. We were old enough to know that the interest of our leaders was not always a good thing.

I nodded obediently, though the day's battle had left me sore and exhausted. I eased myself onto my feet and slipped my plain, unadorned axe through its leather loop at my belt.

The High Priestess headed off into the darkness. I, it seemed, was expected to follow.

Yske grabbed my hand. She and I still shared our fathers' curling dark hair, dense brush of freckles and brown eyes. But by now our progression into womanhood had begun to accent our differences; where Yske had her mother's lithe form, every muscle calculated, every curve measured, I had my mother's compact power.

"What does she want?" Yske asked, low enough to nearly be drowned by a thunder of drums. We both flinched as the warriors of the camp roared with approval and someone began a familiar song in a deep, rolling voice. "What did you do wrong?"

"I don't know," I hissed back.

"Hessa," Svala called.

Yske's hand dropped away. We exchanged one last uncertain glance, then I hastened off into the night.

The songs of the warriors followed us as we left the camp behind. They told the history of the gods, taught to us by Eang herself, of how the Gods of the Old World – their names lost over the millennia – had woven themselves from the darkness of the heavens, borne children, and created mankind from the dirt and divine birth-blood. Eang had been among their offspring, and the Gods of the Old World had quickly learned to fear their most violent daughter.

Svala and I walked until the older woman halted under the shadow of a tree. The firelight could not reach us here, but the stars gave enough illumination for me to make out the planes and shadows of her face – and the runes carved into every inch of the leafless, barren tree at her back.

Svala followed my gaze. "It's a binding tree, Hessa. Have you seen one before?"

Distantly, I heard Yske's voice join the chorus in the camp, vibrant and sweet.

"No..." Cautiously, I circled the tree, squinting at runes for protection and suppression, warning and foreboding. My nerves, already worn, began to fray, but I resisted the urge to draw back. Svala was watching me, and she would not overlook any weakness. "What is bound inside this?"

"What? Or who? It matters little." The High Priestess nodded back towards the camp. Our comrades' song continued to wash out towards us, now recounting how Eang had gathered her cousins and siblings, the so-called Gods of the New World, to overthrow the Gods of the Old. "Eang's power will keep them asleep until the Unmaking of the World, along with the Gods of the Old World and a hundred other enemies besides. But the tree is not why I brought you out here."

I retraced my steps, settling before her at a respectful distance – and letting her remain between me and the hushed, rune-laden tree.

"You killed today."

Tears surged into my eyes, ready and eager. Horrified, I blinked hard and kept my back straight, but I had no doubt Svala saw how the act had shaken me.

She offered me no comfort. Instead she scrutinized me, crowned by the binding tree's stark, wind-blown branches. "I had a vision of you, in the eyes of a dying man. It is not uncommon... Today was your first raid as full Eangi. Your first kill, since you came to us. So Eang showed me your future – a vision from Fate herself."

I remained quiet, squinting away my tears. Fate was the most mysterious of divine beings, elevated and withdrawn from Eang and the New Gods, or any other assembly of gods for that matter. She had no physical form, but there were corners of the High Halls, the high priesthood said, where one could hear the clack of her loom on a starry night, as she wove the destinies of us all.

That Fate had showed Eang a vision of me was both awe-inspiring and troubling.

"I saw a man," Svala said.

"A man?" I could not help myself. I was fifteen and, despite living in close quarters with men of all ages, her words made my cheeks flush. My eyes darted away from her and the lording tree to the chanting masses back in the camp, a hundred warriors releasing weeks of tension. Leather. Muscle. Nerves and grief, clawing for release. Eidr was there, somewhere, singing and laughing.

I shuffled on my feet. "Was he mine? The man in the vision?"

"I don't know." If she saw my embarrassment, she didn't comment. I sometimes wondered if Svala had ever passed through those painful, formative years, or if she had spawned in all her mature, feminine glory. "But he stood with you in the Hall of Smoke, with a hound at his heel and a golden eye."

A few tears escaped my blockade and trickled onto my upper lip. I licked them away. "What does it mean?"

"I'm not sure. But you were a little older, perhaps by three or four years." Svala looked at me askance and, back in the camp, the song entered a resounding, final verse. I thought I saw a rare smile in the corner of the priestess's mouth, but before I could be sure, it vanished into a frown. "When that day comes, you must kill him."

FOUR

I turned away from the baby in my arms and muffled a cough in my shoulder. The Algatt guard who paced around the huddle of prisoners shot me a glare and shifted his grip on his axe.

My captors had brought Sixnit, the baby and I to the horde just after dusk, thrusting me down in the middle of twenty other Eangen. Most of the captives were young women like me, though there were a handful of boys, a smattering of older women and two men. I was the only Eangi.

My body had given into cold and fatigue, the result of Eangi Fire and a night in the rain, but it helped excuse the steady trickle of tears from my eyes. It was a pitiful shield, but it was something; a lesser suffering to focus on while a chasm of loss festered beneath my skin.

Sixnit and her son were the only things that kept that chasm from swallowing me. Sixnit had regained consciousness on the road but had yet to speak, lying with her head in my lap and slipping in and out of consciousness. The infant had recovered, though his breath was still so thin that my heart wrenched every time he inhaled. I wished he would cry, because at least then I could hear the life in him. For all that he moved now, he might have been carved of pale, clammy stone.

I had to save them. They were my one victory, my one purpose in all of this. When I looked at them, I no longer saw Eidr's bloodied, limp hand or Yske's soulless eyes. I saw only a friend and a child who deserved a chance at life. I saw someone I could save.

I gathered moisture from the dewy grass and stroked it across the baby's lips. He began a frail, wheezing lament.

"Let me feed him."

Sixnit slowly sat up, her flat cheeks pale over narrow chin and cracked lips. My heart twisted at the sight of her, but I managed a smile and passed her her son.

The Algatt guard glanced over, but he did not stop her as she unlaced the front of her shift, took the baby in her arms and offered him a breast. He did not latch on, fumbling and flailing feebly, but her skin and the scent of milk soon soothed him.

"Thank you." Sixnit's voice was soft, toneless in a way that told me she was as raw and shocked as I was. She looked at the guards askance, but her eyes did not focus until her son began to feed. Then something of herself seemed to return; she turned her vacant gaze down and stroked his fine black hair.

I thought that she would say more, would at least ask about her husband, but she didn't. She knew his fate, and she knew the reality of our situation as well as anyone else in the tent.

I looked down at my knees. "What did you call him? I… I wasn't there for the naming."

"There wasn't one." In response to my quizzical look, she clarified, "We were waiting for you to come back."

Neither Eidr nor Yske had mentioned that, likely to spare me the burden. I opened my mouth to say something in return, but my words paled. I'd been at the child's birth, so it was appropriate that I would be there at his dedication, but not necessary – especially considering the reason for my absence. It was a gesture of kindness and friendship that, in the end, had excluded the baby's own father from the ceremony.

"Quiet," one of the guards finally commanded, her hard-lined face framed by smears of blue paint – nearly black in the distant firelight – and the axe and short spear she wore across her back.

We lapsed into silence. The other captives glanced at us curiously, but no one else dared to speak. Finally, when the guards had changed and night closed in, an older man broke the stillness. He was Erd, Albor's chief blacksmith and one of my father's distant cousins, though little family resemblance or intimacy remained between us. His muscular arms were bound behind his back – the Algatt had only bound those they perceived as a threat – and the lines on his face permanently entrenched with grey.

"When they realize what you are, they'll kill you, Eangi."

The mention of my title made my skin crawl. My gaze flicked to the guards.

When I didn't say anything, Erd rubbed his bearded chin against one shoulder. "I saw you head up the mountain."

I weighed his words, trying to uncover what he wasn't saying. He didn't know my crime, no one but Sixnit did, but he was the one who cut my collar off. That meant he'd seen just how furious Svala had been with me.

Sixnit watched me quietly.

"I made the climb," I affirmed.

"Why?" the man asked.

I hesitated. If any of the villagers found out that I had been banished for letting an Algatt traveler into the Hall of Smoke, a week before they razed the village, I was as good as dead.

Guilt welled up in my throat. I had offered Omaskat hospitality on sacred ground and blatantly ignored a charge from Eang to kill him. No wonder the goddess had let the town fall.

Gods below. Was all this really my fault?

"It's an Eangi matter. Svala had a vision," I evaded, battling to keep my voice even and that chasm of grief from devouring me. "An owl called me up the mountain."

All Eangen were familiar with Eang's owl messengers. They were not truly owls, at least not according to legend; they were constructs of feathers and divine magic, infused with the final breaths of one of Eang's sisters, who had been executed for a grave betrayal.

"But you gave the dead their rites?" One of the other young women asked, her voice hoarse from crying. "When you came back?"

The guilt plunged back into my stomach, making me want to retch. "No."

My people stared at me, anguish and horror written across their faces. Even Sixnit, already pallid, lost a little more of her color.

"There was no time," I said, desperate to explain my failure to myself and to them. In truth, there was no excuse. I should have begun the rites as soon as I stepped into the village. I had been too focused on Eidr and Sixnit and the baby and escape, and now the souls of our loved ones were bound to the earth until I or an Eangi from another village could release them.

Release them to a High Hall where I could not follow, not until Eang forgave me. But what hope did I have for that, now?

"Eang spared her," Sixnit asserted. "That's why she was up the mountain."

"The Algatt spared her and us, and only for slavery," an older woman, Ama, scoffed. She, like Erd, was another of my distant relations. "Saw that babe in your arms, I say, and think you've got more in you, both of you. You'll be whelping Algatt come mid-winter."

I ground my teeth to stifle a stab of fear. The rest of the younger women looked equally perturbed, though we were aware of our destiny. We had been raised in its shadow as, year after year, women and girls vanished into the Algatt mountains. Most of them were never found.

"Eang spared her," Sixnit reasserted, her voice growing tight.

"If Eang wanted to spare someone, it would not have been Hessa," Ama snapped. "She would have given us Svala or Ardam. But Ardam is dead in the Hall, and Svala's likely just as dead in the woods."

"The woods?" I repeated numbly. Why would the High Priestess of the Eangi be in the woods? Had she been who the riders were searching for, outside the burning town?

"Yes, last anyone saw her, that's where she was. Praying and unarmed." Ama's eyes bored into me for another hateful moment. Then her attention snagged on a miserable little boy, who had begun to cry quietly in a corner of the tent. "So, with Hessa we will die. Don't cry, child. Bravery, now."

The possibility of Svala's escape, and the terrifying hope that came with it, died in the pain of Ama's insult. It burned, yet Sixnit's defense of me burned still deeper. Yes, Eang had spared me – but only for punishment.

That night the rain resumed. The Algatt put us in a tent but permitted no fire and did not lower the flaps, leaving us exposed to the splatter of rain and the watchful eye of the guards. We were given food – rations of bread and hard cheeses, stolen from our own village. The older women organized and distributed it, feeding our bound companions by hand.

Outside the wall of heavy skins, fires flickered. Some of the Algatt sang, recalling the history of their alpine god Gadr, the battles of past years and anticipation of their future rest under Gadr's Great Mountain in the High Halls. Some of their tales blended with ours; stories of how Gadr had been born of the Gods of the Old World and how he, together with Eang and a dozen others, had slain their forebears and claimed the High Halls for the Gods of the New World.

But that was where the similarities ended. Where Eangen songs went on to tell of how Eang came to rule over those Gods of the New World, the Algatt's songs spoke of how Gadr had justly rebelled and come to dominate the mountains of the north. Unable to slay Eang, he set his worshipers, the Algatt, to raid and harry the Eangen until the end of days.

The words made my Fire burn, low and sickening, in my gut. It did not help that the Algatt loved to add slow wails and high yips to their songs – better for echoing down mountain ravines, Yske had once said. The sound was beautiful and eerie. It made my skin crawl.

Later, in the cold of the night, Sixnit shifted closer to my side. She and I huddled together, lending warmth and comfort to one another and the sleeping child.

"We need to dedicate him," I murmured to my friend, eyeing the guards to make sure they didn't overhear. "In case… in case they separate us. I can't give the dead their rites now, but I can do this. Do you have a name?"

Sixnit shifted again, not quite looking at me. "But the High Priestess should do the dedication."

My throat tightened. She was right. The High Priestess – or an elder priest, in remote villages – led all rituals, including the dedication of babies. I wasn't one of them. I was just another Eangi, one of dozens. I was a servant, and an errant one at that.

But I'd seen dedications a hundred times. And this matter, like releasing the souls of the dead, was too important. Even exiled, I belonged to Eang and was bound to fulfill her will.

"Either the Algatt will dedicate him to Gadr, or he'll grow up dedicated to no god. Lost." It was hard to speak those words – the fate of a lost person was eerily close to my own. "If that happens, the gods won't protect him. No one will hear his prayers, and when he dies, he'll never be allowed in the High Halls. He'll be trapped here in the Waking World forever."

Sixnit hesitated another moment. Some of the other captives watched us now, mute and dull-eyed.

"But Vist isn't here." This second protest fell harder than the first. Vist was her husband, dead back in the embers of the Hall of Smoke with Eidr. "Two, for the pledge."

Silence yawned between us.

"I'll… I'll stand in," I offered, as weak and guilt-ridden as the words were. If I'd killed the traveler Omaskat as I'd been meant to, would we even be in this situation?

But Sixnit relented, expression bleak, and placed the child in my lap. "His name is Vistic."

I took this with a nod. I no longer had my ritual knife, but the hairpin I'd picked from the ashes remained buried in the tangled mess of my braids. I pried it loose and set one prong against a newly healed fingertip. It was messy and painful, but I knew the pain would be short-lived. My Fire couldn't heal grievous wounds, but as soon as I burned again this cut would knit, joining dozens of other, finer marks.

Careful to conceal my actions from the guards, I touched the blood to the boy's forehead and lips and loosened the folds of his swaddle to draw a scarlet rune in the center of his chest.

The Eangen around me now watched in vigilant, reverent hush. Each recognized the magnitude of my actions, both in the ritual of the dedication and the drawing of the rune that enabled it.

A rune of blood was the most powerful of all. Blood was magic. Blood maintained life in every living thing. Its loss brought death. Blood carried Eangi power from one generation to the next, wove life in a woman's womb, was spilled once a month and at birth. So it followed that an Eangi's blood, and better a woman's blood, should be sacrificed in the dedication of a new life to a god.

"Eang, hear me," I whispered as the Algatt's songs continued in the background. "Hear my voice on behalf of this child. Bind his soul to the smoke of your Halls and take a drop of his blood in your cup. Prepare a seat beside your hearth for he whom we call Vistic, and when his last day comes, welcome him to his rest."

Then, placing my palm on the child's chest, I let my Fire flow. My bloody finger healed, but this was not a flash of deadly rage or blazing violence like I had unleashed on the raider in the Hall of Smoke. This was a blessing, a baptism, binding the child to Eang and bringing him under her eternal protection. And mine.

Exhaustion came hard and fast, and I took a second to steady myself before I looked up at Sixnit. She accepted the infant back into her arms with a fragile, melancholy smile. I saw tears in her eyes – tears for her husband, I was sure – as I began to sing the blessing song that sealed the dedication.

The backs of the Eangen around us straightened. Even Ama watched us with something less than disdain in her eyes. Then, cautiously, they all joined in. Ama was last, but her voice was strongest.

My voice was not sweet, my throat raspy from cold and sorrow; still, I sang every note. The Algatt's own songs sheltered us, distracting the guards and leaving us in our huddle of warmth and familiarity. Twenty captive Eangen, the last of our town, in the heart of an Algatt horde.

When the song faded, Sixnit held up her son and studied the blood drying on his face. He still slept, exhausted and frail. She cupped the back of his limp head and leant close, so that her breath touched his cheeks.

"Vistic," she said, "I am your mother, and this is Hessa. We bind our lives to yours. We will protect you, however and whenever we can, so long as Eang permits."

So long as Eang permits. I stroked Vistic's cheek, wondering just how long that would be.

I could not stay here. I may have dedicated this child and bound him to myself, but the Algatt would likely separate us.

I withdrew my hand and forced my eyes away from the two of them, hiding my hairpin back in the tangles of my hair. Perhaps separation was for the best. Sixnit's presence consoled me and I hated the thought of being apart, but my duty was to Eang, wasn't it? To the vow that I had failed to keep and my own, uncertain eternity? I didn't need any more obligations.

Whether or not the goddess had responded, whether or not the massacre was my punishment, there was only one way forward that I could see, one way to salvage any hope of redemption and reunion with Eidr in the High Halls of the Gods.

I had to find the traveler, Omaskat. And then I had to kill him.

FIVE

As a child, I watched Yske's mother, my aunt, bind my cousin's dark curls into a spiral of braids. Yske sat patiently on a stool, clad in her finest forest-green dress. The patterns of lynxes and ice blossoms on my aunt's bone comb caught the light as her fingers methodically hooked and brushed.

I hovered nearby. My own mother had long finished my hair, gathering my crop up into a braided tuft before she bade me wait quietly, and went outside.

"Svala is coming?" My father's voice drifted through the open door, on a shaft of golden light that cut across worn floorboards, fresh reed mats and up the far wall, where my parents' shields hung side by side under the beams of the sleeping loft. They were both dark blue, round with glinting bosses, and painted with the lynx heads of our village: East Meade.

I inched closer to the door, my bare feet scuffing on the reed beneath the hem of my grey dress. The mats smelled of summer, warm and dry, and the breeze that came with the light was laden with the scent of the flowers that fringed the overgrown roof.

"You told me the girls would go to Iskir, not the Hall of Smoke," my father protested, still out of sight.

"No, I told you to send her to Albor, but you didn't listen," the headman replied. His tone was soft, far more measured than my father's booming bray. "Svala herself has taken an interest in the girls."

"Good. I said Iskir is too close to the mountains," my mother reminded my father. She sounded exasperated, as always. "I don't want Hessa anywhere near the—"

"She's an Eangi," my father snapped. "She'll be slaughtering Algatt for the rest of her life, in Iskir or Albor or Meade. I hate that woman. Svala is an arrogant witch."

The headman's exasperated hiss followed. "Berin."

"I'd prefer that her life be as long as possible," my mother returned, ignoring the slight against the most powerful woman on the Rim. "And *not* under a Gatti belly."

"Svala is a fair woman," the headman's voice rose, quelling my parents. "A powerful priestess. You know the number of Eangi ordained in the last few generations has… waned. Hessa is obviously Eangi but volatile. She needs a mentor like Svala. As for Yske, her power is more subtle; she could go anywhere. But it is better for her to stay with her cousin, especially as young as they are."

Behind Yske, I saw my aunt's eyes rise towards the door. Since her own husband's death, she had become my father's second wife according to law; the cautious counterpart to my mother's bold.

I could see in her face that she didn't want Yske to go. I wasn't sure how she felt about me, but her obvious love for my cousin made me love her, too.

Anxiety stirred in my belly and I shifted closer to her skirts. She cast me a sad half-smile, but her focus remained outside.

A clamor began off in the village and the conversation between my parents and the headman fell away. My aunt, sensing the change, tied off Yske's braid and fastened the tail of it under the crown with a fine pin. Then, with distracted fingers, she clipped her comb to the beads draped across the front of her apron.

"High Priestess," my mother's voice said. More voices came after, low and deferential.

My heart stilled in my small chest. I had never seen the High Priestess, but I knew of her. I'd heard her Eangi Fire was so powerful she could turn bones to ashes with a scream. I'd heard that she traveled to the

High Halls, in spirit and sometimes even in body, to speak to the dead and hold council with the gods. And when the Algatt raiders came, her Eangi fought and died to protect us, their people.

I held very still as the door swung wide, sunlight washing around the forms of my parents, the headman, and a new, fourth figure. She was younger than my mother, with ebony hair and ruddy skin, like most Eangen. She was tall, evenly muscled beneath a tunic of muted hemlock-dyed red and loose undyed breeches, and her kohl-rimmed eyes reminded me of a hawk – or perhaps an owl. A hooded axe hung through a ring at one hip and a knife sat at the other, its wooden hilt dark and smooth from use.

"These are the girls?" asked the High Priestess of the Goddess of War.

My mother led her forward. The High Priestess surveyed Yske, but as she neared, her attention fixed upon me.

Svala crouched, shifting her axe as she did so, and beckoned me forward. I shuffled up to her knees and she ducked to meet my gaze. "So, you are the child who killed two Algatt raiders?"

My throat constricted. My memory of the event was fragmentary, blurred by the exhaustion that had overtaken me after the fact, but I still didn't like to think of it.

"How did you do it?" Svala asked me.

Over the High Priestess's shoulder, half-silhouetted in the doorway, I saw my mother watching me with her arms crossed. My father stood beyond her, staring outside with an unhappy expression around his eyes.

"I don't remember," I said.

At the sound of my voice, the High Priestess's attention sharpened still more. She studied me for an uncomfortable length of time before she took my hands. Hers were scratchy with calluses and mottled with scars.

"Do you understand what it is to be an Eangi, Hessa?"

I sensed Yske fidgeting nearby, displeased that all the attention had fallen on me. Her status as an Eangi was something her parents had suspected for years – her dreams and visions and unnatural strength were known to everyone in East Meade.

But me? Me, they had not expected.

"Eangi serve Eang," I said, uncertain. "She gives them Fire. They write the runes."

"Yes. You are one. I am one. Your cousin is one." Svala considered my younger, smoother hands. "We are chosen by the Goddess of War to serve her and the Eangen people."

I felt like I was supposed to nod, so I did. My gaze was serious, my hands still.

"We're marked by Eang with the Fire, a piece of the goddess herself," Svala continued. "It's not real fire – you cannot see it – but it is hot like fire. It burns like fire, in the blood and the mind and through runes. Eangi Fire is magic, magic that we can use to kill, to bless, to write the runes and call visions and heal our simple wounds – though we must pay for it with strength. Eangi Fire is power, and that, Hessa is what you used to stop those raiders."

Again, my mind shuttered. I didn't want to remember that night. Not now. Not ever.

I wanted to pull away from the priestess. I was scared. I was scared of her and scared of myself. My eyes darted up to my mother, searching for solace. Her expression softened, but her stare warned me to stay where I was.

Svala tugged me closer. "This world is dark and unkind – no, look at me, child." When I tried to break her gaze, she slapped my cheek lightly. "You may be Eangi, so may Yske, but that will not spare you. Your days will be short, full of violence and difficult choices. I am going to protect you. You will be far from your family, but the Eangi will become your family. You will learn to fight, and you will never, ever, be alone. You will learn to control the fire in your blood. And when the Algatt come down from their mountains to raid, you, child, will protect your people. You will make our enemies fear the name of Eang."

SIX

We were herded into an enormous Algatt encampment before dusk three days after my capture and the destruction of the Hall of Smoke.

The size of the camp made the hair on the back of my neck rise. How many tents were there, clustered between the hills beside the great river Pasidon? A hundred? Two? And how many stolen Eangen boats were beached between them, among the equally stolen flocks and carts and wagons?

I stared at the boats, at their carved rails and ornate figureheads of bears and eagles and stags. These were the vessels that moved Eangen people and goods up and down the river, roughly thirty strong. But now, it seemed, they had borne Algatt south. That meant the north itself was overrun, and, judging by the lack of warning they'd sent us, it had happened fast.

I looked more closely at the inhabitants of the camp. A woman paused in the midst of bathing her baby in a bucket. Her hair was so pale that it was nearly white, smudged with blue about the forehead, but carelessly so – as if it were days old, and she simply hadn't the time to care for herself. She stared at me while the infant shrieked and splashed and, beyond her shoulder, a score of small children herded goats into a corral. Nearby, a pregnant woman leant on a man's arm as they entered a simple hide tent and an old man brushed down a horse. Through them all wove trails of warriors, male and female alike, wearing mail and padded armor over their squared shoulders.

I recalled the dying Algatt's words, back in the Hall of Smoke. Arpa in the mountains. If the legions had somehow thrust their way into Algatt land, driving the clan south, it certainly explained what I saw here. Families. Entire villages. Carts of meagre possessions. These weren't raiders – at least, not all of them. They were refugees.

"If they separate us... Hessa?" Sixnit's voice broke through my observations. She knew exactly what her fate was about to be, but when she looked at me, her eyes were still open, expectant. Searching for something to hold on to. "Hessa. We'll meet in East Meade?"

I nodded. We'd developed this plan over the last few days, along with the other prisoners. The Meades, closer to the western coast, had the best chances of having survived the Algatt tide. Perhaps I held a selfish, naive hope that my father and sisters were alive in East Meade, but it nonetheless gave us a direction to run.

Sixnit offered me a tight, grim smile, but I still saw the pain in her eyes. Neither of us could bear the thought of separation, but that, like so many aspects of our world, was unavoidable. "Good."

In the center of the camp we were herded into a line, all twenty of us. Algatt crowded in to form a wall of beards and braids of blond and red, full of afternoon light.

The hair on my neck rose again and my fingers twitched, wishing for a weapon. My hairpin still dug into my scalp, but though its prongs were sharp, it would hardly carry me out of an Algatt horde.

One of our captors was in charge of the auction. The lean warrior paced down the line of us, toying with a braided cord of leather and horsehair. His own hair was cropped short in the back but left long at the front in typical Algatt style, falling over his eyes in an angular, wind-blown tuft.

"Offers?"

Rough hands turned my face towards the sun and I squinted, shying away. I didn't see the owner of the hands lifting my tunic, but I felt the knot of my trousers jerk free.

Every muscle in my body went rigid. My free hand shot forward, fingers plunging towards my attacker's eyes.

Something slammed into the side of my head. I staggered, disoriented, until gruff hands jerked me upright again.

"I see we've fought before." An Algatt ran his eyes over a large scar on my thigh. "Turn her around."

I stumbled over my own feet as someone spun me in place and I found myself face to face with my captor. It was a woman, a blonde, but I found no solidarity in her compassionless, kohl-streaked eyes.

I glared at her. Then I felt the man's fingers trace three raiding seasons' worth of scars on my back and fear exploded through my mortification. Would he realize I had more scars than the average Eangen? Would he notice the scars on the tips of my fingers and realize I was Eangi?

I instinctively reached out for my Fire, coaxing it into flame, and curled my fingers into my palms. I could shatter this man's bones with a flick of my will. This woman's too. But where would that leave me? Fighting my way through a hundred more warriors to the edge of camp?

The Fire was a berserker's tool, a short-lived burst that would eventually leave me exhausted and weak. It was one reason why Eangi always fought in concert, in pairs or groups, not alone like me. And more than that, as soon as I used the Fire every person in this camp would know what I was. I would burn out, and I'd be left with no weapon but my fingernails and a hairpin.

I had to be more tactful, smother my indignation, and bide my time.

That resolve immediately faltered as the Algatt man slapped my bottom. "Too damaged and too masculine," he declared, and moved on to Sixnit.

The Algatt woman released me, passing on down the line in case Sixnit decided to mount her own resistance. Trying to swallow my rage a second time, I jerked my clothing back into place and eyed my friend.

Sixnit trembled as the man took Vistic from her. I understood why. I half expected him to break the sick child's neck then and there. But instead, he opened the baby's swaddling cloth and noted his sex with approval. Then he nodded for Sixnit to turn around like I had.

She did so without further provocation. She was laced tighter than a bowstring, but her gaze was level and her steps firm.

The Algatt did not accost her like he had me. Instead, he read her body and expression with an experienced eye. "I'll let you keep your child if you cause me no trouble. Keep my bed, my hearth and my children, and you'll receive protection and fair treatment."

Sixnit gauged him, head to toe. I watched her in turn, filled with horrified admiration. My courage was fickle, but Sixnit's was contained and deliberate. She was being sold into slavery, into the bed of our enemies, yet somehow, she had managed to snatch a fragment of power.

"Then I will serve you," she agreed.

With that, Sixnit was sold. I watched the Algatt return Vistic to her arms and wave to an older boy at the front of the watching crowd. The boy led three ewes forward as payment.

I watched Sixnit and Vistic vanish into the Algatt. I met her last, tremulous smile with a helpless stare, uselessly willing Fate to send me a vision, to give me some glimpse of their destinies or to tell me if our paths would cross again. But Fate rarely deigned to answer human cries.

Man after man passed me by. Questions came, hands groped, and my eyes glazed over. Every word, every indignity fed the shard of Eang inside of me until I was sure my blood would boil. Then, without explanation, my Fire died.

Another man had stopped in front of me. Even before I saw the newcomer's face, I knew he was different. The very air around him smelled richer, weightier; like an ancient, creaking forest. His shoulders were broad and easy, set in the manner of a man who felt no need to elevate himself. His skin was sun-darkened – a color I had once mistaken for true Eangen blood – and his sea-blue tunic was embroidered at its slit collar, buttoned with a wooden bead and belted at the waist with a short sword and knife.

But it was his eyes that were the most distinctive. Mismatched. One gold, one blue.

I hurled myself at the traveler called Omaskat. But even as my fingers closed around his throat, he seized one of my wrists and snapped it. I dropped with a screech of pain.

The warrior in charge of the prisoners rebuked Omaskat, but I could not hear what he said. My vision swayed and blurred as the traveler continued to apply pressure to the break. I had no more air, nothing left to scream and no Fire to throw. Black sparked across my eyes.

The pressure released. Omaskat put a hand on the back of my neck and led me away into the crowd, which parted before my stumbling feet like ants before a flame.

"Stay quiet, little Eangi," the man murmured into my ear, "and perhaps I won't tell these wolves what you are."

Omaskat cinched my bindings tighter, securing me to the trunk of a sticky, towering pine.

"I'm your only protection now," the man reminded me, sitting back on his haunches. We were in a corner of the camp, his small plot hosting only a fire, bedroll and an enormous hunting dog. I recognized the creature from their visit to the Hall of Smoke, big and lean and shaggy down the spine. Ayo, she was called.

"If you escape in your condition," Omaskat continued, those mismatched eyes fixed on mine, "the bastards out there will make a sport of you before I can track you down. You look too Eangen."

My eyes flicked to his throat and the fingers of my good hand, tied across my stomach, twitched. But no heat welled up into my mouth. My Fire was inexplicably silent in the presence of Omaskat.

"You led them to Albor," I accused, trying not to dwell on my lack of power. Either something protected this man, or Eang was withholding the Fire from me. Both options were daunting.

Omaskat's head tilted to one side. "I did no such thing."

That made me angry. "There's no use denying it. Why else would you visit the Hall of Smoke a week before your people burned it down?"

Why else would Eang charge me with killing you?

The man rested his forearms on his knees and let his fingers drape down between them. "The horde came to Albor because it was the richest settlement within a few days' ride, and the greatest threat; heart of the Eangi priesthood. There are more than a thousand people in this camp and the numbers grow every day. They're hungry and desperate."

My lower lip trembled – exhaustion, I told myself, not emotion. "They slaughtered everyone."

He paused. No amusement crossed his face, nor disdain. He just leant closer, bringing his dark blond beard an inch from my chin. "The Eangen and the Algatt have lived in crude harmony for hundreds of years, Eangi. But the world is changing. The Arpa have taken the mountains and the Algatt must migrate. Power is shifting, above and below, human and divine; powers older, and greater, than your demon-goddess."

"There is no power greater than Eang," I snapped. I had no interest in whatever heresies the Algatt were concocting to justify the loss of their home. "And she is no demon."

"She is also no god," Omaskat replied, still watching me. "Which you would know, if you had ever encountered one."

The priestess in me ignited, bitter and laughing. The suggestion was so absurd – even for an Algatt – it didn't merit rebuke.

"Eang is God of the New World, is she not?" Omaskat asked. "Begotten by the Gods of the Old? Yet who, young priestess, begot them?"

"No one," I said without falter. "They created themselves, from the smoke and ash of the Last Age."

That was the story I'd been told since childhood, the pattern of existence itself – and the tale from which the Hall of Smoke had found its name. Before the time and world in which my people lived, there had been another. And after its end, the first gods had formed themselves from the remnants of that Old World. They had made the universe anew, the High Halls and the Waking World. They had loved and bred and birthed the Gods of the New World, and they had made humans, from the earth on which their own birth-blood spilled.

Omaskat considered me for another few heartbeats, cool and unflinching, before he relented. He sat back and said in a low voice, "Then I misspoke, priestess. Clearly, you know better than I."

His concession lacked scorn. If anything, it was pitying, which made me angrier.

I ran my teeth along the inside of my bottom lip. Heresy aside, this man had denied leading the Algatt to the Hall of Smoke. I didn't believe him. His visit to Albor made no sense unless he had been involved in the settlement's destruction.

And I was the one that had welcomed him, fed him and given him my bearskin to sleep on. When he had sat at the fireside with us, had he cared that we would all die within a week?

My mouth felt dry. If I killed him now, if I fulfilled the vision Svala had of me three years ago, perhaps everything would be righted. Perhaps Eang would save us. Perhaps I would wake to find this was all a dream in a meadow of poppies.

Omaskat stood up. "The woman and baby sold off today – yes, I saw. Was that Sixnit?"

Taking my expression for confirmation, the man scratched under his beard. His movement was more nervous than casual. "I'm sorry for that. I remember her, from the night I visited your Hall. She was close to her time, then. Very close."

I stared at him, choking on grief and anger and everything in between.

Omaskat turned away, hiding his expression in the night. "I'll fetch a healer for you."

However much I distrusted this man, the thought of being left alone, tied to a tree in an Algatt camp, chilled me to the bone.

"At least tell me your real name," I threw after him, squinting through my pain. "So I can scream it. Or do the Algatt have laws about marring one another's property?"

"Omaskat," he replied without falter.

I glared. "That's not an Algatt name. Are you from somewhere else, then? Somewhere where the people are so ignorant, they believe the gods are not gods?" When he still did not confess, I added, "Someone will tell me who you are eventually."

"They'll tell you I'm Omaskat." He clicked his tongue at the dog, who still waited by the fire, and pointed to the ground at my feet. "Ayo, stay. Guard our purchase."

The hound plunked down, tail brushing against my ankles. She was at least as large as I.

"I'll be back soon."

With that, Omaskat left. I peered around, muscles tensed as though some vile Algatt would set upon me the instant he disappeared. But this corner of the camp was quiet, and the population kept a respectful distance.

The dog rested her head on a paw, watching me as if to say, *do you not trust me?*

"I already trust you more than your master," I replied.

Her tail waved.

SEVEN

E ang was vexed. In the dream, she stood on a battlefield strewn with her Eangi. I knew them, each one. There was lithe Yske. Eidr, his scarred hands limp. Sixnit's husband Vist, open-mouthed in death, together with a dozen others so tied to my days, my sleeping and waking, that it seemed my every memory lay butchered before me; their flesh cold as clay, and their open eyes lain with red poppies.

I saw myself from a distance, sitting next to Eidr's corpse and clutching a bundle to my chest. Our child? No. Vistic. The boy was as motionless as when I found him, little lungs stifled with smoke and ash, and Sixnit was nowhere to be seen.

Eang glared at me through eyes rimmed in kohl. She wore a black tunic without armor or embellishment, save the crossed straps of the brace for the twin bearded axes she wore at her back, framing her head – the fabled blades Galger and Gammler. Her legwraps were splattered with mud and blood and she was beautiful, beautiful in a way that stole the light from the sky and curdled the marrow in my bones. But when she spoke, her voice was surprisingly human, melodic and rounded.

"I should stop the heart in your chest."

My mind scrambled, but there was no defense. Eang was many things, but merciful was not one.

She paced closer to me. "Did no other Eangi survive?"

"Just me," I whispered, though I felt she should already know that. "And Svala. They told me she's missing—"

"Svala is not your concern." Eang's shoulders drew in. Another pace closer. Two. She was so near now that I could smell her: the iron taint of blood, the gust of breath from angry lungs. "Then you are one of the last, Hessa, in this whole wretched land. You! Gods below."

"One of the... last? The last Eangi?" I repeated, numbly. How could the Algatt have killed all the Eangi so swiftly? There was at least one in every settlement, in every corner of Eangen. I gaped at the goddess, fumbling to understand.

"Yes," Eang said, offering me no comfort. "Hear me. Your task was to kill the traveler in the Hall of Smoke. I sent the owl. I gave you three years to prepare and spared you a dozen deaths in between. A dozen! I stopped an arrow from piercing your throat. At Boilingbrook, I put legionaries to sleep who would have worn you and that cousin of yours to tatters. The bear at the Sound? Did you truly think a knife stopped that beast? You," her voice darkened still more, "you could not slay the one man I raised you up to kill."

"He... he tricked me," the protest stumbled from my lips, as pathetic and feeble as my voice. "He was kind and – I didn't know it was him, not for sure. We were under Hearth Law. And I thought that if I was wrong, if it wasn't him and I killed an innocent man—"

Vistic and Eidr and the others vanished, and I stood alone with Eang in the smoldering remnants of the Hall of Smoke. She watched me with deadly intent, one eyebrow cocked as if daring me to finish.

I swallowed hard. Pleading and excuses would do me no good here, much less the borderline lies I was pulling together now.

Because the truth was, I hadn't wanted Omaskat to be the man I was supposed to kill. I'd known it was him, that it must be him, but I had chosen to let him go because he was kind, and I couldn't fathom why Eang would want him dead.

"I can still do it." I forced myself not to cower, to set my shoulders and ram steel down my spine. It didn't matter that I had no idea why Omaskat's death was so crucial to the goddess – it wasn't my place to know and, with my world crumbling, I was willing to do anything that might stem the tide. "Set me free, give me more Fire, and I'll kill him tonight. He's sleeping beside me."

"Set you free?" Eang scoffed. "Give you more power? I will give you nothing. I'll feed you to the next pack of wolves I find. I will blind them with your blood so that they hunt nothing else to the ends of the earth."

"Goddess!" I lunged to my feet, facing her head on. "This is *my* task. *My* right. Let me wake, loose my bonds. Let me do it. Please. Please!"

She still glared at me, but I saw the corners of her mouth turn up in satisfaction. "Very well. But I will neither loose nor arm you. Kill him with claws like the beast that you are, or not at all. Wake."

I awoke to the bite of ropes in my flesh. I jerked against them, heart hammering. I was sweating and cold, wrapped in a blanket against the night.

Then the blanket slipped, and my eyes fell on Omaskat. He slept on his bedroll beneath the stars, facing me across glowing coals with his short, single-edged sword nestled between his thighs, just loosened in its sheath. Ayo leant against his back, ears flicking here and there, chasing sounds out in the darkness. She surveyed me, once, before the screech of a dying rabbit drew her attention away.

My broken wrist was not bound. I lifted it and poked at the knots in the rope, but the pain made my stomach toss and roil. I leant my head back against the rough bark and took a few seconds to breathe.

I couldn't function like this. Despite knowing I would fail, I reached for my Fire. Even if I could take the edge off my pain, I might at least be able to think.

There was no power to be found, however. Not with Omaskat so near.

Something dug into the back of my head, leant against the tree. I cracked my eyes open, trying to remember what it was. The hairpin. Eidr's gift to me, my last keepsake from the Hall. I felt it press into my scalp, each of its three sharp prongs laid out against my skin.

Purpose settled over me. It took three attempts and a bout of retching with pain for me to disentangle the pin and drop it in my lap. I stared at it for a delirious moment, waiting for the ringing in my ears to subside.

Gradually, I became aware of someone watching. I lifted my head and discovered it was the dog, Ayo, her large eyes fixed on my face. We sized one another up. Then she made a muffled grunt, deep in her chest, and commenced scratching behind one ear.

I returned my attention to the hairpin. Pain made me wheeze as I turned it around and braced it between my knees.

Omaskat, disturbed by the dog's enthusiastic scratching, shifted.

I froze. But the man only buried his cheek a little deeper into the pack he used as a pillow and let out a sleepy breath, sending loose dirt skittering towards the embers of the fire.

I waited a heart-pounding minute to ensure he was still asleep, then I severed each fiber of the ropes across my chest one by one. The task was maddeningly slow and at every turn, some weakness of my mortal flesh screamed at me. Hunger. Relief. Pain. Exhaustion. Longing. Grief.

All around, the camp slept in the cool summer night. Occasionally, men and women walked by, talking in low voices. A father led a sleepy child. Two women stifled their laughter and murmured about the antics of a mutual friend, even though one had an arm in a sling and the other's face was mottled with bruises. A goat bleated, a horse whickered, and the lines of a tent creaked. A man wept.

I ran my eyes over the tents, identifying the one where I thought the latter might be. His weeping was contained, not wild and rampant, a familiar sorrow.

I pushed the thought aside, but the keening continued. It clawed at my concentration.

The suffering of the Algatt was none of my concern, I told myself. They chose to worship their god in the mountain – and entertain stranger heresies, if Omaskat spoke true. If their god had seen fit to let them fall to the Arpa, so be it. I, a servant of Eang, had my own task.

It took hours before the rope thinned enough for me to break it.

I arched my back, letting the muscles of my stomach harden against the last strands.

The rope snapped. I stifled a victorious gasp and wiggled out of the remainder of the bindings, leaving them piled around the base of the tree. Then I tucked the hairpin into the palm of my good hand.

I crept across the space between us, listening for each of his breaths. Ayo watched me.

"This is his fate," I murmured to the animal. I slipped the pin into a better grip and ran a thumb over its sharp, silver prongs. "I have no quarrel with you."

I circled the pair, staying beyond the reach of Omaskat and his cradled sword, and stroked the dog's head. I did not want to harm the creature. Besides, if she left Omaskat's side too quickly, he would wake.

I knelt, keeping up a pretense of petting the hound, and watched Omaskat's exposed throat. Vague starlight ran down the prongs of the hairpin as I adjusted my grip one last time and raised my hand for a killing stab.

Omaskat awoke. I barreled him onto his stomach, right knee braced in his back, left foot driving into the earth and my good hand stabbing wildly for his throat. I connected with his jaw instead, grating off bone and earning a frustrated, shocked cry.

The dog yipped and lunged, sinking her teeth into my thigh. I clenched my jaw and ignored the pain, pushing her back with the elbow of my bad arm. I only needed a few more seconds and one good angle to puncture Omaskat's throat. Then he would die, my task would be fulfilled and my atonement made. Then, I was sure, Eang would burn through my veins and I would escape into the night, rescue Sixnit and Vistic and head for East Meade.

Omaskat bucked. He tried to loose his sword, but it was pinned under his body now. I threw all my weight into his back and tried to grab him by the hair with my bad hand, but pain made my vision blur.

Ayo renewed her attack in a cacophony of barking and growling. Before I could raise an arm, she snapped at my head. Something tore.

I struck at her with my free arm and was rewarded by a fraction of reprieve. Blood streamed down the side of my face and, in the second before this newer, fresher pain crashed down, I had the odd sensation of my ear dangling against itself.

Hands hauled me backwards. I screamed from rage and pain and thrashed, trying to keep a hold on the hairpin.

Someone slammed me into the ground. The picket of a nearby tent struck my ribs and the skin gave way with an odd pop.

My hand spasmed and the hairpin dropped.

Omaskat's hoarse voice broke through the clamor. "Leave her! I said leave her!"

The shouts continued.

"Her ear, it's... Mercy of Gadr, it's hanging off."

"Hold back that hound!"

"Brother, are you all right? Can you stand?"

"Kill her! She has to be killed!"

"That is my decision," Omaskat hissed. "I said, leave her."

Through a haze, I watched him stagger towards me. Blood tricked from multiple punctures across his jaw and shoulder, but by the time he grabbed my tunic and hauled me to my feet, his boots were planted and his grasp like iron.

I stared into his face. The veins around his mismatched eyes had burst and there was dirt ground into his teeth. It was a nightmarish thing to see, though I knew that I looked little better.

He dragged me away. All the way through the camp I stumbled, followed by pointing fingers and gaping mouths. I was vaguely aware that people accompanied us for the first part of the journey, but at the edge of the camp, they fell away. This was a master's business now; a master and his slave, and the dog with the bloodied maw who loped behind.

I don't know what I expected to happen. A beating and violation, certainly. Death, probably. But when he threw me onto the muddy riverbank and knelt over me, sword at my throat, I was still surprised at the nearness of my end. And once more, I realized just how unprepared for it I was.

Death had never scared me before. Every Eangen and Eangi died in the knowledge that they were bound for the warm hearths of the High Halls, the company of our forebears and tables overflowing with the food and drink of the gods – a privilege unequivocally denied to the living. But until Eang shrove me, I had no place there and no hope of eternal rest with Eidr, when our days of song and revelry grew weary and we lay down for the Long Sleep.

I'd never see my husband again.

"Why?" Omaskat demanded, his voice cutting over the rush of the river and the distant, settling tumult of the camp. "I protected you!"

"It is your fate. And mine." Pain and anger made me bleary. My good hand slipped in the mud as I tried to push myself upright and his knuckles dug into my collarbone, the flat of his sword cold against my skin. "I have to do it."

"Fate? Eang knows nothing of Fate. You know nothing of Fate." He snorted and shook his head, disgust written across his face. "Ask yourself this, Eangi. If she wants me dead, why not kill me herself?"

I had no reply except what I had been taught: "It's my fate. Ours. I was supposed to kill you in the Hall, back when I first met you. I have to do it now."

He laughed: a harsh thing, all sharps and edges. "Then why am I still breathing?"

"Because I was weak." My voice cracked. The sound horrified me, but I could no longer keep myself together. "Eang left me because of it. She left us and they *all* died. Because of me. I will kill you. Now or tomorrow. But I will make this right."

"A third question for you. Why doesn't she help you? Look at you. You're bleeding everywhere, your ear is on a thread. Doesn't that hurt? I thought you were an Eangi. Turn my bones to dust. You can't, can you? Because my god is truly a god, and Eang's wrath cannot touch me."

I remembered the taste of Fire in my mouth, the way Algatt raiders had crumpled before my sword and gaze a dozen times. But when I looked to Omaskat, that Fire was still terribly, ominously absent.

"Gadr doesn't have that kind of power," I protested.

Instead of countering me he spat on the ground, half spittle, half blood from a punctured cheek. "Gadr isn't my god. Didn't Eang tell you why you're supposed to kill me?"

I blinked up at him, struck by his denial as much as his question. "What?"

"Why am I to die?"

"'Why' doesn't matter. But who do you worship if not Gadr?"

Exasperation burst from him in a scornful gust. "Can you not hear yourself? Or have both your ears gone?"

This second reminder of my ear made my stomach churn. Instinctively, I reached up a weak hand and felt at the dangling wad of flesh. The top of my ear was torn off.

Omaskat flicked his sword. I moved my fingers just in time to avoid the blade as he severed the last thread of skin.

I didn't feel it, but the shock made me scream. I struck out with my bad wrist, and the world cracked into blackness.

The next thing I knew, the rush of the river was all around me. Part of the bank had collapsed and only Omaskat's grip on my tunic stopped the torrent carrying me away.

"Fate has her own mind," Omaskat's voice said. In my disoriented state, I could not figure out which shoulder he stood behind. "You're free to go."

His hand opened and the river swallowed me whole.

EIGHT

I learned I was an Eangi in my fifth year. I remember the night in a child's way – emotions and fragmentary images, now inseparably merged with the stories my elders told me afterwards.

Raiders struck the outlying farms of the village of my birth, East Meade, just after dark. One moment the air was filled with the calls of birds, the scraping of kettles and a father singing a lullaby. Then came the horns and the screams.

That singer was my uncle. He was, by far, the kindest human I had ever known. His voice was like a hearthside in the autumn and sunshine in wheat. My father called him lazy, though I never understood why. He worked, but he did not complain about it as the others did. He sang as he walked, slapping his thigh to beckon the hunting dogs that followed him wherever he went. He sang as he hauled wood. He sang as he strung up deer and butchered them on the edge of the village. And he sang his clutch of children to sleep, every night.

From the loft where my sisters and I were bickering over the braiding of one another's hair and who got to sleep closest to the open shutters, I could see his house. I avoided a flailing limb and crouched, straining to see my cousins through the shutters of their own loft. The grasses growing over the roofs of our houses hung low, laden with summer flowers. But I could just pick out movement in the shadows; young bodies, including Yske, adjusting their mats for the night.

Despite the borrowed lullaby, it took a while for sleep to come. I tried to curl up against my eldest sister Hulda's back, but she complained of the heat and pushed me away. I waited for her breathing to lengthen, then crept back up against her narrow ribs. I knew she would be cuddling me like a doll by morning, which I adored, and so I was satisfied with myself.

After my uncle's voice faded, and the last barking dog had been hushed, the last shuttle tucked into the loom and the last grains set to soak for morning, real quiet fell. I closed my eyes.

Horns. Screaming. Dogs baying. An infant squalling. Hulda dragging me upright.

"Gatti! Gatti! The Algatt!"

I didn't cry. I was too stunned for that. I sat in place, gawking as my mother came up the ladder to put knives in my older sisters' hands. Then she dropped back down to the floor and pulled a padded tunic over her head.

"Stay in the loft," she snapped, then she braced one end of her bow against the side of her boot and strung it.

My father handed her a quiver of arrows and drew his own sword. Then, together, they vanished through the door.

Silence fell inside the house, while beyond, the chaos amplified. Hulda pushed me into the corner with my youngest sister, Etha, and levelled a warning gaze.

"Do not move."

I never forgot Hulda's face that day. There was no fear there – perhaps she did not know enough to be afraid. She was angry as a wounded bear and she held the knife with vengeful purpose. Our last sister, Skay, kept looking to her, desperate to borrow her courage.

My next memory was an Algatt man ascending the ladder to the loft. Hulda slashed his cheek open before he had even seen her. He toppled backwards, shouted, and hit the ground with a stomach-dropping thud.

A woman with a painted face came next. At the same time, a third Algatt grabbed the edge of the loft with an easy grip and hauled himself up.

Hulda shrieked at the woman and threw herself forward, slashing and diving. The woman's eyes widened. She dodged, avoided smacking her head off a beam and snatched Skay around the waist in the same movement. Skay dropped her knife and howled, kicking and wailing until the woman's arm locked across her throat. Her eyes bulged and her face began to redden.

"Drop that," the woman ordered Hulda.

Hulda twisted, trying to keep both Algatt in sight. The male had a lean, loping frame and his eyes were an uncanny green, edged with kohl. He fingered a hatchet warily, watching Hulda's feet, her shoulders, her eyes. She may have only been thirteen, but she was no fool.

Etha clutched at my back, immobilized, eyes round as saucers. She smelled of urine. I pushed her further into the corner.

Hulda threw the knife at the Algatt man without warning. He yelped and staggered back into the roof, loosing a rain of dust, dirt and disgruntled insects.

He recovered and leapt at her. Now unarmed, Hulda hurled a piece of discarded clothing in his face and tried to dodge, but there was too little space. In an instant her shift was wound in his fist and he hurled her out of the loft.

I heard her hit the table below: a scream, a thud, a clatter. Then stillness, broken by the hoot of an owl in the rafters on the other side of the house.

What happened next came to me only through the stories. Skay said that I screamed and the female raider's eyes bled. Hulda, half-conscious, said that another woman came and killed the man with his own hatchet. Etha, her memory thinner than mine, did not remember my presence at all.

All I could remember was heat. Heat in my blood, heat in my mouth, the exhaustion that the Fire left in my bones, and the owl's watching eyes.

"She's Eangi," the headman told my father as the pyres of the dead, including my uncle and three of my cousins, burned at his back. "Send her to the Hall of Smoke in Albor."

NINE

I drifted downriver. Time refused to be measured, but I imagined passing under a great archway of stone. I saw fires atop an endless wall, low mountains wrapped in tatters of cloud, and a rocky shoreline where a creature too large for a bear watched me with quiet, intelligent eyes. I saw the waving tops of cedars stretch into a sky smothered with stars. And then, in the waning light of afternoon, I realized a reed-woven riverman cradled me just above the surface of the river.

Water rushed around us, folding and eddying around his slim frame. Perhaps he had been there all night, or perhaps he had only just arrived. I couldn't recall.

I stiffened. I was barely strong enough to open my eyes, let alone navigate the unscrupulous motives of a riverman. Beings of water and reed, they were creations of the Gods of the Old World, like woodmaidens and humans. They were unpredictable, creatures who long ago slipped through the boundaries of the High Halls and made their home in the Waking World. They were also reclusive, but it wasn't unheard of for them to steal away young men and women for their entertainment, or to mold monsters from stone and clay.

Weak as I was, it took me several minutes to even recall how I'd gotten into the water. My memory returned in flashes, then settled upon Omaskat's face as he loomed over me – that moment when I'd expected to die.

The fear came back, stark and real. Death. Eidr. Helplessness. Anger came hard on its heels, an indignant, blazing spark that sharpened my mind for a blissful instant. But the cold of the river came close behind, seeping into my clothes and thoughts alike.

Why had Omaskat let me go? And where was I now?

I pressed my eyes shut and focused on the arms around me. Riverman. Deal with the riverman first.

"You are kind to me." It was a statement, not thanks; his kind hated praise from humans as much as they hated their questions.

"I have brought you to Oulden's Feet." The riverman's voice was a warm burble, reverberating through his chest of woven reeds and willow wisps. "Tell your patron; I would have her in my debt during this upheaval. And remind her, Eangi, that she is as mortal as the rest of us."

"Oulden?" The question escaped my lips before I could stop it. Oulden was the god of the Soulderni people – beyond the borders of Eangen. "What upheaval? Do you mean the Algatt?"

He set my feet on the silty bottom of the river and vanished under the surface. The water was clear, but I lost sight of him immediately, and he did not reappear.

I collapsed onto a boulder, physical weakness overriding my bewilderment. Now that the riverman was gone, the cold of the water pushed deeper into my flesh. I was numb with shock, my nose streamed, and coughing wracked my chest. I needed to get out, needed to find shelter before nightfall.

But the land around me was like nothing I had ever seen. Narrow hills and forest opened into a plain, bracketed by desolate mountains of iron-colored scrub and dark rock. The river took a slow bend here, broadening out towards islands and banks of fine black pebbles. These banks held back the approach of shoulder-high shrubs decorated with little pink flowers, interspersed with groves of bowing cedars. A bird or two darted among the foliage, but otherwise I might have been alone in the world.

I stared at the shape of the river, trying to recall a map I had once seen.

"This is Eangen." In my memory, a warrior's scarred finger traced across vellum. "Here's the Algatt's mountains, all across the north. This mountain here in the south – below the central Eangen clans like the Rioki and Amdur – that's Mount Thyr, where the shrine of Eang is. Here's Albor at its feet. There in the east, the Algatt's mountains end in foothills of a sort. Iskir is there, guarding the north borders. Now the river Pasidon – no, here, ignore that one, it's been dry for decades. Where are you from?"

I had leant in closer to his side. These were the days before Eidr and I had claimed one another, and I was just awakening to the ways of men and women. I liked this warrior, one of those that often sheltered in the Hall of Smoke. He was older than I at fifteen, his shoulders broadening and his scent that of horse, smoke and road.

"East Meade," I replied.

"So, here." He pushed his finger west and identified the sketch of a lynx face, between Mount Thyr and the sea. Then he leant closer to me and let his hand drift down the Pasidon towards my hovering fingers. "The Pasidon flows south into the Ridings – the grass hills in northern Souldern – past this wall. That's the fringe of the true Arpa Empire. Then it flows down into Souldern proper, the low mountains and valleys. Oulden's land."

My curiosity was genuine. "The Arpa Empire? Have you been there?"

"No." He did not sound disappointed. Turning, he lowered his head over me and toyed with the end of my braid, which hung to my waist. "No desire to, either. We're Eangen. You're Eangi. This land is in our blood and bones. Why would we want to leave it?"

And I had never left. Silently, I cursed my thirteen-year-old self, gawking at a beardless boy instead of memorizing the lines of the map he carried. But from what my people said of Souldern, with its open rock, gnarled trees and blithe shepherds, this river bend could be in its central valley.

Cool dread settled in my stomach. Not only was this land utterly unfamiliar, but Souldern was Arpa-occupied. The archway and wall I'd seen in my delirious journey south must have been the border.

I was in the Empire.

Yet, the riverman had also said he'd brought me to Oulden's Feet. I had no clue where that was, but as a priestess, I could begin to guess. Every god had a place where some of their presence lingered, even if they themselves were not physically present; a place of power, where the living, Waking World bled into the High Halls. Eang had her shrine in the field of poppies. Oulden must have his own holy ground – a place where his people could sit at his feet.

And Oulden, being allied with Eang, might be able to help me.

That thought gave me the strength to wade to the riverbank and strip, coughing and trembling the whole time. The sun still cut over the mountaintops and the breeze was not cold, but my wet clothes would do me more harm than good. Pebbles ground beneath my bare feet as I painstakingly shook out my tunic, loose trousers, leather shoes and woven legwraps. All were torn and stained with blood, though the rugged, birch-dyed brown of my trousers hid it better than the pale fireweed green of my tunic. Left in my linen undertunic, I scrubbed out what blood I could with one hand and threw the garments over a bush in a patch of waning, golden sunlight. Then I washed my aching body.

Finally, I sat down in the sunset. The black rocks were warm, and I closed my eyes, feeling the first strands of dry hair tickle my cheeks.

My hair. My heart dropped and my hand flew up to my head. My hairpin. The hairpin I had brought from Albor, Eidr's gift, my last piece of home. I'd lost it in the struggle with Omaskat.

I ground my eyes shut before I could cry. It was just a hairpin. It was not my husband himself. How could I mourn the loss of an item after all that had happened? My heart might hurt and my eyes sting with tears, but I couldn't let myself crumble over it.

Yet I was crumbling. The memories came now, gaining momentum until my chest ached so fiercely, I thought it might fracture.

Eidr's firm kiss, that night on the mountain by the shrine. Yske. The Hall of Smoke.

I drew in a ragged breath.

My family in East Meade. What had happened to them? Were they gone too?

Could I really, truly be this alone?

It was then, as I stared desolately into the shadows beneath the cedars across the river, that I saw the owl. I scrambled to my feet with a clattering of stones and the complaints of a dozen injuries, but I ignored them all.

There, perched on a low-swinging branch of a great cedar, was a pristine grey owl. He hooted, ruffling his wings, and glowered directly at me.

"Messenger?" I breathed, hardly daring to believe Eang had sent one of her owls directly to me. "I'm listening."

The vision came. I saw Sixnit wailing, her arms empty and her chest caving in with inconsolable grief. The man that had bought her raged, bellowing at their neighbours, demanding to know where the child had gone. Where Vistic had gone.

The image fled. I thought I saw Omaskat in its place, walking over a rise with the hound at his heels, but his face was unclear.

The third part of the vision came with Eang, clad in black tunic and knotted muscle. Her strigine eyes, gold as those of her owl messenger – rather, merged with those of her owl messenger – pinioned me.

"What have you done?"

Whatever hope the sight of the owl had conjured now fled in terror. Tears for Sixnit and Vistic dammed behind my eyes, as constricted as the breath in my lungs.

"You failed again, and you bound yourself to an infant?"

"He's just a baby." The words left me in a shudder, all thoughts of Souldern and Arpa legions vanishing from my mind. Wind stirred my hair, still damp from the river, and my exhausted limbs threatened to drop me back onto the stones. I forced them still.

"Now I must fulfill your vow to protect him," she hissed. "Do you think I have no more pressing matters than chasing down an infant? You've no concept of what this means."

I felt a spark of indignation. I did know what it meant, or I thought I did. I, an Eangi, had dedicated Vistic to Eang and vowed to protect him. In my absence, that responsibility overflowed to Eang. That was normal. Usual. Gods cared for their people and their people served them. That was how the world worked. It was Eang's duty to protect Vistic now, as well as my own. He was devoted to her.

Yet now, Eang raged as if I had committed another vile sin. I didn't dare question her, but I tried to see through her anger, tried to follow the threads of what I knew. Omaskat had spoken of a shift among the gods. The riverman had mentioned upheaval. Eang's people were spread thin, and the Eangi vastly depleted. Eang herself could not be everywhere.

Still, if Vistic was in some simple peril, she could have righted it easily. That meant whatever had happened to the child did not fall into the category of standard human misfortunes – or Eang simply had no care for Vistic's life.

"Where is he?" Caution trickled down my spine. The sunlight no longer felt warm, and the scent of cedar on the wind was tainted with smoke – real or imagined, I couldn't say. "Can you tell me what happened?"

Eang came to stand before me on the bank, the vision of her tall, powerful form overlaying stone, cloud-studded sky and desolate mountainsides.

"Find Omaskat and kill him," she charged. She reached out and put her palm in the center of my chest. Fire laced out from her fingers, worming down into my bones, alleviating my pain and fatigue, and closing many of my lesser wounds. "I give more fire and clarity for the journey, but when you face him, you will do it without my help. Be prepared. The riverman was right to bring you here – go to Oulden's Feet. Even if that bastard is still in hiding, his people will help you."

"Hiding?" I repeated, but Eang's fingers were already fading on my chest.

Her last words came distantly. "Turn around."

With that, she was gone. A dozen desperate questions lodged into my throat as the owl winged away and, by the time I blinked, all signs of the goddess's visitation had dissipated.

"Are you lost?"

I fell over, trying to turn, brace and flee all at once. Somewhere between hitting the ground and getting back up again I seized a rock, my heart hammering wildly, and brandished it.

A girl stood on the riverbank. She was just short enough for the scrub to shield her – ten, perhaps, or eleven years old. She had spoken Northman, like me, but with a tumbling, hitching dialect that I had rarely heard before: Soulderni. She carried a crook and was so darkened by the sun that her skin nearly matched the color of the branches. Half a dozen goats separated from the brush around her, clopping down to the riverside to drink.

My eyes darted around the bushes and my ears strained for signs of anyone else. But other than the goats, the girl was alone. No threat, just a child. And from her unfrightened expression, she had seen nothing of my vision.

"Yes, I am. I'm lost," I replied. My fingers loosened on the rock, but I did not put it down.

The girl frowned from the makeshift weapon to my face. Despite my being twice her size, muscled and unkempt, her crook and better health seemed to convince her I was no real threat. "Where are you from? What happened to you?"

"Eangen," I managed, forcing my shoulders to relax. "There's… trouble, in the north. Can you take me to Oulden's Feet? Is it close by?"

"Nor-th. Nor-teh," she mimicked my accent curiously, then stuck out her hand in a practical, maternal way. "Yes. Come with me."

TEN

Oulden's Feet lay in a small, broad bowl of a valley. There were great trees here, ancient and creaking, with branches that spread low to the ground like descending spiders. Half a league from a waterfall they gave way to patterns of hip-high stones, radiating out in concentric circles from an inner ring and ending in a rim of pillars, weatherworn and taller than two men.

The girl led me to a camp amid the standing stones. There were hundreds of tents, hide and canvas stitched with bright colored threads and supported by intricately carved poles. Some dwellings were girded by worn pathways, as though they'd been there for months, while others were only now being erected; men and women hammered in pegs and corralled herds of goats, gnarled mountain sheep and huge plains horses. Children ran free. Dogs barked, pots clinked, and the eyes of the lean, dark-skinned Soulderni followed my progress around the edge of their settlement.

But no one intervened. No guards stopped us – I wasn't even sure if the pre-pubescent boys and girls, watching over the outer herds, could properly be called guards. I tried to take comfort in this, but my nerves were so raw and my body so exhausted, I almost wished for a hostile welcome. At least then I'd know where I stood.

"What is this?" I asked the girl, who had told me her name was Uwi. My voice was shallow now, raspy and flat with exhaustion, and it took nearly all my focus to put one foot before the other. "Do your people live here? Are you... nomads?"

"No! Well... we do live here during the Summer Solstice, but that's still three weeks away. We live in the mountains, but they aren't... safe, anymore. So we came early." Uwi brushed burnt brown hair back from her eyes and nudged her clutch of goats with her staff.

"Because it is safe here?"

"It is always safe at Oulden's Feet," she stated with the ease of an oft-repeated phrase. "Only his servants can pass the borders."

I began to nod, slowly processing her words. The thought of the mountains being unsafe resonated, but the girl's last sentence presented a more immediate problem.

I slowed, struggling to focus on the nearest standing stone. "I serve Eang, Uwi."

Uwi shot me a surprised look, though it transitioned to one of caution when she saw my blanched face. "That doesn't matter. I invited you in. You're under Hearth Law, Hessa."

Hearth Law was as old as these stones, a code of mutual respect and protection enforced by the enigmatic force of Fate herself to protect travelers and hosts. It was Hearth Law that had led me to trust Omaskat and invite him into the Hall of Smoke, not two weeks ago. But he had broken that law, claiming to be Eangen and lying about who he was – I did derive some satisfaction from pondering what punishment Fate might unleash on him for that. Stories of Hearth Law breakers usually involved lives of ill luck, culminating in bizarre, fatal accidents. I'd heard of one who was mauled by her own, suddenly feral dog, and I thought such a punishment would be particularly fitting for Omaskat.

If Uwi was offering me Hearth Law, it meant I was under the protection of her family and her god, so long as I returned their kindness with truthfulness and respect. It meant that, for now, I was safe.

"Come." Uwi offered me her staff for support and pointed to a nearby tent. "We'll take care of you."

—

I remembered little of the next days save a bed of furs, the scent of herb and honey salve, and the constant, murmuring chatter of Soulderni dialect. The presence of such comforts, rather than alleviating my fatigue, seemed to give it rein. I passed seamlessly from dreams to waking, barely able to discern between the two. Only pain rooted me in reality for any length of time – the pain of my wounds being cleaned, bandages being changed, and memories creeping to the forefront of my beleaguered mind.

At long last, I slipped from a dream of Eidr under the summer sun to a clear, sharp wakefulness. I cracked one eye to see the hides of a tent, sealed with wax and red zig-zag stitches and supported by poles carved with circular patterns. The breeze was cool, and a grating sound came from nearby; a steady rasping, interspersed with the rustle of clothes.

I saw a woman kneeling by a millstone outside the tent. The bottom stone was bellied with age, speaking of generations of Soulderni use. The second stone, held in both her hands and drawn lengthwise across its companion, was equally worn – smooth, and lightened from decades in the sun.

The woman set her stone aside with a deep clunk and swept newly milled grain into a bowl. As soon as she stood, another woman appeared to take her place with a bowl of raw grain, and the grating began again.

"Hessa of the Eangen," the first woman greeted me as she ducked into my tent. Or, rather, her tent. Now that she was closer, I recognized her as Uwi's mother. Her skin and her accent were lighter than her daughter's, clear and almost familiar. "Have you decided to join us in the Waking World? Or shall I nurse you like a babe for another week?"

I couldn't tell if her words were teasing. "A week?"

Uwi's mother nodded. She was clad in a many-layered Soulderni gown of browns and oranges, belted high and hung about with daily tools – knife, scissors, pouch, and a carved disc I thought must be a charm. She stopped across the fire from me, hooked a suspended metal plate and nudged it over the flames to heat. Smoke, captured under the surface, began to seep around its edge in curling grey fingers.

"My name is Silgi," the woman informed me as she fetched several jars and baskets and arrayed them around her bowl of flour. Taking up a jar of oil, she poured some onto the cooking plate as she continued, "My daughter found you by the water, and it is I who have nursed you, and my hearth and family that have protected you. So now, in return, tell me of the trouble in the north."

I met the woman's eyes for a weary, strained moment, and she raised her brows at me. She expected her answers now and was obviously unconcerned by the fact that I was covered in bandages and had just woken up from a week's illness. But though I didn't want to speak, didn't want to remember the events that had brought me here, she was right. After all her family had done, she deserved an explanation.

And I had questions of my own that needed answering.

"The Arpa have driven the Algatt out of the mountains," I began, forcing my leaden tongue around the words and sitting up. I was clad in a linen shift, though I only vaguely remembered putting it on. Beside me, I noticed my own clothes rested on a rock, cleaned and repaired. "The Algatt are stripping Eangen land. The gods are... restless."

Silgi's hands, now sprinkling salt and seeds into the bowl, hesitated. She murmured "Mmm," and began to sift the ingredients together with her fingers. "I thought there have been too many legionaries heading north in the past few years."

I sat up straighter. "What? Why did you not... not warn us?"

She stifled a laugh. "Warn you? Of what, Eangen? Legions pass all the time. We pay our tribute and move on with our own concerns, as you do with the Algatt."

Even weak as I was, the thought made my Fire flare. She didn't know I was an Eangi, but even so – who was this woman to speak me, a wounded guest, in such a way? "We do not pay tribute to the Algatt."

"Then what are predictable raids?" the woman inquired, pouring honey into the bowl in one long, amber stream. On the metal cooking disc between us, the oil began to grow transparent with heat. "You hide what you need and let them find what you can spare. Your Eangi and your warriors spend a few weeks running about, keeping their swords whet and sating your goddess with blood. And the next year it all just happens again."

I sat back, cradling my splinted wrist in my lap and eyeing her grey hair. It was blond between those streaks of silver, and she talked of the north far too knowledgably to be a simple Soulderni mountain woman. Then there was that accent, so clear and familiar.

I felt myself darken. "You're Algatt."

"So was your grandfather or his, like as not." She shrugged, eyeing my face with a new guardedness. Before her heavy skirts, the fire popped, and the oil on the great metal disc began to steam. "A marriage here, a rape there, a forbidden lover. The bloodlines bleed, Eangen, more than we'd like to admit. You Eangen have Soulderni blood from before the Arpa came. I fell in love with a Soulderni traveler and left my people behind. Even my son Iosas is half Arpa. That was my choice; a bargain I made. But he works hard, and his father's god protects him, so for that I am grateful. Life continues."

Her words angered me, but we were under Hearth Law, in the middle of an encampment to which she obviously belonged. Now was no time for hostilities.

"His father's god protects him? What god is that?" I inquired, fighting to keep myself under control.

"Aliastros. An Arpa god allied with Oulden."

"If he's an ally, won't he protect your people in Oulden's stead?" I wanted to know. "Your daughter told me the mountains are too dangerous to live in."

"Oulden is quiet," Silgi returned, adding some water to the bowl and beginning to knead briskly. Pockets of dry flour burst beneath her knuckles. "A new god has been seen; shrines destroyed. But Oulden, and Aliastros, and even Esach, have not stopped it. So, we've fled here, to Oulden's Feet – and at the Solstice, our priests say he will come and put all to right."

This was shocking but I took it mutely, fitting the information

66

together with Eang's words. If there was a new god in Souldern, they must be very strong to send Oulden into hiding. Perhaps he would be no help to me at all. Perhaps I'd be better to beg for a horse and leave Souldern right now.

"Who is this new god?" I asked. "Are they ours, or Arpa?"

Silgi eyed me at the word 'ours' but shrugged. "I'm no priestess, who am I to say? I do not walk in the High Halls or the Arpa courts."

That was fair enough. But where Silgi was no priestess, I was, and though I'd normally have relinquished a concern like this to Svala, I was alone now. Unrest among the gods was my concern and, if I was to make it back to Eangen alive, I needed to know what – and who – I might encounter.

"If I was to guess," Silgi added, "I would say they are Arpa. No, don't ask me who. I don't know. There are too many Arpa gods, and half of them aren't even proper deities. Just heroes or ancestors."

She flipped the dough and shook in wrinkled, sun-dried berries, eyeing the steaming oil and picking up her pace. She continued, "They have a head god called Lathian, as you Eangen have Eang, but no one has ever actually seen him, even his high priests. And only Aliastros has ever been seen in Souldern."

"What does he rule?"

"The wind, elemental and without territory," she replied. "The same generation as your Gods of the New World – like Eang, like Gadr and Oulden. When you meet my son, the half-Arpa one, you'll see… his eyes are different. You, do you serve Eang, or one of her court?"

I watched her shoulders and arms flex as she folded the dough, again and again. Eang had numerous lesser deities under her rule, and many of them governed Eangen clans like the Rioki, the Addack and the Amdur. As an Eangi I answered to Eang alone, but I wasn't about to tell an Algatt what I was.

"My people serve Eang," I said simply. Hearth Law forbade me to lie, but I didn't have to be entirely honest. "I'm from East Meade, between Mount Thyr and the sea."

With a noise of consideration, she looked from me to the oil, then passed me her bowl. "Well, I still worship Gadr, so I'd thank you not to put a knife in my back. I've been away from my people and their raiding for a very, very long time."

I felt my face twitch.

"Now," the older woman said brusquely, "you look well enough to bake us some bread for supper – flat cakes, northern-style, and do not let them burn."

"I need to pay my respects to Oulden," I interjected, glancing from my pile of waiting clothes to the standing stones. I wasn't familiar with Soulderni ritual or Oulden's expectations, but if he was anything like Eang he would require me to present myself somewhere.

"Then I'll fetch my son," Silgi conceded, brushing off her hands. "He can show you to the waterfall."

Iosas, Silgi's son by an Arpa legionnaire, met me in the open ground between the tents. His mixture of Algatt and Arpa blood left him paler than I, and paler than the Soulderni by far – a compact, narrow-eyed young man with skin the color of milk and irises of drifting summer cloud. At first glance, I might have thought him blind. But when his gaze met mine, it was fixed and keen.

"I'll show you the way, Eangen," he said, adjusting the stocky lamb in his arms and nodding towards the waterfall at the end of the valley. His head was shaved and his accent was wholly Soulderni, juxtaposing his decidedly un-Soulderni appearance.

I had never met an Arpa in a peaceful setting, nor one so visibly marked by an Arpa deity as Iosas. So I chose not to speak, ducking my chin and falling into step behind him.

Soulderni parted and churned around us as we passed through the camp. Their women wore high-belted gowns like Silgi, while the men, including Iosas, chose kaftans or tunics, with trousers in the northern style. But while Eangen favored greens and blues and greys, the Soulderni leaned towards fiery, earthen oranges, reds and creams – the colors that their land most readily produced.

The people cast me curious glances, but it was the smiles that caught me off guard. An old woman outright beamed at me. A middle-aged man touched his forehead in acknowledgement, with a nostalgic turn of the lips. Children clustered behind the side of a tent to grin and peer at my short frame, lighter skin and thick, frizzing black hair, and called greetings that I only half-understood.

Their god was missing, and they were hiding in this valley. But they still had the will to welcome a foreigner, far from home?

"Did they tell you about Oulden?" My guide's voice pulled my attention back to him. The lamb rested his head on his shoulder, placidly blinking between me and the crowd.

"A little," I replied, picking up my pace so we could speak more easily. My muscles were stiff from days of disuse and my wounds, pinched and aching, stretched with the exertion. "I know a new god invaded Soulderni land and Oulden's nowhere to be found."

Iosas shifted the lamb in his arms to consider me more directly. "I wouldn't call them a new god, Eangen. From what our priests say, they – he – isn't like Oulden or Aliastros, or even Fang."

"Your mother called him a new god. An Arpa one, too."

Iosas made a discontented sound. "I'm not sure about that."

I brushed my fingers across a tall standing stone as we passed. "Why?"

"Our gods have faces and forms, like us." Iosas slowed as the camp petered off. The waterfall draped over a horseshoe cliff some two hundred meters above us, roaring where it plunged into a pool at its base. But though mist began to condense on my cheeks, we were still far enough away not to be deafened. "They treat, negotiate. They want to be seen and feared and worshiped. But this god has no face. No worshipers. No name."

While I digested this, the man made for a low stone altar beside the pool, stained from centuries of bloodletting. He set the lamb's feet down on the altar. "Will you take the knife from my belt?"

I had more questions to ask, but once the knife was in my hand the presence of Oulden settled upon me. Even if he was in hiding, this was his shrine: his holy ground. The god would hear.

I stilled and breathed deeply, letting the fine mist and clean mountain air rush into my lungs. The shard of Eang inside me swelled to meet it, and I felt the ghostly weight of my lost collar around my neck.

Iosas didn't comment on the change in me. I saw the breath stream out of his lips, sending the mist into eddies, and his hands held the lamb in absolute stillness.

"Greetings, Oulden, from a son of Aliastros," he rumbled under the roar of the waterfall.

"Greetings, Oulden," I echoed, "from a daughter of Eang."

The waterfall continued to crash down, unchanging and unaffected. But I felt the mist press in closer and the noise of the camp grew muffled.

I put the knife to the lamb's throat and slit. The animal bucked and bleated and, when it had quietened, Iosas held it over the pool. Its blood drained into the dark water in a long, languorous stream.

I drew up beside him. With practiced resolve, I slit open a fingertip and let the drops fall beside the lamb's blood for good measure.

"For allowing me shelter in your land, when I was injured and lost," I murmured to the mist and the roaring cascade.

Droplets of blood struck the surface of the pool, one by one. Then they vanished. The water remained dark but clean, all signs of the sacrifice washed away.

"You're an Eangi, aren't you?"

I looked at Iosas askance. I couldn't evade a direct question like this, not without lying. "Yes."

"I've heard only Eangi can make sacrifices among the Eangen. Is that true?"

"Yes."

"Mmm." His pale eyes stared into the distance beyond the waterfall. The drained lamb lay on the altar beside us now, limp and lifeless. "Then, priestess, are you here for a purpose? Has Eang sent you?"

I followed his gaze and let my eyes roam up to the rim of the waterfall. It glistened in the sun, smooth and flashing through a haze of mist. While saying yes might put me in a better position among the Soulderni, it wasn't precisely the truth. Eang had not planned on my being swept into Souldern, and the only charge she'd given me concerning it was to leave again.

But this land was troubled by the gods, and I was a priestess. So perhaps, by proximity, there was a purpose to my presence – however brief I intended that presence to be.

"I can't say," I finally returned. "It was a riverman who found me and brought me to Oulden's Feet. He wanted favor with Eang, he claimed. For the 'upheaval.'"

Iosas went quiet. "Well. The upheaval is here. And I, for one, am glad to have Eang in this camp."

I looked at him sideways, but he was already bending to rinse his hands at the lapping edge of the pool. I mirrored him, hoping the movement would alleviate the need for me to reply.

As I handed the knife back, the young man abruptly asked, "Will you put my family in danger?"

Thinking of kind and trusting Uwi, holding out her hand to me on the riverbank, I shook my head firmly. "No. But I would prefer the camp not know I am an Eangi."

"Why?"

I contemplated him for a minute, then answered candidly, "I need to return north as soon as possible. If your people know what I am, they may expect more than I can give."

Iosas accepted this stoically and took up the dead lamb by the hooves. "Let's head back. You should stay with us until after the Solstice. The gathering will break up after that and I've a cousin who can take you north. He can get you through the Arpa border, quietly."

I hesitated. Summer Solstice was a fortnight away. How could I waste such valuable time when Vistic was missing, Sixnit captive, Eangen being invaded and Omaskat moving on to gods-knew where?

But even as I thought it, the weakness of my body reasserted itself. Loose hair brushed over my bandaged ear. My wrist ached. The dog bite on my thigh smarted and the puncture wound in my ribs protested my every breath. I was in no condition to traverse Arpa territory. Especially with the threat of interloping gods.

As reluctant as I was to do it, I forced myself to nod. "Then I'll stay until the Solstice. Thank you."

Iosas started towards the camp. "Good. In the meantime, Eangi, keep your secret close; I'll not expose you."

ELEVEN

I was sixteen. Yske and I joined a line of women on one side of the long hearth, shoulder to shoulder in our winter dresses of richly dyed wool and thick embroidery, our faces clean of kohl and hair bound in perplexing tumbles of braids, leather and beads.

Across the fire, Eidr caught sight of me and his face broke into a wide, wild grin. He staggered as the other Eangi and Eangen men jostled him, each clad in their own heavy winter tunics and kaftans, skirted and trimmed with intricate, wide braid.

Eidr rejoined their song, hurling verses across the flames toward us women, and I grinned back.

We women replied, familiar harmonies and lyrics twisting up into the rafters of the Hall of Smoke. The men's feet pounded. The women spun and shook out their skirts in a quick, thunderous clap that disintegrated into laughter as a little girl lost her balance. She toppled into a dozen helpful arms, the song ended, and we merged into a second, then a third.

We sang. We chanted. We danced. We lost our breaths and sagged into one another while the winter wind howled through the high chimney and cracks of the huge double doors. But inside the Hall, the air was warm, thick with fire and life, movement and music.

One of the worst winters in living memory was drawing to a close. The elder Eangi murmured that there had been conflict among the Eangen and Arpa gods, effectively silencing Eang for months on end and leaving the Eangen to endure a bleak winter without divine aid.

But Eang's silence, the High Priestess assured us, was no reason to fear for her wellbeing. Nor was it a reason not to celebrate her victory.

We served the Goddess of War, mortal yet undying, and she would return to us triumphant. So, we sang.

At one point, Ardam, war chief of the Eangi, raised his voice over the last of the villagers' lilting strains. The song was familiar, ages old, and it signaled the transition into a different part of the celebrations: the telling of our history. His voice was strong, swelling over our heads as he drew our attention to the front of the Hall.

Eidr pulled me under his arm and leant against one of the Hall's many carved pillars. I eased into him, enjoying the labored rise and fall of his chest against my back.

Ardam's voice took on a chanting quality while we settled in. Children were shushed and a knot of red-cheeked women smothered the last of their laughter in each other's shoulders.

He sung of black waves, and the boats on which our people came to Eangen. He sung of Eang, who saved them from the cold of that first, hard winter. He recounted how she led the Gods of the New World to victory over the Gods of the Old – gods of starlight, shadow and rage. And when his verses finished, Svala's voice rose in his place.

The tempo increased, the melody turned, and a new layer of intensity settled over the onlookers. The High Priestess told of each New God, one by one. Most had submitted to Eang – Aita the Great Healer and Esach the Goddess of Storms, along with lesser Eangen deities like Riok and Briel and Dur. But others had refused, like Gadr and the shape-shifting deity who had once inhabited Iskiri land, Ried.

I closed my eyes as the verses spun on, unraveling the story of how Eang had slain and bound Ried, and how Gadr had fled north to the high mountains.

Then she sang of the struggles of the Eangen. When Svala described the departure of the traitors who became the Algatt, her eyes flashed; the people roared and joined in, ending the tale in a clamorous riot of Eangen and Eangi voices.

"Eang, Eang," we cried. "The Brave. The Vengeful. The Watchful. The Swift."

As the final word rung out, someone screamed. I started, struggling to see over the press of humanity. At my back, Eidr went still.

"What is it?" I hissed to him.

"I can't tell – wait."

The scream died. Eangi elders pushed the crowd back to reveal an Eangi girl, standing rigid at the head of the Hall before the densely carved, candle-laden altar. Ardam moved to help the girl, but the High Priestess blocked him.

"It's Eang," Svala said, her voice oddly thick. "Leave her."

The crowd retreated more, leaving a half-moon of empty floor around the immobile girl. She was no older than twelve.

Slowly, the girl raised her head. I flinched back into Eidr.

Her eyes looked like bottomless wells. The torches around her flared with sudden heat and, for a timeless instant, Eang looked over the masses through the Eangi's eyes. We all felt her gaze, both Eangi and Eangen, like a fire in our blood.

Then she departed, as wordlessly and unexpectedly as she had come. Time slowed, drawing out the space between two breaths. Torchlight flickered. The girl's face slackened and her eyes fluttered closed. And then, at last, she collapsed to the hard-packed earthen floor.

No one spoke. No one moved. Svala, staring at the motionless girl, eased back onto her heels and ran a hand over her lips, collecting herself. Now, I can recall the mix of fear and relief on her face – then the flutter of grief. But in the moment, her disconcertion went without notice. The girl had only fainted, after all.

Svala would not announce until the next morning that the girl had died. It was Eang's gift to a favored daughter – not only a visitation but a swift, painless entry into the High Halls of the Gods and Eang's feasting tables. Deaths like this came every so often among the Eangi. It was the very highest honor.

But in Albor that night, we thought the child had only lost

consciousness. So as soon as the goddess departed, the occupants of the Hall erupted into an elated, worshipful roar around her crumpled form. It filled my ears to bursting.

Eidr stepped forward and threw his head back. As his presence left me, I closed my eyes and cradled my Fire in my chest for a euphoric moment. Then I added my own cry to the throng, unleashing a full-throated howl up into the rafters of the Hall of Smoke.

TWELVE

Over the next two weeks, my shattered wrist knitted and my wounds closed under Silgi's care. I mourned my mangled ear, but only when no one was around to see me touch the ragged flesh and generous scabs. My Fire couldn't return a lost piece of flesh. I could braid my hair to cover it, but that was little comfort. This was not a simple scar – my hearing was affected, and I had lost a piece of my body.

I settled in with Silgi's family, meeting her husband Ceydr and working frequently beside Uwi on whatever household tasks my health permitted. I requested several times to meet the cousin Iosas claimed could take me north, only to be told they had not yet arrived. It wasn't until the night before the Solstice, once evening fires had sprung up, that my question was met with affirmation.

Ceydr, a greying Soulderni man with a black topknot, brilliant red kaftan and a deliberate, smooth stride, led me through the camp. The settlement had swelled since my arrival, forcing the Soulderni to overflow into one another's space. Trying not to trample toddlers underfoot, they greeted one another with kisses and laughter and clustered around laden festival tables.

If I cast my eyes to the sky, I could almost pretend that I was back in Albor for our own midsummer festival. The Hall of Smoke would be thick with incense and visitors. The Eangi women would wear gowns of sky blue and the men forest green, the edges of every garment embellished with braid or embroidery of white and grey and black. I would braid

Eidr's hair and he would pull me down into his lap, kissing me for the entire Hall to see. Yske would roll her eyes. Sixnit would smirk, and her husband Vist would goad us on.

My throat constricted and my surroundings faded. For the barest instant, I caught the scent of Eidr again: smoke and earth, iron and leather, all undergirded by his own warm humanity. I would kiss him and hide in curve of his neck, enclosing myself in him.

I felt cold. I ached for the security of his arms around me, of the laughter of my friends and cousins in my ears. The sense of being one of many, part of a whole.

Here among the Soulderni I was surrounded, but so very, very alone.

"Ceydr!"

My attention drifted back to the present as a woman shouldered through the crowd. Her eyes were the darkest blue I had ever seen, nestled into so many laugh-lines that she seemed permanently on the edge of mirth.

"Euweth." Ceydr kissed her on the mouth and spun her to face me. I blinked. The environment had transformed him from stately patriarch to jovial, impish boy.

She laughed and leant into his shoulder.

"This is a stray Eangen that Uwi found," Ceydr said. "Escaped the bloodshed up north and was delivered to us by a riverman."

"Well." Euweth drew me closer. "After that ordeal, a little time on Oulden's chest seems to have done you good."

I smiled at her. The expression didn't come easily, but these people were my hosts. I needed to keep their trust, no matter the darkness that lingered over me. "Ceydr's family has been very kind."

Ceydr waved over her shoulder at someone unseen and nodded at me. "She needs to get back to Eangen."

"We can take her to the border," Euweth offered without hesitation. "She can regale us with Eangen songs on the way. And tonight. That's my price. Oh, child," she laughed at the expression on my face, "come and take a drink. We don't expect you to sing sober."

Euweth's family was much smaller than Ceydr's. There was no husband, but she had a son of perhaps twenty-five who was not in the company of a wife. He smirked as his mother and Ceydr laughed like children.

"Here." The young man handed me a cup. He wore his black hair short, like Iosas, though most of the older men wore topknots. "Don't mind them. They grew up together and the sight of one another takes them too far back."

I accepted the cup and sniffed at it. It was mead, but not like home. Eangen honey always tastes like pine, so our mead does too.

The Soulderni bent down to look in my face. Whatever he found there, it made him smile. His features lacked his mother's free joy and his black beard was too short, but there was a companionableness about his eyes. "I'm Nisien."

"Hessa. Tell me, Nisien, what should I expect from the next few days?"

He surveyed the gathering. "Well, tomorrow morning at dawn, there will be prayers and dedication. Sunset is when the sacrifice is made and Oulden will bless us… if he comes, but… the priests claim he will. The next two days will be weddings and feasting. Then we head back north and take you home."

"Just as far north as you can," I clarified. "I don't need you to take me into Eangen. Though I'd appreciate advice on passing the Arpa border."

The lightness around his eyes clouded at mention of the border. "Of course. We'll do what we can for you."

I faced him more directly. The wine warmed my stomach, and with it, my discomfort eased.

"You Soulderni are strange people," I informed him, awed that he would help me so easily. "Good people. But strange."

"Life is… sparser, south of Eangen," he admitted, "but also longer. There's little to live on and half of it goes to the Arpa. But what we have, we enjoy, and give to others." He glanced into my cup, discovered it was still three quarters full, and tapped the bottom impatiently. "Drink this and come. I hear you can sing when properly tended."

I shook my head. "Where would you have heard that? No. I'll come with you, but I won't sing."

He relented, offered me an arm and we took a seat beside the fire. Eager to keep away from the topic of singing, I posed a question.

"You and your mother live in northern Souldern?"

"Yes, the Ridings." He settled back onto one palm. "My mother has a way with horses, but the mountains are too rocky for anything more than donkeys. So she, and others like her, congregate on the plains."

I looked around for the animals in question. They were enormous, the plains horses I'd seen on my first night in camp, picketed two tents away in the company of several apathetic donkeys.

"What about you?" I pried. "You talk as though you're not one of them."

Nisien turned his cup in contemplation, then made a sound between a weary exhalation and a laugh. "Maybe I'm not?"

I gave a small shrug, unsure if I had trespassed on overly personal ground.

"I spent ten years in the legions, away from my mother, fighting and taxing my own people. After that, I don't feel that I belong here. But life dragged her to the brink of death while I was gone. I can't leave her again."

My hand stilled on my cup. "You fought with the Arpa?"

He nodded. "Many of the men around here did at one point or another. They take us as boys."

"Not the women?"

Nisien snorted. "No. The Arpa have no women in their army. Their women would never touch a sword, and their men would never let them."

That thought sent me into a pensive silence. The Eangen were pragmatic about gender: whoever could fight, fought; whoever could farm, farmed; whoever could weave, wove. The notion of an entirely male army, and a female population who had never touched a weapon, was foreign to me.

"Do you have an Arpa wife?" I asked, curious to meet one of these unmilitaristic Arpa women. "Did you bring one home?"

Nisien, halfway through a drink of wine, choked. "What? No!" Realizing how emphatic he'd sounded, he added, "I don't intend to marry, so don't mistake my attention."

"Oh, I didn't," I assured him, and it was true. But of its own accord my memory turned back to Albor, back to Eidr's arms, and my smile faltered. I hid my face in my cup. "How did you leave the legions?"

"I earned my release." Nisien sat forward now, bracing his arms on his knees and letting his back round out. "There was a minor... power struggle... among the commanders. I chose the right side. But I'm still Soulderni auxiliary. If there's a real war, I'll be summoned back."

"So the Arpa push into the mountains doesn't count as real war?" I probed.

He frowned, then grunted. "Hah. Well, I wouldn't know. How did they get that far north?"

I shook my head. "No idea. They didn't pass through Eangen lands."

"Must have come up around the Headwaters then." Nisien scratched at the side of his face.

I nodded thoughtfully. The Headwaters was where the Pasidon spawned, a broad expanse of water that bubbled with hidden springs. It looked harmless enough, they said, until you fell into a well and drowned, or were snared by one of a thousand horrors and torn limb from limb. No one lived anywhere near it nor dared to cross it unless it was locked in ice.

"So you can't think of any reason why the Arpa would push into Algatt land?" I pressed.

"Well, it forces the Eangen and the Algatt to annihilate one another, but that's a rather messy strategy for the Arpa, and they've never cared much for anything north of Souldern." Nisien shook his head. "I truly can't say."

Annihilate. I mulled the word over until it soured my stomach, my thoughts darkened, and I stood in the ashes of Albor once more. Was this man right? Would the Eangen and the Algatt battle each other for control of the Rim until one, or both, were gone?

Nisien saw my face change but, mercifully, did not comment. Instead, he offered me one word: "Sing."

I rolled my eyes heavenward and rapidly blinked over-bright eyes. "Gods, no."

"Well, I'm not taking you north if you don't." The man gave a playful half-shrug.

"Perhaps I don't want you to take me north," I replied. "You stink of horse."

He gave me a glare of mock offense, then added in a gentler tone, "Sing something from home? You must miss it."

I made a face at him, but my mind began to turn. There had been no funerals after the raid in Albor, no memorials, no pyres. I couldn't perform death rites from such a distance. But didn't my people, my husband and my cousin, deserve at least one song?

I cleared my throat and shifted onto my knees, letting my chest and stomach open. "All right."

If anyone else watched, I didn't see. I focused inward, recalling Eidr, Yske and Vist. I pulled up the memories of every corpse I had seen and laid it before my mind's eye, like glass beads on a string.

I sang an Eangi song, Eidr's favorite. It was an old one, whose lyrics were wrapped in the obscurity of centuries past; not quite a dirge, though it was by no means joyful. It was a song of passage, of closing, of loss and hope.

My voice was deep for a woman's, not sweet, but easy. I felt each note hum through my ribs, softening as it slipped into husky minors and meandering lengths.

For once, the Soulderni did not openly stare, but their conversations lowered as they listened to the melody. Nisien's eyes followed me throughout, studying me, drawing the words into himself as if he understood their meaning.

When the last note faded, there was no applause. The Soulderni sensed that this was not a song to be commended.

"Are you mourning your village?"

I glanced up at Uwi and was startled to find her face blurry. "Yes."

The girl dropped down to my side and crossed her legs. "Can I sing with you? I don't know the words, but I can sing along."

For a second time that night, I blinked tears from my eyes. "Yes. Yes, you may."

Uwi straightened her shoulders in satisfaction and looked to me, her belly already puffing out with deep breaths.

I parted my lips and began to sing, "The Owl, he watched, his eyes of gold…"

THIRTEEN

At sunset the next day, the Soulderni gathered. They wore their finest clothes, resplendent in oranges and reds and creams. Women bound their hair into twin braids, wrapping them round with embroidered strips of cloth. Men wore their hair free while children shrieked and fidgeted with excitement, hauling around dogs and tugging at their parents' clothing.

I slipped, alone, to a spot in the back of the crowd as Silgi's family merged with two long rows of Soulderni, all singing and shuffling their feet. Skirts swung. Men shook out their hair and women sang to the Solstice sunset, but there was more urgency than joy to their actions. They were a people whose land had been invaded, whose god had gone silent, and all their hope of his reappearance depended upon tonight.

I felt their determination and fear in my bones, pulsing with the beat of escalating drums, tumbling and booming and tapping into a fevered pace. The fervor of the crowd rose alongside, swelling with deep wooden flutes and the sudden blasts of horns.

Straining up onto my toes, I glimpsed a priestess in a gown of palest yellow. Her braids trailed down before her ears, while the rest of her grey hair was piled into a crown and studded with bracken. She was old – likely the oldest woman I had ever seen – but her back was still straight and her gaze clear.

She led a bull towards the altar at the foot of the waterfall, just visible above the heads of the crowd on a nearly imperceptible elevation.

Despite the chaos of humanity and sound, the animal's steps were languid, drugged.

Nisien drew up to my side without greeting and set his stance, arms laced over his chest. He did not sing, but rather watched the proceedings with distant brown eyes.

"Why don't you join in?" I asked.

Nisien gave a half-shake of his head, still focused on the proceedings. "Oulden hasn't spoken in weeks. And I've never been the most pious of men."

I eyed him sidelong, the priestess in me trying to read beneath his words. "You don't think he'll come tonight?"

Nisien shrugged with an air that dissuaded further questioning. After last night I was comfortable with him, but his lack of confidence and the tension in the air made my skin crawl. I brushed at my arms and turned my attention back to the ceremony.

The pounding of the drums eased, the eye of a storm, and the women filled the lull with a new, lilting verse.

As if responding to their summons, the waning sun broke up through the valley and struck the foot of the waterfall. There it hung, transforming the mist into clouds of shimmering gold.

My breath hitched as the priestess raised her knife and the drums picked up again, steadier than before. Besides Nisien and me, she seemed to be the only one not singing. She cast her ancient eyes from the bull to the sunset, blade poised, chest rising and falling in time with the music.

A horn blasted and the Soulderni priestess struck. The head of the bull bowed, and his broad horns dropped from sight beneath a wall of howling faithful. Though I couldn't see, I could imagine how the blood gushed onto the altar, overflowing the rocks and into the pool.

The drums and flutes stopped. The last horn died, and a hush fell over the crowd as the mist continued to dance, iridescent and alive.

Time stretched on. The Soulderni didn't move, didn't speak. The back of my neck prickled and Nisien's brows contracted inwards, his lips turning in a half-formed frown.

Slowly, the shaft of light left the pool and began to travel up the waterfall, taking its golden glory with it.

"Oulden," the voice of the priestess rose. "We beg your presence."

Beside me, Nisien shifted again and I noticed more than one person glance at their feet. The ground here, I saw for the first time, was covered with a fine clover of sorts, laden with buds.

"They bloom," Nisien leant down to murmur in my ear, "when Oulden is near."

But, judging from the mood of the crowd, the god was late again. Sunlight reached the top of the waterfall and slipped over onto the ridge beyond. Whispers laced through the Soulderni, some low and cautious, others thin and frightened. Nisien crouched, staring at the buds, and I remained poised, every instinct preparing to fight or run.

Someone cried out. Then another and another. Across the ground flowers began to bloom, buds unravelling with unnatural swiftness. Their color was equally strange, not a color at all but a lack of it, insubstantial and empty. A shadow. The heart of a mountain.

Nisien recoiled and I lifted my feet, staring at the plants in confusion and a growing, heart-pattering dread.

"What?" I asked. "What's wrong?"

There was no time to answer. Cries ruptured into screams and, as the last flower unfurled, the waterfall ran dry.

People bolted, snatching up children and crying for missing family members. I stayed where I was, drawing up Fire in my chest and winding it through my body like ivy.

Nisien stepped closer, narrowly avoiding collision with a fleeing girl, and grabbed my arm. "We should go!"

"No," I said. Lost in the Fire, my voice was emotionless. While the human side of me would have run in an instant, even abandoned the camp and headed north, it was the Eangi, the priestess, who was in control now.

The Soulderni thinned around us, leaving the priestess and a pair of acolytes at the side of the pool. I knew that whatever was happening, whatever was coming, I should be with them.

I pushed Nisien's hand away and stepped back. "Give me your knife."

The horseman put a hand on the long blade at his hip. "Why?"

"I'm an Eangi," I said. "A priestess of Eang. Give me your knife, please."

To his credit, he pulled the weapon from his belt and handed it over without hesitation. At the same time, he became incredibly calm. "Tell me what to do."

"Do not let anyone leave the valley." Without waiting for confirmation, I turned the knife into a familiar grip and ran towards the pool.

The old priestess didn't see me. She was praying, quick and rapid. Two followers hovered a pace behind her, long knives bared, their faces thin masks of composure over wild-eyed fear.

One of them threw up a hand towards me. "Stop! Run! The other way!"

"I'm Eangi!" I called back. "Let me help."

The priestess lifted her head and looked at me over her bony shoulder. Her lips never stopped moving, but her eyes closed, once, in affirmation.

My shoes splashed into puddles of blood as I took up position at her side. The purification that the waterfall had wrought over Iosas's and my sacrifice had stopped. Now the blood of the bull congealed, creeping into the pool in curling tendrils.

No mist met my face. There was no roar of the waterfall to smother my senses, just the lap of tiny waves while the bull lay nearby, horns angling his head at an unnerving angle towards the sky. It was a sky without texture, a blanket of unearthly dusk and odd, diffused light.

As the screams of the Soulderni grew more contained and distant, the priestess's hissing prayers became the loudest sound.

"Eang," I breathed, touching my throat where my collar used to be. "Eang, hear me. Goddess of War, Watchful Goddess, speak to me. I know you are displeased with me, but I need you now. Tell me what is happening. Show me what to do."

I slit open my bad hand – it still wasn't strong anyway – and held it down to my waist, letting the blood pool in my palm. I murmured familiar Eangi words, over and over. "Let me see, let me see."

Before I could complete the ritual, before I could look for a vision in the blood, someone spoke from behind us. But it wasn't the old priestess or I they were speaking to.

"Oulden, where are you?"

The priestess and I turned as one. A man, a creature – a god – stood between us and the camp. I couldn't describe him, because there was no way to actually look at him. He was shadow. He was nothing. Like the tainted flowers at our feet, he simply was.

This had to be the interloping god, the one tormenting Souldern. But how could he be here, at Oulden's Feet? How could he pass onto the other deity's sacred ground?

"You." The priestess's voice did not waver. "Why do you trespass at Oulden's Feet?"

The being remained motionless, but I sensed him draw closer. His presence billowed out like silent thunder, rushing across my skin.

It took all my will not to flinch away, but I couldn't help a fluttering blink. In that brief space between my eyelids closing and opening again, the priestess's acolytes evaporated. One moment they were there and the next they burst into ash, ash that rippled and blew into my face. I gasped and spluttered and covered my mouth with a sleeve as the rest of the ash fell upon the shadow flowers at our feet. There, the blossoms shuddered and bloomed broader, greying and becoming more... substantial.

The priestess seized my hand. Her knife, still slick with the blood of the motionless bull, tangled between our fingers. There was no need to communicate; we served different gods, but together we were stronger.

"I have come to kill your god, old woman," the being declared. His voice ground through me, making my bones and teeth ache. "Come, Oulden, protect your servant. See how many long and grey years she has given you. See how your people cower!"

I kept my gaze focused on the stranger, trying to ignore the ash – the remains of two people – caught in my hair and smeared across my tongue.

I could see now why Iosas had said this god was different than Oulden, or Eang. He was formless and faceless, intangible but powerful. So very powerful. Powerful enough to disintegrate humans in a breath. Powerful enough to trespass on another's sacred ground.

That realization sent fear rocking through my chest. What was I doing, standing here with an old woman in a land that wasn't even my own, while an unknown deity stalked towards us?

When he received no answer the being laughed, a human sound caught in a landslide of divine disgust. "He is *hiding* from me! Hiding, still! Even in his own temple! They cower, they cower, the New Gods. The young, the weak. Can you not bear the power of the Old World?"

Before I could process these words, a rope of blackness lashed towards us. I instinctively ducked, pulling the old priestess down with me behind the bloody altar.

But my movements were too hasty, and the other woman too slow. My foot slipped in blood and I nearly careened into the pool. The priestess stumbled, emitting a crackling, piercing wail.

Our hands broke apart. The ceremonial knife clanged off the rocks and toppled into the water with a soft plunk and a ripple – both nearly drowned by the other woman's shrieks.

I stumbled halfway to my feet, soaked in water and smeared with blood. The old priestess clutched at the altar above me, contorted and shuddering like a speared rabbit.

I cried out. The woman *had* been speared, but not by any weapon of this world. The interloper stood on the other side of the altar now, his hand buried in her chest as if he grasped her lungs. Shadow poured into her in a constant flow, solidifying into a humanesque, muscled arm.

All amusement fled the being's voice when he spoke again. He bellowed out towards the mountains, "Oulden!"

I heard the woman whimper. My gaze flicked from her legs, just within my reach, to the strange god. He hadn't marked me as a threat yet, even with Nisien's knife still clutched in my good hand. If I was going to run, now was the time.

But even as my baser instincts urged me to bolt, I reached out one bleeding, Eangi hand. My fingers found the woman's thin ankle and I dug my nails into her skin.

My Fire rushed from my body and into hers in a blessing, cleansing burn. The deity's arm jerked back, and the woman dropped like a sack of grain onto the rocks.

The strange god's head snapped towards me, recoiling his smoke-and-shadow arm. "What? Spawn of Eang, here? Oh, I shall catch your mistress too. Oulden and Eang, fallen at the feet of Ashaklon. The bindings fray!"

Finally, he had a name. Ashaklon. But it meant nothing to me. Was this one of the Arpa gods or… No. A God of the Old World, he'd called himself. One of the divinities Eang had bound, long ago?

Then, as my mind raced, my knees dug into bloody rock and the old priestess struggled for breath, Oulden appeared.

The god of the Soulderni was a middle-aged man with wild hair, his body clothed in a tunic of the finest weave and his muscular thighs bare. He wore a pelt over his shoulders and bore a herder's staff. Everywhere his feet fell, the flowers transformed to brilliant Soulderni red, shedding Ashaklon's darkness in a fine mist.

At the same time, a great crash of water sent me reeling into the altar. Deafened and half-drowned in spray, I had just enough time to realize that the waterfall had reawakened before my senses were overridden by Ashaklon's delighted, gut-melting laughter.

The Soulderni priestess, huddled behind the altar beside me, reached up to clutch my arm. Her voice gurgled with blood and grey rimmed her eyes. "Where is Eang?"

The question rung in my ears, more meaningful than the priestess knew. Where was Eang? Where was she when Albor fell, when the Algatt poured out of the mountains, and when I knelt here on the ground of a foreign land?

I had no answer, except that my goddess was too far away right now, and I was an exile. But I bowed my head onto the stone slab all the same, still slick with blood and spray, and prayed to the darkening sky.

The waterfall continued to roar, Oulden and the formless god raged, and the old priestess choked, but my prayers met nothing but silence. Eang would not or could not hear, even on Oulden's holy ground, where the High Halls bled into the Waking World.

But Eang had to hear me, here as I faced down an unknown deity – it was her duty, her role as my goddess and as an ally of Oulden. And I'd spent enough time in Svala's shadow to know what the High Priestess would do now.

My fear faded into a grim, blinding brand of indignation, and there in the warm blood on the altar, I began to draw runes. Eight symbols, at eight points; symbols of opening and tearing, of the human world and the divine, and of Eang. Brave. Watchful. Vengeful. Swift.

I did not know what to expect. But as my finger left the blood of the final rune, languid and nearly black in the waning light, Eang rushed into my lungs like the flurry of wings. There was no time to be afraid, no time to remember the Eangi girl I had once seen possessed and die in the Hall of Smoke.

My self, my thoughts, all that I considered my own, stepped back through a veil. And then... there was Eang.

She tasted like iron on my lips. She was the coldest hour of a winter night and the brazen heat of the summer sun. She overwhelmed me, roaring through muscle and veins, marrow and bone, until that fire, that presence, was all I knew.

My vision sparked with a golden-amber haze, and I stood. My cuts and scrapes closed over and I watched Ashaklon tear the earth from under Oulden with a drop of his chin. Oulden leapt, his staff transforming into a spear as he charged. One slash. The haft shattered. Three of the tall standing stones around us exploded in plumes of dust and shrilling fragments.

In the debris, Oulden hurled himself into Ashaklon's chest. The two went down, humanesque god entwining his spectral fellow in arms of corded muscle. Beneath them, the flowers turned from grey to red in a path of divine rancor.

I – Eang – left Nisien's knife on the altar and began a slow approach. With every step she sunk deeper into my limbs and I into her mind, her thoughts and instincts laid out like the valley before my eyes. There was will, hard and unyielding. Anger and frustration.

And fear. True, fluttering fear.

The feeling was there and gone, hidden away from me, but not before I'd sensed its direction. It wasn't fear of Ashaklon, but fear of something greater, something vaguer – something he heralded.

Still, Eang strode forward. Amid the stones Oulden and Ashaklon struck one another, the shadow deity's darkness slipping seamlessly between anthropomorphic blows and spectral retreats. Oulden came back at him with earth and stone, the very ground itself moaning and bowing, bending and cracking at his whim. More standing stones, sacred and riddled with magic as they were, burst. The grass, dirt and rock beneath my strides shuddered, the air in my lungs thinned and the water of the pool behind me trembled, every element reacting to the clash of gods.

I stopped to pick up the remnants of Oulden's staff. The wood felt as solid as rock, but the break was total; a hundred splintered ends gaped at me, refusing to meet again.

I took one end in each hand and crept after the thundering gods. My wrist protested, tendons straining, barely healed bones grinding. But this was Eang working, not me, and the goddess did not blink at suffering.

Ashaklon backed away from Oulden, his hidden muscles roiling, building for a ferocious charge. I circled to the side, my eyes lingering on his exposed back.

"Oulden," I called with the voice of Eang, and my throat burned.

Oulden looked up, the flowers beneath his feet shuddering black, then bursting into a brilliant, violent red. I hurled him half of the staff and bolted, rounding Ashaklon just as the being lashed out at me.

I drove my half into his spine. At the same instant, Oulden sprung, his half of the staff meeting mine in Ashaklon's stomach.

Ashaklon shrieked. Eang's presence or no, my flesh was still human; the sound blasted me backwards in a blur of sight and sound. I struck a standing stone and my world fractured into blackness.

The next thing I knew, I was coughing. Dust rained around me, choking and obscuring. Beneath my bruised ribs, Eang's Fire had gone out. The goddess had left me. Dizzying, cloying exhaustion came in her place and I trembled as I pushed myself upright.

Through a veil of dust, I saw Oulden heft Ashaklon like a skewered rabbit and plunge one end of the staff down into the earth. The crook had grown significantly, thickening and extending, wrapping snaking roots around Ashaklon's writhing form and creeping into the earth like the roots of a tree. At last, the God of the Old World folded from sight, and stilled.

Relief gushed through me. The threat was gone, Eang was gone, and I was still drawing ragged breaths into my lungs.

But something of the goddess remained, curling in the back of my mind. It was that fear I'd sensed, that vague and fleeting dread that Eang had tried – and failed – to keep from me. It was so genuine, so human, that it left me disarmed. I knew, in that moment, that I'd learned something of my goddess that I was never intended to know.

The Goddess of War was afraid.

Distantly, I heard the Soulderni erupt in a wave of lamenting, tremulous cheers. "Oulden! Our god! Oulden!"

I let my head droop onto the mossy earth and closed my eyes.

FOURTEEN

Eang came to me as I slept. She met me in a vision of the Hall of Smoke as it once was, in a quiet corner where I stood alone, kneading dough at a long table.

"You did well," she told me. She was not angry today. Rather, she seemed reserved and thoughtful, clad not in her warrior's garb but in a simple gown, black as the heart of the poppies in her meadow.

Her praise filled me with warmth, but my memory of her fear came hot on its heels. I kept working with my head down, concealing my own thoughts from her. "Thank you for hearing me."

Out of the corner of my eye, I watched her run a distracted hand over the stomach of her gown. The gesture was reflexive, self-calming, though her expression was a veil of impassivity. "Did Svala teach you how to use those runes? To reach me at such a distance?"

I shook my head, face still lowered. "Not directly. But it seemed the right thing to do."

I felt Eang's eyes linger on me, cloistered and calculating, but she said no more on the topic. "I have found your charge."

My head shot up. "Vistic?"

"Yes." Eang glanced across the Hall. Faceless Eangen and Eangi, little more than memories now, went about their business, oblivious to us. "There... there is more to the situation than I knew. Why did you pledge yourself to the child?"

My hands paused at their work. "He's Sixnit's son. His father was gone, so I stood in."

Eang didn't look at me, her face inscrutable.

"Why?" I pressed. "Is he all right?"

Asking any question was a risk, but she did not snap at me. She simply returned my gaze, unspeaking.

I tried another route. "Is there trouble in the High Halls?"

She nodded. "Yes. But the appearance of Ashaklon revealed much."

I remembered her fear again. "Who... was he?"

"A God of the Old World," Eang replied. "Whom I, Oulden and Gadr bound long before your people came to these shores."

"Then how did he escape?"

"That is my concern, not yours. Besides, he was a lesser god – a mere servant. And now he is bound again."

A mere servant? All at once, her fear made sense. Ashaklon had been strong enough to trespass on Oulden's holy ground, challenge him, and required the intervention of two gods to subdue. If entities like him had been servants among the Old Gods, how powerful had their masters been?

Powerful enough to make the Goddess of War afraid.

Eang let silence hang between us before she spoke again. "You were right to call to me, but you are not forgiven. You must return to your original task. It is crucial, Hessa. I do not write fate, but I have interpreted her words, and you are destined to kill Omaskat."

"Why?" As soon as the question fell out of my lips, I knew I'd gone too far. I froze, hands covered with sticky dough and coarse flour, and raised my gaze to hers.

Eang's chin drifted to one side, eyeing me like a crow might a corpse. When she spoke it was with deadly, forced calm. "Because I told you to."

I braced, but there was no violent reprisal, no more harsh words. Eang, it seemed, was trying to control herself.

Finally, the goddess shook her head. "I should leave you to suffer, but it's impractical. You must get north as quickly as you can. I will call in a favor with Aita and send her to see to the worst of your injuries while you sleep. Also, there are those among the Soulderni who have decided you are, in fact, me. Do be clear that you are otherwise. Now, wake."

I awoke to the light of high noon, alone in Silgi's tent. I squinted up at the tight bonds between the roof hides, sealed with resin and studded with their red zig-zag stitches.

The camp was much quieter than it had been before the attack, but there was a peacefulness about it. Oulden was still here; I could sense him. I sensed others, too. There was a heaviness upon the wind that was Ashaklon, imprisoned within the tree grown from Oulden's staff; now a fully established binding tree, as I'd seen with Svala on the night I learned I was to kill Omaskat. Then there was iron, clinging to my skin and the air around me: a remnant of Eang. And lastly, I caught a whiff of balsam and lavender – the tell-tale impression of Aita, Healer of the Gods.

Given the extent of the divine presences around me, I felt no surprise when I saw Eang's owl perched high on the central pillar, her talons wrapped around a carved branch which normally held clothing. I watched her and, in response, she closed the golden coins of her eyes in an unhurried blink.

I eased upright. I was still clad in my ash-streaked tunic and trousers, with my braid in tatters and tufts of hair sticking out from my head.

I flexed the fingers of both my hands without pain. My wrist was completely healed. I turned it, expecting to find some new limitation in movement, but it never came, and my skin smelled strongly of Aita. The cuts on my palms were thin white scars. The tightness in my thigh from the dog bite was gone, and the tender puncture wound was little more than a tiny, gnarled knot.

A spark of hope sent those scarred fingers up to my ear. It was clean and free of scabs. But it was still mangled – an intentional sigil, it seemed to me, of my failure.

I swallowed my disappointment and, smoothing my expression, turned my attention back to the owl.

"So," I asked dispassionately, "why are you still here?"

The animal only blinked in response.

The Soulderni held the year's weddings that night, a great mass of couples holding hands between the remaining standing stones. The waterfall crashed down behind them, sending billows of mist to surround the stark blackness of the newly planted binding tree. I saw the owl there among the branches, a puff of grey feathers amid a lattice of ebony.

Though I could not see them from this distance, I knew that the tree was scrawled with runes. The Soulderni's high priestess, her restored body also scented with lavender and balsam, had carved them with me mere hours ago. They were runes of silence and subduing, of Eang – jagged, simple and overlapping – and Oulden – circular and tangling.

Beneath the tree and across the valley, Soulderni-red flowers blossomed. No place where my feet trod was free of them, yet no matter how many times their cool petals bent, they remained undamaged.

"Under sky and over earth, I bind your souls." Oulden didn't raise his voice over the heads of the crowd, but every ear heard. "I charge you to serve one another, all your days; the husband to the wife, the wife to the husband; flesh to flesh, blood to blood."

With that, the couples were bonded to one another and Oulden presided over a dusk feast of unnatural proportion. The wine was red and strange, the meat never grew cold and the bread was studded with fruit and nuts.

More than once, I caught the god's eye. I expected him to call me over, to explain his hiding and sudden appearance – at the very least, to express an interest in my presence. But beyond those glances, he did not interact with me, and when I held his gaze a moment too long, he looked away.

I drew up to Nisien as torches flickered to life. "Your god will not speak to me."

He tore his gaze off Oulden, whom he had also been scrutinizing. "Perhaps he's embarrassed."

I started to shake my head, then stopped and surveyed the Soulderni's god again. He had leant back down towards a clutch of children, hands waving in the manner of a grandfather spinning yarns.

"Saved by Eang, on his own sacred ground?" Nisien gave a stunted, half laugh. "He'll endure enough ridicule in the High Halls over that, without being shamed before his people."

"Perhaps." I hefted the bulk of my hair off one shoulder and let it fall down the center of my back. The dress Silgi had gifted to me – for she refused anything less – was a tempered red like the flowers at our feet, grounded in gold and laced at the sides. "Will you and your mother still take me up through the Ridings?"

"You think we would do otherwise? After last night?"

"I thought you might be reluctant to travel with an Eangi," I admitted.

"You helped slay a god." Nisien didn't look at me as he spoke. He was watching Oulden again, but it was not with worship. "I'll take the aid of Eang any day."

"We didn't slay Ashaklon – we rebound him. That's a binding tree. As to the aid of Eang, that's not quite how it works," I cautioned. "I'm no more than a warrior with Eangi Fire. Eang herself must intervene for me to do something like last night."

His eyes drifted to my mended wrist. "Does she always intervene?"

I didn't reply.

"Well, the gods are gods; they are powerful and fickle and flawed." Nisien rubbed at his jaw, glanced at Oulden one last time, and faced me fully. "In any case, we'll still take you north. Can you be ready to leave after breakfast tomorrow?"

"I'll be ready."

~

Goodbyes were simple. I bowed low to Silgi and Ceydr, grasped Iosas's wrist, and, lastly, laid a few light fingers on Uwi's shoulder in thanks. Then, with saddlebags laden with gifts and supplies and a new Soulderni-style sword – shorter than I was accustomed to, curved, without a cross-guard and suspended horizontal across the hip – I rode out with Nisien and his mother.

For the first two days, we journeyed with others from the Ridings; a dozen families, their horses hung about with bows and children. I watched a woman ride past me, a baby strapped to her back and a toddler between her thighs. His pudgy hands sunk into the horse's braided mane, unafraid.

That toddler, it turned out, was a better rider than I. By noon my legs screamed with the effort of holding myself upright and my horse, displeased with my lack of skill, tossed his head and broke into a spontaneous trot.

"I can see riding is not considered a necessary Eangi skill." Euweth drew up beside me and snatched at my mount's bridle. Her hips rolled easily, her body acclimatized to the horse's movements. "I'm going to have to lift you off tonight."

"Our horses are smaller," I protested. My hips, spread far too wide for comfort, agreed heartily. "And we don't ride. Not like this. Our forests are too thick and the Algatt steal all the good horses, anyway."

"Or," Euweth suggested, "you just can't ride."

She was right. I couldn't even mount and dismount on my own. I managed to get myself down at our noon break, but by dusk my muscles were so torn I could barely stand. Nisien took one arm and Euweth the other as I toppled from my horse's back. The blanket and leather pad that served as a saddle came with me in a fluttering clump.

Nisien laughed and hauled me upright with the amused practicality of a father. "All right, little Eangi, slayer of gods. One foot down, then the other. Take a walk."

I set myself hobbling around the camp, earning smirks and good-hearted insults from the neighbours. I relieved myself at the designated area without collapsing, which I considered a great victory, then stretched as best I could in the shelter of the scrub. My hips popped like honeycomb while the grey owl watched from the bushes, wide-eyed and emotionless.

Two more days passed in similar fashion. Travelling with the group was an easy, comfortable thing – before the burning of Albor, I'd never truly been alone in my life. The chatter of the group, and lying my bedroll beside Euweth and Nisien each night, kept my loneliness at bay. Occasional smiles crept back into the corners of my mouth. My riding improved and I even mastered the art of springing up onto the horse's back without aid or a strategic rock.

Yet, despite these gains, worry toyed with my heart. The owl continued to follow me, but for no discernable reason. In the day she would appear in a tree, or on the wing. At night her ululations rippled over the creak of the crickets and stilled the rustle of mice in the grass. But she ferried me no more visions, and when I spoke to her, she only blinked in return.

The landscape changed. The twists and turns of the Pasidon sheltered ever larger stands of fragrant cedar and gave way to the occasional low island. To either side, the scrag and rock of the mountains lowered into windy grassland that rippled like waves.

"Two more days to the border on horseback," Nisien told me one afternoon as we plodded along something of a road. The river flowed off to our right, broad and glistening under the sun. "One night at home, and then we'll – or I'll – take you up to the Spines."

The rock formations called the Spines marked the Arpa border between Eangen and the Ridings. I gave the barest nod and tried not to think about the fact that, beyond them, I'd have to travel alone once more.

"Will the Empire outposts cause me any trouble?" I asked.

Nisien opened his mouth to dismiss my concern, then hesitated. "I know a quieter path," he said at length. "You should pass without notice."

We both glanced up as Euweth wheeled her horse around. She made for us at a canter, the smallest of her braids twirling in the breeze.

"Nis," the woman addressed her son. "That cave you used to visit, is it close by?"

I saw the man's brows contract. "Yes…"

Almost at the same time as the word left his lips, the wind cooled. My horse tossed his head unhappily, jerking me forward in the saddle.

"There's – ach, steady there – there's a storm coming in," I said.

Without a word, Nisien nudged his horse into a trot and pulled ahead. His mother and I fell in behind.

"Storms around midsummer are bad out here," Euweth called to me. "The storm goddess can be vicious. We need a roof over our heads. Fast."

"We're an hour's ride away," Nisien said over his shoulder. "Follow me."

FIFTEEN

The temperature plummeted. The air charged with power, raising the fine hairs on the back of my neck and making the horses skittish. A flock of starlings startled from the grasses and wheeled south, undulating ribbons against a darkening sky.

Before long the first flashes of lightning illuminated the western horizon, brief and muffled. The thunder was still too far away to hear, but every flash brought the storm one step closer.

Nisien took us down to the river's edge. We splashed through a shallow ford and up the opposite bank, joining a little-used path through the shivering cedars.

"How close are we?" Euweth called to her son, up ahead. Her eyes darted up through the trees, searching the consistency of the clouds.

I ducked low to the saddle and peeked out under the boughs. Beyond the rushing expanse of the river, the sky pulsed with a sickly, irregular heartbeat. Thunder billowed nearer; the travail of Esach, Goddess of Storms.

"Close," Nisien answered.

A few harrowing minutes later, we led our horses into the moisture-laden blackness of a cave. As I entered, the owl swooped low over my head with a muffled flutter of wings and I slowed, watching its grey blur precede Nisien and Euweth into the murk.

I heard, more than saw, Nisien leave his horse and approach. My nerves fluttered as he loomed, visible one moment in a flash of lightning, wrapped in shadow in the next.

"Get this lit?" He pressed a pouch, iron, flint and torch into my hands and took my horse's reins. "I'll help my mother with the horses."

Anything I might have said was drowned in another bout of thunder, so I simply complied. Oil-soaked reeds darkened and flared, and I hefted the newborn flame high.

The cave was enormous, so enormous that my circle of light could only find one of its walls. The horses' hooves *tak-takked* as Euweth moved them to the most level part of the cavern, Nisien's boots splashed as he disappeared into the shadows on the far side, and, beyond them all, the owl's eyes hung like a pair of harvest moons.

Nisien's voice called from the black, "Hessa, can you bring the torch here?"

My footsteps echoed as I traversed the chamber, my orb of light illuminating puddles, a flash of Euweth's focused expression and the anxious walnut eyes of the mounts. Nisien produced two more torches from a crude barrel, lit them off mine and left me again without a word, moving off to wedge the lights into makeshift sconces around the driest area of the cave.

"How does he know this place?" I asked as Euweth passed me a saddlebag.

The woman smiled, but there was a falseness to it. "Hid here every time the legions came. I never knew where it was, just in case..." She sniffed and wrinkled her nose. "Well. The local lads still use it to hide, by the looks of those torches."

I glanced at Nisien. There was an anxiety about him, an inability to stand still. He moved quickly, stepping up onto a ledge and wedging another torch into a notch on the wall. Judging from the discolored stone below the notch, Euweth was right. It was well-used.

"Here." The man reached down and pulled the bag from my arms. He set it down on the ledge. "I'll go out and find us some wood before the rain comes."

"I'll come with you," I offered.

"No, stay and help me, child," Euweth interceded. She said to her son, "Stay close."

Nisien ducked his chin and dropped off the ledge with a crunch of rock.

Euweth waited until he was outside before she looked at me. "It's best to let him go alone. He may be grown, but this place holds no good memories for him."

We set up camp while I turned the implications of what she'd said over in my mind. I thought of Nisien as a child, spending days hiding in the dark while the legionaries exacted taxes and scooped up boys like him. Had he had a father back then? Or siblings?

Nisien returned four times before the rain hit. On the first, he brought an armful of cedar boughs to layer upon our ledge. On the next two, he brought wood and kindling for a fire. On the last, he hauled a fallen tree and set to chopping it, just outside the cave mouth.

Euweth cast him more than one concerned look, but she didn't intervene. She and I started a fire in a stone circle – also blackened from use – and covered the cedar boughs with our bedrolls.

"Little use sitting up 'til proper nightfall," the woman decided. "We'll sleep as much as we like tonight and get on the road at first light."

I nodded. "You must be eager to get home."

She flicked out a travel-worn wool blanket. "More than that. We need to relieve those we sent into the high pastures with the herds."

"Oh." I paused. "Will you still take me to the border?"

"Yes. Nis will." She sank back into her heels and looked over her shoulder at me. "I've decided not to come – I'm tired, and I need to get home. You're all right to travel with my son alone?"

I nodded again.

"Good." Euweth shifted up into a crouch. "Pass me my pack so I can see to the horses."

Nisien came in just as the rain hit, raking droplets from his short hair and setting up the last of the wood to dry beside the fire. He didn't speak and his mother let him be.

The storm settled in overhead and we settled in for the night. As true darkness fell, I sat down on my bed, ignoring the prying eyes of the owl and offering a few scattered prayers. My companions had yet to complain about the bird, but I did not miss the glances they cast it.

Finally, Nisien looked up at me. "I need to move. Will you train with me?"

I looked between him and his mother. We had two swords and I missed the rhythms of training, but his tone worried me. I saw the tension written across his frame, the way his hands fidgeted and his eyes refused to rest.

Still, I agreed. "Yes."

Euweth watched without a word as we both took up weapons and dropped down to a smooth section of the cave floor.

"No shield?" I asked, lifting my left hand and waving my empty fingers. "You'll have me at a disadvantage."

Nisien shrugged. "It will be good for you to try a different style."

"Arpa or Soulderni?" I clarified.

He smiled. "Arpa cavalry, mostly Soulderni recruits."

I nodded in appreciation. "Then you can learn Eangen." I settled into my feet, letting my mind run over each muscle of my body, calculating the distance between our bodies, our weapons, and the extent of his reach. I was far from home, but this – this was familiar.

"I've fought your people before," he replied.

Cold trickled down my spine. "Oh?"

Nisien inclined his head. "Begin. But please don't actually try to kill me?"

"I wouldn't need a sword for that."

I moved, attacking first like a good Eangen. I darted forward and slashed, met his blade, sidestepped and slapped the point of his sword away as he lunged after me. His blade caught the light in a devious twist of the wrist and the cave echoed with a short clash of steel, our quick breaths, and the splash of my foot in a puddle as I swept past him. I snapped my blade down at the exposed back of his knee – just close enough to press the fabric of his trousers into fine, thin skin.

"Mine," I declared, opening up the space between us and levelling my sword in a long, extended guard.

He raised his hands out to his sides in concession and turned to face me. I watched him, wary of reciprocal attack, but he simply adjusted his stance. The tension in his face smoothed into focus. His eyes lit, his lips parted, and I saw the anxiety slide from his limbs like oil.

"Eangen tactics work well with a Soulderni sword," I suggested, loosening my grip on the hilt of my weapon and settling my shoulders. "Or you're out of practice."

His eyes crinkled. Slowly, I started to smile back.

Right in the middle of the expression, he attacked. He came in with three strikes, high and quick like lashes, his blade moving so fast that I barely managed two fumbling parries before I darted out of reach.

Nisien came after me. I saw his muscles coil and stretch, his blade begin to arc back and up in a fluid sweep. I blocked, but no sooner had our swords met than I felt the tip of his curved blade hook around the underside of my wrist, gentle, cool and final. I froze.

"Mine," he said.

I nodded rapidly and backed off. We took stance at distance from one another and I sucked in a breath, resisting the urge to touch my wrist and turning over his movements in my mind.

I could already sense a disparity with Eangen tactics. We found our power in mass, in fear, aggression and intimidation. We burst upon our prey with sword and shield intent on paralysis, ferocity and quick dispatch. But Nisien's movements were smooth and concise; he refused to be shaken or lose control. For all his confidence, he might have had an entire legion at his back, but his focus was narrow. Two bodies. Two swords.

Frustration flared in my gut. I had no shield, and no hatchet to throw from a distance. Using my Fire would be underhanded. Yet I was fighting a man twice my size.

But did that matter? I turned my sword in two slow, looping arcs, imitating the cuts I'd just seen him perform. I'd overcome greater odds than this before, surely.

"Perhaps some slower drills to begin," I suggested. "Apparently I'm the one out of practice."

He eyed me, then, deciding this wasn't a trick, nodded.

For half an hour, we passed through Arpa maneuvers. I studied everything about him, from the placement of his feet to the direction of his gaze. Outside the cave mouth, the thunder rolled, muffled by the trees and the hill above. All the while, Euweth watched us from the pile of cedar boughs and furs, her expression inscrutable, and the horses shuffled on their tethers.

My body warmed and my movements became more fluid. When I felt that I had a better sense of Nisien's ways, I stepped back. "I'm ready."

"Are you sure?"

"I'm Eangen." I shifted into a lower stance. "We're not a patient people."

We faced off. I howled. The single note turned and echoed about the chamber, falling into discord with the thunder outside. The horses' ears swivelled and one tugged at her tether, hard.

A startled, almost delighted grin flickered over Nisien's face.

I crossed the space between us in two long strides, bringing the sword up to execute one of the cuts he had just taught me. Our blades met and I immediately moved again. Strike. Block. Strike. Sidestep. Block. The blows came fast and quick, and with each one he held back less. Soon I focused on deflecting, drawing him out, tempting him towards the edge of his legionary's control.

I saw the moment that control broke. Aggression spilled out of him in a frustrated hiss and his whole countenance transformed. I responded in kind. He was still a giant and the blade in my hand still foreign, but now we fought on Eangen terms.

He used me, all the same. I saw it in each new attack. He relished each resistance I posed. He tested my limits, pressing for the point where his aggression was too much: where I would flinch and shy and concede.

More than once, he almost succeeded. I knew there was no way I could actually win – all things were not equal; I was weakening and several of his blows fell too close for comfort. But he needed this outlet, so I gave it to him.

That was, until he nearly took my head off.

"Nisien—" I deflected a blow that sent pain all the way up my shoulders into my jaw. "Nisien, enough."

"Nisien!" Euweth's reprimand boomed through the chamber.

He levelled his sword at my face, chest heaving, and blinking sweat from his eyes. "Mine."

I lowered my sword, keeping my attention on his face. Some of his anxiety toward the cave and the storm – a host of memories I could not see – had already crept back into his gaze. But it was rawer now, closer to the surface.

"Nisien." Euweth's voice was edged with iron. "She's just a girl."

"There are no girls in the north, Mother," Nisien replied. He watched me too, as if he still expected another attack. "I think that's plain enough. I'm going to wash. Hessa?"

Together, we laid our swords on the ledge. Then he strode for the cave mouth, dragging fingers through his sweaty hair as he went. I followed a step behind.

Rain struck my face. Nisien led me to a torrent of rainwater just beyond the cave, where he splashed his face and filled his mouth.

When he stepped back, I stuck my whole head under the flow, drowning Nisien's startled laughter and the pounding of blood in my skull. I tilted my face up, relishing the fleeting, blissful forgetfulness that came with the cold water.

I spat as I re-emerged. "You would have made a good Eangi. But… I promise I won't goad you again."

"You shouldn't have been able to goad me." Nisien let out a long breath and turned his face to the thunderous sky. "But thank you, Eangi."

Lightning cracked overhead; thunder followed instantly.

"Gods!" I grabbed Nisien's sleeve. "Come on, back inside."

He let me draw him back into the gloom of the cave.

A frayed-looking Euweth stretched herself out between Nisien and I in the flickering light. I studied the lines around her eyes as she slipped into sleep, her mirth forgotten in the wake of her son's troubles – and, I reflected, her own.

Nisien's broad shoulder rose beyond her, but I could tell from the rhythm of his breathing that he wasn't asleep. If I'd been forced to spend day after day in this damp darkness as a child, I doubted I would be able to rest here either.

I considered staying awake out of solidarity, but that was foolish. Nisien was a grown man and needed no such profitless concern. Besides, my body had other notions. I buried my nose into the cedar and drew a deep, steadying breath. Soon, Euweth's face, Nisien's shoulder and the sporadic silhouettes of the horses faded into oblivion.

I awoke to the chink of armor and reverberating voices.

"Whose hearth?" an accented voice called.

I snatched up my sword and staggered upright. Nisien already stood, blade in hand. Euweth was a second behind me. I heard the clunk of wood, then the woman's face glowed as she blew on the low-burning coals and rested a torch inside them.

The torch flared and my stomach lurched. Twenty men came into focus – at least twenty, for the darkness could conceal more. There were half a dozen horses, too, whickering in the shadows.

Light glinted off the finest armor I had ever seen; layered plates streaked with mud and rain, helmets with short crops of sodden horse-hair running from forehead to the back of the neck. They bore both swords and spears, uniform and glinting, and slung large rectangular shields across their backs.

Arpa.

One of the men sheathed his sword and, opening his chest to us, took a step forward. As he did, he unclasped the strap that held the cheek plates of his helmet closed. They swung wide, revealing a clean-shaven jaw, flushed red with exertion and chill. "We do not mean to trespass."

Nisien stepped forward and replied in what I guessed was the Arpa tongue.

Hard-edged relief flickered across the speaker's face; an expression shared by more than one of the men behind him. They all looked haunted and harried, but hungry too. Their eyes flickered over our supplies and fire.

Their leader asked a question in Arpa. I didn't understand, but I could guess what he wanted: shelter.

Nisien paused. I considered Euweth in the pregnant silence, searching for signals in her face. She was straight-backed. Stoic. But she was also shivering, a deep tremor from her very core.

She realized it too. Slowly, so as not to startle the legionaries, she slipped forward and passed her son the torch. Then she retreated into the shadows, within reach of her short horseman's bow.

Unsettled, I stepped back to join her. Our arms brushed and I heard her shuddering exhale.

"If they come for you, don't fight," she murmured in my ear. "Don't you put my son at risk."

I recoiled in indignation, but there was no time to respond. Nisien had nodded to the legionaries. Their leader raised a hand and the men relaxed, moving to unload the horses and pulling helmets from their heads. Faces appeared, most of them young and unscarred. Too young to have been on the Rim for long.

My brows furrowed. Not one of these pale creatures even had a beard – a day's shadow, at most. They wore little more than arcs of golden, black and mild brown fluff upon their scalps. Like infants.

These were the great legionaries, subjugators of the world? Most of them were little more than boys, far from home and afraid of an unsettled sky – though, I had to admit, that fear was well placed.

Nisien turned to his mother and me, and I noticed how his close-shaven head reflected those of the Arpa. He hadn't been among the legions for years, but he still wore his hair like them?

"They will stay with us until the storm passes," Nisien said, careful not to show any reluctance. But before the legionaries came into earshot he added rapidly, "They and their gods do not hold Hearth Law. Take nothing they say for truth and do not lower your guard."

I squatted at the fire and rested my sword across my knees, watching them settle in with a shuttered intentionality I had learned from Svala: no hostility, no fear, no curiosity. Simply vigilance. But when their eyes passed over me, my skin still crawled.

The legionaries' leader and another man stepped up onto the ledge. They each grasped Nisien's forearm in a practiced gesture while Euweth stoked the fire and set water to boil.

"Perhaps we should speak your language," the leader suggested as he sat down and set his helmet aside. "For the sake of your mother and…"

Nisien's eyes flicked to me. "Slave."

I barely stopped my face from reacting. He knew the legions. I had to trust him.

The Arpa leader's eyes trailed over me. His gaze was appraising and distasteful, even though his eyes were vivid as a summer sky, wide and lovely. His hair was longer than the others, dark brown curls pasted to his forehead with sweat and rain.

"A slave with a sword," he commented.

"She's Eangen." Nisien seated himself beside the fire. "You know how their women are."

The Arpa snorted, an action incongruent with his apparent authority. "Woman or no, I wonder why you'd trust any barbarian with a weapon?"

I glanced at him but managed to keep my expression passive. I knew the Arpa despised my people – this was no surprise.

"I trust her," Nisien assured him.

"Well then, names?" The leader shrugged and rubbed open palms on his knees. "We should observe the local custom, should we not? Hearth

Law? I am Castor, a captain of the Fourth. We are heading north to reinforce the Eangen border. This is my second, Estavius."

The other man, pale-haired and paler eyed, looked between all of us – even me, I noted with interest – and touched his heart.

"Nisien," Nisien replied, "and this is my mother, Euweth."

"Thank you for your hospitality," Castor said. "We were caught on the road during the worst of the storm. Two of our men were struck by lightning and died, including our commanding officer. I've taken his place."

I sat back slightly. So Castor had not originally been in command of this frightened, rain-soaked band. That made more sense.

Then the rest of his words caught up with me. His comrades, struck by lightning?

Castor continued to explain, "Several more were burned when they tried to shelter under a tree – which, unfortunately, was also struck. Tell me, woman, are you a healer?"

Euweth shook her head and forced out a single, "No."

I blinked at the Arpa. He spoke about the death of his men with obvious regret, maybe even a little grief, but not nearly enough fear.

Words spilled out of me: "Have you offered sacrifice to Esach for their souls?"

Castor cocked his head. "Esach? One of your heathen deities?"

"Esach *is* the storm," I insisted. "If she struck your men, their souls will be bound to her unless you appease her. You are trespassers on this land and your gods may not have enough sway to intervene."

Castor passed his gaze from me to Nisien. "Vocal, for a slave."

His blond companion, Estavius, gave him a sideways look. The other man clearly understood Northman but had yet to speak.

"Yes. But she may be right," Nisien offered. "It might be wise to offer Esach a sacrifice in the morning."

I surveyed him. The Soulderni man's back was straight and his expression calm, but he was cowed. 'Mays' and 'mights' did not suit him.

Estavius, still unspeaking, covered a hand that was raw and blistered with burns and, from the paleness of his face, he was likely hiding more. But he was admirably bright-eyed and the glances he cast me were more curious than anything else.

"Nisien," Castor said, "you said you served in the Third. You must have participated in the Southern Campaigns?"

"I did." A muscle in Nisien's throat twitched, but there was a ghost of wistfulness around his eyes.

"Ah. What would you have been at the time? How old?"

"Fourteen. Until my twentieth. Then I was posted to the Rim."

"Formative years to be hip-deep in blood," Castor commented. His eyes traveled to Euweth as she added herbs to the pot over the fire. "What is that?"

She paused, then held out the pouch for him to inspect. "Sweet Tear. For your men's nerves."

Nisien clarified the name in Arpa and added, "Northman's balm."

Castor sniffed at the pouch, then nodded and handed it back. Euweth tucked it into her pocket again.

Estavius spoke up, asking something in Arpa. His voice was appealing, rounded and warm, and inquisitive.

"I've been on reserve for three years," Nisien returned in Northman as he eased back onto one palm. That wistfulness I'd caught earlier had deepened now, and his gaze took on a distant quality. "My gratitude to my general is… was, well, I think of him daily. He was an admirable soldier – and the best of men."

Castor gave a thoughtful nod, and memories flickered behind Nisien's eyes until Euweth leant forward to stir the tea. His expression shuttered.

"I knew a captain from the Southern Campaigns, called Telios," Castor said. "He had command of the cavalry, as far as I remember, but never… made general. Did you know him?"

Every line of Nisien's body went taut. Whoever Telios was, Nisien definitely knew him. And he did not like him.

"Yes," the Soulderni replied, his voice flat and emotionless. "He was one of my commanding officers."

Castor's eyes lingered a fraction too long on Nisien's face. "Admirable soldier."

Nisien nodded, but without feeling. "Admirable soldier," he affirmed.

"Now." Castor glanced back over his shoulder, something of the leader he was supposed to be slipping back into his tone and posture as he sighted his men. "Share some of our supplies. All we have are soldiers' rations, but I'm sure you're used to that."

Nisien nodded again.

Food and tea were distributed and Euweth shared her portion with me. My stomach had not taken well to being jarred from sleep but I ate anyway, knowing my muscles would be sore come morning.

"Tell me," Castor said at one point. "Do you travel from the north or the south?"

"South," Nisien replied. "From the gathering at Oulden's Feet."

Estavius asked a question in his own tongue.

"Yes," Nisien answered in Northman. "There was a disagreement between Oulden and an interloping deity."

I stiffened. If these men knew about the unrest at the ceremony, they may also have heard about the Eangi who helped bind the interloper. They may even know that she traveled north into the Ridings, which made me more interesting than I wanted to be.

Castor put a chunk of stale bread in his mouth, gazing at me before he asked Nisien, "Did you see what happened?"

If Estavius was a dog, his ears would have pricked.

Nisien began to nod, then turned it into a disappointed shake. "Not much. I was near the back of the crowd. But I watched the waterfall die – that was… unnerving. Then everyone ran."

"You too?" Castor asked him.

Nisien replied with a wry grin. "I've no right to interfere in the battles of the gods."

"Wise…" Castor relented. "But what a tale that would have been."

Estavius leant forward and produced a stream of questions, to which Nisien shrugged and replied in his own language.

I shifted uncomfortably. I hated this lack of understanding on my part, this blatant ignorance. All the peoples of the north spoke a common tongue, though our accents and dialects might make an outsider think otherwise. Only priests used more cryptic languages, harkening from thousands of years gone by, and I knew the Eangi's. Yet now these men spoke right in front of me and I understood nothing.

I considered Euweth out of the corner of my eye. She had relaxed fractionally, her focus on the tea she was ladling out into the battered cups of one legionary after another. She gave no sign of understanding the men, either.

I fidgeted. I needed to stretch, to walk, but the rain continued to pour outside, and the cave was too thick with men. I forced my breath out through my nose and began to tend the fire, like a good slave.

The hours between the legionaries' arrival and dawn were long. Once all the men's bellies were full, they began to seek dry spaces to lay out their bedrolls. Several produced folding frames that proved to be cots, making their beds right over puddles and wet rock.

The cave filled with the smell of men and equine piss. My attention shifted from sound to sound; a snore here, a murmured conversation there, the rush of a horse relieving themselves and the steady rasp of a sword being sharpened.

When Nisien finally eased himself down beside me, I sat up. "What were you talking about?" I whispered.

"The north." He drew a self-conscious hand over his beard. "They told me something strange."

I waited for him to go on.

"They claim there are no Arpa in Algatt territory."

I recoiled. "What? That's absurd. They're lying."

Nisien turned his head reluctantly. "Castor insists the rumors of Arpa in the northern mountains are false and… Gods, I'm far too tired for this… I can't figure out why they would lie. It serves no purpose, unless the invasion wasn't sanctioned…"

"Or Castor just doesn't know," I offered, my dislike of the man plain in my voice. "He's no war chief."

Nisien shifted to brace his back against the wall. "Can you…" His voice lowered further, "Can you not look for a vision? Or ask Eang?"

"Ah, yes, master." I nodded vigorously. "Right in front of the heathen Arpa."

The corner of his mouth twitched. "I'm sorry about that. But you're obviously Eangen and I'm rather famous among the Soulderni for not having a wife."

I relented with a grudging nod. "Well… I can ask, but Eang may not answer. And I can't just look whenever I want to. They say for every vision we call, an Eangi sacrifices a day of life. What we use, we must pay for – in strength or blood or life."

Nisien's chin drifted to one side in concern. "I… see. What about the owl?"

That was an idea. I scanned the darkness, but no eyes flashed back at me. I saw only horses and Arpa and the vague, gloomy mouth of the cave.

"She's gone."

SIXTEEN

By the time the first light of dawn drifted into the cave, we were ready to leave. While Nisien and I shouldered the saddlebags, Euweth untied the horses and led them past the sleeping soldiers. Few of them stirred, subdued by exhaustion and Euweth's tea.

The air outside was fresh and crisp, still laden with Esach's power. Storm clouds dispersed over the waving tops of the cedars, backlit by the pink and orange hues of the coming day. More than one nearby tree was blackened, their split and charred trunks glossy with rain.

No one spoke until the horses were ready and Euweth already up in the saddle.

"Thank you for your hospitality," Castor said from the mouth of the cave, one hand on his sword. I wondered if he had taken it off. "Nisien, perhaps we will meet again."

"Who knows the will of the gods?" Nisien replied as he mounted up. "Until then."

Castor's eyes drifted to me. "Until then."

It was hard to shake the feeling that we were in flight. We rode harder than usual and didn't stop until the sun had passed its zenith. Then, after only a brief rest we pressed on, crossing the river and breaking north-west.

"Let's camp here for the night," Euweth drew up her horse in sight of a small copse. The sun was still a full hand above the horizon.

Nisien reined in. "We can still reach home before moonrise."

Euweth shook her head. "And risk the horses? No. We camp here. You know there's no better shelter between here and home."

Whether he agreed or not, Nisien dropped from the saddle. I followed suit and took up my usual role of unloading the saddlebags and clearing sleeping spaces while Euweth saw to the horses. Nisien unfastened a hatchet from his saddle and started off through the low trees in search of firewood.

"No fire tonight," Euweth pulled the blanket and leather pad from her horse's back with a little too much force. "I'll not have those Arpa taking our 'hospitality' again."

Nisien paused, caution in his eyes. "Mother, they won't follow us. They'll return to the Arpa roads."

"No fire."

Nisien took a step back towards us. "I know last night was—"

Euweth's countenance darkened. "No fire."

That was the end of it. We chewed on cold, soaked grain and smoked meats before turning into our bedrolls early. No one looked for conversation.

I couldn't sleep. I turned from one position to another and prayed, but sensed that Eang did not hear. By the time the moon rose my thoughts had blackened. Sixnit and the baby. My parents. My sisters. Had East Meade survived, or was it a charred ruin like Albor?

In my mind, I walked again through the Hall of Smoke and crouched down beside Yske's contorted body. I laid her out properly and closed her gaping eyes. I wiped the bloodied red hair from Eidr's face and arranged him, too. I imagined the faces our children might have had, the warmth we might have shared, and the home we might have made. Those thoughts were so agonizing, so painful, that I couldn't breathe.

I stood up and made for the edge of the copse, brushing unspent tears from my eyes and forcing even breaths out through my nose. In the light of the moon I unsheathed my sword, laid it to my palm, and let it well up with blood.

"Eang." I looked down at its murky heart. My voice shook like a frightened child's. "Let me see. Let me see East Meade and what is in the mountains."

Moonlight glinted off red liquid. My palm smarted and I squinted, willing the rooves of my birth village or a glimpse of the high Algatt mountains to appear. Even if Eang herself was occupied, I should've had enough power in my Eangi blood to see something.

I did. I saw an Arpa shield emblazoned with the head of a great, maned feline, its jaw wide and its eyes open in a lifeless stare. I saw a murder of crows lift off from a sea of blinded bodies. I glimpsed a mountain peak, imperious and isolated from its fellows in a girdle of black cloud. I saw bees swarming a tree laden with overripe fruit.

Lastly, I saw Omaskat. He waded into a lake so thick with minerals that it was the color of milk, his tunic floating around his waist. Before him, the regal peak of that same imperious mountain divided the clouds.

Reality slammed down upon me. I shook the blood from my hand and stared out across the rippling grasses, silver and palest green under the moon.

"Omaskat is in the mountains," I whispered to Eang. "Or will be? Why? And what about East Meade?"

"Hessa."

Euweth approached. Even before she spoke, the pile of saddlebags and blankets in her arms told me why she was here.

"You have to go," she said, shoving the items into my arms and laying Nisien's hatchet on top of them.

I wavered. My throat felt too thick to speak but I managed, "Why?"

"If my son takes you north, I'll never see him again." She spoke the words with utmost certainty. "And I will not lose him a second time, to the north or to the Arpa."

My stomach twisted. "Euweth…"

The woman's gaze was as cold as winter. "My son came home a shattered wretch of a man."

I clutched my bundle tighter, trying not to drop the hatchet or bleed on the blankets.

"It took a full year for him to stop screaming in his sleep." Her eyes flashed. "They used him and broke him, and they put a restlessness in him, girl. You saw it too. I will not let you drag him back into that life."

I remembered Nisien's face, that first night at the fireside; his devotion to his mother, the weight upon his shoulders. Then I recalled that subtle flicker of nostalgia that I had seen when he spoke to Castor.

"I understand," I said, though it felt like a knife in my gut. I'd known all along that Nisien's – and Euweth's – companionship was temporary, but it did not make the idea of setting off alone, in the dark, any easier.

"Then take a horse and go," Euweth said, turning away. "Nisien's horse, Cadic – she will serve you best."

I couldn't speak, so I walked away.

I rode north. The night was clear, the moon illuminated my path and placid Cadic was resigned to my inadequacies as a rider. But my eyes burned with unshed tears and my heart ached more fiercely than I wanted to admit.

Sixnit. Uwi, Iosas. Nisien and Euweth, even Silgi. They had only been temporary reliefs from the reality that I was alone in my task.

The thought of East Meade lent me some small comfort. My vision had been inconclusive about its condition, and that left room for optimism. But the village was at least five days' detour off my path north, and something more than pessimism warned me that I could not expect aid there. Even if their Eangi survived, they would not help an outcast. I couldn't go to them until my task was finished, and Eang's favor restored.

Wind rushed through the grass and the horse plodded on. No hoot rippled out through the night. No white-grey shadow came to me on the wing. The head of Nisien's hatchet dug into my side and my Soulderni sword bumped against my thigh. I let my hand fall to the latter's hilt and ran my fingers over it, taking comfort in its smooth leather and cold pommel.

"Eang?" I began, intending to pray, but no more words followed. Why bother, when she likely couldn't hear me? Or might choose to ignore me?

Soon, all I could think of was the fear Eang had felt at the sight of Ashaklon. I battled to reconcile that emotion – so raw and human – with the supposed indomitability of the goddess in whose shadow I'd been raised. But I found no resolution, and, deep in my soul, a seed of doubt burrowed down with Omaskat's assertions that Eang was not worthy of worship.

Doubt, however, would do nothing to help me. It did not matter how I felt about Eang's fear; I belonged to her. I was still an Eangi, and I had only one way to redeem myself.

I had to press on.

I saw other riders on the horizon three times over the next two days: a pair meandering east, a train heading south and four drivers bringing their herd to water. Each time I avoided them, heading for lower ground or waiting in a stand of trees until they passed.

Sometimes as I rode, I sang. When we were girls, Yske and I would sing together constantly; a trait she had learned from her father and kept in his memory. Now I kept it in hers.

The songs secured me and reminded me of my place in the world, my obligations as an Eangi. I sang through all the deeds of the daughters of Risix – ancestor of all those with red hair, including my lost Eidr. My heart ached as I sang of how one daughter discovered the herbs that healed the eternally wounded bear Aegr, how another had bartered her voice for a flask of the High Halls' pure water, in the hopes of healing her wounded lover. Both she and her love had perished in retribution, for no living human was permitted to drink from the High Halls. And I sang of Ogam, mischievous son of Eang by a winter storm, and his travels from the western inlets to the Headwaters.

The tales of Eang herself stuck on my tongue – accounts of her leading her people into battle against the former Algatt kings, of her slaughtering a thousand Arpa at the Pasidon, and how she stole one of her sisters' breath and transformed it into her owl messengers.

On my second night away from Nisien and Euweth, I made camp in a hollow. The ground was becoming rocky again and I guessed that I would reach the Arpa-Eangen border sometime around noon the day after. I saw to Cadic, divided the last of my food into two paltry portions, and filled my belly with hot water.

When I heard the flutter of wings, my heart leapt. I stood up, turning full circle in search of their owner. Uneven rock faces rose on every side, ledges laden with ferns and moss and the occasional stunted tree.

Cadic watched me for a blithe moment, then turned her attention back to grazing.

"I'm listening," I called.

"For me? How kind."

A man stepped out of one of the many passages into my campsite, his knotted white hair brushing against overhanging ferns. Despite the color of his hair his face was youthful, with large blue eyes and perfect, nearly feminine bowed lips within his braided beard. He wore a calf-length grey kaftan, latticed with silver and red embroidery, and the unmistakable, overpowering aura of the unveiled divine. A god might choose to hide that aura when they were physically in a human's presence, but this one let his fill the air like an oncoming storm, unmistakable and bold.

I jerked the hatchet from my belt – my sword was with my bedroll nearby – and demanded, "Who are you?"

He smiled slyly and adjusted a rope hanging over one shoulder. "You've sung to me so sweetly these last few days."

I took a step towards Cadic, still unable to name the stranger.

The man gave me a bemused frown. "I thought you'd be quicker than this."

"Ogam?" I rested a hand on the horse's neck. Could this be Eang's son? He looked the part, from his snowy eyelashes to his broad shoulders and crooked smile. But no one had seen Ogam, son of Eang by Winter, in centuries.

The newcomer nodded. "Yes. Rather foolish of your teachers, Eangi, not to warn a young woman against singing my name so often. It gives me ideas."

My muscles stiffened, ready to leap for the horse. "Did your mother send you?"

"My mother?" Ogam barked a laugh. "No, I just told you, you called me. Though perhaps I should not tell untruths, not so close to your hearth. In a way, she did send me, and your song helped me find you a little sooner. I'm looking for her."

I forced my fingers to loosen on the haft of the hatchet. I doubted Eang's son would do me permanent harm, but I knew the tales about him well enough not to risk it. "She's not here."

Ogam began a sauntering circle of my fire, closing on me. I retreated into Cadic's flank.

The Son of Winter raised his nose in my direction and inhaled deeply. "I smell her on you. But you're the only vestige of her I can find."

"You can't find Eang? Why? What's happening?"

Ogam stopped two paces from me. "I don't know. I've been away."

My eyes narrowed. "Will you keep Hearth Law?"

Ogam took a moment to think, then pressed an open hand over his heart. "I swear it."

I relaxed, though not entirely. I returned to the fireside and refilled my small iron pot from a waterskin, then set it on the stones beside the fire. "All I can offer you is information."

"A god expects to provide." He swung the rope from around his shoulder and held up a fat skinned hare. His clothing, however, revealed no blood, no sweat or other signs of a hunt.

Hunger ignited in my belly, but I made myself hesitate. "That's very generous."

"I know." Ogam inclined his head. "Give me a moment to find a suitable branch, and I'll have it spitted."

Reluctant as I was to let him leave my sight, I hung back as he vanished into the shadows.

"Eang," I murmured. "Your son is here."

"She can't hear you," Ogam called through the clefts.

I pinched my lips shut. In the songs, Ogam was a hero, if an unpredictable one. He wasn't truly a god, despite his claim, but we had no other title to give him. He was singular within creation – the son of a goddess and the elemental Winter. His feats were as prolific as his illegitimate offspring, though I hadn't heard of any woman bearing a son of Ogam within living memory. As he said, he had been away.

"Where were you?" I asked the empty air.

"In a land of vast herds, magic drums, winters without day and summers without night," Ogam replied. He re-entered the firelight with two crooked sticks and a long spit. He sunk each stick into the earth with efficient jabs, speared the hare, and laid it over the flames. "And women with hips as round as the moon."

I snorted at the last. "Then why did you come back?"

Ogam dropped into a crouch across from me. "An owl came to fetch me. But when I called to my mother, she didn't reply."

I took this information with a slow nod and rested the hatchet on one thigh. "Then I have a lot to tell you."

SEVENTEEN

O gam stayed in his crouch. "Go on."

I gave him a brief account of my failure to kill Omaskat, his buying me as a slave, the binding of Ashaklon and his mother's last visit to my dreams.

"That was the last I heard of her," I finished. "One of her owls followed me for a few days, but then it vanished, too. Three nights ago."

"Under what circumstances?"

"We spent the night with a detachment of legionaries."

Ogam's eyes drifted to the horse. "Did these legionaries... oh, I don't know. Set up an altar, offer more than a handful of prayers – something that would have sent the owl away?"

"Not that I saw."

"Were they all human? Was there a god or hidden creature among them, perhaps?"

"What?" I looked at him sharply. "They were just men."

"Well then. That's strange. Now, let me see..." Ogam rotated the spit. Fat hissed and popped in the flames. "You disobeyed a direct charge from my mother to kill an 'Algatt' wanderer. You devoted yourself to someone else's baby, which upset my mother and sent her off on an apparently dangerous quest. Ashaklon, a God of the Old World who's supposed to be bound, attacked Oulden and is now a tree. And last, there is unrest in the High Hall of the Gods, likely connected to Ashaklon's rise. Yes – I've heard rumors."

"And the Arpa," I added. "They've pushed the Algatt south, but they claim they're not involved. Wait – if you came south, didn't you pass through the northern mountains?"

"Not precisely." He squinted at the hare and craned to see its crisping belly. "I passed over them."

"From where? The Hinterlands?"

Ogam's gaze levelled. "Yes."

Interest warred with the dozen practical questions I should have been asking. "What's it like?"

"Empty," he said. "And thus, I have spent little time there. There are no humans to save or fight or seduce."

At his last word, my fingers brushed the hatchet.

Ogam noticed and smirked. "The gods may have their moral failings, Hessa, but honestly, lying with a servant of my mother's is a touch too unwholesome – as interesting as you are. Freckles. A peculiar Eangen feature. And so thick…"

I forced myself to relax.

He added slyly, "Unless she doesn't know…"

"Hearth Law," I reminded him coldly.

Ogam shifted his stance, coming onto one knee and one palm. He peered into my face like a curious fox. "That only holds if you're unwilling."

"The hare is burning."

Ogam jerked our dinner away from the flames and blew it out with one frigid, curling breath. He grumbled, "Human females. You're beautiful for such a short span of time. A fruit plucked in its season is so much more satisfying than one that is eternally ripe."

"And now the hare's cold," I noted.

Ogam scowled at our supper's sudden skin of ice and laid it back over the fire. After a moment, it began to drip again.

"Ogam," I said, trying to pull him back on course. "Your mother's people are being slaughtered. My people."

His frost-colored brows knit together. "Yes."

"So? Are you going to do something about it? You're Eang's son."

"Don't talk to me of duty, woman, it will not sway me." Ogam rocked forward into his toes. "That being said... I'd go to the High Hall, but I have a feeling that's what my mother did and now... well. No one can find her. What of Oulden? What did he say?"

I shook my head. "He wouldn't speak to me."

Ogam gave me a reprimanding look. "Oulden's an unsocialized goatherd. You need to be more direct. Did you even try?"

I gaped. "I wasn't about to demand counsel from the Soulderni's god; that's disrespectful. Besides, your mother will tell me what I need to know."

At my first sentence he started to roll his eyes, but at the second, his expression sobered into something close to pity. "I... see. What about the rest of the Eangi? Or this High Priestess, Svala? My mother said she could not be found?"

I hesitated. "She didn't say that exactly, she just said she was none of my concern. If... if she is dead, Eang would know, right? Frir would tell her?"

Eang and Frir were close, and not only because they were sisters. The Goddess of War and the Goddess of Death naturally labored hand-in-hand.

"Yes," Ogam affirmed.

"Then how..." I shifted into a kneeling position. "How could the Algatt hide her?"

"The Algatt have Svala?" He asked the question like a teacher, suggesting there was an answer I hadn't thought of yet.

I paused. "I don't know. She wasn't with the other captives, and I think I saw them looking for her in the forest. Could Gadr have taken her to set a trap for your mother?" That would be entirely in character for the Algatt's skulking mountain god.

"If I find him, I'll ask." Ogam reached up and unbound his hair, mussing it out with crooked fingers. "Braid this for me. The hare will be thawed soon. Oh, don't be so full of pride, Eangi, it's not befitting a human. Come, come."

127

Deciding it was better to curry favor with Ogam than irritate him, I slipped the hatchet pointedly through my belt and came around the fire.

His hair was as soft as rabbit's fur but as thick as a horse's mane, and cool as the first snow of winter. I braided it up from one side of his face, then the other.

"How will you find Gadr?" I wanted to know.

He made a contemplative sound. "If I can find one of his priests, I might be able to locate him through them. But there's never been many of them. Gadr likes to keep his power to himself. And tracking one down is something my mother will have already done."

I took up the locks over his forehead and twisted them together with the braids, in a long tail. "Do you have a leather?"

He held up a leather thong in a manner that reminded me of Sixnit, who asked for her hair to be braided at least twice a day. I swallowed and wrapped the length of his hair in the cord before tying it off between his shoulder blades.

"Then what?" I inquired, coming back around so I could see his face. "After you track down Gadr?"

"That will depend on what he has to say." He leant forward and eased the hare off the fire to blow, ever so gently, over the meat. "What of this Omaskat? Did my mother tell you why she's so bent on his destruction?"

I shook my head and reached to pluck a piece of meat. It was perfect, despite having been frozen.

"It's strange," Ogam mulled. "When you failed, she should have struck the both of you down and been done with it."

My stomach fluttered. "I saw him in the mountains, in my vision. Maybe he's connected to all this. I just can't imagine how."

"Is he human?"

I hesitated, greasy fingers reaching out to pluck more meat from the thinning hare. "Yes. I sensed nothing unnatural about him, except... I can't use my Fire around him. I think your mother is withholding it."

"'Unnatural'." Ogam's mouth twisted into a grin. "We gods created you. You are the ones that did not naturally arise. That is odd though, about your Fire. My mother is petty at times, but not quite so."

I remembered Omaskat's heresy about the gods being created by divinities even more powerful than they, but I refused to get sidetracked. "As far as I could tell, Omaskat is as human as the next Algatt."

"And Vistic? This baby?" Ogam pressed. "Is he human?"

I let my hand drop. "Why do you keep asking if people are human?"

"It is a question no one asks enough. Do you know how many gods are posing as humans at any given time, meddling and mating and spying? No. Of course you do not. You've never been taught to ask, and oh, how the gods love to masquerade, how good they are at it. Learn to ask the right questions, Eangi, and you will go far."

"Vistic is just a baby," I protested. "I attended his birth. His mother is my friend and I've known his father since I was a child."

"That means very little. Who is he, really? What will he be?" Ogam asked the air as much as me. "You're likely correct… but whatever happened to him caused my mother a great deal of stress, so it cannot be a simple child-snatching or hungry lynx."

All those suggestions made me ill. "He was the last thing she mentioned."

"Well," Ogam tore off one of the hare's haunches and bit at it, revealing immaculate teeth. He chewed and swallowed before continuing, "I'll visit this Sixnit, then, and find the baby's trail. And if I find a priest of Gadr along the way to interrogate, I will."

"Be kind to Sixnit," I begged. "Help her, please, if you can. She has suffered so much."

A flash of genuine reproach passed through his icy blue eyes. "Have I been gone so long? You petty creatures. All you care to recall are blood and sex. I am not a compassionless beast."

I sank back. "Forgive me."

"You say that," he waved a finger at me, "but you don't mean it, Eangi. Ack. There's more than one reason why the other gods don't give pieces of themselves to their worshipers. It chokes them with pride, not to mention her Fire burns you out like candles. Don't look at me like that. I'll question my mother as much as I wish. I, unlike her, am truly immortal – an unforeseen side effect of my father's blood, or lack thereof. She cannot slay a winter storm, let alone one from her own womb. Believe me, she has tried."

I stared at him, unable to think of a single thing to say. Besides, the thought of Eang trying to kill her own son was concerning. Not for the first time, I swallowed my unease at the goddess's choices.

I forced my shoulders down. "Can you advise me? What should I do next?"

That seemed to appease him somewhat, though his gaze remained cold. "Kill Omaskat. There is a reason my mother unleashed you on him. It must be important."

"But in my vision, he was in the high mountains," I pointed out. "I... That's three weeks' travel, alone. And by the time I get there, summer will be waning. What if I don't find him right away? I can't winter in the mountains."

"Was the vision you had of him now, or in the future?"

I paused. "I couldn't tell. It wasn't that clear."

He tilted his head in consideration. "Fate rarely is, that manipulative old hag. Well, you should make your way north, in any case. Are you asking me to come with you?"

"No," I snapped, beginning to fray. "I just..."

"You're lost." Ogam set the spit back over the fire and leant closer to me. The iciness in his eyes retreated. "My mother molded you to serve her and now she's abandoned you. I can understand that. You were raised as an Eangi, always surrounded, back to back, shoulder to shoulder. Now they're all gone."

I hadn't expected such sympathy to come from him. It made my next question, a startled, tremulous thing, slip more easily from my lips. "What do you mean, all the Eangi are gone? Your mother said... she said I was one of the last but..."

"Well, you're the only one I've been able to find."

"What about the western villages?" I pressed. "West Meade? By the sea? There has to be at least one or two Eangi that far out. How could the Algatt have gotten so far so fast?"

Ogam shrugged. "I have no answers, Hessa. Not yet."

Tears pricked at my eyes. "Eang... she wouldn't have let any of this happen because of me, would she?"

Ogam's eyes widened a fraction, flicking between surprise and amusement, and I saw the laughter build up in the crinkling of his cheeks. Then he seemed to register the rawness of my own expression, and his humor fled. "You're serious?"

I flushed with grief and embarrassment.

"It's not your fault." Ogam leant in close again, all at once the warmth of a winter hearth instead of the cold wind outside. "I assure you, my mother does not think nearly enough of you to deliver such a punishment. All of this happened because my mother hadn't the chance or will to stop it."

I wanted to take comfort in that, but the suggestion that Eang hadn't been able to save us, or hadn't bothered to, was nearly as terrible as my fear of culpability.

I wrinkled my nose and let out a long breath. "I'll find Omaskat, whatever the cost."

"Yes. That's your charge from Eang, and it is your highest priority, no matter what else happens," Ogam affirmed. "Forget Ashaklon – leave matters of gods to the gods. But I will offer you one piece of advice. Do not go back to East Meade."

I met his gaze. He didn't elaborate, but I saw more than warning in his eyes. And I, for all my supposed pride and strength, could not bring myself to ask why.

That was, until something else occurred to me, something that made my lips numb and my chest ache. "But I could go to Albor and release the dead."

"No. It would add too much to your journey," Ogam said with finality.

"They'll have to wait. Besides, time is different for the dead, Hessa. Stay focused. Find Omaskat."

With that Ogam looked back to his meal, and neither of us spoke again.

Despite the weight on my mind, I slept long and deep. By the time I opened my eyes again, the colors of dawn had faded, and a blue sky opened above me.

I searched for Ogam. The space across the fire where he had slept was still rimmed in ice, but he was gone.

As if sensing my gaze, the son of Eang strode out from a cleft, clad in nothing but his loose trousers, tied at each hip with simple knots.

A flush rose up my cheeks. Growing up Eangi, I had seen men of all types in less than this – but no one to compare to Ogam. His masculine perfection was casual, not overburdened with muscle, yet every line of him was clean and defined. His skin was the only thing that detracted from his appeal, ethereal and cold.

"Braid my hair," he commanded.

I paused. Eidr was there at the back of my mind, like he always was, and as the memory of him swelled so did a spark of anger. Braiding hair was an intimate gesture among the Eangen, something families and close friends did for one another. Last night had been one thing, but to ask again? The shirtless Ogam's request bespoke overfamiliarity.

But he was my patron goddess's son. I likely didn't have a choice.

"At least give me time to relieve myself first," I muttered.

Eang's son wrinkled his nose in distaste. "Very well, but hurry back. Then I'll tell you what I discovered last night."

That convinced me. I quickly took care of my necessities, splashed my face in the stream, and returned to him within a few minutes.

"Well?" I asked. "What is it? What did you discover?"

"I visited Oulden," Ogam revealed nonchalantly. "And he – come, braid my hair."

I complied. "And he?"

"Had word from Esach."

My hands slowed at their work.

"The Storm Goddess says the legions have been pouring north via the Arpa roads, to the Eangen border. But she did affirm that none of them seem to have actually crossed that border since last harvest."

"So if there are legionaries in the mountains, they went north last year."

"Precisely." His broad, bare shoulders shone in the sun below me. "And wintered in the mountains or the Hinterlands. Also, Esach has quite set her face against the Arpa. Several of their gods, it seems, have been encroaching on her territory too. Another god, starlight and shadow, challenged her just a few days ago. While she labored over the harvest. They did battle."

"In the storm?"

"Yes."

"Another God of the Old World, like Ashaklon?"

"How am I supposed to know? Maybe. Are you almost done?"

"Almost."

I hooked and twisted, turning over this new information in my mind. Finally, when I'd finished braiding, he stood up.

"Sit," he instructed. "Your hair looks like sparrows tried to nest in it."

I narrowed my eyes.

"While I return you to a moderate state of refinement, I'll tell you about my mother."

The temptation was too strong. I sat and tried not to flinch as he dropped my beaded leather tie in my lap and began to work his fingers through my hair. They were cold, but pleasantly so: like cool stone on a hot day.

"When my mother conceived me, she was furious," Ogam began. "She strode to the High Hall and demanded that Aita, the Great Healer, remove me. So Aita did. She carved Eang's belly open and handed her my tiny, naked self. Eang's wound healed as I screamed, and she left the

133

High Hall, striding past all the rows of gods and human dead while I wailed in my birth-blood. Then Eang climbed the highest mountain and left me there to die. What happened to your ear?"

It took a moment to register the question. "What? My ear? Oh... a dog bit it off."

"Pity." Ogam fingered the frayed tip and tsked, then plunged back into his tale. "But I did not die. For a hundred days, my mother returned every dawn, hoping I had perished in the night. Still, I lived, and at the end of those hundred days, I won her respect. She took me to her breast and paraded me back through the High Hall. 'Look,' she crowed, 'I have birthed a true immortal. The cold could not kill him, and the wind could not kill him, and sun and storm and time could not kill him.'"

Despite the reminder about my ear and the overall heartlessness of his tale, the gentle passage of his fingers made my scalp prickle with pleasure. My eyes drifted closed.

Eidr used to do this for me. We'd sit together on cool evenings and he would run his fingers through my hair, just like Ogam did now, and hum under his breath.

My heart contorted and my eyelids flickered. Clenching them shut, I forced out a long breath and turned my thoughts back to Ogam.

The Son of Eang continued, oblivious to my pain. "She kept me with her for... oh, I'm not sure of the years. I never had a need to count them. She taught me to fight and she relished my strength. She loved seeing herself in my face. And that, my little Eangi, is how you came to be."

My eyes cracked open and I turned my good ear towards him. "What?"

"My mother decided she liked seeing herself in other beings. But the gods were reluctant to lie with her and Winter turned her away – apparently, I was something of a disappointment to him. Human mates would do for entertainment, but she would not carry their children. Instead, she wandered through the villages and began to choose her Eangi from the Eangen people. It was a bad habit, if you ask me, something she picked up from one of this land's old gods. Ried did such things – I'm sure you know of him, a rebel my mother slew and buried in Iskir. Binding himself to so many other lives made him rather difficult to put – and keep – in the grave."

I stared across the camp, my pain forgotten in these revelations. I knew, distantly, that I should be getting on the road, but this was not the kind of information one came across twice in a lifetime.

I said into a pause, "But the Fire is in our blood now. We're born with it or we're not… like red Risix hair."

"Yes and no," Ogam acknowledged. "My mother's Fire can only be ignited in someone dedicated to her. But back then things were more… intentional. Those first Eangi were unstoppable. And your presence made my mother far too strong, like Ried. Fate forbade her to make more, but the Fire was in the blood by then, as you say. Short of annihilating all Eangen, it could not be stopped. But it did thin, with the understanding that, eventually, it would cease altogether."

I nodded inwardly. Everyone knew that there had been fewer Eangi born in the last generations. "So the Eangi make – made – Eang stronger? Like Ried's followers made him?"

"Yes." His fingers continued to weave, drawing the hair back from the sides of my face in meticulous lines. "The Eangi make her nearly immortal, between your blood sacrifices and other… services. Nearly. Anyway, as I said, bad habits from old gods. She was stopped."

I took a minute to digest this. "And with… with the Eangi gone, is your mother weaker?"

"Yes. Her life is tied to you little creatures, and without you, her power wanes. Think of it as a tree… My mother is the oak, your worship – especially your shed blood – waters her, and you yourselves are the roots."

"I see… What about all your children," I wanted to know, "do they make you stronger?"

"Stronger?" He chuckled. "I'm immortal. I need no one but myself, no need to visit the Halls – not like *they* do. And I do not give bits of myself to worshipers."

"Halls?" A shadow slid between my brows at his choice of words. "Do you mean the High Halls?"

"Of course," Ogam returned.

"Then what do you mean, the gods need the High Halls?"

Ogam started to smirk, then the expression waned into a grimace – as if he'd said something he wasn't supposed to. "Well yes, and no. It's more nuanced than that. I assumed an Eangi would understand."

"I'm no High Priestess," I said defensively, though the concept of the gods needing the High Halls, instead of simply dwelling there, was absurd. Ogam had to be toying with me.

"Ah, well, you don't need to understand. As to my children," the god said, tugging the conversation back around, "would you like one? They're adorable, I promise, and many of them are immortal. Parenthood is so much less stressful when they're immortal."

Irritation flared in my belly. "You're wasting my time. I need to leave."

"Ah, yes," he agreed, sounding as if he had forgotten this fact. "You shouldn't ride over the border. You'll attract too much attention, a lone woman on a valuable horse. The Algatt are as thick as flies on a dung heap and the Arpa are arresting anyone near their outposts."

I recalled Nisien's promise to direct me to a quieter path. "Where should I cross, then?"

"I'm not all-knowing."

I tried to glance up at him, but he prodded my head back into position.

"I will take your horse for you."

My gaze darted to Cadic, steady and trustworthy. "I need her."

"You need to pass unnoticed," Ogam corrected. "And I like horses."

I wanted to protest, but he was probably right. And I knew there was little use arguing with an immortal. "Can you take her back to the Soulderni?"

"No, I need her. She can have the privilege of being my valiant steed for... however long horses live. I get your lifespans all confused."

"Fine," I agreed. I licked my lips nervously; whether or not I liked or trusted Ogam, I needed allies. "But in return, I want a favor."

"Yes, you can bear my child. Just let me finish your hair, first."

"I want you to hear me."

He paused in the midst of gathering my braids at the nape of my neck. "Hear you?"

"If I'm in need, hear me. Offer me counsel, if you can. Not as a duty in place of your mother, but as yourself."

Ogam finished his work, came around, and pulled me to my feet. Thoughts flickered through his eyes and I thought he might be genuinely lost for words.

"I agree," he acquiesced.

I smiled an almost genuine smile and lifted my hand to touch my hair. It was elaborate, multiple smaller braids pulling my hair back from my forehead and merging into a thick, leather-bound plait, but it was practical. "Thank you, Son of Eang."

Ogam nodded. "You're welcome, Hessa. I…" He considered the horse. "I may have a suggestion."

The positivity in the air wavered. "Oh?"

"It seems that we both have need to cross the border. So, let us ride together."

I narrowed my eyes at him. "I thought riding across the border was too conspicuous. That's why you're taking my horse."

"It's too conspicuous for you alone," he waved a dismissive hand. "So it occurs to me that I would do better to take you with me… just until we're in my mother's lands."

I crossed my arms over my chest. "You're as difficult as the stories say."

Ogam's only reply was a slow, dry smirk.

EIGHTEEN

I rode behind Ogam as the Spines came into sight. Larger, grander and deeper versions of the cleft where I had camped, they brought the rippling grasses of the Ridings to an end and served as a natural border between the outer limits of the Arpa Empire and Eangen – difficult to navigate but easy to defend. On the other side were the thick forests, lush farmland and meandering rivers of home.

"Where are the Arpa outposts?" I asked Ogam, keeping my voice low.

"There's one just over the ridge in front of us."

I stiffened. "What?"

"We need to pass," Ogam said reasonably. "But we can't very well scale the wall with Cadic now, can we?"

I forced an irritated hiss back down my throat. "The horse – Gods. You said… oh, never mind. But they won't let us through. Worse – they'll kill us. Or me, rather."

"Hessa," Ogam reached down to pat my calf. I moved it out of reach. "Have you forgotten who I am?"

"I think I have." I leant around him and tried to snatch the reins. "Hold up. I'll take my supplies and go on alone."

Ogam held the reins out of my reach. "Woman, I'm as much a god as Eang, no matter what my mother and her court say. I can talk my way through a gate."

I dropped from the saddle. My indignant departure was hindered by the fact that I lost my balance on the uneven ground, but I recovered. Jogging along beside the horse, I reached up to dislodge the saddlebags.

Ogam reined in and grabbed my wrist. All jesting departed his voice as he barked, "Hessa! For all I know you're my mother's last Eangi. I would not put you at risk. That's why I decided to cross *with* you."

I tried to jerk away but his fingers didn't budge. "I'm not walking through an Arpa gate."

"You'll ride if you get back up here."

I slipped the hatchet from my belt. I wasn't sure immortals could lose limbs, but I wasn't above finding out.

That was the precise moment when an Arpa patrol rode over the hill in a ripple of hooves and flash of steel.

"Up. Now," Ogam snapped.

I was already halfway back in the saddle, left hand dug into his belt for grip.

"Let me speak," Ogam told me as he nudged the horse back into movement. "The only woman an Arpa respects is the one that birthed him."

I shifted my hips, feeling the press of my sword and hatchet. "Then I already know one of their weaknesses."

Ogam's chest rumbled with a low laugh. "Good, Eangi. Now hush."

The Arpa patrol split before us, three to each side.

"Halt," one of them called in butchered Northman. "Who are you? What is your purpose?"

"I am Ogam, Son of Eang."

A shiver raced up my spine. As he spoke a cold wind whisked around us and his skin went frigid. Furthermore, Ogam's voice had changed. It was low and somehow hollow, like an expanse of slumbering forest on a midwinter night.

Cadic's flanks rippled and she shuffled backwards beneath us. The Arpa horses reacted similarly, tossing their heads and dancing away. More than one of the riders darted glances at their leader as they struggled to calm their mounts.

The leader rose higher in his saddle. This was a man who had spent decades on the Rim, his face carved by hardship and sword alike. He was clean-shaven and wore a helmet, but his eyebrows betrayed tarnished grey hair.

"My lord," he said in a tone that held just enough deference not to be offensive. "I will escort you to the gate. I must, however, alert my general before we allow you to pass."

"To pass into my own land?"

My eye snagged on Ogam's braids, hanging just above the level of my eyes. They were crusting over with ice.

"There is great unrest in the north. We have orders to—"

"I am the north. Do you presume to tell me something I do not know? If you hold us back, none of you will rise from your beds come morning."

The leader's horse danced sideways in the high grass, though her rider's face remained calm. "I beg you, sir. You may be a god, but I am not. I must answer to my general."

"Then he will answer to me." Ogam nudged our horse into movement. "Come."

The Arpa hastened to catch up. As we crested the rise, their leader spurred his mount to the fore.

I caught my breath. A wall the height of the Hall of Smoke stretched from east to west against the backdrop of the Spines' rocky formations. In its center was the largest stone fort I had ever seen. This was no outpost. This was a city. Its twin gates faced us, bracketed by square towers and ramparts capped by wooden rooves. Roads of fitted stone converged at the gates, again from the east and west.

Sunlight glittered off plate armor as watchmen noted our approach and ran for the towers. A bell began to ring and, at a wave from the scouts' leader, one of the gates opened.

I felt the color leach from my face. "What is this place?"

"The Ilia Gates, a border outpost," Ogam said.

"But…" I swallowed. "It's… it's huge."

Ogam was silent for a moment. "This is only a shadow of the Arpa, Hessa. A full legion, a touch more if you add slaves and priests and the like. I have not been south for centuries, but even when I saw them in their youth, they were… impressive. Now? I can only imagine their strength. Legions and ships and cities with more inhabitants than there are stars in the sky."

The weight of this revelation threatened to crush me. I hadn't known there were that many humans in existence, let alone in one place. "That's impossible."

Ogam didn't reply as we passed under the shadow of the gate and the legionaries came into file with us, before and behind.

The gatehouse was easily half a dozen paces thick. My skin prickled as we clopped through the shade, dreading whatever we would find on the other side.

Cities with more people than stars. Fortresses of stone, larger than any building I had ever seen. It made me feel small and ignorant, and I hated both.

"Why haven't they conquered us," I whispered to Ogam, "if the Arpa are so mighty? Why would they fear anything in the north?"

"My most formidable and dauntless mother," he shrugged. "The Hinterlands, and the whim of Fate."

The end of the tunnel approached in blinding light. With Ogam's words echoing in my ears, I straightened my spine and suppressed all emotion. I was an Eangi, I reminded myself, chosen by the goddess who had held back this tide for hundreds of years. I would not cower under the sight of stone and beardless men.

Still, when the burning sun fell upon us, I faltered. A great courtyard opened, lined with shaded porticos and thick with men. Soldiers walked past boys in tunics, who bore sacks and bundles. A blacksmith's hammer clanged. A fountain burbled into a long trough built into the back of the gate itself, where horses watered and a pair of road-worn messengers lingered in the shade.

The air smelled wrong. Where was the scent of mud and manure, the husky warmth of wood? There was the metallic mingling of iron and fire, smoke and human sweat, but this place was too clean. There was something else there, too, running through it all. A musky, heady scent that refused to disperse.

Following the smell, I saw a stone slab tucked into a recess to the right of the main gate, mirroring the fountain on the left. Bowls smoked before a collection of wooden panels, painted with faces and interspersed with bronze and wooden idols: an altar to an Arpa god, or gods.

As I stared, movement atop the great wall, over the shrine, caught my attention. A man loomed between me and the blinding summer sky, his short grey robes held in place by a belt and crossways chest straps, partially hidden by an armful of cylindrical white objects. These had wooden handles on each side and, when he adjusted his arms, I saw they were rolls of something like thin bark, but smooth and seamless.

"What are those?" I whispered to Ogam. "And who is that?"

"That's a priest, and his scrolls. They mark their runes on them."

I resisted the urge to twist and get a better look at the priest. Despite the fact that we were obviously speaking of him, he had not moved, staring down at me with a guarded, calculating gaze.

"Runes?" I repeated. "On that? What's it made of?"

"Pressed reeds," Ogam returned absently, his focus once more on the crowd ahead.

The man with the rune scrolls turned abruptly, vanishing along the wall into the nearest tower.

The leader of the scouts lifted a hand and dismounted. A boy in a tunic and wrapped sandals darted forward to take his horse while the rest of us remained astride, waiting.

I fidgeted as more and more stares fell upon us. The blacksmith had stopped his hammering and come to stand at the end of an alley, arms crossed over his chest, a slave and an apprentice hovering behind him. More men appeared from doorways.

Then I saw him. Estavius, the curious blond Arpa I had met in the cave, peeled from the crowd. Nisien had mentioned Castor and his men would continue north on the Arpa roads – but could those roads really have brought them here so fast?

The scout leader reappeared with another man wearing a draped garment, tucked around his hips and thrown back over one shoulder across a polished breastplate and red tunic. He rested one hand on his scabbarded sword as he walked, his defined, hawkish nose lifted high. A commander of men, through and through.

Castor strode at his shoulder, his gaze fixed upon Ogam with cautious interest. He hadn't recognized me yet, so I took the opportunity to scrutinize him, from the sword at his hip to the squint of his lovely, untrustworthy eyes.

"My lord," the general in the red tunic addressed Ogam in a gravelly voice, as if he had spent one too many days bellowing across a battlefield. "You do us honor. I am Athiliu, General of the Outer Territories."

"Let my companion and I pass, and I will not spoil this fine occasion by spilling your blood," the Son of Eang replied calmly. "Bow."

Athiliu's back remained straight. "We bow to Lathian and his court alone, Ogam, Son of Eang. But I offer you my deepest respect."

Ogam's hair crackled with ice. I braced, preparing for his assault. But the Son of Winter merely nudged Cadic forward until the beast could have cropped the general's grey hair between her teeth.

Everyone in the crowd watched us now, even the guards patrolling the wall.

I found Estavius again and met his quiet gaze. His eyes, I noticed for the first time, were so pale in the sunlight that they might have been colorless. Like those of Silgi's son, Iosas. Was he a servant of Aliastros, allied with Oulden?

Aliastros. Lathian. How many gods would there be over a nation so vast?

Castor inquired in a tone that implied he already knew the answer, "Who is the barbarian traveling with you, my lord?"

"She is one of my mother's priestesses, an Eangi."

I felt a small thrill as the press of Arpa rippled. Clearly, my people had a reputation.

That thrill faltered as Castor's gaze narrowed fractionally. I kept my expression smooth, but I felt a twinge of distaste, and unease – he recognized me. That meant that he knew Nisien had lied to him, and I was no slave.

"Eangi?" Athiliu repeated. He shifted sideways to get a better view of me. "I have met your kind in battle, woman. I offer you my respect."

I inclined my head, hard-pressed to hide my disbelief. I hadn't expected to find any respect here, not among the Arpa.

I wasn't the only one surprised by Athiliu's words. Castor's gaze flicked to him and his upper lip twitched with displeasure.

"One does not survive thirty years on the Rim without learning to respect the gods of the north and the Eangi," the general said, casting the crowd a slow, stony gaze. "In fact, my Lord Ogam, let us hold a feast in your honor."

Castor's head whipped around. "Sir, she's a barbarian, and he's—"

"What am I?" Ogam prompted, deathly calm.

Castor's mouth sealed.

"We will hold a feast in honor of Ogam, Son of Eang," Athiliu stated in the same voice that brought battle-crazed men into line and ordered the razing of cities. "If, that is, you would condescend to sit with us."

Ogam slid down from the saddle with easy grace and stepped towards the general. As his presence departed the heat of the day returned. I was left feeling exposed, a thousand eyes pressing upon me and five hundred thoughts moving my way.

I slipped down after the god.

Ogam faced the general, a full step closer than was polite between mortals. While the deity glared and deliberated, I drew up to his shoulder and kept my expression passionless. Tension hummed through the air and blood thrust through my veins with an almost ecstatic force. I could taste the approach of violence, and the Eangi inside me craved it.

"Let us pass," Ogam ordered. His voice split the air like a tree burst with frozen sap.

"Do us the honor of a feast."

"Why do you keep us here?"

The general kept his gaze steady, though he had to look up a good six inches into Ogam's face. "I doubt I could keep you here, even if I wanted to. But. You are a god. Why would you pass through this gate if you did not want to draw attention to yourself? Please. Let us feast, Ogam, Son of Eang. Then you can tell me why you've come."

I turned on Ogam once the flap of the tent closed. We had been led to open ground where a hundred semi-permanent tents sat: the camp of the Arpa's northern guard.

"'Why you've come'?" I threw at Ogam. "What is this? A game?"

"No." Ogam, for once, was calm and free of humor. "Do you want to know what's happening in those mountains? This is where we learn. This is the largest Arpa settlement north of Souldern and General Athiliu is the highest officer on the Rim. He's also known for being open-minded, as you may have noticed, but he's an intensely devious man. If the Arpa have crossed Eangen to get into the mountains, he will have had a hand in it."

"You lied to me." Anger and anxiety churned in my gut. "I never would have come with you if I'd known."

"Of course," he acquiesced, shameless.

"Gods above and below, I'd already be over the wall if you hadn't dragged me into—"

"Eangi, calm yourself." Ogam arrayed himself in a carved chair. It was one of several in the room, along with a large bed, a table and three braziers. This was not an average soldier's tent. "I'll protect you."

Heat rose in my chest. "You have limits."

"You're afraid," Ogam stated. "Today you learned that there is a world beyond your borders more powerful than you ever dreamed and your greatest enemies are more numerous than the stars in the sky. That powerful world also thinks you are less than a feral dog. It's understandable that you're upset. Just give yourself time to adjust."

I fidgeted with my sword as my Fire swelled. I swallowed it hard and tried to ignore the feeling that the tent was about to smother me. "Send me away. You can stay here, just... use your power to get me out."

Ogam laughed. "What? I don't have that kind of power, Eangi. Do they say that I do? I should listen to the new songs about myself more closely. Can you sing them again for me?"

"You went over the mountains," I protested.

"Alone." He looked at me again. "Not with you. Not with a horse. Can you turn into wind and water? No?"

Fire curled up into my mouth. I felt caged. Trapped. "Ogam. Let me leave."

I heard the change in my voice. It deepened and broadened, rolling from my tongue like waves before a storm. Eangi Fire.

A single drop of silver-tinted blood escaped his inner eye and trickled down his face, shimmering and slow.

It took him a moment to feel it. Not realizing what was happening, he lifted a hand and brushed the droplet just before it crept into his moustache.

Ogam let out a startled bellow and launched to his feet. "What are you doing?"

I stood there, quivering with fear and shock. I'd never known Eangi Fire could do something like this. "I... It's... You're a god. How—"

"Yes, I am," he roared. The tent shook and I heard footsteps beyond the canvas. The walls were so thin, I was sure the entire camp could hear us. "Do not use your petty Eangi tricks on me. You may be able to turn a man's brain to milk, but you will only irritate me."

Ogam strode forward and wiped the rest of the silvery blood on my face. I flinched away.

"Be grateful, human," he said icily. "If you'd crossed alone your chances of making it into Eangen were fragile, at best."

"I knew that." I intended the words to be a growl, but they emerged as a mutter instead. "It was my risk to take."

He snorted. "Well. Feast with the commanders and me tonight if you wish. Dine with a god and the most powerful military men on the Rim. Help me learn the secrets that might save your people. Or…" Ogam turned and strode back towards his chair. "…you can hide in here and pray that no one in this fort takes out their hatred of barbarians on you."

NINETEEN

I sat against the tent's central pillar and stared at the closed flap, hatchet in one hand and the other on my sheathed sword. Ogam had been gone for an hour or more and the day was growing late, the rays of the sun stretching over the horizon and filling the canvas with yellow light.

A shadow stopped before the flap and scratched. I was tired from my journey, exhausted by my fear and sapped by the Fire, but I gathered my frayed wits and rose into a crouch. "Who is it?"

To my shock, a female voice replied in indecipherable Arpa.

I edged closer to the door flap. "Who are you?"

The voice came again, tentative and unintelligible.

I pushed the flap open. A young woman flinched back, shoulders hunched, head bowed. Two passing soldiers gave us pointed looks and I noted one's hand drift towards his sword. What did they expect me to do? Kill her for no reason in the middle of the camp?

"Come, please," she beckoned in accented Northman, drawing my attention away from the soldiers. "Please."

I didn't move. I understood, but I wanted a closer look at an Arpa woman: one of these southern females who could not – would not – fight. She did not look half as soft as I anticipated. Her arms were leanly muscled from labor down to the metal circlets at her wrists, etched with Arpa runes – the mark of a slave? Her hands were rough, and her posture had a guardedness to it, like a rabbit prepared for flight.

She looked foreign, too. Her masses of frizzing, light brown curls were bound back from her face, framing a nose that ran straight down from her forehead without dip or falter. Until today I hadn't seen enough Arpa to realize this was a hereditary trait.

She was staring at me in terror. I raised my hands in what I intended to be a calming gesture, only to realize I still held my hatchet. I thrust it through my belt and opened my empty palms. "I'm sorry."

Every line of her body remained taut, but she ceased to cower.

My eyes lifted back to the soldiers. A handful more had gathered, amused comments passing between them. The casual, predatory way some of them eyed us made my skin crawl and reinforced my conclusion that this woman was a slave.

An Arpa slave on the edge of the world. I stared at her for one more minute, trying not to imagine the details of her life. Still, the images rose up.

I remembered the line of men who had passed me in the Algatt camp. I remembered their hands and their faces and wondered what my life would have been like if Omaskat hadn't been the one who purchased me, or if he had treated me like an average slave-owner would have instead of dumping me in the river.

Sixnit's face flashed through my mind, and with it a pang of loneliness and worry. Was she still there, in that camp? Had she escaped and gone searching for Vistic?

"Please," the slave interrupted my thoughts.

"I will come with you," I relented, half out of pity, and half to escape the soldier's eyes.

Relief melted the girl's features. She skittered down the well-worn path ahead of me, sandaled feet scuffing as she went. I strode behind her, past tents and appraising Arpa.

The air was full of the smell of food and fire, men and oil and metal and horseflesh. The tents themselves were square things, uniform in shades of dun and grey and interspersed with fluttering crimson flags, each emblazoned with the heraldry of the men who lived under them – an eagle, a boar, crossed spears. Their campfires burned in communal spaces, and trails of smoke partially obscured my view of the fortress proper.

Still, my heart contorted at the sight. The fortress, with its lording walls, arched gateways and hefty towers, was a monument to my own smallness.

The feeling solidified as we entered the cool of the massive structure. It was a maze of cloisters and curtains, echoing halls and gates. We passed courtyards where nearly naked legionaries wrestled, barracks hung with rectangular Arpa shields, and countless alcoves with incense-laden altars to gods I did not know, populated by idols of bronze and wood and stone.

By the time we entered a large, covered courtyard, my feeling of smallness had become coiling resentment.

"Here," the slave said.

Thick candles on black iron stands stood about the table where Ogam and half a dozen men reclined on elongated chairs of fine wood and soft cushions. Three more slaves – two women, one man with rune-etched cuffs – stood against one wall with pitchers and bowls in hand, unmoving.

My guide motioned me towards a side table, where I saw a number of Arpa swords already laid out – the same length as my Soulderni blade, with pommels modeled after eagles, a narrow-eyed boar and a great, roaring feline.

The slave held out her hands and looked at me with no small degree of pleading.

I glanced at the men. They hadn't cast me more than a sidelong glance yet, their bodies turned inward in conversation. None appeared to be armed, but this was their world, the seat of their power. I bristled at the thought of setting aside my weapons.

"Please," the slave said quietly.

"Ah, my pet Eangi!" Ogam broke in, waving me over. He stretched out on his cushioned chair like the other men, though he was out of place with his grey kaftan and icy complexion. "Oh, put those trifles down;

everyone here knows you do not need weapons to kill them, and nor do I. Are you hungry?"

I was ravenous. My eyes dragged across a table laden with the stripped ribcage of a boar, heaps of half-eaten vegetables and stacks of breads.

I handed my weapons to the slave, who nodded with gratitude. As she set them aside, I rounded the table, making for Ogam as all the men's eyes trailed me. I did my best to ignore them, searching for somewhere to sit – but all the seats were occupied. I did notice, however, that Castor was not among the company. That was something.

Ogam sat up higher in his chair to make room and slid his plate towards me. It looked as though he had just refilled it, but run out of appetite two bites in. Casting a casual glance at the watching Arpa, I reluctantly eased onto the edge of Ogam's chair and took up a three-pronged fork.

"Have the Arpa properly honored you, my lord Ogam?" I asked as I stabbed a chunk of boar with the fork. I remained composed, but, even hungry as I was, I was nearly too uneasy to eat.

Ogam leant back and patted his belly. "Yes."

"And? What have you spoken about?"

One of the other men leant forward. No one bothered to introduce themselves; I was too lowly to even know their names. The speaker's eyes passed over me in an insolent, dismissive sweep. "We've spoken about the north and the trouble in the mountains, Eangi."

"Where your men are driving the Algatt into my homeland?" I asked. I knew I trod dangerous ground, but my hostility kept my nerves in check.

General Athiliu replied, "As I have been telling Lord Ogam, whatever is happening in the mountains north of Eangen is entirely unsanctioned."

"Everything you do north of the Spines is unsanctioned," I replied. "You have no right to be there at all."

Ogam rested one finger on my back, so cold that pain lanced up my spine. I understood the warning and shut my mouth.

The pain retreated and my companion spoke: "General Athiliu has decided, with my permission, to send a detachment into the mountains to investigate our allegations of Arpa in the north. And, if Arpa are found, to stop the bloodshed."

I nearly dropped the plate and fork. "You did what?"

"I will send soldiers north with Commander Polinus. A special detachment, hand-picked." Athiliu gestured to one of the other men at the table. "Polinus, here, is Second on the front and I trust him to uphold my directions. This is a peaceful foray; violence will only be used if violence is met."

Polinus inclined his head low, letting a wave of dark brown curls fall over his forehead. I made sure to note his face, with its wide mouth and deep-set eyes; if he was truly heading north, there was a chance I'd see him again.

"It is my pleasure, sir," Polinus said.

I did not miss the looks the other men shot him.

"Anyone who sees you will kill you," I pointed out. "Algatt or Eangen. Eang herself."

"This has already been decided. If you wanted a seat at the table, you should have come down earlier," Ogam told me tiredly. He waved at the slaves and one of them approached, filling the god's cup quickly before he retreated to the wall.

My chest burned. Sensing the rise of my Fire, Ogam reached out and took my wrist in one cool hand. I twitched.

"Curdling their brains will not help root their men out of the mountains," the Son of Eang said.

Athiliu's eyebrows rose and the other men exchanged glances.

"I didn't realize the consistency of my brain was in peril," one of the oldest men at the table chuckled. He was bald and kept a dinner knife conspicuously close at hand. "Though I have heard stories about the servants of Eang. Perhaps you could..." his mouth quirked up, "...give us a demonstration, later."

I forced myself under a blanket of calm. I needed to think clearly, not snap and overreact.

"Did you swear upon your own gods to uphold your word?" I asked, looking at General Athiliu. "Upon your... Lathian, and his court?"

Athiliu inclined his head. "We will even make a sacrifice before you leave in the morning."

Dread pooled in my stomach. In the morning? I might have known we wouldn't be escaping this place tonight.

"I also have a proposal for you, Hessa of the Eangi," Polinus leant forward, his eyes shadowed in the torchlight. Among his companions, I noticed, he and Athiliu were the only ones that didn't find me amusing. His expression held no condescension, and I found myself meeting his gaze without hostility. "If you travel north with us, our passage may be eased. A priestess of Eang sanctioning our way through the land?"

I shot a look at Ogam. Had he told them I was going to the mountains too?

His face remained impassive.

I hesitated. Traveling north with the Arpa would let me ensure that they kept their word. Yet, though the matter of the Arpa and the mountains was like a millstone around my neck, I had to find Omaskat. And in order to do that, I needed freedom.

"I have duties elsewhere," I declined. "Besides, I would do you little good. If my people saw me collaborating with you, they'd just kill me."

"I will mark you instead," Ogam offered the foreigners. "If it does not offend your tender sensibilities. It will give you some measure of protection."

"What do you mean by mark?" Polinus asked.

"Other gods will be warned to stay away from you, along with unnatural beasts and other threats. Like the blessing of your own gods, but more effective in the north."

"I would want to consult with Quentis first," Athiliu spoke with equal measures of respect and caution. "Our head priest. But I am sure it will be acceptable."

Ogam shrugged. "As you will. Now, Hessa, eat. Athiliu, do any of these slaves play music?"

Fifteen minutes later, my plate was clean. Two soldiers had been fetched, one with a double flute and one with a curious stringed instrument I didn't know. The latter's fingers danced while his companion raised a gentle, nondescript melody. Whatever the song was, I dearly hoped that the lyrics were elaborate, otherwise Arpa music was maddeningly dull.

My focus broke as the priest I had seen on the fortress wall, the one who had carried the rune scrolls, entered. He noted me, where I sat cross-legged on the end of Ogam's couch, then he bowed to Athiliu and greeted him in Arpa. His voice was deeper than I had expected, with a pleasant crackle, like a low-burning fire.

The general inclined his head and transitioned into Northman. He reviewed the agreement he and Ogam had come to and Ogam's proposition of 'marking' the company headed north.

"What is this marking? Please, tell me more." The priest addressed Ogam in flawless Northman. Back on the fortress wall he had seemed tall and imposing, but now, standing before the Son of Eang, he looked small and waxen. Human.

While my gaze lingered on Quentis, Ogam licked the inside of his gathered fingers and pressed them unceremoniously to my cheek. I jerked back in shock and, without realizing it, pressed my dinner knife into his belly.

"That." Ogam settled back, away from my knife, and waved his hand at me dismissively. "Examine her, if you like."

Quentis eyed my blade. I lowered it and he circled the table, his head preceding him like a curious dog. It only retreated when he stood right in front of me, eyes slitted. His breath smelled of some strange alcohol, chewed mint, and that heady Arpa incense I had noticed in the street.

Discomforted by his proximity, I let a touch of my Fire flare.

Quentis's next breath was a thin, strangled whine. He recoiled, bumped into the table and sent a fork clattering to the stone floor.

Every eye in the room darted to us and the music stopped. At the same time, I withdrew the Fire I had just pushed into the priest's lungs and pulled it back into my own in one, deliberate breath. I held the man's bulging eyes the entire time, my own level and calm – an expression I'd learned from Svala.

"Forgive my pet," the Son of Eang drawled. "She's not domesticated."

Quentis's mouth thinned into a line. Behind him, I saw the old man who had prodded me to showcase my Eangi skills murmur to one of his companions and Athiliu signaled the musicians. They clumsily resumed their song.

Ogam slipped closer, bringing his shoulders level with mine and looking at Quentis. His eyebrows rose, prompting the priest: "The mark. What do you think?"

"It seems harmless enough," Quentis relented, though he still stood a solid pace from us.

"I don't see anything," the grumpy old commander snorted.

"It's only for… certain eyes." Withering disdain flickered across Quentis's face, but at this angle, only Ogam and I saw it. He looked at Ogam. "What will this deter?"

"Beasts. Lesser demons, and such ilk. Other gods who might otherwise disregard the dedication of a southern deity."

"Demons?" The old commander let out a full-bellied bark of laughter that made the flutist sour a note. "My word. It's true, what they say of the north. What good are your gods if they cannot even keep demons down?"

Athiliu cast him a look, as if noting the man for later rebuttal. Then he turned seamlessly back to us. "Quentis, if you have no objections? No? Then we accept your offer, Ogam, Son of Eang."

Instead of being returned to the tent, Ogam and I were escorted to a well-ornamented room in the main fortress. Gauzy curtains covered a window overlooking an interior courtyard and the comfortable bed-chamber had a lived-in feel, out of place on the northern front. Whoever had been evicted for us to stay here, they had impractical taste.

Ogam retired to the bed while I laid out my bed roll, fetched by a slave from the tent, on the floor.

However peaceable he had seemed with me in front of the commanders, Eang's son was still angry I had contradicted him. He did not flirt anymore. Irritation rolled off his skin long into the night and when morning dawned, he did not demand I braid his hair. He simply swept it up into a knot, belted his kaftan with an emphatic jerk, and stepped over me on his way out the door.

After the Arpa made their sacrifice, we rode out of the fortress and into the Spines under an escort of a dozen men. The air down here was cool and laden with sweet moisture. I chose to walk instead of riding with Ogam, striding in the middle of the group and watching spires clad with moss and fern pass by.

The Arpa-built road we traversed was level and smooth, bringing us to the other side within one short hour. My heart ached, sudden and fierce, as Eangen opened below me. Thick forests and rolling hills filled my eyes, unbroken until the distant fields of Urgi, while to the west Mount Thyr loomed towards the clouds.

I let out a thin breath and closed my eyes, tasting the pine and wildflower familiarity of the wind. For one blissful moment, I was able to forget that the distant mountain no longer marked home, that there was no more Hall of Smoke. No Eangi. No Albor. No Eidr or Yske.

I directed my gaze north, burying that pain in a knot in my chest. I blocked out Thyr and imagined I could pick out the Algatt's mountains in the north instead. They were my goal: my road to Omaskat, destiny, and absolution.

We crossed a wooden bridge over the broad trench that formed the northernmost fortifications of the Empire. It was guarded by two wooden watchtowers, which sent twin trails of smoke into the morning sky.

Then the Arpa retreated, the bridge was withdrawn, and Ogam and I were alone. I stared at Eang's son, any thanks I might have offered sticky on my tongue.

"I want to trust that you did the right thing," I offered finally. "Letting them go north."

He dropped to the ground before me with a lightness that did not suit his size. "I have every right to kill you for the way you've questioned me. Do remember that. The fact that you've a task to perform is the only reason you're alive."

"I understand." I adjusted the strap of the saddlebag I had modified into a pack. "Goodbye, then?"

He grunted and smoothed a few hairs escaping my braids, redirecting his displeasure towards my hair. "We'll meet again. If I have anything important to tell you, I'll send the wind."

I held still, refusing to retreat under his touch. My trust in the Son of Eang had certainly faltered since yesterday, but the knowledge that he would still be in contact was consoling. "Thank you."

With that Ogam mounted back up and nudged Cadic into a canter. The forest roads swallowed them within moments and I was left alone on the Arpa border.

I looked north again, then west and back north. Omaskat. Thyr. My people. Omaskat.

I thought my heart might rend in two. Ogam had advised me not to go home, but how could I not? How could I continue north when my family in East Meade might be in danger or even dead, and when Sixnit and I had promised to meet there? How could I, once again, forfeit the chance to release the souls of the dead in Albor?

You are Eangi. The voice inside my head was my own, yet not. She was the harder side of me, the zealot, and the priestess. I could not even consider making the long journey to Albor and East Meade, not when I would be unwelcome, and it would jeopardize my charge from the goddess. That charge took precedence over all.

And perhaps, in the deepest corner of my heart, it was Albor's dead, and the thought of facing them, that made me grit my teeth and start walking north.

TWENTY

My route north took me in the vicinity of Urgi. I held a thin hope that the town had managed to survive the raids, being so far south, but I could not risk my life and freedom on hope. So I kept off the main paths and moved carefully, still wrestling with my decision not to go home.

At the slightest movement in the trees, I paused. A trio of deer here, a curious fox, a bird rooting about in the deadfall. These were normal occurrences, consoling and natural, but the further north I delved, the more I sensed all was not well. Something was amiss in the fall of light and the scattering of songbirds.

Still, I could not decide precisely what it was until I found the dead, charred tree. Once, the tree might have easily been eight feet thick, but the years had hollowed it out, leaving a shadowed interior visible through a high, triangular split. Weather had stripped the outside of bark and worn the trunk to a smooth grey beneath swaths of black char.

The hollow tree was unique, but three things stood out as unnatural. Firstly, the doorway was of raw, newly torn wood. Second, there was no deadfall inside – no branches or refuse – only a smooth, earthen floor.

And third, it was covered with runes. From knotted roots to cracked, battered branches, the tree was rife with markings for safety, protection, warding and suppression, just like the ones the Soulderni priestess and I had carved into Ashaklon's tree. But these were far older, weathered and bleached by the sun.

I circled the tree with hatchet in hand, each step carefully placed and a prayer to Eang ready on my tongue. Reaching out one finger, I brushed at the burned wood.

Charcoal outlined the swirls of my fingertips. The fire had been recent, at least since the last good rain. Perhaps around the very same time that this binding tree had been torn open.

My eyes fell on the four biggest runes, hidden among their fellows right above the doorway.

Eang. Binding. Death. Urgent, warning danger.

I left without another word. I did not question my decision. I simply adjusted my pack and put as much distance as I could between that tree and myself before nightfall.

Just like Ashaklon had been bound within a binding tree at Oulden's Feet, something, someone, had been bound inside this grey trunk in the name of Eang. It was a binding that should have lasted for centuries but had now been broken with force and fire. Eang's absence in the land was taking its toll and, short of the knowledge of a high priestess and the intervention of the goddess herself, there was nothing I could do.

Whatever had once lain within that tree was now loose upon the world.

On the second day, fear of the woods – and whatever had broken free of the binding tree – drove me onto the main road toward Urgi. Here I found more signs of disturbance, both mundane and bizarre: a shattered waystone, a broken cart, and a burned farmhouse.

I encountered no other human beings until I found an abandoned watchtower on the edge of the forest, within sight of the riverside settlement of Urgi. It was twice the size of Albor, its fort and surrounding town made wealthy by lush farmland and trade up and down the Pasidon.

But now it was surrounded by the Algatt horde which had captured Sixnit, Vistic and I. The once Eangen settlement had been expanded, tents and temporary dwellings clothing the hillfort in a living, writhing skirt of humanity. The river also hosted the stolen Eangen longboats I'd seen in the camp by the Pasidon, and smoke from a thousand fires drifted up into the blue summer sky.

"Turn around. Turn around and throw us your sword."

I stilled and slowly, slowly, looked over my shoulder. Four Algatt were tucked amid the trees, two at the fore with bows drawn, and two at the back bearing a dead doe between them. Hunters.

"Your sword," one of the archers repeated, gesturing with his half-drawn bow to the Soulderni sword across my hip. He noted my hatchet and added, "That too."

My mind raced, calculating chances and variables, the direction of arrows and the speed of my road-worn limbs. Fire, ready and willing, curled on my tongue.

But I hesitated. I hadn't seen another person in days. These Algatt, I realized, might be more of an opportunity than a threat.

"Where are the people of Urgi?" I asked, making a show of drawing my sword and hoping they could not see its slight tremor. However much I silently consoled myself, however much the Fire smoldered, the sight and sound of my people's murderers affected me.

Albor. Eidr. Sixnit. The Hall of Smoke. A blade at my throat.

"In Urgi," the man replied. "As slaves. Or fled west."

"West?" I repeated, steeling myself against my memories.

"To the sea." The other archer, a woman, advanced two paces. "So they say."

I tossed the sword to the ground, concealing the depth of my relief behind a hard mask. So, Sixnit and the survivors of Albor hadn't been alone in their goal to flee west. I'd half expected the Algatt to execute a full Eangen genocide, but if enough people had managed to flee, perhaps there was hope.

Still, the distant bulk of Mount Thyr loomed. My emotion was genuine when I asked, "What of their Eangi?"

"Dead," the woman replied. "Of course."

My stomach dropped.

"The axe," the male archer reminded me. "If you've got questions, ask your own people. You'll be with them soon enough."

With that, temptation rushed over me. It would be easy, so easy, to let these hunters drag me down into Urgi. I could search for Sixnit, ask when and where Omaskat had gone – perhaps I could even find relatives among the captives. I could try to recruit people to accompany me north, instigate a rebellion among the slaves, save my people from servitude within their own homes...

But the risk was too great. I hadn't managed to escape the first time – why would the second be any different? Besides, Eang had instructed me to do none of those things, valiant as they were. My task was Omaskat alone. Once he was dead, once I regained Eang's favor and secured my place in the High Halls, then I could move on to other tasks.

"The man called Omaskat, when did he leave your camp?" I asked, pulling my hatchet free and dangling it, unthreateningly, by two hooked fingers under the head.

The woman raised her bow and drew three-quarters. "The axe, now. And get on your knees."

No more conversation, then.

I flicked the hatchet up, snatched it by the haft and hurled it in one movement. It slammed into the man's thigh at the same time as I willed Fire into the woman's eyes, boiling them instantly. Her bow sprung, arrow lodged into the dirt and the two other hunters dropped the doe. In a spurt of inglorious self-preservation, they fled.

I launched forward, throwing an Eangi battle cry after their scrambling forms for good measure. The sound echoed through the trees, as alone as it had been when I faced the raider in the Hall of Smoke.

I snatched up my sword and jerked my hatchet from the archer's thigh with a squelching crack. The man screamed but the woman was too stunned to make a sound, convulsing and covering her bleeding face with both hands.

"Omaskat," I repeated, sheathing my sword. My pulse thrummed in my ears; it would likely be a few minutes before anyone else arrived, but I needed to be long gone by then. "Blue tunic, mismatched eyes. Hunting dog. Threw his slave in the river last month. Whoever tells me first will live."

"The traveler went north," the man croaked immediately. "Weeks ago."

"Where was he headed?"

"That's all I know! Let me live, I beg you, please—"

A flick of Fire turned his begging to a choke, then a burble as his ribs collapsed in upon themselves. The woman I left alive, but not before stripping her of her bow and arrows and casting one last look at the far-off rise of Mount Thyr.

I jogged off north with a new bow and a belly full of conflict as Algatt horns bellowed from Urgi. But by the time they reached the body and the wounded woman, I had vanished into the forest.

On the fourth day after I left Ogam, I crossed a tongue of the Pasidon and diverted east, avoiding open farm fields and scattered hamlets. Most of the settlements were occupied by Algatt, so I kept to the forest and lit no fire when I camped. Alone in the night, I watched the mountain people's lights glisten through the windows of Eangen houses.

By all appearances, the Algatt were settling in for the season. They inhabited Eangen farms and could be seen in the fields, tending crops and flocks. They hadn't just taken our goods or our lives; they'd taken our homes.

The knowledge of that, the weight of it, ached in my stomach. It was the same feeling I had when I thought of Sixnit or my family in East Meade and the leaderless, priestless refugees heading west towards the sea – that I was turning my back on my people. I was abandoning them all for the charge of a goddess who hid fear in her heart, and who had vanished from the face of her own land. A goddess whose bindings were breaking. A goddess whom I had disobeyed, and who, it seemed, had little time for her people.

I kept trudging north for Eang, but everything in me screamed to turn back. I prayed and sacrificed, sending droplets of blood into the few fires I dared to light. I encountered more signs of unnatural unrest in the land – broken standing stones and a collapsed cairn – but Eang still did not respond to my inquiries.

Once, while washing, naked and knee-deep in a creek, I even contemplated making yifr – the drink which the Eangi High Priesthood used to leave their bodies and visit the gods and the dead. The sickly sweet scent of yellow widow's soap flower, growing on the bank nearby, reminded me of Svala. I saw her again, eyes red-rimmed and cheeks painted with runes, spouting visions of the High Halls. The drink, and visiting the High Halls, were forbidden to common Eangi – but what if I made it anyway? I would be careful not to attract attention, and so long as I broke no laws, like eating or drinking or lingering too long, I might avoid reprisal. I would simply search for Eang and get answers to my questions. It was what Svala would have done.

No. I splashed cold water on my face and scrubbed the impulse away. Svala was a High Priestess – honored, faithful, and wise enough to tread the realms of the Gods.

I was none of those things.

On the fifth night, a vixen came into my camp. I smelled her before I saw her, musky and dank and circling the coals of the fire.

I sat up slowly and reached for my sword. I didn't expect a fox to pose a real threat, but animals were not always what they seemed to be.

"I have no food for you," I told the creature.

She kept pacing, her eyes pools of captured, low firelight. Behind her, I heard the rush of a creek and the mournful lilt of a night bird.

"I said, I have nothing for you. What do you want?"

Another rustle sounded in the undergrowth, so faint that I almost missed it.

I came fully awake and stood, sword in hand. "What do you want?" I demanded again of the fox.

Her lips peeled back in an unnerving grin. She yipped, once.

A second fox peeled from the shadows, then a third and fourth. I recoiled, narrowly missing the tail of a fifth as it darted past my legs. A sixth's eyes glinted from beneath a fall of ferns. A seventh strode the length of a branch ten feet above the ground, displaying elongated claws.

I raised my sword, forcing my breaths to stay steady and deep. "Who do you serve?"

The first fox stalked around the fire in my direction, tail drifting out straight behind her.

A whisper separated from the darkness at my back. I whirled, but there was no one there. A breath touched my cheek, on the side of my mangled ear, and I spun again, terrified of the sensation and my own diminished hearing. But there was still no one.

Then a tongue stroked the back of my neck; broad, humanesque, and leaving a trail of moisture that stung like nettles.

I stifled a shriek and leapt towards the fire, levelling my sword at the shadows. More light, I needed more light. I snatched up dry branches from my shelter with my free hand and threw them onto the coals. Burning lines crept up the leaves, but all they did was curl and smoke.

"Who are you?" I demanded, urging my limbs into a more defensive stance. "I am a servant of Eang."

"Eang?" The voice, far from menacing, sounded melancholy to my ears. It had a female lightness, sweet and drifting, and though she was not speaking Northman, I understood her words. "Eang, Eang... Is this her blood in the land? Why has she not come to me?"

I was not about to tell this creature, whatever it was, that my patron goddess was missing. I'd been devoted to her as a baby, just as I'd dedicated Vistic – her name should be enough to protect me.

The stranger, however, had sounded more curious than daunted.

"Please," I said, "tell me who you are so I can pay you proper respect."

"Shanich," she said her name like a question. "I've... been asleep."

"Greetings, Shanich." I turned, trying to find her in the shadows and keeping my good ear towards her. All around me the foxes paced, tails mingling, but staying out of sword's reach. "Did I wake you? If so, I didn't mean to disturb you."

"I am awake," she stated. "Where is Eang? Call her for me."

My throat tightened. "She will be angry if I call her now."

"Why?" the unseen creature asked innocently.

One of the foxes let its tongue loll between glistening white teeth.

"She has business with Gadr," I said. "But her son, Ogam, is nearby."

That was a stretch to the truth, but Ogam was more likely to respond in force than Eang.

"Ogam." The name dripped off her tongue like honey. "Who is this Ogam? Is he the one who marked your cheek?"

I took a few steadying breaths. If Shanich had not heard of Eang's son, she had been asleep for a long time indeed. Ogam's mark, like Eang's name, might not deter her if she meant me harm.

"The most handsome of the gods," I enticed her. "The immortal son of a winter storm."

"Oh," her voice quavered. "I remember Winter. I remember when the Four gave him life."

The Four? That was a term I had never heard.

"Who?" I asked before I could think better of it.

"The gods, the Four, the ones who came before," Shanich tittered at her own rhyme. "The Four Pillars of Creation, those who made all life, in the beginning. In the black. Thvynder and Eiohe, Imilidese and the Weaver. But Ogam, him I do not know. Is he a Miri? Perhaps I will have you summon him... but not now. You." I felt her attention sharpen. "You. What are you? Who are you?"

I'd never heard of the gods she mentioned or the Miri, but the way she stared at me left no room to ask more. "I am human," I said, withdrawing further and struggling to keep my extended sword from wavering. A fox brushed past my heel.

"A human?" The word clearly meant nothing to her. "What is that? Whose daughter are you? Not Eang's… You do not smell as Miri do. There is power in you, but you are not like us… A dangerous mixture, I think."

"Miri?" I repeated the unfamiliar word this time, turning over legends and songs in my mind. "Are you saying you're a Miri? And Eang is too?"

"She is, I am," Shanich trailed after my retreating steps, "but what are you?"

I pushed the new word aside as a remnant of a forgotten age and searched for another word for human, one equally as ancient. "Clay? My kind was formed of clay, clay and birth-blood of the New Gods."

"There are no such creatures."

I paused, stunned and at a loss. "We serve the gods. We are mortal. We… only bear children through coupling… Our lives are short and we age with years."

"You serve the Four Pillars?"

I hesitated. All of a sudden, Omaskat's talk of powerful gods who begot the Gods of the Old World rushed back to me. Were these Four Pillars what he meant? Were they gods that had existed before the Old World, and this woman who called herself a Miri remembered them?

"I serve the gods like Eang," I repeated, cautiously. "Shanich… are you a god?"

She burst out into laughter, a delighted, crackling descent of notes. It filled the air around me, directionless and disembodied. "Oh, oh! No, I am no god! A flame to a forest fire – that is what I am to the Four. But oh, little slave, I remember your kind. How you have grown. How strong you are, and yet still so blind."

Slave? Her choice of words chilled me. But this was no time for debating history, theology, or the possibly skewed memories of an ancient being.

If I understood, Shanich was a creature from a time before the Gods of the New World had bound the Old. Whatever she was – miscreation, monster, abomination – she had been asleep long before the Eangen had landed on these shores or the Arpa came from the south. Perhaps she had slept in something like the broken binding tree, or the collapsed cairn I had seen on the road north.

"May I ask," I ventured, "how you awoke?"

"I do not know." Her voice drifted again, as though she circled me. The foxes continued to glare, unwavering. "But I am very thirsty."

A hand ran up my spine, and it was not figurative. Shanich was behind me.

I fought down a wave of panic. "Ogam—"

An arm clamped over my mouth, thin and grey and strong as iron. I screamed and bucked. My feet struck the fire and sparks burst up into the night, illuminating the foxes and a thin shoulder at the side of my vision.

I bit down. The flesh did not bleed, but I heard a shriek and the arm released. In its place, the foxes flew at me in a chaos of yips and snarls and flashing eyes.

I ran, abandoning fire and pack and bow. There was nothing else I could do. I leapt through the forest with the thoughtless panic of a fleeing rabbit, ignoring the claws and teeth and the nettle-like hands that scrabbled after me.

The foxes followed. They streaked across the ground and through the trees, leaping and chattering in an unearthly chorus.

"Ogam!" I screamed at the wind. "Ogam, please!"

A fox leapt at me from the side and sunk its tiny teeth into my neck. I snatched at its tail, ripping it away and slamming it into a tree as I passed. It yelped and crumpled.

Fire burst through my veins, loosening my limbs, strengthening my muscles and sharpening my mind. I pounded across the earth, leaping obstacles and ducking branches. I plowed through a meadow in choking clouds of dandelion fluff and lazy fireflies, then dove back into the shadows.

"Hush," a voice hissed in my face.

I skidded, lost my balance and landed hard on my back.

Shanich crouched over me. I could barely see the lines of her; thin and emaciated, feline in her poise.

"Oh, little slave, hush…"

I threw Fire up into her bones, trying to shatter them, but she barely flinched. So I hacked with my sword instead.

It bit into her side. She screeched and leapt away in the shambling, curling clamber of a wounded spider. Again, the foxes took her place. I swatted and fought my way to my feet, yelling and crying and raging all at once. Two crumpled, their skulls ruptured by my Fire, but the rest kept coming.

I found my feet and ran, stumbling, falling, and losing my sword. I pelted over the earth until the ground dropped off before me. An arm of the Pasidon looped some twenty paces below, placid and swift under the moonlight.

Foxes burst from the forest, blocking off any escape to the left or right but keeping their distance. Trapped, I turned, tugged my hatchet from my belt and braced for Shanich's final attack.

But it never came. Back in the trembling shadows of the trees, I heard a roar – the great, gut-watering rumble of some fell beast. The foxes scattered with yips and cries and I stood frozen on the cliff, petrified eyes wide, wondering what could waylay a being like Shanich.

I could never be sure, but I thought that something too large for a bear passed between the nearest trees. All I truly saw, aside from a great shadow and a broad rustle of branches, was an ursine face. Intelligent eyes gazed out at me around a maw smeared with blood and grey fox fur, recalling a night spent in the very river that flowed past my back, the night I'd been swept down to Soulderni in the arms of a riverman. Had I not seen a creature just like this, among the trees?

Whatever it was and whatever had caused our paths to cross a second time, that beast should not have been in the Waking World – but nor should Shanich.

Still, that was no reason not to show proper respect to my savior.

Slowly, tremblingly, I bowed to the forest. I heard a deep, whuffling grunt that might have sounded satisfied, then heavy footfalls moved away down the tree line.

Before the beast could change its mind, I turned on my heel and fled for the river.

TWENTY-ONE

Water stung my open wounds as I crossed the Pasidon. I fought against the current, gasping and shaking in a way that I hadn't since my first skirmish. Raiders, I could face. Wild beasts, I could manage. But a demon with a thirst for humanity and a beast that could frighten her off were more than my nerves could bear.

And I'd faced them alone. Always, always alone.

I climbed out onto the opposite bank and collapsed. My body shook, but no tears ran down my face. I was too shocked, and too drained by the Fire.

I remember little of the rest of that night. Eventually, the sky blushed with the approach of dawn. I realized I was walking – stumbling – south. The wrong way. Next, I was waist-deep in a slow-moving section of the Pasidon and submerged myself.

The current dragged locks of hair across my face and pulled it out behind me, turning my braid into a tangled mat. But slowly, like grains of sand melting into glass, my wits began to return.

I waited until my lungs cried out for air before I rose and dragged in a deep, shuddering breath. I wiped the hair from my eyes and stroked my forehead and my cheeks. I found cuts and bites that made my heart pound – my Fire had not managed to heal them all before it burned out – but the feeling of my own skin, warm with life and cool with river water, anchored me.

I was alive. But nothing could describe the depth of my despair. Neither Eang nor Ogam had helped me. I had lost everything except the clothes on my back, the shoes on my feet and the hatchet in my belt. I had no food. No cloak. No tinderbox. No one to stand at my shoulder.

"Eang," I croaked. "Eang, if you can hear me, I need you."

My goddess did not reply. I ground my teeth to suppress another wracking sob and slit the end of each of my fingers. I held my hand out in front of my face and watched the blood drip down into the water, languid and bright.

"Eang, hear me."

Drip, drip, drip.

"Goddess, please."

Drip, drip.

"Eang!" I screamed. The name echoed over the river and up into the sky, but there was no response. No hoot of an owl. No vision.

I sank down upon the bank. My palms met the cool stone first, bleeding fingers twitching, the exhausted sinews of my wrists straining. My legs gave out next, jittering into one another as they collapsed. Round river stones clattered against my hip and knee, hard enough to bruise, but I was beyond feelings as irrelevant as that.

My vision narrowed and, in its place, grief swelled. It brimmed and overflowed, as broad and yawning as the sky above, and as deep and drowning as the river below.

Eidr came into that vastness first, simple, sweet and unadorned. Then the memories followed, screeching and cavorting into my thoughts like a flock of vengeful crows. Eidr on our wedding day, laughing in the firelight. Eidr brushing hair from my eyes in the warmth of our bed, on a cool autumn night. Eidr lying butchered in the ruins of our home.

I tried to stand back up, clawing at the rocks as if I could physically distance myself from the memories. But all I did was smear the stones with blood and earn myself a dozen more bruises. I gagged, trying to steady my breathing, trying to stop my chest from heaving and my heart from racing, but there was no end to it. Not this time.

I cried. I screamed for Eidr, for Yskc and my family. I cried for the Eangi. But most of all, I wept for myself, because I was alone and afraid, and I did not want to inhabit a world without them; a world where the goddess I'd served and worshiped all my life would not hear me.

Dawn found me listlessly trying to rebind the wounds on my legs with shreds of my undertunic. The rough weave of my outer tunic grated against my skin, but I hadn't the will to care.

"Woman!"

I raised my head.

"We mean no harm. Woman? Can..."

I blinked as the man dismounted and pulled a fringed helmet from his head. He held out a warding hand and halted ten paces away, his brown eyes wide with shock.

"Hessa, put down the hatchet."

I stared into Nisien's face for a long, stupefied minute, then disintegrated into hitching, hysterical laughter.

Nisien hovered as I sat under the care of an Arpa healer. Together with eighty other Arpa, the healer was part of the expedition into the Algatt Mountains that Ogam had initiated and General Athiliu had sent from Ilia. And Nisien, it seemed, had joined them.

The rest of the legionaries, led by Commander Polinus, were currently breaking up camp beyond a stand of birches. The leaves of the trees shimmered gold in the dawn, indifferent to the road-worn men that moved around the peeling white trunks.

"I came after you," Nisien began.

I flinched as the healer applied paste to another wound on my thigh. The thin man was not pleased to be tending a barbarian, but Commander Polinus, as unruffled by me as he had been back at the Ilia Gates, had ordered him to do it.

"My mother had no right to do what she did."

While I appreciated this, I offered the Soulderni no reply. After what I had endured the night before, I was having trouble remembering how to speak.

"I worried you wouldn't make it through the border, so I went straight to Athiliu at the Ilia Gates. Apparently, I missed you by half a day." Nisien brushed at one of his cheeks. He was clean-shaven now, and it was strange to see familiar eyes in such a naked face. I couldn't help but think, when I glanced across the line of his jaw, that Euweth's fears for her son had been all too valid. Despite his darker skin, he looked... Arpa.

"I didn't know what to make of your traveling with that that god, Ogam, either." Nisien watched the healer wind another bandage. "I wanted to help you. But the only way General Athiliu would let me cross into Eangen was if I joined the party heading north. So, I agreed and... well, we rode out two days after you and Ogam."

I studied the horseman. The thought of him coming north for me, crossing the border and putting himself at risk, warmed my heart. But I'd seen the nostalgia in his eyes when he spoke to Castor; I doubted Athiliu and I were the only reasons he'd rejoined the Arpa.

When he didn't speak again, I cleared my throat. "You only joined because Athiliu made you?"

Nisien scrubbed at his cheek now, discomfited by my scrutiny. "No. I wanted to. I owe you, after what my mother did. She broke Hearth Law. Perhaps Fate will be merciful to her if I help you."

"Then Oulden must have brought you to me," I decided. However clouded Nisien's motives might be, there was no need to speak of them now, in front of the healer. "And for that, I'm grateful. You weren't punished for lying to Castor?"

Nisien shrugged. "Athiliu is First in the north and Castor's only a captain. I'll be fine. Where's Cadic?"

My heart turned at the thought of his horse. "Ogam took her. I'm sorry. If I'd known I would see you again—"

He waved a dismissive hand and looked away, but I could see the lines around his mouth tighten. It left me with the hope that, beneath this Arpa garb, Nisien was still a Soulderni of the Ridings.

"Did you run into anyone along the way?" I asked, though I feared the answer. "Algatt or Eangen?"

Nisien hesitated. "Yes."

I waited for him to go on, watching the way the sunlight settled in his black eyelashes.

"We encountered Algatt twice. One group were villagers, so there was a small stand-off, but everyone left alive. The second was a raiding party. That ended more violently, but we didn't lose anyone. If there were Eangen anywhere, they're well in hiding. We saw footprints here and there, a figure in the distance. Nothing more."

I took this soberly. "The Algatt are settling in."

Nisien's nod of agreement turned into a wince as the healer moved on to the bite on my neck. Both men leant closer, examining the tooth marks with a perturbed kind of interest. "Ah… Harvest is only a couple months away and there's no reason for them to starve when the fields are ripe."

The healer tsked, muttered in his own language, and poked at the holes in my flesh. I strove not to flinch and held my leather-wrapped braid out of the way.

"Then they've conquered Eangen," I concluded grimly.

"Well." Nisien still watched the man work. "If more beings like Shanich and her… creatures… are roaming about, the Algatt might not be able to stay either."

I shivered compulsively. I tried to hide the tremor in a scowl, but my façade was thin. "Eangen may become too dangerous for anyone. I found a broken binding tree, and other signs of unrest."

"Is that why you're this far north?" The way Nisien spoke made me realize he'd been holding this question back. "I hoped to find word of you in the south, but I gave up days ago. Did Eang send you here? Does this have anything to do with the god you bound in Souldern?"

It dawned upon me that I had never told Nisien about Omaskat or the real circumstances that had brought me to his land. I glanced from him to the healer. I wasn't sure I wanted to divulge the whole truth yet – especially with Nisien clad in smooth cheeks and Arpa plate armor – but I trusted the healer even less.

"Your mother was a goat," I suggested casually to the older man.

The healer rolled his eyes and told Nisien something in his own language.

"He doesn't understand you," Nisien clarified with the hint of a smile.

"I am going north for Eang," I said. The next part was harder to divulge: "And yes, it may have something to do with Ashaklon and the trouble in the High Halls. All I'll say is that I'm looking for someone."

Nisien took this in stride, and if he was hurt by my lack of candor, he didn't show it. "I see."

"I..." I looked beyond the stand of birches, where the rest of the Arpa were almost finished breaking camp and the gold of dawn settled into a clean, summer brightness. They loaded the horses now, calling to one another and tossing saddlebags between them. A flutter of panic passed through me.

"I've lost my gear," I fumbled. "Can you leave me with—"

"Come with us," Nisien said before the last word had left my lips. "This is no land to be traveling alone, Eangi or not."

"Would Polinus agree?" I hesitated. "They offered to take me with them at the border, but I... I never expected to meet something like Shanich."

"Polinus is a good man. He wouldn't abandon you here." Nisien stood up. "I'll speak with him now if you like."

I paused for the span of two breaths. But the thought of being left alone on this riverbank, without Eang or Ogam or my own strength, was too much.

"Please."

And so, I came to travel north through Algatt-overrun Eangen in a company of legionaries.

I rode with Nisien, pouring all my focus into staying astride the horse. I paid the Arpa little attention and bore their interest passively, holding onto Nisien's belt as we plodded up a well-traveled road.

"There's a town, Lada, nearby," I said at one point and gestured to a carved stone up ahead. "That marks a three-mile distance from a temple."

Nisien nudged our horse into a trot and wove up to the fore of the group, where Polinus rode in deep discussion with another man. As we drew up, I realized the second man was no legionary at all, but the priest, Quentis. He was robed and carried a knife but was otherwise unarmed and unarmored.

Quentis forgot whatever he had been about to say and, for a second, we stared at one another.

"Servant of Eang," he acknowledged in an indecipherable tone.

"Servant of..." I glanced him over, but if there were clues to his patron god in his grey robe and its crisscrossed leather straps, I couldn't recognize them.

"Lathian," the man finished for me.

I levelled my shoulders and considered him with a new, cautious respect. He served the Arpa's chief god directly, just as I served Eang. Yes, I had caught him off guard with my Fire back at the Ilia Gates, but this man was my equal. Who knew what kind of power his god had gifted him with?

Slowly, I inclined my head. He did the same.

Polinus and Nisien, meanwhile, had begun to speak.

"...supplies." Polinus tilted his helmet back and squinted up at the sun. "You, take a man and scout ahead. Go."

Two soldiers dropped from their saddles, passed off reins, and jogged away up the road.

As they vanished, Polinus looked at me. "I'd like you to tell me all you can about this region."

I considered lying, but I needed these foreigners now. And as far as Arpa went, I didn't mind Polinus.

"This village is one of three on the road to the mountains," I explained. "They're farmers, like the rest of us, except for Iskir. That's the town furthest north. There is... *was* a large group of Eangi there. It was probably the hardest hit by the Algatt. If there is anyone left, they will be hostile. Iskiri are the wildest of the Eangen."

"Human threats we can manage," Polinus said, his tone impassive and practical. "But what of this Shanich? Is the area known for beings like her?"

I shook my head. "She'd been forgotten. The only name I know in this area is Ried, an old god. His bones are buried beneath the Hall of Vision in Iskir, but he's been dead a thousand years."

"Ah. Did this trouble in your 'High Hall' disturb Shanich?"

I wasn't about to admit Eang's power was waning, and along with it, her ancient bindings. "Maybe."

"Then how can we defend against her?" Polinus turned his gaze between Quentis and me.

"Pray," we replied in unison, though my response had a doubtful undercurrent. No one else noticed it.

"I gave Shanich what should have been a mortal wound," I added. "It only irritated her."

"I can cast a ward over the camp tonight," Quentis offered. "It will do little against the Algatt, but perhaps the creatures will be deterred."

When Nisien glanced over his shoulder at me quizzically, I shook my head. "Eangi don't do witchcraft."

"Witchcraft?" The priest shot me a half-disgusted, half-pitying glare. I saw the insult poised on his tongue – barbarian? Heathen? Savage? "Then what are your runes and your Eangi Fire?"

I scowled.

"Place your ward then." Polinus eyed us like a disapproving parent. "We'll stop within the hour, depending on what word the scouts bring back. Then the two of you can discuss what we should do if Shanich or her ilk attack."

The scouts returned with word that the village of Lada was abandoned, so we made our way there.

My heart clenched as we rode past gaping doors, overgrown gardens and empty pathways. There were no burned buildings or bodies, and that lent me hope that the population had fled in time. But there were still signs of violence – shattered shutters, a door torn off its hinges. The Algatt had swept through on their way south, and little of value remained behind the houses' gaping windows.

When I caught sight of the temple through the narrow paths between the houses, I tapped Nisien on the shoulder.

"Slow down. I'll be back."

Before he could protest, I slipped from the saddle, pushed aside a cascade of hanging grasses and made for the temple, hatchet in hand.

The simple building resided on the edge of the village. It looked much like the shrine I had visited on Mount Thyr, but this one was larger and walled with weathered grey cedar boards. Winters were harsher in the north and its people practical about the burden of cold and snow in their worship.

I took a second to compose myself. The emptiness of the village oppressed me, lingering at my back like an unspoken threat. Despite this, insects hummed in the grasses around my shoes and the sun on my scalp was warm, almost pleasant.

I stepped into the shrine. Inside, the scent of wood, smoked and weathered, sunk deep into my lungs. My eyes closed and my lips parted in a prayer so instinctual that I hardly noticed it.

"Eang, Eang. The Brave, the Vengeful, the Swift and the Watchful. I come to pay respect and beg your eye fall upon me."

I crossed the worn earthen floor. Offerings lay scattered across the ground: idols of owls and female forms; bowls that had once held honey wine or blood; animal's teeth; owl feathers; wooden beads; and intricately carved bones. Anything more valuable was long gone, carried off by the Algatt.

Rage burned in my chest at the desecration. But at least they had not burned this holy place, as they had the Hall of Smoke.

Carefully, I gathered up all the offerings and set them back on the altar. Then, as I glanced down into the basin of ashes and dead coals, I saw an irregular shape.

It was a collar. An Eangi collar, slightly warped by the heat of the flames and so old that its runes had vanished. It had been modified into the shape of a torc, turning its severed ends into smooth swirls of bronze.

Gently, I lifted it from the ash and brushed my fingers along its curve. This was a far northern style of collar. Normally, an Eangi collar was made to be permanent and irremovable – only to be cut off when an Eangi had done something so heinous it merited casting out. But in villages like this, which would only have one priest or priestess for the entirety of that person's life, collars could be passed down, like a chieftain's brooch or a mother's beads.

For a short time, I knelt in the temple and cradled the collar in my ashy fingers, lost in bittersweet memories of Albor and Eidr and the Hall of Smoke. I longed to slip this collar around my neck; to rise redeemed and burn my path through the world. To be a true Eangi again, fearless with hope of the High Halls and reunion with my lost people before me.

But I was still unforgiven. What right did I have to wear such a thing, even one as warped and tarnished as this?

I wanted that right back. Fire lit in my chest, more of a throbbing than a blaze. One day soon, I would wear this collar proudly. And I would see Eidr and Yske again.

With determined, grim movements, I cleaned the bronze circlet and tucked it through my belt.

TWENTY-TWO

I t wasn't until I sat down to eat my midday ration that I realized Castor and pale-eyed Estavius were among the company. In truth, I hadn't bothered to study any of the soldiers. They were all untrustworthy under their helmets – that was all I cared to know.

But when I settled myself in the shade of a tree, I saw Castor, the captain, watching me. His light brown curls were stiff with sweat, dragged in furrows from his flushed forehead. Estavius, the inquisitive one, sat next to him on a bench, his attention directed toward his food.

My eyes darted around for Nisien, but he was out of sight. Why hadn't he mentioned that Castor and Estavius had joined the mission?

Riding the grim determination I'd found in the temple, I met Castor's gaze and nodded in acknowledgement. Estavius noticed too and returned my nod, relief and interest passing through his pale eyes.

Castor, however, did something quite different. He drew back his upper lip and curled his tongue around his teeth in a lewd sneer. Estavius, who had already looked back to his food, didn't notice.

A fracture laced up my calm exterior. My heart thudded against my ribs, once in unease, twice in anger, then I calmed. I delivered Castor the snarl I usually reserved for Algatt.

He choked on a laugh. That caught Estavius's attention again and his gaze flicked between the two of us. Seeing the end of my snarl, he demanded something of his companion.

Castor chortled out the last of his amusement and flapped a hand dismissively, but Estavius's gaze was cautious from then on – though I couldn't be sure if it was directed toward Castor or me.

When Nisien sat down at my side, I pointed to the pair. "What are they doing here?"

The Soulderni followed my gaze. "Ah. They volunteered."

"After a month of marching, they still volunteered to cross Eangen?" I couldn't decide whether to be impressed or disdainful, particularly given the burns Estavius had taken during Esach's lightning storm. Though, now that I noted his hands, I saw they had healed remarkably well.

"They're currying favor. It will be a smart move if we survive." Nisien threw the pair a discreet look. "The Rim is a good place to make your name and those two – they're rich men's sons. Estavius's father is High Priest of Aliastros and Castor's is a senator." When I gave him a confused glance, he clarified, "A powerful man, a politician and a spokesman for the people."

"Ah," I said. "That explains his… attitude."

Nisien gave the ghost of a grin. "Well, the commanders on the Rim are harder on men with a comfortable background. But now Athiliu knows their faces personally, as does Polinus, and if the mission is successful the story will go right to the Ascended Emperor Himself."

"Then there must have been a lot of men vying to come."

Nisien understood my meaning. "Yes. But as you may have noticed, they're all pure Arpa. They're legionaries. Not auxiliaries. My… fluency in Northman is why Athiliu insisted I join – that and my reputation. I was surprised, honestly."

"What do you mean by reputation?"

The Soulderni fingered the dense bread and dried meat in his hands. "I made a name for myself in the far south, like those two are doing now. I was a scout, sometimes a messenger, sometimes a spy."

I eyed him. "A spy?"

Nisien grinned. "The southerners are dark, like Soulderni. I drew less attention."

I let my head tilt to one side and examined his face. By now, the seed of nostalgia I had seen in him back in Souldern had blossomed into something near hunger. There was still a shadow behind his eyes, like any sane man recalling a season of violence, but he missed it, too.

I thought of Euweth's expression when she sent me away – a mask of anger and determination that had covered her terror of losing her son, and her own loneliness. She had been right to fear, even if she had brought that fear to fruition.

The sight of Quentis striding past tugged my thoughts away from the Soulderni. Polinus had instructed us to collaborate during the rest, but from the way Quentis kept his eyes focused ahead of him, he had no intention of doing so. I didn't, either.

"Tell me about the south and the Empire," I invited Nisien.

Nisien settled his shoulders back into the tree's trunk. "Only if you tell me about being an Eangi."

I leant back beside him, leaving a gap between our shoulders. "You first."

"Well…" The horseman gathered his words together. "The Empire is vast. Far more than I ever imagined. Going there as a child, straight from the Ridings to the capital, it was terrifying. So many people, people from all over the Empire, all packed into high houses and narrow streets."

I considered this before I asked, "Did you try to run away?"

Nisien stared into the distance. "No. There was no opportunity – I was just so far from home. But I wasn't alone. I was with dozens of other boys in the same situation. We became brothers. I never stopped missing my mother, or vowing to return to her, but I didn't hate the legions. I was welcomed. Respected. I belonged."

I watched unspoken memories flicker through his eyes. "If it wasn't for your mother, would you ever have left?"

His focus remained on that distant point. "Circumstances are never that simple."

I glanced around the village, at the legionaries sitting or standing all around us. The thought of Nisien willingly living among these people, belonging to them, chilled me.

"In the Empire…" I asked, "did they let you worship Oulden?"

Nisien shook his head. "No."

"So you…" I sat straighter. "You didn't worship Oulden for ten years?"

"Everyone in the Empire bows to Lathian and the Emperor, who is his… well, the Emperor to Lathian is like an Eangi to Eang, a vessel." The horseman picked at his nails. They were torn to the pink, I noticed. "That's the way it is. You don't worship gods outside the Arpa Pantheon. One of my commanders enforced that. Some don't. But he did."

"Who was he?"

Nisien's face clouded. "He's called Telios. One of Lathian's zealots."

I recalled the name from Nisien's conversation with Castor, that night in the cave in Souldern. This, combined with the tightness around my companion's eyes, told me I was inching towards something important. "Lathian's zealots?"

The young man's expression darkened. Telios, it seemed, was not someone Nisien wanted to remember. "Soldiers absolutely devoted to Lathian. Zealots, like the name suggests."

His words, said and unsaid, hung in the air between us. I searched his clean-shaven face for clues, both about Telios and the state of Nisien's soul. Had Oulden really accepted him back after ten years of worshiping foreign gods?

"Now," Nisien said abruptly, "your turn. Tell me about the Eangi."

That evening I stood by as Quentis worked his Arpa witchcraft. Mixing drops of his own blood with powders and herbs from a bag, he took a reed and proceeded to flick it onto the trees around the camp. Occasionally, he used the paste to draw a symbol and muttered over it.

"What is this supposed to do?" I crossed my arms over my chest. "Do you put Fire in the runes?"

He frowned at me in disgust and scooped out the last of the mixture with his fingers. He used it to mark the forehead of each horse. They shuffled and danced around him, unnerved by the smell of blood.

"They're not runes. And no, I don't put *fire* in them. They have power in themselves, sourced from Lathian."

I bristled and fingered the hatchet at my belt – the only weapon the Arpa let me carry. Everything about this priest, from his measured strides to the smooth rumble of his voice, made my skin crawl and my hair stand on end. He was in my home, the land of my goddess, but he did not seem the least bit cowed.

"It will deter anything unholy from coming upon us." Quentis neatly avoided a falling hoof and cast me a second, more lingering glance. "And if you do not stop watching me, I'll ward you, too."

"Eang's blood is in this land," I returned. "You can't 'ward' me."

He gave me a tired look and circled around, making for the tents. There were eight of them, simple structures arranged in a neat, inward-facing circle around several cookfires. For all their faults, the Arpa were industrious; a whole night's worth of wood was already stacked, and several men had begun to cook the evening meal.

Abruptly, Quentis turned. "Eangi."

"What?"

"Why are you going north?"

I let the silence hang between us for a while before I said, "I serve my goddess. As you serve your god."

He took a step back towards me, his bowl in hand, fingers stained with paste and blood. "How do you serve her?"

It was my turn to step closer to him. "That doesn't matter to you."

"To me? Yes, it does. Perhaps not to Polinus, but we are different men, with different… sensitivities." He was a pace away from me now, bloody fingers poised as if he might reach out and touch me. "Why would Eang send one of her priestesses into the mountains, alone, in such dangerous times?"

"Why would I tell you?"

His lips pinched into a sour, thoughtful expression. Without another word, he turned and strode away.

I waited until Quentis was gone from sight before I rolled the tension out of my shoulders. The priest had left me unnerved, but I had no time to dwell on him.

A voice came to me upon a twisting strand of wind. "Hessa."

I turned around and scanned the trees suspiciously. "Ogam?"

"Come."

The cold wind tugged me forward by a lock of loose hair. I ignored the disconcerted stare of a legionary and followed it outside the camp. A few minutes on, the lock of hair fell back against my cheek and I halted in a small clearing of jutting rocks, knotted roots and bursts of hip-high ferns. In a forest of waning summer sunlight, this place alone was cool, smelling of snow and long, dark nights.

"Where are you?" I asked, not bothering to hide the accusation in my voice.

"Far away. You called to me?"

"Two days ago." My throat thickened at the memory of that night – hunted by Shanich and near madness. I turned slowly, scanning the clearing in the mottled evening light. "I nearly died. Didn't you hear me?"

"I was occupied. Tell me what happened."

"A creature called Shanich attacked me."

"Shanich… Shanach…" Ogam tasted the name, turning it on his tongue and trying to find a sound that registered in his memory. "Shanalch?"

"Shanich. She tried to…" I felt my face paling. "She wanted to… drink me."

"Your blood, spirit or tears?" he inquired.

I gaped at a disembodied patch of orange sunlight, galled. "Blood, spirit or— Gods above and below, Ogam, you do realize I can die? Only once?"

"Yes. So which was it?"

"She didn't say," I retorted.

"Hmm…" Ferns rustled in a circle around me, moving contrary to the rest of the forest in Ogam's icy breeze. "Likely your blood, for its life-magic. If so, I've heard of her, but only just."

"What is she? A demon?"

"Yes." He hesitated. "Of a sort – she is something that never should have been. A child of one of the Gods of the Old World, but that god perished long before her kin were bound by my mother and the other New Gods. They say that before her death, terrified of her mortality, that goddess tried to secure her children eternal life. It went… awry. And the first generation of demons came to be. And they bred."

I waited for him to go on, angling my good ear in the direction of his voice. When he didn't, I ventured, "Shanich mentioned a group of gods I've never heard of. Well… she seemed to think *only* they were gods, actually. She called herself and Eang Miri and the 'gods' the Four? Pillars, I think? A Weaver and Thvynder, and two others?"

Ogam was silent for another second. Then he made a derisive sound. "She's slept for a long time, Hessa. Her memory has likely skewed. Don't let her madness trouble you. But…" he added thoughtfully, "if she is from as far back as it seems, she's not with Ashaklon. My mother must have rebound her at some point, and now that her power is fading, Shanich walks again. Still, she may not be able to leave the area you found her in. Yet."

The thought of Eang's waning power stole any consolation from his words, or lingering interest in the Four. "I found a broken binding tree, too. And a cairn and shattered standing stones."

"Unsurprising."

"And there was a creature. A bear, maybe? Bigger. It's what scared Shanich off."

"Really?" Ogam sniffed. "I heard Aegr escaped the High Halls… but so many have. What a time we live in. Demons breaking ancient bonds, Gods of the Old World causing a ruckus, legendary beasts clawing back into the Waking World!"

Aegr. I'd sung of the great bear in the Ridings, hadn't I? Cursed with an eternal wound, the ornery bear had been healed by a daughter of red-haired Risix. Since that healing, he'd become a gentler figure of Eangen lore, but he was supposed to dwell in the High Halls.

Ogam sounded nonchalant as he mentioned the bear, and the creature had saved me. Still, the thought of anything escaping the High Halls was discomfiting.

"Then I might encounter more things like Shanich and Aegr?" I summarized.

The wind hovered for a pensive moment. "It is possible, though Aegr's a paternal fellow – maudlin, too – so he's hardly a concern to you. If my mother came back to Eangen she could likely do something about them but... well."

"She's not in Eangen?" I asked, though I dreaded the answer. "At all? You're sure?"

"Not sure, but reasonably convinced." Ogam's voice lowered and the wind pooled in front of me. "You're still all I can sense of her. She's either far away or hiding very well."

Eang, hiding? I remembered how Eang's fear had felt, as we faced down Ashaklon. Perhaps Ogam was right, and Eang was hiding just like Oulden had.

Disconcerted and more than a little indignant, I protested, "She can't do that. We're her people. Her duty is to protect us."

"She can do whatever she pleases. Haven't you learned that by now?"

I pushed down another rush of ire. Ranting about Eang's actions to Ogam was not only dangerously heretical but would not get me any closer to the High Halls. And I still had questions to be answered. "Fine. Then what should I do if we meet something like Shanich again?"

"We?"

I paused. "I've joined up with the Arpa. After Shanich... I had no choice. Traveling alone was too dangerous."

Ogam's laugh made the leaves tinkle in a full circle over my head. "See? I did make the right choice. Trust the immortal Son of Winter, Eangi."

"But you didn't come." I tried not to sound like a petulant child and failed. I reined myself in. "You said you would hear me. You promised."

"I was occupied," he said again. "I've found the trail of the child, Vistic."

I hadn't expected that. "You have? Is he all right? Did you see Sixnit?"

"She's with me now," Ogam replied, and relief washed over me like the warm evening sunlight shafting through the canopy. Before I could respond, he carried on, "As to the child, he was taken."

"I know that," I strove to be patient. "By what? Or who?"

"As near as I can figure, Gadr."

I gaped at the forest. What did the Algatt god want with an infant? "Gadr? Himself?"

"Yes."

"Why?"

Ogam's tone turned irritated. "Do you realize how many questions you've asked in the last minute of conversation? If I was a riverman I would have stuffed you in a muskrat den by now."

I stilled myself. "I'm sorry."

The wind tugged at my hair again. "Gods below. Stop using words you don't mean."

"My questions are justified," I pointed out. "I need to know."

"All you need to know is your own task. I'm being generous by even speaking with you," he replied. "If you encounter another creature like Shanich, try to soothe them, keep them calm. Sing. They'll be groggy and may be convinced to go back to sleep. Other than that, just be cautious and stay away from binding trees. And graves."

The air pressure dropped as if something had vacated the space around me. "Ogam?" I called, and realized it sounded like yet another question. "Ogam."

"'Thank you," his disembodied voice prompted from somewhere far away.

"Thank you," I relented.

His presence faded and the cool wind retreated, letting the warmth of the fading sun slip back into my little corner of forest. Slowly, I let out a breath and closed my eyes, sorting out what I had learned. Eang, absent from Eangen? Vistic taken by Gadr? But why?

Ogam's voice, a memory this time, rang through my head.

Are you sure he's human?

I thought about the tiny infant Vistic, curled into Sixnit's chest in the ravaged Hall. The thin breath in his lungs, the limpness of his head; could he be anything other than human? But he had survived, the son of an Eangi, the only living creature in the Hall of Smoke besides his mother. Maybe there really was more to him.

I took a few more moments to collect myself, then rubbed the back of one hand over my eyes. I couldn't work this through alone. It was, I realized, high time I brought Nisien into my confidence. Maybe the Soulderni would have fresh insight.

It was then that I heard footsteps. They were distant and many, so soft and cautious that I could barely distinguish them from the usual rustle of the leaves. I dropped into a crouch in the ferns, cocking my good ear towards the sounds and keeping my breaths quiet, measured and deep.

The footsteps continued at a steady distance, passing me and heading in the direction of the Arpa camp. I crept forward, sheltering behind a root-draped rock, and peered through the forest with a hand on my hatchet.

Shapes crept through the trees. They moved low, traversing the rough terrain through shafts of nearly horizontal sunlight and swaths of shadow. Round shields preceded them, their bosses smeared with charcoal to keep them from reflecting the sunlight, as were the heads of their axes and their swords. Their cheeks, pale in the waning light, were painted with telltale blue and yellow.

The Algatt had come.

TWENTY-THREE

I watched the Algatt progress, two halves of myself awakening and vying for dominance. One was a memory, an Eangi girl with forty shields locked with hers and the dauntless, unquestionable leadership of the war chief Ardam ringing in her ears. That Eangi had faced a force like this many times. She had little fear, surrounded and guided by her people. One of many. Part of a whole.

But the other half of myself, the louder one, knew she was alone. All she could remember were the remnants of the Hall of Smoke where every one of those companions lay.

Those two halves collided into a flush of fear and rage. My breaths shortened and Fire clawed up my throat, livid and scorching. My eyes flicked over the shapes in the woods, counting a dozen, two dozen, three. More came on; I heard them all around. In moments, I would be surrounded.

I hunkered lower, allowing myself one more second to think. Hurling myself at this many Algatt raiders was certain suicide. But as the seconds slipped by, my rage coiled tighter and the odds mattered less and less.

The camp had to be warned. If the Arpa watchmen hadn't sounded the alarm by now, perhaps they'd already been silenced. An Eangi war cry might carry the distance, but I'd be killing myself in the process. I needed to get closer. Fast.

An Algatt stepped into my clearing. He didn't see me immediately, narrowing his eyes against the last of the evening light and stalking his way through the ferns. He was red-haired and bearded, like Eidr had been before Algatt, like this one, had murdered him.

I made no conscious decision to move. My limbs simply unfurled and I rose halfway, hatchet in hand and Fire falling from my lips like hot coals from a brazier.

The Algatt crumpled like a sail without wind. The ferns swallowed him, settling with a gentle rustle.

Keeping low, I darted over to him and picked up his shield, shifted my grip to test the strength of my arm, then shoved my hatchet through my belt and took up his longer axe instead.

I allowed myself the briefest moment to let their weight settle into my limbs. The shard of Eang inside me reveled at the action, pulsing and radiating. Her euphoria, her hunger, met with my turmoil and began to hum through my every muscle, every vein.

My head lowered, my shoulders loosened, and I ran. I sprinted back through the forest toward the camp, flitting through beams of dusky light and passing right by a clutch of startled raiders.

I darted and wove, but no arrows chased me. Between my speed, the Algatt shield and the ensuing twilight, they likely couldn't tell I was Eangen.

But they followed. Algatt whoops and howls filled the forest behind me and their soft, shushing progress broke into an outright charge. We'd be on the camp in moments – I recognized that rock, that tree, and streaked past two of Quentis's wards with Algatt as my escort.

I nearly laughed, then choked as one of the closest invaders, a woman with yellow streaked into her sandy hair, diverted to run right beside me.

She saw my face at the same time as I saw an Arpa shout in the distance – a watchman?

"Eangen!" The Algatt raider gaped at my darker skin and hair, recoiled in shock, and then threw herself in front of me.

There was no use hiding now. I screamed, but the voice was not mine. It never was, not when the Fire possessed me like this. The Algatt crumpled and two more took her place, diving to intercept me with howls of desperate challenge – and dread.

"Eangi! Eangi!"

I burst out into the Arpa camp and the world slowed again. My gaze passed from the charging Algatt to the Arpa, scrambling into quadratic formation in the center of the camp, shields locked and eyes glinting behind their helmets. Their cookfires burned and, overhead, twilight turned the leaves into a rustling canopy of violet-grey.

Raiders surged between the tents and surrounded the southerners in seconds, howling and lunging and yipping, but they hadn't forgotten about me. Four attackers closed in, cutting me off from the Arpa and the safety of their formation.

One Algatt charged me, shield at his left shoulder, weapon hidden from sight out behind him. I raised my own shield and braced.

We met with a teeth-jarring clatter. He used his height to flip his shield over mine and thrust the rim towards my throat with a violent scraping. His sword followed an instant behind, flashing towards the back of my thigh in the light of the nearest fire.

I gave way in one quick step, enough to let the edge of my shield slip free and avoid his strike. I dropped, hooking his ankle with my axe and hauling. The man went down, and I spun to face my next opponent.

A sword thrust rammed into my shield. Its wood nearly cracked off my forehead but I was already dropping again, spinning the shield to tear the sword from my attacker's hand. I shook away the pain, knocked her shield aside and lashed my axe at her knees. Down.

I straightened to find myself chin to chin with a berserker, all but his beard and kohl-rimmed eyes concealed by an owl-eyed helmet. His bloody hands seized both sides of my head and twisted me forward. I let my body follow the motion, rolling, and by the time I'd come into a crouch, red liquid seeped down his neck. He tumbled into the arms of another warrior, who let out a horrified cry and buckled under him.

My consciousness settled deep inside me, sheltered while the Eangi burned. My movements became more distant, even to me; each thrust of my sword, each sprint of pursuit, each grind of my heel and blow against my shield.

This was every raid I had ever participated in, grim and distant. The Algatt I faced now, I had already defeated. The blows I took, I had already taken.

I saw Yske. Her face flickered across my vision as I struck down a rabid Algatt woman, little older than I. Her mass of white-blond braids spun as I sidestepped, caught her across the back of the neck with my shield and knocked her sprawling.

Someone grabbed me from behind. Simultaneously, I brought up my shield to stop the downward blow of a huge, bearded war axe. My shield cracked and the handle slipped from my fingers.

I shouted and the woman wielding the axe recoiled, clutching bleeding eyes.

I tried to knock my head into the jaw of the person holding me and met shoulder instead. My shield arm was crippled with pain. My attacker pinioned my right wrist, squeezing it so hard that I dropped my axe.

An arm locked around my throat and I heard a female voice shout some command. Her spear thrust towards my stomach.

Nisien barreled her over. A second later the arm left my throat as pale-eyed Estavius jerked my assailant free and drove a sword into his gut.

I stumbled forward, raking air into my lungs. A hand hauled me upright and I blinked gratefully into Nisien's face.

Without a word he grabbed my fingers and pressed a sword into them.

The shard of Eang hurt me now, tearing my muscles and making my bones ache. This was the end of the Fire. When the blaze faded, I would be left with only my physical training and pain.

Between Nisien and Estavius, I fought my way to the shield wall. It distantly occurred to me that there had to be at least a hundred Algatt, which, subtracting the twenty strewn across the ground, was still a formidable force.

I fought until my knees gave out and my head swam. Finally, as I knelt in a forest of boots and wounded legionaries, Commander Polinus's voice broke over the waning chaos. I didn't have to speak Arpa to understand their meaning.

"Hold! Hold your ground!"

Pounding footsteps, shouts and a frantic horn signaled the Algatt's flight. The legionaries maintained their position, eyes fixed outwards, heels braced against the churned earth.

I eased my hips into my heels and wheezed. No one spoke yet, though several of the injured moaned and sobbed. I looked away from them and glimpsed Nisien's head, free of his helmet and silhouetted against the sky above. He glanced at me and, to my surprise, grinned.

Bands of firelight fell across me. The soldiers let their shields part and stepped outwards, guards still raised, swords and spears prodding each body they passed.

Estavius lay on his back not far away, head tilted to one side, eyes closed and his breathing shallow. Instinct, and an unexpected flutter of pity for the quiet man, made me reach out and loosen the scarf that protected his throat from chaffing. His eyes didn't open, but he breathed more freely after that. Satisfied, I patted his armored chest and started to sink back onto the earth.

But as I moved, my eyes snagged on a cut on Estavius's cheek. For an instant, I would have sworn that his blood glistened with an odd, amber hue. But when I blinked again, it was gone. Just a trick of the firelight and my own exhaustion.

Nisien sat down beside me, chest heaving. He smeared blood away from his mouth, then flopped backwards and let out a quavering laugh. The laugh strengthened after the first few hitches and turned wild; a mix of relief, elation, and shock.

I gazed at him. My consciousness had returned to my body now, creeping out of her sheltered corner and stretching back into my limbs.

She was numb, she was weary, and she hated the taste of blood.

"Gods above and below," Nisien spluttered, throwing red-streaked fingers towards the night sky and turning them about dazedly, "I've missed this."

We buried ten legionaries at dawn the next day. As the men labored over shovels, Polinus approached me. He didn't comment on my actions the night before, but there was a new candidness in his deepset eyes.

"What should we do with the dead Algatt?"

His deference gave me a little strength.

"The Gatti will come back for them, after we leave," I told Polinus, surveying the rows of Algatt corpses and pulling on the padded vest I had stolen from the dead blond woman. I had a new axe and shield, too, not to mention pairs of proper throwing axes, boots, and legwraps.

I felt like an Eangi again, and yet, at the same time, strangely other. I refastened the warped collar I'd found in Lada to my belt and set my shoulders. "We'd dishonour the bodies if we buried them."

"I see," Polinus said. It looked like he had taken a set of claws to the face and, judging from the spacing of the fingers, I suspected they were female. "Are they likely to retaliate?"

"Yes. But it won't be tomorrow." I fumbled with my belt. My Fire had knitted most of my scratches and bruises before it died, but my shield arm was weak enough that I couldn't tighten my fingers. "The Algatt are… skirmishers. They attack and run, tend their dead, gather more men, and attack again."

"I see. So next time we might anticipate a larger force?"

"If one's available." I grimaced at the ties of my belt, frustration flaring. "Definitely. They'll rally and hunt us down. But we should be in the mountains by then, and there's a chance they won't follow."

Polinus accepted this and offered me his empty hands. "If I may?"

I nodded and moved my arms out of the way.

As the older man fastened my belt, he informed me, "I've assigned you a horse. See Castor before we ride out."

Half an hour later, I unwillingly tracked down the legionary.

"She's yours." Castor threw a blanket over the back of a mare and hefted the saddle into place. He adjusted it, bent to find the girth, and tightened that. His tone light, he asked, "So, you turn men's bones to dust? Is this a common barbarian practice?"

I ignored him and moved to meet my horse's eye. She lifted her head from the grass and shook away a buzzing fly, her short white mane rippling in the morning light against a coat the color of creamed honey.

I didn't look up until I felt the captain's eyes run across me. Arrogance remained in the curl of his lips, but it didn't quite reach his eyes.

"It was impressive," he admitted. "What you did last night."

"I'm Eangi," I replied simply.

Castor fitted the bridle over the horse's head and tucked the bit into her mouth. She shuffled on her feet and shook her head again, this time accompanied by the ring of tack.

"You're Eangi," the legionary prompted.

"Yes. That, last night, that's Eang's gift. Her power is in our blood."

"Ah." One of his eyebrows arched at this. "I see. So, your parents are Eangi?

"No." I absently scratched my horse's neck, under her mane. "It doesn't work like that. Does she have a name?"

"Who?"

"The horse. Does she have a name?"

"Melid. It means honey."

I glanced down at the animal, who had gone back to lipping at the grass. "A fierce name for a warhorse."

"Mmm," he agreed, watching me. "What does Hessa mean?"

His sudden friendliness made me uncomfortable. I edged around his broader frame, choosing to step behind him instead of passing through the space between him and the horse.

As I crouched to shift my possessions into Melid's saddlebags I replied, "'Hes' means boat. 'Sa' is… well, it's not anything really. Not anymore. 'Nae sa' is what we say when someone is married or moves away. Or dies. 'Nae sa – don't look back.'"

"Then… 'Look back to the boat'?" Castor offered. "'Remember the boat'?"

I finished repacking the saddlebags, slipped them over Melid's back and made sure they were secure. "Directly, yes. But the sense of it is more… 'remember the past', or 'remember where we came from'. It's an old name, from the time before we settled here. Before the tongues changed or we began to worship Eang."

"Who did you barbarians worship before then?"

I rankled at the insult but tugged at a strap and replied with a dismissive, "No one remembers."

In the back of my mind, however, Shanich's words about greater gods, older gods called Thvynder and the Weaver and Eiohe, prodded at me. Had my people once known those names, too? Might Eang know them? And if so, why had she never told us?

Just how much might the goddess be hiding from her own people? The possibilities were too huge, and too heretical, to contemplate.

Castor took this with consideration. "Weren't the Eangen and the Algatt one people, in the beginning? Before you started slaughtering one another?"

I straightened and gave him a cool stare. But he was taller than me and, by the twitch at the corner of his mouth, my gaze was less than intimidating.

"Yes," I replied, taking him by surprise. The priestess woke in me then, armed with centuries of lore and song and prayers. Eangen history was courageous and proud, and I refused to be ashamed of it. "Before we came to carve out a life for ourselves. Before Eang came to us in the snow of the first winter. Before the Algatt found their god in the mountain and chose to live there, to worship him, instead of staying where the land was fertile and where Eang ruled. Long, long before your Empire."

Castor nodded sagely. "Ah, yes. A heroic history. Yet you still defecate in the forest, build your houses from sticks and send your women to fight?"

My anger struck in a fierce white flash. It raced up my throat like a snake in the grass, evasive and uncatchable.

Just before it left my lips and struck the legionary down, Nisien stepped up to my shoulder. I closed a mouth full of heat and swallowed hard.

"Castor, leave the Eangi be." Nisien banished the other man with a jerk of the head.

Castor shot a look between us, gave an over-ingratiating half-bow and strode away.

Nisien and I stood poised until the Arpa was out of earshot. Then Nisien let out a ragged breath. He retreated from my shoulder to lay a hand on Melid's neck, looking like a man who had talked down a hungry bear.

"Did I just save that bastard?" he asked, both incredulous and unnerved.

I brushed hair from my face with both hands and filled my lungs with as much cool morning air as I could gather.

Taking this for an affirmative, Nisien examined me. "Castor's rattled," the Soulderni finally said. "So he's trying to rattle you instead. You unnerved them last night, and that's on top of losing so many men. I think only Polinus and two or three others had ever seen an Eangi fight. It's savage, to them. Demonic. Not to mention the fact that you're a woman."

"If Polinus lets me take the horse, I'll go on alone," I suggested, more weary than offended. My offer was a reasonable one, but as soon as I made it, I hoped he would dissuade me. Whatever Nisien and I meant to one another by this point, whether friends or allies or comrades of circumstance, I desperately didn't want to be alone again.

"If you kill Castor, you'll have to go anyway," Nisien quipped with a little too much truth to be humorous. "And if that's not enough incentive to stave you, it will not end well for me either."

"Well, if I did harm him, I'd make sure you weren't connected. I won't let you suffer for my sins." As soon as the words left my mouth, I remembered speaking them to Eidr and Yske in a rainy night on Mount Thyr. I fidgeted with the contents of the saddlebags again, angling my face to hide a rush of grief.

Melid lifted her head and watched us through the walnut depths of her eyes, then flicked one ear. Nisien, lost in his own thoughts and unaware of the weight of my words, reached out to scratch her neck.

"I've been meaning to ask," I forced myself to switch topics. "Have you officially rejoined the army, or are you just here for me? Will you return to your mother when this is over?"

Nisien took the bridle and held the horse steady as I swung up into the saddle, though the placid mare needed no such direction.

"I'm here willingly," he said. It was obvious that my question had sobered him; his preoccupied look slipped into a weighted, sightless stare. "Beyond that, I don't know."

Around us, the rest of the men were mounting up. More than one of them noted Nisien's and my proximity, but neither of us cared.

"You want to rejoin," I observed after a momentary silence.

He scratched at Melid's jaw. The first riders moved onto the road, leaving Nisien's own horse conspicuously unoccupied.

That was when a flash caught my eye; sunlight reflecting off one of the men's rectangular shields as he slung it across his back. Tugging his mount towards the road, he presented me with a clear view of a maned, feline head with a yawning mouth and a dead, empty stare.

The vision. I had seen that shield in my vision, the night I left Nisien and Euweth at the grove. The rest of the men carried shields with other symbols, majority being a boar with elongated tusks, while Estavius's and Castor's had a pattern of wings.

Nisien noted the direction of my gaze. "What is it?"

"Your shields. What do the different symbols mean?"

"What? Oh, each legion has one," he replied, startled and maybe even a little hurt by my sudden distraction. "When I was in the Third,

199

mine had two horse heads. The boar is General Athiliu's. The wings are academy-trained, like Estavius."

"And the mountain cat, with the mane?" I pressed, overrunning his last few words.

The Soulderni scanned for the shield in question. "The border legion east of the Pasidon, I believe, at the Nivari Gates. Why?"

"Aux, mount up!" Polinus bellowed.

We were about to be left behind. Nisien cast me one last glance before he crossed to his horse in four quick strides. He mounted with seamless grace and I nudged Melid in beside him.

"Eangi," Polinus's voice cut again over the uncoordinated ripple of hooves, swish of tails and creak of leather. "To the fore."

TWENTY-FOUR

Polinus kept me at his side throughout most of the day. Since I knew the road and the land this was a valid request, but it kept Nisien and I separated.

During those long hours of silence and indecipherable Arpa conversation, my thoughts were my own. I contemplated my vision of the feline shield and what it might mean. Inevitably, I recalled the violence of the night before, but my mind shied away from that. Instead, I considered Eang, Ogam and Vistic. I wondered where Omaskat was and how I might find the milk-white lake, once I finally reached the mountains.

And I thought of Nisien. Thoughts of him were insidious, rising and diverting even my most focused of contemplations. His blood-drunk laughter after the attack worried me. I felt responsible for dragging him away from Euweth, for opening the door that brought him back to this life. There was no romance in that connection; I had no interest in men beyond Eidr and his loss, but Nisien unnerved me, concerned me and consoled me in the same breath. I was an Eangi without a Hall, a young woman without a family, and Nisien's friendship was all the camaraderie I had left in the world.

Still, I knew I'd likely need to leave him soon. Once we reached the mountains, the Arpa would go on their way and I'd go mine, searching for the white lake. Given the choice, I wasn't sure if Nisien would come with me – or if I would even allow him to. My quest was an Eangen matter, and Nisien, despite his friendship, was an outsider.

But for now, I permitted myself to cherish the simple truth that I wasn't alone.

We rode until near dusk, fed on trail rations and lit no fire. As we settled in, I glanced from my bedroll to the tents, at a loss. In the Hall, all the Eangi slept in close quarters. Privacy between the sexes was a luxury that no one could afford, even if it had meant much to us. During raiding seasons, matters were even more practical: Eangi and Eangen warriors slept wherever we could.

But the Arpa were not Eangen. I did not trust the legionaries.

I turned my eyes to the sky. I doubted it would rain that night – the moon had a warm red glow and the sky was almost clear, so I went to the base of a pine and pressed my foot into the bed of moss and needles around it. It sunk in but didn't meet hidden moisture.

I rolled out my bed of sheepskin and wool, slipped my pack under the head as a pillow and tucked my sword beneath the edge. I had just set my shield up against the pine when Nisien dropped into a crouch a pace away and unfurled his bedroll.

I stared at him. "What are you doing?"

Nisien set his pack between us. "Sleeping here."

My heart swelled uncomfortably. When I didn't protest, he shrugged off his shield, unfastened his armor and laid it atop the pack within easy reach. Then he sat down and jerked off his boots before arranging them at the end of his bed.

There was a familiarity to the routine that spoke volumes about the portion of his life he had lived on the road. As sun vanished over the horizon, he dug around in his pack for an oily wax to rub into the leather parts of his armor and his boots, and settled in.

The rest of the men finished up their own evening routines. They had not bothered to close the tents completely, and the sun-bleached canvas breathed in the wind. I could see the rows of men lying inside, keeping to themselves or murmuring, but there were no jests or laughter. One lit incense on a folding wooden altar. Another set a bronze idol out at the head of his bed, kissing it once, and I wondered if it represented Lathian.

Darkness settled in, drawing the shadows closer and thinning the last twilight colors into blacks and greys. Nisien finished his work and returned wax and cloth to the pack. Out of the corner of my eye, I saw his face turn my way. "Goodnight, Eangi."

"Goodnight," I returned.

He turned his back and lay down, forming a wall between the Arpa and I, and I curled up on my bed. Mutely, I watched his side rise and fall, recalling hundreds of nights spent this way with other Eangi, with Yske. With Eidr.

The darker it became, the easier it was to imagine that Nisien actually was my husband, alive and breathing, close and familiar. The thought of Eidr, the dusky scent of his hair and the warmth of his skin, became so vivid I could not push it away again.

I rolled onto my back and forced my eyes closed, but the movement only reminded me of how empty my bed was, how cold the place was where Eidr should have been. Nisien's presence ceased to be a comfort.

What if Eidr could have lain here with me? What if I could have felt his chest against my back right now, his arm draped across my waist? What if I could have felt his lips press into my ear, warm and soft, as he bade me good night?

What if we could have endured these past weeks together?

What if, back in that field of poppies, I had simply asked him and Yske to stay?

The land changed over the next week and, slowly, we began to climb. Forest and farmland gave way to the lakes and windblown pines of the true Eangen north. Huge swaths of exposed, smooth rock rose out of vibrant mosses that alternatively deadened and accented our horses' hooves. Wetlands gathered between old-wood groves, thick with clouds of blackbirds and towering reeds.

We saw signs of other humans but encountered no one. We found fire pits with ashes solidified from rain. Though the rocks concealed most signs of passage, the occasional stretch of sheared grass and churned earth showed where herds had passed. But by the time we saw them, they were already returning to a natural state.

The next village on the road north was called Gilda. Resting next to a broad, glistening lake that eventually emptied into the Pasidon, the cluster of forty houses sat abandoned. Its temple was intact but sat out on a rocky island some hundred paces into the lake, inaccessible without a boat or very long swim. And there were no boats to be found, nor were there signs that any Eangen had been present when the Algatt came through.

"There's a good chance they escaped." I stood on the lakeshore, a great shelf of pinkish rock, laced with quartz. Racks for drying fish sat nearby, as did a few piles of netting and a long jetty of rough-cut timber. The sun was partially clouded, but frequent bursts of light speckled the lake and heated the rock under our feet. "No burned houses, no fresh graves."

"I hope you're right." Nisien unstopped his flask and considered the water.

Inspired, I tugged off my boots and stockings and tied my trousers up above the knee. My bare feet eased onto the warm stone as I held out my hand. "Let me. It's colder further out."

He gave me the flask and I waded into the lake, placing each step with care. The lake remained shallow until over a dozen paces out, where I noted the sudden drop in temperature and halted. On the edge of an unseen rock shelf, I pushed the flask a full arm's length under before I let it fill with blissfully cool water.

I straightened as Nisien splashed up and handed him the flask, which he accepted.

"I don't think it's too much to hope that many of your people escaped, here and in other places," he offered, resuming our conversation. "They're just in hiding."

I nodded, recalling the refugees the Algatt had told me of, heading west, and suppressed an ache in my heart. I accepted the skin back from him and drank, letting my eyes roam out towards the temple on the island.

Though the architecture of Gilda itself differed little from other Eangen settlements – weathered wooden houses and low thatch rooves – the shrine was unique. It was a one-storied octagon with a strong timbered frame and a vaulted roof that rose into a high gable, all layered with cedar shingles and accessed by a narrow door. Even at this distance, I could see wooden carvings, bones and feathers dangling from the birches around it.

I wasn't aware that a silence had fallen until Nisien broke it. "Did you often travel this far north?"

I emptied the skin and reached to fill it up again. Water lapped up over my knees, but I wasn't concerned. The day was warm enough that my trousers would dry quickly.

"Every raiding season," I said, capping the flask. I handed it back to him again and wiped my hands on my face, enjoying the cool water. "They usually only come in spring and autumn, but I spent whole summers up here. We'd keep watch, stopping them from ranging too far south. Sometimes they'd slip by, but usually not."

Nisien pulled the strap of the flask over his head. "How many years have you fought?"

"Three," I replied.

"So how old were you when you began?"

"Fifteen. We still come north when we're younger, but we don't participate until Svala permits. There's no specific age when we start; it's based on ability."

A teasing glint entered his eye. "So were you older or younger than the average?"

"Older," I admitted. "I wasn't strong enough."

"Even with your…" He pointed at my mouth, lacking the right terminology.

"The Fire," I supplied. I nodded to the right and we started wading back to shore. "Yes. Even so. But my cousin, they let her fight at thirteen."

Nisien kept his eyes ahead. "Is she gone?"

"Yes," I replied hollowly. I stepped out of the water and bent to squeeze out the bottom of my trousers and legwraps. I planned on saying more, but the words congealed in my throat. I focused on clenching the wet fabric and watched trails of water pool around my feet on the warm rock.

Nisien lingered in the shallows. "Tell me."

"Tell you what?" I didn't look up.

"Tell me what happened. Tell me the feel and the smell of it. Tell me what your cousin looked like."

I straightened to gape at him. "You're sick," I accused.

He strode out of the water, leaving a trail of splashes and wet footprints. "It will help."

"No." I flinched away. "I— No."

"What did it smell like? The village?"

I continued to gawk at him, too shocked to be angry. "Why are you asking me this?"

"Because a month ago your entire village was slaughtered, your home burned, and you were enslaved." Nisien sat down on a hip-high boulder and slicked the water off his legs with a hand. "I can see in your face that you haven't talked about it. It's scabbed over and festering."

I clamped my jaw shut and snatched up my boots. I hadn't forgotten Euweth's words, that it had taken almost an entire year for Nisien's night terrors to stop after he came home. Perhaps he knew what he was saying. Or perhaps not.

"I can't believe I'm hearing this from you," I said, exasperated. "What about that zealot commander of yours, Telios? You won't talk about him, but I haven't interrogated you."

"Fine." He lifted his head. "Do you really want to know?"

I did, but I snapped, "You keep your pain to yourself and I'll keep mine."

Nisien rested his forearms on his knees and shrugged.

Something in me hated that he'd given up so easily. But perhaps I should have been more concerned for him than myself.

"You had the blood-hunger the other night," I pointed out.

"And you didn't?" He let his eyes fall into mine, open and deliberate.

"That doesn't mean I wanted to," I said. "That's Eang. You chose to put that armor back on. But I was five years old when I went to Albor and I killed two Algatt to get there. I've never had a choice. I've never known anything else."

It was only as I spoke the words that I realized what I was saying. I had never had a choice. I'd been bound to Eang, to her wars and violence, since childhood – and until now I'd been content with that, secure in the knowledge that my service had value, that I shed blood for a goddess who would always protect me and my people in turn.

But she hadn't protected us, had she? She was in hiding. Her bindings were breaking and her land – *our* land – was full of unchecked enemies. So why did I kill for her? Why did I risk my life for her?

The thought unsettled me so much that I took a step back. I couldn't truly think these things, could I? I couldn't feel this way?

The wind picked up. Clouds passed over the sun and the day's heat faded. Nisien inspected me as we were thrown into shadow, the sunlight passing off his grim face in a clean line. But his eyes, they were transparent and filled with… what? Melancholy? Understanding?

I didn't flee, but I left. I turned and half-ran through the streets of the village, barefooted over rock and sunbaked earth and wooden bridges. I passed a score of startled legionaries, riffling through homes, and stopped on the far side of the village in a stand of trees.

I thought of myself, fifteen years old, facing Svala in the firelight while the warriors sang around us. There, still raw from my first intentional kill, she had handed me the charge to slaughter Omaskat. Then, when I had fallen for the kindness in his eyes and failed to fulfill that charge, I had been stripped and outcast. I had returned, desperate to serve, and instead suffered the rage of Eang – the goddess who had, until now, preserved my people for centuries, yet left her infant son to die, helpless and screaming, on a mountaintop.

I leant back against the smooth bark of a tree and stared out across the rock and sparse fields of Gilda. My carefully trained mind balked at the thoughts that I entertained now, but that didn't mean they weren't there.

So much violence. So much danger and loss. What would happen on the day when I couldn't fight my attackers off? It would come. Eangi Fire or no, my life was destined to be violent and short.

I fingered the Eangi collar at my belt, vacillating between disillusionment and hard, unwavering dogma. Finally, unable to reconcile the two, I pushed them both down and went to apologize to Nisien.

TWENTY-FIVE

F ive days after I joined the Arpa, we came to Iskir. We were in Eangen's far north now, and the Algatt Mountains swept across the horizon in a great, brooding wall of stone and snowy peaks and tattered cloud. This was the home of the Iskiri, a land of rock, dense mossy forests and waving, reedy marshes. This was where I'd spent months of every year, first watching for, then eventually hunting Algatt raiders. I knew the road we traversed as well as I knew Albor. I knew the waystones that marked our way and the bends of the rivers, the glisten of the lakes. I knew where the fog bellied in the ravines, where the marshes could be traversed, the best places to camp, to hide, to ambush.

And I was alone in that familiarity. However close to me Nisien rode, he had no memory of this place, no sense of its importance and history. He couldn't understand what it was to be an Eangi, side by side with Eidr and Yske and Vist, running these forests and scouting from these ridgelines – all in service of the goddess who had let them die.

I lost myself in remembrances until we reached a well-trodden road alongside a marsh.

"Iskir is in a hidden valley up ahead," I warned Polinus.

The commander called a halt and sent scouts, combing the country-side for any sign of life while we rested in the warmth of the evening sun and the rustling of marsh grasses. As we waited I battled a rebellious, desperate optimism: the Iskiri were the wildest, most violent of the Eangen. If anyone could have held out against the Algatt, surely it would be them.

But what little hope I'd conjured faded upon the scouts' return. They spoke to Polinus in Arpa, but from the calm and dismissive language of their bodies, it was clear that the village was uninhabited.

My stomach lurched. I fought to keep my emotions down, my face impassive. It made sense, after all. If there were any Eangi alive in Iskir, Eang would have been wrong and Ogam would have found them. Iskir was gone, just like every other settlement in the Algatt's path.

That night we camped on a wooded rise near the town. Nisien was on watch so I rolled out my bed in a more secluded location than usual, behind a large boulder and a cluster of pines so low and gnarled that they draped like a curtain. The wind whispered through their boughs as I rested my shield against the tree, cleaned my boots and drank a little from my water skin.

The presence of Iskir tugged my eyes west, down the hill. I had not been able to see the black scar of the town during our ascent, but I knew where she was. I knew the hill we camped on. I even knew the rock I sheltered under. I'd sat atop it as a child on sentry duty, bickering with Yske and braiding her hair.

The night settled in. I sat with my back against the boulder, inhaling the scents of pine, warm stone and distant lakes. The Arpa risked no fire tonight and kept conversation low, but when the wind turned, I caught threads of their voices.

They were calmer, now. The shock of losing companions in sudden violence had ebbed into a bruised, wary resignation. None of them were strangers to battle.

Nisien was the exception. Since our conversation by the lake in Gilda and the memories it had stirred, he had slipped into such a dark and shuttered mood that nothing could rouse him. Yesterday he had nearly come to blows with a legionary over some matter in Arpa and Polinus had put him on constant watch duty ever since.

I considered pressing him but knew that he would only dig into my troubles in return. So I left him be.

The moon slipped free of a heavy bank of cloud, three-quarters full and brimming with light. It fell across the landscape like the passing of a divine hand, elongating the shadows of the pines and outcroppings until it found Iskir.

The town had inhabited a grassy section in the valley, guarded by high walls and centred around their own Hall of Vision, a lesser version of the Hall of Smoke. Rock was plentiful here, meaning that many of the buildings, including the Hall, had been more than half stone. Thus, the charred remnants of Iskir were still layered with the organized outlines of homes.

When I slung my weapons and shield back on and headed downhill, I wasn't conscious of what I did. All I could think of was the bleakness of the town under the moonlight. I glanced back more than once, but either Nisien and the lookouts were slack tonight, or they decided to let me do whatever I intended to do.

I found the first body within ten minutes, though I smelled it long before. He or she – the half that remained was ambiguous – lay strewn alongside a field of rustling barley, torn and putrid and riddled with beetles. I covered my face with a sleeve and murmured the final prayers with overflowing eyes.

The next body – or the parts of it that remained – had clearly been there longer. They were nearly skeletal, as was the next, and the next. I stopped to pray for each, the tourniquet around my stomach twisting tighter and tighter.

Finally, I stepped through Iskir's charred gate. There were too many bodies now, sunken into layers of rain-sealed earth and ash. Too many rites to perform. So I picked my way through debris, tufts of brave new grass and walls of charred stone, to what had been Iskir's Hall of Vision, the second greatest Eangi Hall.

The lines of its carved stone doorframe stood out against the cloud-studded sky. I ran a hand over intricate latticework and runes, the stylized owls and representations of Eang with helmet and her bearded axes, Galger and Gammler. Through the archway, I could see nothing but collapsed beams. I was sure there were bodies there, friends and comrades and distant relations, but they were long beyond recognition, and my grief remained obscure.

Still, I leant my head against the stone and fought back a wave of despair. The smell of char and rot washed over me in waves, merging with my memories of Albor. I dragged in a few shallow breaths to keep my stomach down, but the wind gusted through the ruins. Fine ash rushed into my lungs, making me cough and twist away.

"Eangi."

I raised my head and choked.

Eang approached through flurries of dust and ash, setting her feet around stones, beside a corpse's reaching hand, over a fallen beam. She wore helmet and armor of burnished bronze plates over a tunic of pure black. Her fitted trousers were muddied up to the knee and her upper arms were bare, revealing corded muscle and a web of bleeding scratches, as if she had been caught in brambles. Her head was framed by the blades of her two bearded axes, just like the carvings.

My heart exploded into a panicked, joyous canter and I dropped to my knees. "Eang!"

The goddess raised a hand to silence me. Stricken, I cast my eyes down and forced them to remain there as she strode forward. One step at a time, her muddy, blackened boots entered my line of sight.

"They cannot rest," Eang's voice sounded hollow and disjointed. "Sing the rites, child."

With a shaking hand, I tugged up my flask and took a drink to clear the ash from my tongue, still not daring to look at her face. Eang, here, after all this time? After so much silence? Perhaps all my doubts had been wrong. Perhaps Eang had returned to the land, Shanich and her ilk would slumber again, and Eangen would be restored.

I sketched the runes I needed in the ash and stood. I cleared my throat. Then, closing my eyes, I lifted my chin and began to sing a broad, sweeping version of the final rites.

My voice quavered and rasped. It died at the end of the first line and agonized stillness descended upon the ruins. I clutched an arm across my chest and began again, singing more softly. The words were old, the oldest – like my name, like the stones, like my people's memories of the boats that had brought us across the sea.

All the while, Eang's gaze bored into me. Once, when I cracked open an eye, I saw the weakness of her posture, the openness of her hands at her sides. Her own eyes were invisible behind her helmet, but blood clung to the line of her jaw, dripping and fresh. Blood running down from a concealed wound.

The sight struck fear and helplessness into me, as if I were a child watching my parents weep. They had wept over my sister the day the Algatt threw her from the loft, and it had terrified me more than Hulda's stillness. But even that paled in comparison to watching the Goddess of War bleed.

I finished the first song, then the second. When I began to pray, Eang tilted her face up towards the night sky in relish.

The ground beneath my feet eased. There was no other way I could describe it. All the blood, all the sorrow in the earth released like a sigh and was caught up in the wind with dirt and ash and dust.

At the same time, something else departed. I had not sensed it until the void opened; the presence of a thousand souls, the souls of my people, clustered about me. And once they were gone, I stood alone.

Eang laughed, shedding tension with every note. She rolled her shoulders and arched her back, drawing Galger and Gammler in a smooth, simultaneous movement. Their bearded blades caught the moonlight, legendary iron glinting with embossed golden patterns and runes.

The relief welling up inside me soured as she took another step forward. Her footfalls made no sound. Why not, if Eang was truly here?

Fear struck me like a stave in the chest. "Ogam?" I whispered, recoiling. Trustworthy or not, he was still the only one I could think to call upon. "Hear me. Please."

Eang's head snapped down like a snake. "Who did you call?"

My hands twitched towards the throwing axes at my hips. "Goddess,

I mean no disrespect. May I see your face? My road has been long, and it would ease my soul."

She paused for one moment, then pulled the helmet free. Her black hair was shaved down to the scalp in a hundred ragged cuts, supplying the blood I had seen on her jaw. Her eyes were restless hollows, her lips dry and cracked, and the richness of her skin dulled by... illness? Once more, her face was wrong. This was not Eang's mouth, Eang's nose, or Eang's cheekbones. They were crude and raw, like a half-finished carving.

A cold pool of dread trickled into my gut. I reached for the shard of the goddess inside me. It lit, but not with the strength and ferocity it should have so close to Eang herself.

Understanding struck me with far more grief than fear. This was not Eang at all. My goddess was still absent.

As desperately as I wanted to break down or fly into a panic, one sheltered quarter of my mind retained its clarity. Sing, Ogam had told me, if I encountered anything like Shanich again – and for all I knew, this imposter was precisely that.

I opened my quivering lips and began another song. It was still a funerary song, but it rolled and lilted like a lullaby.

The creature that would be Eang loosened her shoulders. As she moved her body changed, waist thickening, hips thinning, shoulders broadening and breasts retreating. Her hair remained cropped, but the female lines of her face fell away; her jaw broadened and a beard unfurled.

Last of all, the thing before me grew. It gained two feet in height and its clothes changed to match its new form – broadening, tightening and transitioning.

The imposter stretched out his newly formed chest and unleashed a rivalrous battle cry to the stars.

The ground beneath my feet trembled. I staggered back into the doorway of the Hall of Vision, still singing, battling to keep my voice level and my panic at bay as dust and ash dislodged from the lintel in a grey, choking veil. But it gave me no shelter. The creature's gaze fastened on me and my throat closed over.

He stalked forward and took up position just outside of the arch's shadow, leaving me with a thin hope that he wouldn't dare step on Eang's sacred ground.

I coughed, blinked ash from stinging eyes and started to sing again, louder this time, repeating the same song until my voice began to falter and crack with numbing, dull terror. He watched me, his face not so much aggressive as intent. With every passing moment, his skin became more radiant, his muscles harder and his stare sharper. He lifted his feet and tested his limbs, eyes still fixed on my face. They were an incredible blue now, dark as the sea and iridescent as the moon hanging over his shoulder.

"Where is your mistress?" the being demanded.

My voice died.

All at once, one of his hands was free of an axe. It shot out with inhuman speed and seized me by the tunic, jerking me from the shadow of the doorframe. I bit off a scream as he slammed me back against the stone wall outside, shield and all.

His fingers closed around my throat. I let out a whistling shriek and retracted my legs, trying to use my own weight to drop free and kicking him in the process.

At the same time, my Fire flew. His hands contracted and his body bent under the force, but he did not fall. Whoever this was, my shard of Eang was not enough to deter him, and my frantic kicks might as well have been raindrops.

His grip strengthened again, stronger than iron, stronger than anything I'd felt before. All I succeeded in doing was nearly popping off my head and scraping my shield against the stone with a frantic, grinding clatter.

"Eang!" the man growled, directing his words into my eyes. "Come to me, usurper."

I fought my hatchets free, hurling one into his face and sinking the other under his arm.

He avoided the first with a duck but the second bit deep. I lifted my feet again and drove them into his chest with all the force Eangi Fire could lend. He staggered backwards and I crashed to the ground in a stunned heap. I couldn't breathe. I toppled to the side and twisted my head, trying in vain to find some narrow passage of my throat that wasn't crushed. A thin strand of air whisked into my lungs and I pulled at my Fire, repairing some of the damage – but at a cost. My strength flickered and waned, and I barely managed to sit up against the charred wall.

Through a blur of eyelashes, I saw Quentis stride into the space before the hall, beyond the interloper's hulking form. There were more figures there too, legionaries with shields raised, swords and spears glinting in the moonlight. Another appeared at a run and fell into a bracing position, then another and another.

Clutching his side, the being that was not Eang turned on the newcomers and screamed in rage. The sound cut through me, making me jump and scramble backwards. But I still could barely breathe.

Arms slipped under mine and hauled me back into the shelter of the archway. I blinked at the newcomer, expecting to find Nisien, but it was Estavius instead. With remarkable calm, he unfastened the strap of my shield. I leant into his chest with a hand as he tugged the strap free.

I let out a frightened gasp as his hands closed on both sides of my head, holding it straight.

"Breathe?" he asked in accented Northman.

I drew in a ragged breath and dragged my eyes sideways. Quentis stood in the center of the village now, facing the creature with one of his bowls in hand. I would have laughed – or wept – at the absurdity of the picture, but I hadn't the strength.

Quentis began to chant. He dipped his fingers into the bowl and held it out in a warding gesture.

The wind picked up with sudden, unnatural force. The creature raised his axes – now dull, no longer Eang's legendary weapons – and began to close the space between himself and the priest in a disgusted, menacing stride.

I grabbed the collar of Estavius's breastplate, fingers folding around warm steel and sweaty cloth. "No," I wheezed. "Stop. Him."

Estavius shook his head and said something in Arpa.

I leant my head back into the stone and stared at the scene before me, knowing deep in my soul that I was about to watch Quentis and his useless bowl be cut to pieces. Then the creature would turn on the legionaries and, lastly, back to Estavius and me.

My eyes darted about for Nisien. His face was impossible to distinguish from every other helmeted head, but I thought I recognized him behind Quentis, legs braced, sword poised, eyes glaring.

Again, Quentis dipped his fingers in the bowl. This time he flicked dark liquid at the creature. It shook its head, disgruntled, and for the space of two mad heartbeats, silence reigned over the village. Then our attacker charged Quentis.

The priest did not move. He poured the remainder of the bowl on the ground before him in an arc, heedless of the fact that each pounding footstep brought his doom closer.

The imposter raised his axes, two steps from Quentis. His body began to coil and turn, preparing for a lunge that would end the priest in two coordinated blows.

But he never struck. As soon as his foot touched Quentis's concoction in the ashes, he screamed and collapsed.

I stared, heedless of the fact that I was clutching the top of Estavius's armor. The legionary stared right along with me, his pale eyes fastened on the spasming being and the Arpa priest.

Quentis stepped up to the creature as it roiled and bucked. He nudged one of the axes out of his path with the toe of a boot and crouched behind the attacker's head. Then, with calm gravity, he placed his bloodied palm over the man's forehead.

The huge being stilled. I sensed something else in the village then, the presence of another god whom I had never met or tasted. The presence wrapped around our attacker like invisible bonds until his chest ceased to rise.

Quentis remained crouched, murmuring and holding his palm to the man's forehead.

"Lathian?" I asked Estavius. "The power... Quentis used..."

He nodded and looked at me sideways. "Breathe?"

My lips cracked into a wan smile. I detached my fingers from his breastplate.

"I can breathe," I affirmed. In fact, breathing came a lot easier with Estavius nearby.

After a few minutes, Quentis stood up and nodded in the direction of several legionaries. A form that I recognized as Polinus strode forward and they began to confer. At the commander's word, several men jogged back towards the camp.

Now that the threat was gone, Estavius left me. I pressed back into the stone of the arch and closed my eyes, focusing on my breaths. Somewhere in the back of my mind, I wished Nisien would come to me. But the more rational part of me was glad when he did not.

No one came at all, not until the legionaries had dug a grave in the center of Iskir and lowered the limp form of the creature into it. Then they replaced the dirt, Quentis watching the proceedings with a calm, calculating eye.

I sat up a little when the priest stopped before me.

"Come, I'll help you back to the camp," he said, and offered me a hand. "You and I clearly need to speak."

TWENTY-SIX

Quentis placed a cup of water in my hand and sat cross-legged before me. The healer, who until now had been scowling at my neck and applying a numbing salve, spoke to him in Arpa, picked up his small clay pot, and left us.

"When did the creature appear?" Quentis asked without preamble.

"As soon as I came to the Hall," I told him in a raspy croak. There was no sense in holding anything back. As unsettling as the other priest was, he and his god had just saved my life. "It came to me as Eang."

Quentis's eyes widened at that. "Really? As your goddess?"

I gave a slight, wincing nod.

"That is galling." Quentis drew a knee up to his chest, under his robe. A note of caution entered his voice: "Where is Eang, Hessa?"

"I don't know," I answered, flat and honest.

Quentis was silent for a long minute. "Do you understand what a Vestige is?"

I half-heard his question. My eyes had lifted to Nisien as he shouldered out of a tent and joined a knot of legionaries. My friend met my gaze momentarily and offered a small, relieved smile before he followed the others off on patrol.

"Hessa?"

I coerced my attention back to Quentis. "A what?"

Irritation flickered through the Arpa priest's eyes. "Where is Eang?" he asked again, emphasizing each word.

"The High Hall. The mountains, hunting Gadr. I don't know." My own irritation flared, both at his tone and my own lack of knowledge. I couldn't resist adding, "It's not my place to know."

Quentis considered this. "And what of Ogam?"

"He's busy."

"Hessa," the priest leant forward, "I know there is far more going on than you're telling me. I may be able to help. Lathian may help."

"Your gods have no power here," I ground out through gritted teeth, though I already knew that wasn't true. "No right to be here."

Quentis fell silent. He glanced down at his hands, scrubbed clean of blood and ash but still stained. "You're young, Hessa. Too young to carry whatever burden the goddess has put on you. I want to help."

I levelled a cold stare at him, still battling not to wince at the pain in my throat. "You want the north."

Quentis raised a hand and pointed down to the village. "An Eangi on sacred ground could not touch that creature, nor detect whatever Vestige it used to crawl out of the grave. Yet I subdued him without violence."

Vestige. I still had no clue what that was, but I wasn't about to admit it.

"That was my weakness, not Eang's," I stated, though the words rankled me. Was it really my fault? Eang's power should have been enough to dissuade that creature – and protect all Eangen from the horrors we now faced.

"Hessa," Quentis bit out my name. "Listen to me. Our lives could hinge on the information you refuse to share. I need to know what's happening in the north. Nisien says you are on a quest from Eang to find someone in the mountains. Who? Why?"

Nisien? I ground my teeth and swallowed a flicker of betrayal. Clearly, I had done well not to confide more in him.

"What is a Vestige?" I finally asked in deflection.

"You know gods die," Quentis began. He watched my face carefully, searching for any reaction. "But when they do, it is possible for them to come back to life through an anchor, a piece of themselves that they infuse into an object blessed with human blood – a great deal of it – or a living person. That object, or that person, is a Vestige, and it can be used to crawl back out of the grave."

Grave. The word tugged at my memory. Ogam hadn't just told me to sing if I came across something like Shanich. He'd warned me to stay away from graves. But as I'd mentioned to Polinus on the road days before, one of the gods that Eang had slain was buried beneath the hall in Iskir. A shape-shifting God of the New World, Ried, who'd refused to bow to Eang.

Quentis continued, "That man in the village was the shadow of a dead god. If I am correct, the bindings over his grave must have failed – bindings Eang cast, like the matter with Shanich. Yet the weight of the souls there, of your fellow Eangi in particular, constrained him until tonight. But when you released them, this god was able to access a Vestige somewhere and begin to journey back into life."

I looked down at my hands to hide my unease. Moonlight traced the dark scabs and smooth, thin scars of my fingertips. "It was Ried."

Quentis cocked his head. "Who?"

"A God of the New World who refused to ally with Eang after her rise to power, so she slew and bound him." I gestured at the stone beneath us. "This was his land and he's... they say he's buried under the Hall of Vision, down there, in Iskir."

The priest of Lathian cast his gaze back in the direction of the town. "Ah. Yes, that makes sense."

"What do you think he tied his life to? To make this... Vestige?"

"I don't know, but whatever it was, it's been used up and Lathian rebound Ried. Properly. Even if he has more, Lathian will keep him subdued. He is our highest god for a reason, Hessa, and even if Eang is dead he can protect your people. I can help you, if you will let me."

"Trust me, priest," I returned, "Eang is not dead."

My voice was steady. Despite my recent doubts, in the face of a foreign priest my faith was instinctual, if dispassionate. If Eang was dead her sister Frir, the Goddess of Death, would know, and thus Ogam would know. She was simply weakened.

The priest levelled his chin. Whether or not he believed me was unclear. "If your people worship Lathian, he will protect them. That is the way of conquest and the pattern of the world."

"The Eangen will never worship an Arpa god." Drained and injured as I was, I stood and glared down at him, my dispassion hardening into something tired and sore. "And I will tell you nothing."

"Very well, then." Quentis stood and looked to the right. I realized Polinus stood there, watching our conversation with Castor and half a dozen others. The priest transitioned into Arpa and spoke to the commander, delivering a short discourse in a rational tone. He finished it with a question.

Polinus appeared to consider. The two of them fell into conversation, at the end of which they all advanced.

I retreated a step, realizing too late that I was without weapons. My eyes flicked between the commander and the priest. Their expressions – Quentis's satisfied, Polinus's grim and guarded – made my blood run cold.

I bolted, but my exhausted limbs didn't get far. Castor caught my arm. I threw what little Fire I had left into his face and followed it with a fist, but the blow missed and the Fire only staggered him. His expression faltered into shock and a spark of fear, then a mask of anger. He redoubled his attack, grabbing for my hair and my tunic at the same time and spinning me around.

Quentis stood before me. Before I could burn, before I could draw another breath down my bruised throat to speak, the priest put a hand on my chest.

Cold. Cold seeped down through my bones and my legs crumpled. I sagged into Castor and he lowered me to the ground.

Arpa voices merged over me as Quentis leant in. Someone handed him his bowl. I squirmed, horrified and indignant, as he dipped one finger and began to draw symbols across my skin.

One, at the base of my throat – the Fire died completely. Two, over my lips – my tongue became lead. Three and four, on my cheeks – my vision blackened, and my senses closed in.

I tasted something acrid on my tongue. Henbane. Mandrake. Something else, something worse: widow's soap. Then, oblivion.

I squinted down the raised path, dirty fingers hanging down over my temple. The setting sun washed the fields to either side of me in golden light, igniting the wings of insects like sparks as they hummed through the vegetation. There were two-pace strips of beans, knee-high corn, a flush of young barley, cabbage, turnip and so on in repeating rows, all the way to a farmhouse on the western edge of the forest.

Quentis stood in the field, watching me between waving stalks of corn. I noted him but had no real understanding of his presence. This was my memory, after all. He was not really here.

Omaskat walked beside me, slowing his long strides to match mine. His hound Ayo sniffed at the skirts of my daily working dress and apron, rounding us twice before she deviated off the road and nosed through a patch of young cabbage leaves.

"From where have you come?" My own voice came from a great distance. I held my apron high, packed with the herbs I had spent an afternoon gathering in the forest.

He smiled. "You'd do better to ask where I've not."

I grinned back. It was a typical traveler's response. "Well, we have a bed and a meal for you in the Hall, if you'll take it."

This was the way things went. Offers of hospitality were usually given before names were exchanged – that way, both sides were bound to Hearth Law before most lies had a chance to be told. If someone tried to circumvent this process, it was both suspicious and rude.

"I'll gladly take it. My name is Omaskat."

"Hessa."

We sat in the Hall, now. The sun had set, and the majority of the Hall's inhabitants had already headed down to the river to bathe. So I sat alone with Omaskat and the dog, listening to the crackle of the fire and the chirr of crickets outside the Hall's great open doors.

I fetched us bread and cold meat and handed him a plate. As twilight faded, we heard laughter out in the village. People began to return, flowing around us, asking who the stranger was, rubbing their hair dry and scratching the dog's ears. They picked up their food and sat down around us, talking amongst themselves and prodding Omaskat to tell them stories.

"Who's this?" Eidr asked, dropping down beside me. He rocked on his seat, jostling me good-naturedly. His clothes still smelled of the fields, earthy and green and rich, though his dark red hair was wet from the river.

"Omaskat," the traveler said.

"Eidr," my husband replied. "Omaskat. That's an old name."

"As old as the boats," Omaskat said. His eyes crinkled and he glanced between the two of us knowingly. The way we sat and the ease with which Eidr had inserted himself into the conversation both indicated our claim on one another.

Eidr sat forward. "Would you tell us your story, then, Omaskat?"

Omaskat lifted his plate out of the reach of the dog as she nuzzled up, lips already pulled back for a delicate try at his meal. "Gladly. But if you give me leave, I'll eat and bathe and regale you all with my travels once I no longer stink."

Eidr nodded, and Omaskat turned to his food.

I gave Eidr a reproachful look that failed to be remotely reproachful. "Leave the man be. He's my guest," I hissed.

He leant forward to whisper in my ear, "And you're my woman."

I tsked my tongue, but before I could properly reply he ground his wet beard into my cheek. He fled my swatting hands and retreated, making conciliatory gestures, until he walked right into Yske's slap across the back of the head.

Omaskat looked up and grinned, looking grandfatherly despite the fact that he was only ten years older than I. It was that expression, that simple smile on a warm, early summer's night, which made me like him so much.

He turned that smile upon Sixnit as my friend, full with child, sat down nearby and accepted a bowl of food from her husband. Sixnit smiled back, a sheepish, weary smile, and patted her belly.

"You're a few days early, traveler," she quipped, "otherwise you could have met my little one."

"Indeed I am." Omaskat gave a second, more wry smile and raised his cup. "My mistake."

Two more Eangi appeared and stoked the fire, temporarily blocking my view of Omaskat's face, but I saw his eyes linger on Sixnit's swollen belly. Then, as the firelight swelled up into the rafters, I saw the color of those eyes: one gold, one blue.

I stared. In the dream, in the memory, I recalled the way my heart had threatened to jerk from my chest, the way I'd felt absent from my own body. How had I not seen his eyes on the road? Had they changed, just now as he looked at Sixnit?

If Omaskat sensed a change in me, he did not mention it. He finished his plate and stood with the hound at his heel. I scrambled to my feet too, facing him across the flames. My heart contorted – this was Svala's vision, the one she'd given to me that night when I was fifteen. After three long years of knowing, of waiting, this was the day.

But how could that be? It was so common, so full of sunshine and normality. I'd always imagined we would meet on a battlefield or on a stormy, legendary night, perhaps at a moment when all hope was lost, and his death would turn the tide. And this man – he was too kind, smiling and relaxed and gracious. I'd assumed the man I was to kill would be threatening, a shield-biting berserker or a murderer of children.

But today? Him? It made no sense. Why would Eang want him dead?

"The river is west of the village?" Omaskat asked.

I nodded dumbly. "North-west. By the lake."

The vision shifted. I lay in my bed and stared at Omaskat's sleeping form beside the low-burning coals. The early summer night was cool, and wind whisked through the open door of the Hall, drawing the scent of smoke and a hundred sleeping bodies up through the narrow window slits below the roofline.

Could it truly be him? He was so... amiable. He had spent an hour telling us about his travels, of meeting a beautiful wavewoman on the coast, talking his way out of a confrontation with the Arpa and a night spent in a glade so thick with flowers that the scent made him drunk.

I continued to stare, suppressing a deep tremor. I could not kill this man with laughter in his eyes. There were so few like him in this world.

Maybe I was wrong. If Svala were here she could have affirmed his identity, but she was gone to Urgi. What if I killed the wrong man, under Hearth Law? Who knew what Fate would do to me?

Just then, I saw someone silhouetted in the doorway of the Hall of Smoke. I stared, unable to decide who it was, until a distant part of my mind understood it was Quentis.

Quentis? The Hall blurred and the priest stepped forward, as if to stop the scene from changing.

The dream shifted again, but I was too aware of it now. Images fled as soon as they took form, no matter how Quentis grabbed at them. I saw Eidr's body. Sixnit, wracked with grief. I stood in the line of slaves before Omaskat. I stabbed the hairpin at his neck. He snapped my wrist. I cradled Vistic in the destroyed Hall. I floated in the arms of a riverman.

Somehow, somewhere in the chaos of the memories, I found an anchor. The anchor was Svala's face on the afternoon the blacksmith cut off my collar with two laborious clips.

"You were given a charge directly from the goddess," her voice was like the crack of ice underfoot. "And you chose to disobey, Hessa. She gave you a task. Until you fulfill that task or make atonement, you are no longer welcome in this Hall, or the one to come."

I held the vision there, at that moment. I saw Quentis over Svala's shoulder, bowl in hand, bloody fingers weaving something in the air.

Svala's hand shot towards my wrist. I stifled a gasp and recoiled.

This was not part of my memories.

"Run, Hessa," she hissed, low so that Quentis could not hear. The Fire in her eyes burned into my skull. "Run as soon as you can. Run into the mountains. You will find Omaskat where the waters run white and the sky bleeds into the mountain."

I clutched at her. She felt so real, sounded so real. "Where are you?" I rasped.

The vision closed like a clap of thunder. I lashed out, still in the throes of the drug. I was bound, bound to a tree – I felt rough bark and sticky sap – and men fought nearby. The tension in the air made me struggle all the harder. I heard bones pop and felt my muscles stretch beyond bearing, but there was no pain.

"He's killing her!" Nisien's voice raged. "Look at her – gods above, she's going to kill herself – what did you give her? Quentis! *Quentis!* You bastard, I swear if you don't—"

Quentis touched my eyelids and all went dark.

TWENTY-SEVEN

Castor held Melid's reins as my mare plodded along behind his. I hunched forward in my saddle, eyes slit against the sun and battling the worst headache of my life.

The headache never eased. Quentis's witchcraft ensured that. Sometimes I was permitted to walk; other times I was so stupefied by drug and pain that I had to be tied to the saddle. I lolled and I wilted, snatching at fragments of thought but unable to pin anything down.

At some point, I registered that the mountains were close. I saw the line of them soar above the tops of the trees, snow-crusted crags sweeping into the clouds. The sight consoled me before I slumped forward over Melid's neck and vomited.

Melid, to her credit, reacted well. She danced left but didn't bolt or dislodge me.

Moaning, I buried the side of my face in her neck. "Take me away," I whispered to her in the oldest Eangen. "Run, Melid."

That night I found myself tied to a tree again, hopelessly disoriented. I dreamt of Svala, charging me to flee again and again. I dreamt of Eidr and the warmth of our bed on a winter night. I dreamt of Yske and I as girls, braiding flowers into one another's hair beside the river after a day under the Eangi war chief Ardam's brutal instruction.

The next morning as we rode, I heard Ogam's voice on the wind. But I was so addled that I couldn't make sense of it.

"I can't hear you." I stared upwards, watching a pair of sparrows flutter by. "You sound too much like your father."

Castor smirked at me, catching my languid gaze. I lacked the will to scowl back.

That night, Nisien, with Estavius at his side, convinced Polinus not to tie me to a tree. I was allowed to lie in my bedroll close to my friend, under sight of the watch and near to Quentis, who stalked me ceaselessly.

I rested my bound hands on my stomach and tried to pick out constellations among the tattered clouds.

"The bear's chasing the hart," I commented absently, "but the hart is too fast… and the hind is too fast for the hart… But the bear is here now, did I tell you that? The great bear is in Eangen. I saw him, twice."

Nisien, cleaning his armor, glared between me and Quentis. "You're going to ruin her mind," he snarled at the priest. "She can't take much more of this."

"She can," Quentis stated. "I'm close."

It didn't occur to me to wonder what he was close to.

"It's all right." I rolled over to face Nisien. "I'll get away."

Nisien rubbed the back of one hand across his brow. If I'd had my wits about me, I would have seen how burdened he looked, how worn and divided. But just then, all I noticed was that he had three days of beard on his chin and the hair on his head was growing longer. It made me smile.

I waited until Quentis left before I reached out and tugged at one of Nisien's trouser legs. I hissed, "I mean it. I'll escape. You can come with me."

He lifted his eyes but kept working. "You should try to sleep."

"We can escape together."

"It's not so simple. They don't trust me enough."

"Nisien—"

Quentis returned. "Sit her up."

I saw Nisien lace with tension as another legionary crouched and hauled me into a sitting position. This happened every evening and morning now, so I was used to the routine, and fighting it only used up what little strength I'd managed to gather.

Still, I couldn't help a small, petty spark of rebellion. I focused on keeping my eyes level with Quentis's. "I won't drink it."

He held his bowl in hand, undeterred. "Hessa, please. Listen to me. I've seen enough now to know whatever you're hiding is vital, and I will do anything to honor my god and protect my people. By tomorrow, perhaps the day after that, I'll have learned how to kill that fragment of Eang inside of you. Then you will tell me anything I want to know – so why not spare yourself the trouble? Talk to me. Now, freely."

The relevance of this fought its way into my befuddled mind. Kill my Fire? That was impossible, wasn't it? But I supposed that made little difference. The core remained; he was going to drug and poison me until I posed no threat to anyone.

Quentis grabbed my chin and lifted the bowl. "Drink."

I turned my head away, fear cracking through my numb façade. I squirmed to the side and toppled over Nisien's pack, forcing my captors to haul me back into place.

Quentis grabbed me by the hair and upended the bowl into my mouth. I blocked it with my tongue until the priest clapped one hand over my lips and pinched my nose, forcing me to choke and swallow all at once.

I toppled into blackness.

I lay among poppies, in the shadow of a shrine, and watched the wind tug at a shroud of mist. I could see nothing beyond it; it smothered the sky and coiled through the tree line to every side, condensing on the fine needles of conifers and drooping deciduous leaves.

Yet, somehow, I did not feel stifled by it, nor could I sense Quentis nearby. Sunlight still filtered through, warm and full of promise, and the moisture that swept into my lungs was sweet and heady.

The shrine here, in my dream-skewed memory, differed from true life; it was less weathered, and untouched by the rigors of the real world. Moisture darkened its beams, fresh-hewn and smelling of cedar, and turned the rattle of its bones and carvings and feathers into a muted tinkle.

If I didn't think too hard, if I didn't reflect on recent events or the goddess the shrine represented, I remained content. So I lay there, impassive to the hum of a few brave bees, and watching the poppies dip under their weight of dew.

But the longer the dream went on, emotions began to crop up. There were no thoughts attached to them, only feelings: anger, fear, urgency, and, beneath them all, confusion.

"Svala," I asked the sky, "are you here?"

"Hessa."

Ogam dropped into a crouch before me. His snowy skin nearly merged with the fog, and his hair was in mild disarray. Irritated, he swatted at the mist and leant down to get a better look at my face.

"Hessa, what is wrong with you? Why are you here?"

I stared up at him, still lying on my back. I laced my fingers over my stomach. "The priest of Lathian drugged me. Am I imagining you?"

"No, I'm here. What did he drug you with?"

"Widow's soap. Henbane." I pronounced the words thoughtfully. "Mandrake… It tastes like yifr might but… not. How do I know you're actually here if this is a dream?"

"You are in the High Halls," he replied. There was not a scrap of amusement or playfulness in his voice. He looked like a father hovering over a sick infant except more… angry. "You should not be here."

I laughed. "I'm not in the High Halls, Ogam. I'm in a dream. A memory."

"These are the High Halls, Hessa. And this bedamned mist knows you do not belong." Ogam glanced at the fog in a resurgence of irritation and stood up. With a few flicks of his fingers, he drew something and blew on it. The rune for sight and clarity appeared, crystalizing in the moisture-laden air, and the mist vanished.

The rune hovered above me against an utterly unearthly sky. To my baffled sight, it was not one sky, but four – or eight, or more. I couldn't truly count them, for there was no place where one ended and another began – only a new and bizarre wedding of the two.

The most distinct skies inhabited the four points of the compass. In one direction – west? – a quarter moon hung in violet twilight, while opposite the sun sank into smoldering amber cloud. In what should have been the north, white light slashed up into a midnight sheath of black, dancing and burning and swelling – a colorless, liquid rendition of the Northern Lights.

I turned, craning to see the peak of Mount Thyr and what should have been south. The mountainside stretched up into a winter day of thick and obscure snow cloud, waterfalls of ice reflecting the violet and amber and opal light of the other directions.

"It's… it's more than just a Hall." Ogam broke through my awestruck silence, crouching back down and putting himself into my line of sight. As he did, his rune disintegrated into snowflakes and nothing remained between us and the ethereal sky. I reached out, catching the flakes on my hand and dazedly watching them melt.

"Hessa, are you listening to me?" Ogam pressed. "How long have you been here? Gods below – you have not eaten or drunk anything here, have you?"

My head felt like it was full of creaking, mud-caked wheels. His last sentence slipped by, empty in the wake of the uncanny sky and the revelation that I sat, living and breathing, in the world of the Gods.

Even as an Eangi, I knew little more about the High Halls than the average Eangen – most knowledge was restricted to the High Priesthood. Only they were allowed to traverse this world before death. But I knew that the Halls were where the gods dwelled, held court, and where strange creatures resided. It was a surreal reflection of the world below, where mortals went after death to rejoice and tell of their deeds while they waited for their loved ones, whereupon they could lie down together under Frir's care until the Unmaking of the World – when, they said, all of history would begin again.

"This can't be the High Halls," I protested. "Even if the drink

Quentis gave me acts like yifr... it can't be. Where are the souls? And the gods? I've only seen you, and Quentis, and my own memories." Belatedly, I added, "And Svala. Does that mean she's... Ogam, does that mean she's dead?"

Ogam surveyed me for a substantial minute. His eyes were a touch too round and the muscles of his shoulders bunched with tension. "You saw Svala? She's here? In body or spirit?"

"I don't know, I couldn't tell," I admitted. There were two ways a human could enter the High Halls: without their physical bodies, by means of yifr or death; and bodily, through a rift between the two worlds.

My heart twisted in guilty, raw hope. If this was the High Halls, my mother should be here somewhere – along with countless others who had already perished.

It was also where Eidr and Yske would have been, if I'd given the dead their rites back in Albor. If I hadn't failed them. But they were still trapped in the earth, and I'd no idea how my mother, how my people gone before, would react to my presence. Would they know of my disgrace? Would they welcome me if I saw them, comfort or curse me?

"Ogam, if this – if these – are the High Halls, where are all the souls?" I asked.

"Frir has been shepherding them to her Hidden Hearth early. Yes – that's Death, over there," Ogam flapped a distracted hand at the violet quadrant of the sky, his thoughts clearly elsewhere. He either failed to notice how my expression faltered at this, or he didn't care. "There's too much happening right now to contend with humans underfoot."

I cleared my throat. "Then I need to leave too."

"Yes, you do. But I still don't understand why you're here in the first place. Why has this priest drugged you?"

"He's trying to... kill my Eangi Fire." Even the memory of Quentis made rational thinking harder. "He wants me to tell him what I'm doing – looking for Omaskat – and where Eang is. He comes into my visions, or comes to visit me here, I suppose. And he watches my memories. Can he do that? Kill the Eangi in me? Watch my memories?"

"Many things are possible in the High Halls that are not in the Waking World, if you know how to… utilize them," Ogam answered, but he had gone very still. "What do you mean, kill your Eangi Fire?"

I frowned at him. "That's all I know."

"Is there anything else in the drug?"

I stared past his shoulder, considering this, but the sight of the uncanny sky threatened to drag my mind towards the souls of the dead, my mother, and the emptiness of the High Halls. "I think it's different every time. He's trying things. And… he has real power, Ogam. Ried came back from the dead and Quentis and his god sent him back to sleep."

"Ah." Ogam shifted to kneel in the grass before me, countenance wrapped in concern. The poppies bent out of his way, like peasants before a king.

I leant forward in turn. "How can his god be so strong in Eangen?"

When he didn't immediately reply, I opened my mouth to repeat myself. But the Son of Eang held up a hand. I pressed my lips together, and silence fell.

After a few thoughtful moments, I began to fidget. I bent the head of a poppy towards myself and stared at its black heart in the varied celestial lights – black to grey to fringed with gold. I felt at the petals, delicately so as not to tear them. Then I let the poppy go and watched it sway.

After my fourth time setting the poppy swaying, Ogam's hand closed around my wrist and set it in my lap.

"I still haven't found Eang, Hessa," Ogam began, "but I did find Gadr. He's… not himself, skulking about the mountains, hiding. I also found the bodies of two rivermen at the Pasidon. Someone – or many someones – are hunting the gods and anything like us."

"The gods are hunting gods," I observed, unruffled and eloquent in my stupor. "Like Ashaklon was hunting Oulden. But the rivermen aren't proper gods."

"No, they didn't dwell in the High Halls long enough for that," Ogam muttered, so low I barely heard him. "I think they are hunting the Eangi too. I have yet to find any alive, but I did find… bodies with

Eangi collars, pierced by arrows of bone. Those weapons did not come from the Waking World."

My gaze grew glassy, the weight and emotion of this revelation seeping through my inebriation. I'd met every Eangi in the land at one point or another. "Who?"

"Chief priests from the coastal Addack villages. I don't know their names."

"And… who, who killed them?"

The Son of Winter shook his head, eyes drifting across the meadow towards the amber sunset in the east. It had nearly vanished by now, deepening into a twilight that mirrored the western Realm of Death.

"I don't know that either," Ogam admitted. "I don't even know where my own mother is – I've searched every corner of these Halls, and nearly all of Eangen. I can't sense her life, nor her death. If you've seen her, Hessa, you must tell me. Hessa?"

"I'm listening," I protested, though my addled wits were over-whelmed. Only one thought managed to crystalize. "Ogam, you have to help me escape."

"I cannot."

"Of course you can. You should. You're Eang's son, and she's my patron. In her stead, I'm your responsibility."

Ogam scowled. "You may be stupid with widow root, but I am still a god, and we've been through this before. Do not instruct nor command me. There is much you do not know."

I laughed at that, bitter and more than a little unhinged. "Then why won't someone tell me?"

"Because you have your task, and that is all that should matter to you, Eangi. Go kill Omaskat."

"But how am I supposed to escape? Quentis keeps me drugged." My bitterness boiled into righteous indignation. It was a frightening feeling, lined with guilt, but grounded in the pillars of the religion Eang herself had handed us. "I'm an Eangi. Your mother should hear me, should come to my aid. But she can't, or won't."

Ogam snorted at the last. "And she shouldn't have tried to murder me at birth, but here we are. Well, perhaps it will comfort you to know *why* I cannot help you. I am with the child and Sixnit."

"Really?" A fragile, reckless smile found its way onto my lips. "They're together? They're safe?"

"Yes, Gadr had the baby in the mountains. But now I cannot leave them exposed." Ogam ran his hands agitatedly through his hair. "I need to find a safe place to hide them before I can do anything else. Gods below. Svala. You said you saw her here in the Halls. Where?"

"In a memory, by the blacksmith in Albor," I told him. "But the way she acted, what she said – she wasn't part of my original memory."

For a second Ogam's expression remained strained. Then, like the dawning of a new day, revelation struck. He stood up. "I have to go."

I scrambled upright. "Where? To find Svala?"

Ogam ignored my question. "I am sorry, Hessa."

"Sorry?" I repeated, my voice thin. I'd never felt so blind, so utterly without guidance. "Sorry for what? Ogam, wait. What am I supposed to do?"

Ogam had started to walk away, but at the last moment he spun back and gesticulated at the expanse of the High Halls around us. "Do you remember what I once told you, about the gods needing to dwell in the High Halls?"

A shadow crossed my face. He'd mentioned that in Souldern. "Yes. You were toying with me."

"Was I?" Ogam challenged, arching one snowy eyebrow. "You know what? Feast, little Eangi, feast and drink the splendors of the High Halls while you yet live. Feast like the gods and the immortal dead. Then let's see how long that misled priest can keep you under his boot. The rune I used to disperse the mist; do you know it?"

"Yes."

Ogam smiled with a dark, satisfied mischief in his eyes. "Then fill that human belly of yours and give it a try. The mist will return – it's trying to hide the Halls from you, in a way, because you don't yet belong.

But once the magic of this place is in your belly and blood, everything will change."

I stared at him, ensnared between indignation and hope and a dozen new questions. But for once, I was almost glad for Quentis's potions muddying my mind. Then I might not have to consider what any of this actually meant.

"In fact," Eang's son continued as he turned away, "I think you'll find all your runes more useful here than your own world – though do be careful. Time and space are malleable here, and many of the rules of the Waking World may not apply."

"Ogam," I called again as he reached the tree line and ducked under the rustling leaves of a grey poplar. "I can't do this. It's forbidden."

"And I'm unforbidding it," he shot back. "I'm granting you a privilege, as is my right as a god. You want me to act like Eang's son, honor her pact with you? There. I grant you the privilege of feasting in the Halls while you live."

My conscience creaked, torn between dogma and need. "Please don't lie to me."

"I am not." He scowled back at me with such gravity and candor that I couldn't help but believe him. "I truly am not."

I swallowed. "All right. And what about Quentis's poison?"

"I'd say that the more you eat and drink, the less it will affect you." Lifting a finger to his lips, he added with a spark of his legendary mischief, "Just do not tell my mother. Or my aunt. Or anyone else, for that matter. Agreed?"

He pushed aside another branch and was gone.

TWENTY-EIGHT

After Ogam's departure I sat with my back against a pillar of the shrine, staring up at the unveiled sky and waiting for my thoughts to sort themselves out. The division of the heavens had changed slightly; the amber sun had completely set and stars had come out, though the north still rippled with patterns of white light and the moon in Frir's realm had become full.

To the south, above the peak of Mount Thyr, the afternoon waned. The shadow of its heights and crags toppled all the way down the forested mountain to where Albor should have lain, obscure now in the darkness.

I preferred it that way. With the village out of sight, it was easier not to wonder what my former home would look like here. Unseen, it did not matter if the town was whole, as in my memories, or as burned and charred as it was in the Waking World. No one I loved was there to welcome me.

Gradually, my mind began to grasp more practical, manageable matters. So, Ogam had invited me to eat and drink of the High Halls, yet I was to hide it from Eang and the other gods?

Even my dull mind was sharp enough to question the need for secrecy, and to mistrust the mischief in the Son of Winter's eyes. But what else could I do? No one was coming to help me. I needed to cure myself.

I climbed back to my feet and turned full circle, surveying each tree around the meadow. There was still enough light from the waning southern afternoon to see berry bushes here and there, and when I cocked my good ear, I picked out the sound of a stream nearby.

I began to forage, keeping close to the meadow. I nervously ate berries off the bush and, crouching in a pool of golden evening light, I drank water from a creek of clear meltwater. As my confidence grew, I stuffed my pockets with mushrooms and dug up root vegetables from a corner of the meadow. I made no effort to hunt – I didn't have tools for cooking, and for all I knew, any of the rabbits or fowls that fled my path might be something far more powerful in disguise.

By the time something like full dusk unfolded over the High Halls, my belly and pockets were nearly full. Satisfied, I began to head back to the meadow on a narrow, winding path.

A low hum caught my ear. I turned, squinting into the shadows between the trees. There, barely discernable in the gloaming, a thousand sleepy bees converged around an ancient, hollow ash.

I crept closer, leaving the path and picking my way over gnarled roots, lichen-covered rocks and pockets of moss. The bees ignored me, attending their tasks while I paused at the base of the tree.

Honey streamed down the bark in amber waterfalls, rimed with a hardened crust and rivers of ants, before it disappeared into a yawning hole among the roots. I stuck a finger into the flow and licked it. Sweetness burst across my tongue, thick with the taste of forest and home, of pine and mountain flowers, and for an instant homesickness overwhelmed me.

But so did strength. It prickled through my fingers, my veins, and infiltrated my heart itself. My heartbeat intensified and my vision sharpened a fraction.

I slowly licked my fingers clean, taking stock of every sensation, every subtle change in my mind and muscles. Eventually the feeling receded, but I felt better than before. I cracked off dried pieces of honey to take back with me and retreated to the meadow.

The next morning, I awoke from a restless sleep to find the fog had returned, though not so thickly as it once had. I ate and drank and tried to draw the rune that Ogam had used the day before to disperse the miasma, but it did not work for me.

Another day came and went. Haunted by fog, I stayed close to the perceived safety of the meadow. I foraged and drank and slept, hoping that the next morning I would awake to find my mind clearer and my body stronger.

But when my eyes opened again, Quentis had come. I didn't see him immediately; instead, I knew he was coming, as naturally as seeing him approach. He was a subtle change in the air, almost a draft, as if an unseen door between the Waking World and the High Halls had opened and closed.

I climbed to my feet, moving with habitual care, but my limbs felt lithe and strong, and my head was blissfully clear.

Careful not to betray my new strength, I faced Quentis over a swath of dew-heavy, closed poppies. Mist tickled across my cheeks, but it was even thinner than the day before. If anything, it seemed to be here for Quentis, and it formed a barrier between me and my enemy.

"What do you want?" I asked.

The Arpa held his mixing bowl in one hand and regarded me like the Eangi war chief, Ardam, would when I lost yet another training bout. His other hand was stained with a mixture of muted orange, embedded now in the creases of his knuckles. As I watched him in return, he raised the hand to his lips and licked at it absently.

"What do you want most in the world, Hessa?"

"Leave me alone," I hissed. Nonetheless, my thoughts flickered through a series of hopes and recollections. I saw my sisters and me as girls, cuddled safe against the winter's cold. I saw Eidr, pulling my head gruffly into his chest on a bloody battlefield. Yske, singing. The Hall, rebuilt. Vistic as a grown man, at Sixnit's shoulder.

But these thoughts, as poignant as they were, stuttered when my eyes drifted to the shrine. Eidr and Yske were dead. Perhaps my sisters and father were too. The Hall of Smoke would never be rebuilt, not without Eangi to fill it. Sixnit was so far away and Vistic, this child I had bound myself to, how could he survive the world as it was now?

The High Halls were all that was left to me. This field of poppies, the world beyond, they were my hope of being with my loved ones again. This place was my eternity – elusive and strange though it was.

That thought bloomed and turned until I forgot Quentis altogether.

If I killed Omaskat, Eang shrove me and I lived through the entire ordeal, what would the rest of my life look like? Eangen was scarred and scattered, her people fleeing towards the Western Sea. As one of the last Eangi, it would fall to me to help lead them – me and Svala.

That reality was a weighty one, rife with challenges – not least of which was the reliability of the goddess we served – but I didn't shy from it. What if Eangen could be saved? What if I could not only absolve myself, but restore my people before I returned to this meadow and sought out Eidr among the trees?

The hope was a frail one, stubborn and thin as a winter sapling, but its roots sunk deep.

"Now let me show you something," Quentis said in a way that made me realize he had been watching my thoughts the entire time. "Let me show you the Arpa Empire."

The meadow shuddered beneath me and vanished. Quentis and I stood on a cliff overlooking a great, sprawling city of sunbaked red stone. Mist still clung to the corners of my vision, but the night before us was clear, and the lights in the city were as numerous as the stars in the eastern quadrant of the sky. Towers with silver, gold and tarnished copper domes reflected the light of the moon and in the center of the settlement, I saw a circular palace with more arches and walkways and gardens than I could count. To the north-east and west, elevated canals brought swift water down from mountains layered grey and purple against the heavens.

"Where is this?" I asked Quentis.

"One of my own memories, of the Arpa capital. Apharnum."

Our perspective shifted. We stood in an afternoon street, surrounded by a crowd so diverse my eyes could not alight on one thing before another tore them away.

I saw people paler than an Algatt and darker than a Soulderni. Some of them were slaves. Some of them wore rich clothing. I saw

Arpa women with fine-draped clothes and their hair pinned in swoops and curls and coils. I glimpsed a barefoot girl with bells about her ankles, dancing before an appreciative crowd. I saw soldiers, relaxed and at ease. Fathers with children in hand. Mothers with plump, healthy cheeks. Elders who must have seen four generations. Together. Fed. Safe.

Quentis pointed up the street. Before I had even lifted my head to follow his finger, we stood in a temple.

I took an involuntary step back. The stink of Arpa incense filled my nostrils and the dome of the ceiling lorded over me, fixed with a hundred small windows of colored glass. They cast a geometric pattern on the floor beneath my feet, centering around a square altar and a single statue.

"This is where our emperors are crowned and ascend..." Quentis bowed low, reverence humbling each line of his body. "Where the power of the Arpa Empire is sourced... the Temple of Lathian."

I froze, staring into the statue's impassive eyes. Somehow the power of the place resonated in my blood, pulsing from the tiles beneath our feet and up into the statue before me. It was the same power that had swept through Iskir after Ried was rebound, and it made my head ache.

A distant part of my mind registered the details of Lathian's representation – his draped clothing, his impeccable form, the handsomeness of his face and the grave kindness of his expression. But what I saw in those eyes was deeper and more compelling than simple attraction. It was power. It was perfection.

"We all worship Lathian, though we may devote ourselves to one of his divine followers. He is the head, the hub, the root." Quentis faced me, the pattern of light from the ceiling falling across his face. One shafted directly into his bowl, making the orange paste within glow. "You feel it too, do you not? The pull of him? The power beneath our feet?"

I did, and it terrified me. I took another step back, prying my feet from the stones as my eyes sought a way out. But there were no doors in the temple, at least, not in the version I saw here. Instead, I saw alcoves filled with statues of lesser gods, their sandaled feet wrapped in trails of creeping, telltale mist. Everywhere I looked, another Arpa deity stared placidly back.

"Let me out," I demanded, spinning back on Quentis.

"Fall before him, now," Quentis urged. "Devote yourself to him. Guide your people under the hand of the Empire, and they will be safe, Hessa."

"Safe? They'll be slaves," I laughed, thin and frail and high. Did this man truly think I'd believe that Lathian would help my people or that we would submit to him, the god of one of our enemies? "You Arpa despise us your god will be no different. Eang is ours, our god. We belong to her. We serve her. I serve her."

Even as I said the words, uncertainty flickered through my mind. We served Eang because she had chosen us and protected us, but now Eangen was overrun with Algatt, ancient bindings were buckling, and Eang herself seemed pettier by the day.

Here, now – this was not the time for such thoughts. And if there was an answer to Eang's failure, it wasn't Lathian.

"No," Quentis corrected. "You serve the Eangen. Serve them, by bending before Lathian."

I spat at Quentis's feet.

He held his ground, eyes flashing with wrath. "Your goddess will die, Hessa. Choose what is right for your people."

"It is not Lathian."

Quentis's expression contorted in malice. He stepped forward, his stained hand raised in a bold, warding gesture.

Immediately, my knees began to weaken and buckle. I instinctively reached for my Fire, but it was nothing more than a memory here, while Quentis's magic still quelled my living body and I was in the seat of Lathian's power.

I could, however, taste honey on my lips. I acknowledged the sensation delicately, measuring it like a foot testing autumn ice.

The force driving me down abated. But rather than fight, rather than reveal the new weapon I'd found, I allowed my knees to sink onto the smooth marble of the floor. I would use my new power, but not until I was sure of its potential – and the time was right.

"This is what you want from me?" I asked. "To convince my people to submit?"

"Yes," Quentis returned, his eyes glinting with greed.

Distantly, I recalled Nisien's comments about Estavius and Castor. They had come north looking for glory, to make a name for themselves on the Rim. Clearly, Quentis had done the same.

"Kneel." Each of Quentis's words battered me, but the sweetness on my lips remained like a shield. I bowed my head, hiding my face from his impassioned, nearly euphoric gaze. "Join us. When Eang is gone, Lathian will bring peace to the north."

His last words echoed up to the domed roof of the temple as heat crept over my skin and the marble beneath my knees turned to ash.

I jerked my head up. The ashes and charred beams of Albor spread around me, still radiating heat and curls of smoke and the ever-present, insidious mist.

Quentis was gone and I was alone in the ruins of my former life. There were no bodies, not in the High Halls' version of this place, but I saw them in my mind's eye – butchered, broken and charred.

If Quentis had intended this transition to be his final blow, it succeeded. The sweetness of the honey turned sour on my tongue and a keen tore up from the roots of my lungs, dragging every scrap of my strength and courage with it.

I could not be here. Not this place. I had to get back to the meadow, to its silence and refuge. There, this pain could be held back. There, I could let myself slip away into delirium and forgetfulness. Just for a little while.

But with these ruins before me, the thought of the meadow suddenly held no solace. It belonged to Eang, the goddess who had let this horror befall her own people.

I couldn't go back, so I began to walk. I walked until I came to a lowland forest of smooth-barked trunks and leaf-filtered light. Birds flitted and lilted through the canopy, their songs a mingling of familiar and strange. Eventually the woods ended, and I found myself on the rocky shore of a lake near Albor, reflected here in the High Halls. Cedars stretched through the mist over placid, clear water, and gradually, its stillness calmed me.

Mist tickled the inside of my nose. I screwed up my face and raised a hand, pointedly sketching the same rune that Ogam had used to disperse it two days ago. Nothing happened. I blew on the unseen rune – or the space where it had been – but my breath, of course, could not freeze the mist into the symbol's shape.

I glanced around myself, red-rimmed eyes scanning cedars, still water and shoulders of rock, until I spied a patch of muddy earth down the shoreline.

I went to it and crouched, drawing the same rune in the cool, damp dirt. At the same time I flexed my will, exerting honeyed power through my touch as I might with Eangi Fire, and sat back.

The fog vanished, between one blink and the next. I couldn't understand what I'd done, but it thrilled me – and unnerved me. I'd found a way to wield my new power, just as Ogam had said I would. But unlike Eangi Fire, this one was hidden from Eang's sight.

I sat down on the rocks, under the High Halls' uncoordinated sky. And then I began to plot.

After that day by the lake, the fog never returned. Whatever was happening to me, whatever this new power meant, the High Halls now recognized me as its own. The truth of that both enticed and frightened me. What were its limits? How long would it last? What would happen if Eang found out?

But with a child's fascinated audacity, I kept on eating and drinking, and every morning I awoke stronger, sharper, and more determined.

My goal, quite naturally, was escape. I spent the next two days sketching runes in the earth to that end, runes of cleansing and release and breaking. I imagined returning to my own body in the Waking World, but the runes and my new magic failed to take me there, and my Fire still lay out of reach. Either I wasn't strong enough yet to break Quentis's curse, or I didn't have the experience or knowledge to properly wield my newfound magic.

I began to roam further afield, searching for another way out. The High Halls seemed to bend around me, taking me inexplicable distances one minute, while the next I remain trapped in the same patch of woodland. I considered searching for Svala or Ogam, or anyone that might advise me, but Ogam's caution not to tell the gods about my feasting hung heavy on my mind. And with each passing day, the advice they might give me seemed less and less vital.

In the end, I'd little need to fear discovery. I saw no gods in my wanderings and encountered few creatures. I saw a herd of sable deer one morning, led by a huge stag with antlers the breadth of a grown man's height, but they fled my voice. I heard howls in the distance that might have been canine, but saw nothing. Birds were as common as trees, brightly colored and singing strange songs, but they ignored me.

I was alone in a world that should have been rife with the beings of mystery and lore. And I couldn't help but fear where they'd all gone.

There were only two options: Frir's Realm of Death in the darkness of the west, or the Waking World. Having seen Aegr the Bear, I was inclined towards the latter. Was the war among the gods so great that all the Hall's denizens were fleeing, or were they simply taking advantage of the gods' distraction?

Haunted by unanswered questions and a growing restlessness, I wandered north. Of all the directions, its perpetual white lights seemed the most unnatural, so I thought the magic of the High Halls might be stronger there. But the closer I came, the more blinding the light was, and the world began to grow... sparse. There were no trees here, only an expanse of exposed grey-pink rock as far as the eye could see, with the occasional low marsh and rustling reeds like Iskiri and

Orthskar territory. Even the rock seemed oddly opaque, as if the white light bleached them like bones under the sun. Whatever this part of the Halls was, I'd never heard of it, and lingering in a fading realm seemed unwise.

I turned west, the fabric of space and time bent, and I came to the sea; the Halls' reflection of Western Eangen, the land of Addack where Ogam had found the murdered Eangi and many Eangen refugees had fled. But there were no refugees in this reflection, only a beach of fine multi-colored pebbles wrapping a winding coastline, topped with rustling grasses and hulking, perfectly round boulders.

From there, calf-deep in the cool waves, I looked out towards Frir's Realm of Death: the Hidden Hearth, and my people's final resting place. It was closer now. I had to crane my head back to see the sickle moon in the sky, and violet light surrounded me. But the sea lay between that realm and me, deep blue and clothed with white-capped waves.

There were legends of mortals who had crossed that expanse, trying to rescue perished loved ones, seek the counsel of the dead, or speak to the Goddess of Death herself. But I did not plan on being one of them. At least, not yet – Frir was Eang's sister, after all, and not to be trifled with.

The sea breeze raked hair into my eyes. I clawed it back and glanced down the shoreline, momentarily at a loss for what to do. It had been five days, by my reckoning, since I'd seen Ogam. I doubted that time flowed the same here as it did in the Waking World, but the Arpa might be in the mountains by now. I needed to wake up.

Then I heard the moan. The cry quickly faded and the wash of the waves resumed their dominance, but I waded back to the shore and scanned my surroundings in alarm.

A second moan drifted up the beach and turned into a fragile wail of pain. It was female, and I had attended enough births over the years to realize what was happening.

Gathering my new power in my belly, I began to follow the sound. My feet crunched on the pebbles and the wind rose, twisting the woman's agonized cries up through the sea spray and into the violet-grey sky.

There, built into the side of a low cliff, I found a door. Or rather, what had once been a door. The single wooden plank had long rotted off its hinges and the bottom showed signs of being eaten by the tide.

The door creaked open at my touch and my shadow stretched into a cave. There, a woman lay on a cloak, her great round belly proclaiming just what kind of discomfort she was in.

I fell to my knees on the damp pebbles. "Esach."

The Goddess of Storms dropped her chin onto her glistening chest and stared at me through dull, broad-set eyes. "Where is Aita? Does she come to me?" she panted over the tent of her knees. Red blood stained her shift, fresh enough to ripple with a strange amber sheen.

I jerked forward at the pain in her voice but caught myself. One did not simply rush to the aid of a goddess. "I don't know."

Esach's head fell back, the muscles of her jaw and throat contorting as she suppressed another wave of pain. When it had passed, she sank onto the mat in exhaustion.

I found my fists clenching with uselessness. "Goddess, may I serve you?"

She dropped an elbow over her eyes. Her response, when it came, was thin. "Yes. Water."

As soon as I turned away, I let the fear pass over my face. The birth of Esach's yearly child both foretold the prosperity of the autumn's harvest and blessed its outcome. But it was too early; she should not be bearing until well into the ninth month and even then, Aita and the other goddesses should be with her. Even Eang was known to attend.

But here was Esach, laboring alone. I was devoted to Eang, but I could not abandon the Goddess of Storms.

I searched the cave and found a flask, abandoned with Esach's belt and outer clothing on a nearby rock. Then I went back to a stream I'd crossed earlier, emptying into the sea, and filled the flask.

When I returned Esach lay on her cloak, exhausted, her face slick with sweat and the collar of her shift askew. I knelt and helped her sit, making each of my movements cautious and leaving her with plenty of time to reject my help.

But she did not. Esach sagged against me and let me pour a dribble of water over her parched lips.

For the first time, I caught a good look at her face in the light from the door. She was old for motherhood, her mouth lined with wrinkles and her hair grey – the multi-faceted grey of storm clouds shot with the white of lightning. In her prime, she would have been glorious. But now her hair was clustered with sweat and her eyes swollen with strain.

"Where can I find Aita?" I asked. "I'll fetch her for you."

"The Hall. She will be in Eang's Hall."

TWENTY-NINE

I left Esach in her cave and paused with the waves tugging at my ankles, trying to corral my thoughts into order.

In all my wanderings, I'd yet to glimpse Eang's own Hall, the place where she held her court. That wasn't unintentional – it hadn't seemed wise to seek out the seat of Eang's power, not when the gods were being hunted down and I shouldn't even be in the High Halls. But if Esach believed Aita would be there, I had to go.

I found a spot up the beach where the colorful pebbles and round boulders gave way to a swath of smooth sand. Kneeling, I steadied myself with a breath and began to draw symbols for sight, discovery, and direction. The sand was cool about my fingertip, giving way in gentle furrows until each symbol was in its place.

Leaning forward and praying for luck, I planted my palm in the center of the triangle and reached for my new power. I imagined Eang's Hall, piecing together legends and stories into one image.

The quality of light changed. The sand warmed beneath my hand and the wind shifted direction, gusting past my mangled ear and sweeping stray hair into my eyes.

I sat back, leaving only the tips of my fingers in contact with the earth, and gazed after the wind.

A Hall now sat on a hill overlooking the coast, where a moment before there had been only boulders and resolute, shuddering grass.

Hardly able to believe my runes had worked, I stood and started towards it. The closer I came the more I slowed, turning my urgent steps into cautious and respectful. I summoned all my strength and poise, expecting someone to greet me – or at least, stop me. I was, after all, a reprobate with a belly full of stolen magic, encroaching on the most sacred of spaces. But no one appeared.

More details of the Hall came into focus. The building was smaller than I expected, no bigger than the Hall of Smoke in Albor, with a hefty wooden structure greyed by weather. Square-hewn trunks formed its doorway, each impressed with the finest carvings I had ever seen. Endless knots coiled into the forms of animals and unrecognizable symbols, and each time my gaze shifted, they reconfigured. Carvings also adorned the gables of its high triangular roof too, and each beam ended in the head of a beast: wolves, bears, eagles, lynx and foxes.

I was a pace from the door by the time I realized it was slightly ajar. My heart, already fluttering, began to pound.

"May I enter?" I asked, unconsciously taking on Svala's welled, rounded tones.

Silence met my inquiry.

"Eang," I murmured in instinctive prayer, then pushed against the ancient wood.

The scent struck me first. It smelled of wood smoke and iron, ancient oak and beeswax. Sound came next, barking and scrabbling as two huge hounds thrust past me out the door. The dogs, combined with the steady crackling of a fire, were the only sounds in the High Hall of the Gods.

The light was muted. At first glance, I noted pillars of carved wood, a high ceiling with exposed, smoke-darkened beams, and a long central hearth. But on second glance, the hearth was gone, and a long table stood in its place. It was bare except for row upon row of herbs: yarrow, sumac, motherwort, mint, willow bark and widow's soap.

"Aita," I called the name of the Great Healer. My voice did not echo in the warm, now herb-scented air, but remained trapped in the space around me.

I peered left and right. Where I expected to see walls, I found endless rows of pillars, each decorated with carvings, cedar boughs and garlands of holly. The Hall appeared to be far bigger inside than it was outside.

Disoriented, I cleared my throat. "Aita?"

When there was still no response, I left the security of the doors and moved past the table. The crackling of a fire rose up again and the pillars broadened, leading me towards a central space where a dozen thrones surrounded a hearth of blackened fieldstone.

At first, the thrones looked to be empty. The fire burned low, sending more smoke than flame up into a pillar of light from the chimney. But when I looked again, two were occupied by limp, lifeless forms. One was instantly recognizable by her looping braids, mossy gown and black-lined eyes, which gaped at the pillar of smoke: Riok, governor goddess of the central Eangen Rioki. The name of the second corpse appeared in my mind a moment later: Dur, god of the Amdur, another central Eangen people. He sat motionless, his thick chest pinned to his throne by three raven-fletched, bone-white arrows.

Both were Eang's subordinates, members of her court for all of Eangen history. Their deaths would irreparably alter my world. But it was the third body that filled me with the greatest dread.

A male god lay on the ground beside the fire, the backs of both knees hacked apart, an oak shield shattered, and his wild hair and fine tunic caked with blood.

Oulden, the god of the Soulderni. Dead.

I ran a few steps closer before a force struck me. It hit my chest like a warding hand, stopping me in my tracks and sapping my knees of their strength. I tottered into a pillar and clutched at my ribs.

This pain was terrific, but my new magic – *my* magic – responded in kind. It surged through my body, chased by wisps of dormant Eangi Fire, and the pain abated. My senses cleared and expanded, and I sagged into the pillar.

I heard footsteps, low breathing and the light tap of fingernails against wood.

A female figure stalked around the circle of thrones, ornate white bow in hand, but the tapping had not come from her. A lean, pale man stood three paces away from me, his face defined by an out-thrust chin and eyes smeared with black. He rested one hand against a pillar, his long, canine nails tapping out a distracted rhythm.

As our eyes met, his lips parted to reveal red-rimmed teeth. Then he tucked his tongue up and let out a strange, hissing whistle.

My gaze flicked back towards the doors. The dogs that had shouldered past me not a minute before returned, ears pricked, snouts raised. At some unspoken command, they began to pace across the doorway with their heads low. Barring me in.

"The taint of iron and the stink of sweat," a female voice noted. This was the figure with the bow, her beautiful face lit with interest over the collar of her weathered huntsman's clothes. "Rioux, we've found another Eangi."

I stood my ground, though everything inside me howled to run. Another Eangi? They'd encountered my kind before?

"I'm almost disappointed! Hunting down your brethren has made such excellent sport." The lean man, Rioux, began to approach. He took each step with lanky indifference. "Oh? Did you not know?"

I stared, turning the trembling of my lips into something like a snarl. Ogam had said he'd found murdered Eangi on the coast, pierced by arrows of white bone – just like the ones that pinned Dur to his throne and clustered in the archeress's quiver.

"You killed them?" I demanded, fear and caution lost in a rush of fury and grief.

"Well, those that the Algatt didn't kill for us," the archeress replied, scrutinizing me from head to toe. "Are you the one from the Fall of Ashaklon?"

I didn't reply. Rioux made a contemplative sound and the archeress drew her bow, turning her approach into a broad circle to flank me. I watched the overdeveloped muscles of her arms flex, holding the white bow – no, not just white, a skeletal bow, the weapon impossibly formed of ornately carved bone – taut in a way no human could.

"It must have been you," she concluded. Her accent was light and high in the mouth. "How many of your kind are left, priestess? There cannot be many, not between us and Eang clawing her way out of the grave so often. Once we kill you too, she might finally stay dead."

Rioux's laugh echoed around her last sentence. "Look at her face! Oh, Eangi, we've killed your goddess before. Didn't you know that? I opened her belly like a fish just two moons ago."

Their words rattled in my ears. Eang, killed? Two months ago? That would have been right before Omaskat came to Albor, during the quiet normality of early summer. The High Priestess had mentioned nothing at the time, and I'd seen Eang since. How could she have died?

A horrible suspicion crept up the back of my neck, even as my eyes remained fixed on the interlopers. Ried. Vestiges. Ogam had said his mother learned how to make Eangi from the gods she had displaced, gods like Ried. Ried, who had ensured they could come back to life through Vestiges.

What was it Ogam had said, when he first came across me?

"You're the only vestige of her I can find."

"I'll do it again when I have the chance," the lean god added. His voice took on a mocking tone, but with each word, it clouded with a new level of hatred. "The ranks of the Gods of the New World thin, Eangi. They grow weak, while we, the Old, regain our strength. So call your goddess. 'Eang, Eang, the brave, the vengeful' – the cowardly, the deceitful, the traitor!"

We, the Old. Gods of the Old World. I was face to face with not one but two Gods of the Old World. Gods who had just butchered Oulden, Riok, and Dur, and who claimed they had slain my goddess at least once before.

The goddess's eyes slitted, thin and harsh as the head of the arrow she trained upon me. "Rioux, what do you see on her face?"

"Fear," her tall companion quipped. "Desperation. Confusion. Courage so thin I—"

"The Son of Winter marked her," the Archeress realized, holding my gaze, and a trickle of relief passed over me. Was there a chance that Ogam's name would finally protect me, even if Eang's did not? "He wouldn't do that without good reason. Why?"

Without warning, Rioux's arm shot towards me. He was still out of reach, but I felt his nails dig into my gut, jerking and pulling and twisting until I couldn't help but cry out. My knees buckled and I grabbed onto the nearest pillar.

Rioux crept closer, chin thrust out and eyes glinting. "Are you carrying his spawn?"

I could barely breathe. I locked an arm over my stomach, wondering through gritted teeth if harm I suffered in the High Hall would transfer to real life. It seemed stupid to find out, particularly if I was one of Eang's last anchors in the living world. No wonder Quentis was so curious about Eang's condition and the nature of my Eangi Fire.

Eangi Fire. My fingers twitched against my tunic, yearning to throw Eang's power into Rioux's leering eyes and burn them away. But the barrier of Quentis's magic remained, clenched as tightly as the pain beneath my flesh.

The magic of the High Halls, however, was free. It swelled without conscious prompting, sweet and clean and liberating. The pain in my stomach retreated, the gallop of my heartbeat slowed, and I straightened slowly, stunned but determined.

Rioux, still gloating over my suffering, retreated a step. His expression snapped from sneering to wary and his outstretched hand flexed, trying and failing to overpower me again. I felt no more than a brush of fingers against my skin – impotent and harmless.

One arm still pressed over my stomach, I set my shoulders and looked from him to the Archeress through a haze of amber, honeyed magic. My heart drummed steadily against my ribs and my thoughts ran rapid, but I understood one thing.

My new magic had shielded me from Rioux's power – the power of a god.

The Archeress's bow creaked as she raised it an inch higher and said to Rioux, "Best back away from the Eangi, brother. She's clearly been taking what doesn't belong to her. But an arrow will still put her down."

Rioux stepped aside and I was left facing the Archeress and her bow of bone.

My eyes flicked to Dur again, the man with three arrows buried in his chest, and a rush of fear clawed up my throat.

With it came instinct. I snatched at my new magic and threw it out in a lash.

Liquid amber light burst between the gods and me. I screamed in surprise and ducked, throwing up my arms to protect my head – from my own magic and the thrum of the Archeress's bow.

I didn't see the effect of my lash, but I heard Rioux bellow in rage. An arrow blurred through the corner of my eye, so close that I felt it whisk past my forearm and snatch at my hair. It buried itself halfway through one of the hall's great carved pillars with a crack.

"Our master is coming, Eangi!" A hand seized my wrist and jerked my arm down. I'd barely time to register Rioux's face, smeared with scarlet-amber blood – ichor, I realized in a flash, the blood of the gods – before he drove a knife down at my chest. "And even the Goddess of War cannot stop them."

A gale tore through the Hall. It stole the air from my lungs and staggered Rioux, just enough for me to sidestep, grab his wrist and jerk the knife away. He howled in renewed fury and I dashed for cover, sprinting past three rows of pillars before darkness crashed around me.

I dropped into a crouch and tried to see through the raging black. I sensed, more than saw, Rioux bolt away, one layer of darkness blurring with another. The Archeress was too far away to be seen, but I heard shouting, a scream, and the squealing of one of the dogs as it died.

My mind sputtered and blanked, unable to follow what was happening, but I had to escape. There was a new power in this Hall, and I wasn't about to wait to find out who it was.

Eangi instinct took over and, almost without thought, I slit open one of my palms. As the wind buffeted me and the darkness tripled,

I drew a clumsy rune in my own blood on the slate floor of the hall. Freedom.

I slammed my open palm down into the middle of the symbol and let my magic roar through. The wind muted, the sensations of the Hall – stone, wind, slick blood – retreated, and I had the bizarre sensation of sinking down into nothing at all.

Only as the last shadows of the High Hall faded did I notice that the blood rune around my hand glistened with amber magic, just like Esach's had in the cave, and Rioux's not a minute before.

My blood glistened like the blood of the gods.

I cracked open sticky eyes. Quentis crouched over me, backed by the Waking World's uniform, if stormy, sky. Clouds billowed and boiled over one another in masses of grey and black, and the wind was sharp with coming rain.

"Hessa?" Strong arms pulled my shoulders back into someone's chest. Nisien. "Hessa, are you awake?"

"I'm all right," I croaked – my throat was still bruised from Ried's attack, of all things. Without thinking, I pushed myself away from him and sat up on my own, though I still clutched his fingers in my good, right hand – anchoring myself in this moment and this world.

Rioux's knife was gone, but the gash I'd made in my left palm remained. Scarlet blood oozed between my fingers, still glistening with amber. But as I watched, the secondary color retreated, replaced by a familiar, invisible heat. Quentis's curse was broken, and my Eangi Fire surged back to life.

At the same time, I sensed the magic of the High Halls sinking, retreating and stowing itself away in the marrow of my bones, bowing to an older, angrier force. I tried to stop it, tried to snatch at it, but my Fire only surged in response.

Resigned, I curled the fingers of my injured hand in, hoping Quentis hadn't seen the fading amber gleam and wouldn't think the cut significant. He hovered closer, wind from the oncoming storm tearing at his hair and robes. I realized now that I could see the Algatt Mountains behind him, so close and so high I'd mistaken them for more clouds. They were a day away, at most.

"What is happening?" Quentis demanded. "Why are you awake? This storm is not natural, woman. Tell me what's going on. Who is doing this?"

"Esach, Goddess of Storms," I replied simply, hoping he would take that as explanation for my waking too, and turned to Nisien. I took the Soulderni's hand with renewed urgency. "Nisien, Oulden—"

He cut me off, his voice low and sober. "I felt it."

Distantly, irrelevantly, Estavius appeared in the corner of my vision, his helmetless hair windblown and unkempt.

Quentis reached to grab my tunic, but the look I cut him made him pause. He dropped his outstretched hand, fingers still poised and a new wariness about his eyes. "What… what are you saying?"

It took a second to breathe, piecing my memories of the High Hall back together. They were a cacophony of revelation, unanswered questions and violence, but I understood one thing clearly. Three gods, allies or servants of Eang, had died in the High Hall.

I looked at Nisien. I barely registered his Arpa armor or his clean-shaven cheeks. All I saw then was a kinsman, a man of the north, devoted at birth to the god of his forebears. It did not matter that Nisien had turned from him for so many years. Oulden was the heart of the Soulderni people, and it was he who kept Nisien's body and soul – both through the evils of this life, and into the ease of the next. Without him, Nisien's afterlife was as unattainable as my own.

Oulden was dead. Nisien was devoted to no god.

THIRTY

I stared up at the mountains through slitted eyes while the Arpa made camp. I sat beneath a birch tree nearby, half-sheltered from the fine, misty rain with my hands bound in my lap – left one bandaged, right one clasped on my opposite forearm. A new dose of Quentis's poison made my mouth taste sour and my stomach ache, but my reaction was purely physical. It no longer sent me spiraling back into the High Halls.

The magic of that world, however, remained quiet. I still tasted honey on my lips, and I felt it within me, protecting me and granting me a new, heightened sense, but it was inaccessible – a sleeping limb or a forgotten name. Eang's Fire burned under my skin instead, clean and hot and familiar as the sun. Its presence was a relief, but I could not help but feel that I was being denied something important; something outside of Eang's control. Something that, even if it was stolen, was now mine.

The Arpa, of course, knew neither of these things. Since I awoke that morning, I'd maintained a bleary façade, pretending to doze and slip out of my own mind while we plodded north and I plotted my escape. But between the presence of the legionaries, Quentis's near constant watch, and a lack of opportunity to speak to Nisien, I'd yet to make a play for freedom.

Now the repetitive pinging of tent pegs jarred into my skull. I closed my eyes and leant back against the smooth, raspy bark of the tree, trying to force my muscles and mind to calm. But most of my thoughts were as unwelcome as the world around me, harsh and repetitive and wearing me thin.

I remembered the dead gods around the thrones. I recalled the Archeress and Rioux, the bow and the knife and the runes. I thought of Vestiges and saw Svala's face, the night Eang had possessed the Eangi girl in the Hall of Smoke. I recalled her fear and grief as she watched the child crumple.

She had understood, before anyone else, that the girl was dead. But had she known more? Were they matters for a High Priestess alone?

"You're the only Vestige of her I can find."

"Oh, Eangi, we've killed your goddess before. Didn't you know that?"

"The Eangi make her nearly immortal… bad habits from old gods."

And, as reluctant as I was to do so, I began to understand. The ache in my stomach compounded and I drew my knees in more tightly.

The Eangi were Vestiges of Eang. Rioux had said they'd killed Eang many times before, most recently two months ago – right around the time Omaskat came to Albor. The goddess must have used an Eangi in some far corner of the land to claw her way out of the grave, just as she'd once done with that young girl in the Hall of Smoke. Otherwise, I would have heard of their death.

Now only Svala and I were left, it seemed. If Eang perished again, which of our lives would she extinguish to keep herself alive?

I suspected the answer, at least once Omaskat was dead, and it made my emotions roil. I knew that if I'd brought this matter to Svala, she would have insisted dying for Eang was a privilege, in any context. But I could not believe that, not with my goddess so distant and my circumstances so grim.

I had to escape. For all her faults and deceptions, Eang was still ruler of the Eangen and I was her Eangi. I needed her to ensure I had a place in the High Halls. Then, and only then, could I reconcile my questions of Vestiges and faith.

So my purpose remained, as simple and inexplicable as it had always been – find and kill Omaskat.

The sound of laughter brought me back to my surroundings; my sheltering tree and Arpa companions. The tents had been erected and men vanished into them, swinging off packs and talking good-naturedly while others kindled fires and tended horses – Nisien among the latter.

But I didn't look at my friend, or the Arpa. Instead, I observed a train of mountain goats leaping from one ledge to the next on the rainy mountainside, oblivious to the two-hundred pace drop below them. Their destination was a ravine, overgrown with brush and cutting deeper into the mountains. As I watched, they vanished one by one into its fold.

My eyes flicked back to the legionaries, then my bound hands. I didn't need free hands to disappear into that ravine myself, but I would need the cover of night to reach it. Or a good distraction.

It was then that I saw the blood staining my trousers, beneath my rumpled tunic; thick, dark and spreading. The aching in my lower stomach intensified and I blinked down at myself in dull despair.

My bleeding. I had forgotten about my bleeding. It had come when I was in Souldern, but with all the stress and anxiety of the last few weeks, female cares had entirely left my mind.

I did not need more weakness in my body, not now.

I dragged myself upright. The movement caught Quentis's attention, as I'd known it would. He left the shelter of the rock face, pulling up the hood of his cloak as he went.

"What is it?"

"I need cloth and privacy," I told him with as much dignity as I could muster. Before he could question me, I pulled up the front of my tunic and showed him why.

Quentis staggered back as if I were contaminated. "Aux," he called over his shoulder.

My heart lifted and my cheeks burned with embarrassment as Nisien came forward.

"See to the woman," Quentis clipped, still refusing to look at me, and strode away.

Nisien, to his eternal credit, kept his eyes level with mine. "Wait one minute."

True to his word, a minute later he came back with bandages from the healer and what looked to be an extra pair of his own trousers. He took my arm.

"Come, little Eangi," he said, "let's find you a private spot."

The muscles of my legs had forgotten how to coordinate, and the cramping did little to help. I stumbled and wobbled, but by the time we reached a stand of rugged, shoulder-high scrub, I'd recovered a little.

"How are you?" I asked him, the priestess in me making a cautious appearance. "Considering... Oulden."

His expression grew stony. "Oulden spent months in hiding. As far as I'm concerned, he deserted me long before he died. My only fear now is for my people – especially with Ashaklon in their midst. Will the binding hold?"

"Eang's side may... for a time." I hesitated, thinking of Silgi and her family and wondering just how truthful that statement was. So many of Eang's older bindings had already failed. "But without Oulden, what will become of the Soulderni? Where will your dead go? Did Oulden have any Vestiges he could come back with, like Ried?"

Like Eang has me, I thought.

"I don't know. Those are questions for priests, not me. Here, let me unbind you."

He pulled a knife and went to work.

"You need a new patron," I warned Nisien. "You can't go about devoted to no god, especially at a time like this. Weakened or not, Oulden's name has protected you since you were born. And what of your High Halls? How will the Soulderni get there if Oulden doesn't vouch for them?"

He made a noncommittal grunt and the rope fell away. "I don't know, and I'm not sure I care. I'm tired of the gods, Hessa. The day I see one worthy of worship, I'll bow. But I refuse to grovel before another selfish, cowardly being just because they are more powerful than me."

Despite myself, I thought of the power of the High Halls, amber as the gods' own, sleeping in my bones. If a mere week in the High Halls had transformed me, a human, what had it done to the gods over millennia? Where might the inherent powers of the gods end, and the magic that they'd surely harvested from the Halls begin?

Was this, then, what Ogam had meant by the gods needing the High Halls?

Heresy. That line of thought was the purest form of heresy I had ever contemplated. I shoved it aside but it remained all the same, curled up at the back of my mind with Omaskat's assertions that Eang was no goddess, Shanich's whispers of the Miri and the Four, and the amber blood of the gods.

Nisien was still speaking. "Or because they claim to control my eternity," he added.

Now doubly perturbed, I rubbed at my wrists and I accepted the bandages and new trousers. "It doesn't matter," I snapped, more vehement than I intended. "This world, our souls, are owned by the gods. You must serve someone."

At the last, I reached to take the knife too, but Nisien held the blade away from me. "No, Hessa. No gods. And I'm sorry, I can't let you have that."

My mouth fell open. I hadn't intended to use the knife for any devious purposes at least, not yet. "I need it to cut fabric—"

"No."

"Why?"

"Because killing someone or making a foolish attempt to escape will not help you," Nisien replied, but he could not hold my eyes. He added more quietly, "Or me."

"So you're willing to let Quentis kill me?" I retorted before I could think better of it. "You're so loyal to the Arpa you'd let him poison me to death?"

"I would never let him kill you!" Nisien protested, alarmed at the accusation. "And I can't just— Hessa, when, if the time is right—"

I shouldered into the bushes before he could finish his sentence – or see the betrayal on my face. Ensconced in foliage, I kicked off my boots and unbound my trousers with angry, uncoordinated fingers. But only half my anger was directed towards the Soulderni. The other half burned against myself, my traitorous doubts and Omaskat's insidious statement that Eang was no true god.

Eang controlled my eternity. What else was a god?

Through the lower half of the scrub, I saw a second pair of legs join Nisien's in a companionable stance. I paused, scowling and listening to the sound of misty rain on the leaves until the second man spoke. Estavius.

I quickly made suppositories and saw to my needs, glancing around as I did so to make sure I wasn't being watched. But though this section of scrub offered little protection from the fine rain, it was high enough to block me from sight. It was also vast and thick, spreading to the east down the foot of the mountains, while to the north it crept into a ravine. The very ravine which the goats had vanished into.

I paused and studied the spot, gauging the distance between it and myself as my pulse began to thrum. I could run, right now. Yet if I did, I would leave Nisien vulnerable and bearing the blame of my escape.

But however kind he'd been, he had refused to give me the knife.

My heart clenched. Euweth's fears for her son were coming true. He might be my friend, but perhaps his loyalties were too divided.

My forehead itched, clawing at my concentration. I scrubbed at it with the back of a hand, and one of Quentis's runes, still painted on my face, came away in a streak of rust. I stared at it, at this stark reminder of the other priest's broken power, and felt a rush of grim determination.

I could not control Nisien's choices, but I could make my own. I began to knot my new trousers and wind my legwraps, mentally charting my path towards the cleft.

"Hessa, you'd better hurry," Nisien said, reminding me how close he and Estavius stood. My heart slammed in my throat and my movements slowed. "Estavius here is trying to convert me to Aliastros."

"No Arpa gods," I retorted. "You're a Northman, Nisien. And I need a few more minutes."

Estavius said something that I couldn't understand, and I felt a flash of resentment. Yes, the pale-eyed legionary had saved my life before and, in the right mood, I might even admit that I was starting to like him. But if he was trying to sway Nisien to foreign gods, that changed matters.

The legionary's voice came again, soft and urgent. Pleading.

"What's he saying?" I asked, tying off one leg-wrap just below the knee and moving on to the next. I didn't have time for this.

"That Aliastros was allied with Oulden," Nisien translated. "He has sway in the High Halls and the Arpa Pantheon. That he's the better choice, apparently."

"You're a Northman, Nisien," I repeated, hoping against hope that that sentiment would stay with him and keep his wavering loyalties in check. "Call on Esach. Please."

"I'm not calling on anyone."

The two men fell into quiet discussion, and my attention was dragged back to the mountain.

I could wait no longer. I submerged a shot of regret and guilt, left my blood-stained trousers behind in mockery of Quentis, and began to work my stealthy way towards the cliff.

One step, two. A sparrow chattered as it darted over my head and branches tugged at my hair. Three steps. Four. I entered the shadow of the cliff. Five. Six. Seven. Eight. The ravine opened, narrow and filled with fallen rock. But the scrub ended some twenty paces ahead. From then on, I'd be exposed.

I broke into a run, moving as quietly and quickly as possible. Eang's Fire awoke, coursing through my veins over a suppressed, honey-sweet taint.

"Esach," I panted at the clouds above, "Goddess, I know your pain, but if you have any thought to spare, I could use some cover."

Thunder immediately rolled. I was so shocked that I lost my footing and fell, smashing one knee into a sharp rock. I cursed and pushed forward, crawling up a former landslide.

I reached the top before I heard shouting. I did not look back. Instead, I took off across a ridgeline and ducked into another ravine, heading deeper into the mountain.

Further and further I pushed. The sky opened and thunder cracked, deafening me. Esach was not only alive, she was furious.

The rocks became slick and my progress slowed. At a section of even ground, I broke into a shambling sprint. I startled the herd of goats I'd seen earlier, now sheltering under an overhang, and their alarmed bleats chased me around another bend.

This path turned and ended in a cleft so steep all I could do was stare, aghast. There was a ledge some ten feet up, but I couldn't reach it.

Footsteps pounded into the ravine at my back. I spun and drew up my Fire, ready to unleash the last of my strength on whoever appeared around the corner.

Estavius stumbled into sight. Whatever he saw in my face and stance, he threw up his own arms and took a step back. The storm burst around him as he did, billowing up the cleft and blinding me with rain. But though the wind buffeted him, he stood steady and unperturbed.

Behind his splayed fingers, he glanced from me to the far side of the cleft.

"Up?" he asked in his heavily accented Northman.

I gawked at him, blinking rain from my eyes. "What?"

"Up." He lowered one hand cautiously, pulled a knife from his belt and held it out, hilt first. "Take and go."

I might have remained there, gaping, had another jaw-cracking thunderclap not burst overhead. I jumped and braced as wind burst over us with renewed force, but Estavius still stood fast, unfaltering as wind and rain cavorted. His calmness unnerved me, a pillar of humanity in the violence of the unnatural storm. But his god was the Arpa God of Wind, was he not? Why should he fear the wind?

Echoing my thoughts, Estavius began to speak. But his words were not directed to me. They must have been a prayer, for the gale returned to the sky in one long rush. Estavius relaxed, pushing hair from his eyes with one hand, and offered me a nervous half-smile. With the other, he still held out the knife.

The sight spurred me. Whatever kindness Estavius was showing, whatever sway he held with his Arpa god, I needed to go.

The thunder still reverberated as I snatched the weapon, shoved it through my belt and began to climb up the narrow end of the ravine. The Arpa, meanwhile, trailed after me.

My fingers wrapped around wet stone. Rain streamed into my eyes and my boots scrabbled, but no amount of determination or will found me a proper foothold.

"Wait."

I found Estavius no more than a pace away, hands laced into a stirrup.

I accepted the gesture without hesitation. He grasped my foot and hefted, boosting me up over the height of his head with a tight-jawed grunt. I scrambled onto the ledge and looked back down at his pale, serious eyes, suppressing a rush of gratitude – and sudden loneliness.

"Why are you helping me?" I asked him.

Estavius smiled and locked a fist over his heart. "Nisien," he replied simply, then pointed to my cheeks, where Quentis's runes had been. In vastly improved Northman he said, "Do not let the gods see that you stole their magic."

With that, he turned and ran.

I scrubbed rain from my eyes and squinted after him. I remembered kneeling on the ground beside him after the Algatt attack, and how, just for a moment, I'd thought I'd seen a flicker of amber in his blood.

I laughed aloud, a short, stunned sound, and rubbed more rain from my eyes. Perhaps Estavius truly knew something about stealing from the gods. Or perhaps Aliastros blessed his worshipers in ways Eang would not.

But there was no time to wonder how much he knew or what it meant – or the revelation that he spoke more Northman than he'd pretended.

I reached the top of the cleft a few minutes later. The premature darkness of the storm hid me as I stumbled and leapt across the mountainside, descending here, ascending there. Finally, when I could go no further, I crawled into the shelter of a clutch of stunted pines and hunkered down.

After a few minutes, my frantic heart began to calm. With that came the Fire's predictable fatigue, and I collapsed on a bed of damp deadfall, arms clasped around myself and the knife in one hand.

No one came for me. Alone and undisturbed, I rested until the rain eased, the clouds parted, and the eerie gloom of the storm transitioned into the true dark of night. Then, lulled by the retreating rumble of Esach's rage, I nestled my cheek into a fragrant, sticky bed of pine needles and slept a true, deep sleep.

I awoke grudgingly. Light met my face and my consciousness peeled itself from the recesses of sleep, slipping back into my fingers and toes and forcing my eyes open.

I had just enough time to roll sideways before bile hit my teeth. I vomited a thick black substance onto the ground. Coughing and spluttering, I wiped pine needles and bile from my face and sank onto my bottom, trembling from head to toe.

It was dawn. Considering I had also fallen asleep at dawn, this disconcerted me until I realized that the ground was nearly dry. I had slept through an entire day and night.

Now I was starving, and bleeding completely through my trousers again. It was time to move on.

For the first hour, I skulked like a wary animal. But the mountains in late summer were laden with food, and there were only the beasts to share it with. I ate berries and leaves and drank from creeks until, around mid-afternoon, realized I was following a path. Even then, it took the sight of a circular stone building to understand that the path was, naturally, made by the Algatt.

I darted for cover behind a boulder and peered out at the building. Its stone walls sat under the deep eaves of a wooden roof, where firewood was layered in upside-down triangles all the way to the rafters. The heavy wooden door was closed, and there was enough debris gathered at its feet to tell me it hadn't been opened in a long while.

I crept across the open space and reached for the latch. It was high on the door, little more than a wooden handle dangling from a cord of braided leather. I pulled.

The latch lifted with a squeak and the door swung inward, letting a slice of twilight into the murk beyond. I stepped outside the patch of light and waited for my eyes to adjust, clinging to the knife.

The building was a stable or a herder's hut. A raised oven in the center of the room yawned open, revealing old coals. Racks of beds, four in total, sat at head height while the central chimney let in a circle of light. The smell of livestock clung to everything.

I stared at the beds for a long time. They were little more than shelves, but they were off the ground. I could start a fire. I could rest and tend to myself. Like as not, there would be fresh water nearby.

But could I afford to linger? I scrubbed at my tired eyes with the heels of my hands and sagged back against the wall, trying to force myself into a wise decision.

Then I saw supplies tucked up under the eaves. I hauled myself onto one of the beds and, perched on its creaking frame, unwrapped a tinderbox, blanket, water flask and pouch with bone awl and gut.

There was no decision to be made after that. I built a fire, filled my belly with hot water, and went to sleep.

I slept until the middle watch. Unable to return to slumber, I rolled over and stared at the glistening coals in the oven. Orange twisted across their surfaces, and, occasionally, a pop of bright flame illuminated the hut with its stone walls, wooden struts and hard-packed earthen floor.

Perhaps it was the warmth or the hush of the night, or the reality that I was finally free, but I felt calmer than I'd been in two months. And in that calm, I reflected upon my new circumstances and the road ahead.

My first concern was Quentis. Assuming he was the driving force behind my captivity, I hoped that Polinus would not spare the men to hunt me after the first night. If I happened across them by accident, I had little doubt that I would be recaptured. Otherwise, only Quentis and his Arpa God of Gods, Lathian, posed a lingering threat.

Secondly, the Algatt. I could not act on the assumption that they had *all* fled the mountains. If any were still here, they would be doubly dangerous.

Thirdly, the supposedly rogue legionaries that had started all of this by slaughtering the Algatt. If they were still alive and still here, I needed to avoid them at all costs.

Fourth, the Gods of the Old World. I had no idea who had attacked the Archeress and her companion in the High Hall, or if they had lived, but I could not disregard the fact that the Gods of the Old World might come after me.

Our master is coming, and even the Goddess of War cannot stop them.

Rioux's last words crept up in the back of my thoughts, forgotten amid shock, flight and fear. Eang herself, when she'd visited me after the defeat of Ashaklon, had mentioned Ashaklon was only a lesser god, a mere servant. So which God of the Old World did he and the others serve?

I swallowed tightly and scrubbed at my eyes. I had no answer for that, and no way to find one. For now, I had to think of Omaskat. I needed to find the white lake and the place where the sky bled into the mountain, and hope that somehow, his death could save my crumbling world, my people and me.

THIRTY-ONE

I came to an Algatt village at noon the next day. Worn trails in a conifer wood converged into a central road, passing hunters' racks and a stinking, fly-ridden tanning hut before I came to the village proper.

The houses were like nothing I had ever seen. They were two-storied, built of rock and merged directly with the mountain. The ends of beams protruded a meter out from their walls, braced and stacked with V's of wood, as they had at the shepherd's hut. These beams supported rooves which, unlike those on Eangen homes – nearly flat and lain with sod – were built at steep angles to shed the snow.

I crept toward the nearest home. A quick survey found the bottom to be a barn and storage area – stripped clean – while the upper floor, accessed by a ladder, was for human habitation.

The floor creaked as I climbed, guided by light from small, shuttered windows. Bed racks stood at the back of the room, near the entrance of a genuine cave. The oven sat at the edge of this cave, large enough to sleep atop and with a wide, yawning mouth.

I glanced around and, noticing a hatch in the low ceiling, I opened it to a rush of light and alpine air. Sunlight poured across the worn planks and into the cave, where I spotted a water basin carved into the rock and a series of long workspaces. Rows of jars and vessels showed little sign of disturbance, though the rest of the home had been emptied of basic necessities.

I hovered beside the shaft of sunlight. This, I realized, was how the Algatt survived harsh mountain winters. With their flocks below, their oven before them and the beams of the ceiling packed with goods, the storms could berate their stone homes with minimal effect. It was, admittedly, impressive.

But the presence of so many supplies unnerved me. These Algatt had left in calculated haste, taking only what they needed for the summer. It almost looked as though they expected to come back.

I plucked at the strings of a forgotten loom with a single, muted thrum and turned about. I recognized Eangen-made cloth and barrels in the rafters, but the worst sight was a row of Eangen shields hung like trophies on the wall. One bore the two twisting whales of Addack, on the coast; another wore the Rioki's moose antlers; another, the lynx head of East Meade, my birthplace.

I tore them down and set the one with the lynx near the stairs. I would take that with me.

The new light had also illuminated the rim of the cave. It was carved into an intricate arch with layer upon layer of stylized trees, animals and representations of Gadr. A bearskin about his shoulders, he looked up to the curve of the arch. There, mounted warriors progressed towards a great owl, perched in a forest.

I trailed a hand over the owl, momentarily lost in thought. Burgeoning hatred made my vision feel thick, like a finger drawn through oil. Algatt. Algatt had built this. Algatt had stolen my life away. Why was I standing here when I could be burning this village to the ground?

Then I heard it – a low hoot, echoing through the cave. The sound was like hearing Eidr's voice after a battle; relief coiled with desperation and love. It was like Yske's songs or Svala's emphatic prayers – they drove through me, dredging up every spark of determination and will I had ever had. The sound was hope.

But though my heart responded in pure Eangi instinct, thundering against my ribs, my head remained cool. If Eang was coming to me now, I doubted it was out of kindness.

I tilted my good ear towards the sound and paused, waiting for a rustle of feathers or the voice of Eang. Neither came, but the owl hooted more insistently. She was in the cave, and I, it seemed, was to go to her.

I glanced around the house until I spotted a candle, burned so low it had been left behind. I cracked it off a polished clay platter and fumbled around the hearth with my tinderbox.

As soon as my candle was lit, I shouldered past a half-open door and into a tunnel. The owl hooted a third time. I started down a set of stairs, so worn that they bellied in the middle. The air was cool but pure and my candle flickered, lively in the draft.

The passage levelled out after a handful of steps. I slowed as more staircases joined, all coming from the right – the direction of the houses. They were all connected, back here under the skin of the mountain.

The owl's steady hoots guided me down to what I guessed was ground level. I glimpsed a large, double door outlined with daylight, but the owl's hoots came from the opposite direction. I walked on, following an even, well-maintained tunnel deeper into the mountain.

Except where I expected to find endless rock, I saw light, and where I expected cold, I encountered warm, humid steam. The air became sweet and heavy, prickling down into my lungs in a way that reminded me of the High Halls' mists.

Pools covered the floor of the caves and stalactites and stalagmites had merged into pillars throughout. The steaming pools emptied out the far side, sliding into daylight over a sheet of smooth rock before merging with a pond under the summer sun.

I picked my way to the cave mouth and stared out. Brave pines clung to ledges, reaching towards a blue sky, while moss and ferns lined well-worn paths through a small forest before me. Carved, painted standing stones stood out among the trunks and layers of burnt-orange pine needles, quiet and unobtrusive.

The valley was so hidden, I wondered if it was a piece of another world – or a doorway between them. With that thought came a memory of amber and honey, coiled beneath Eang's Fire, and I saw a division in the air among the standing stones. It was barely noticeable, like a fine crack in a clay pot, but it was there.

I had never seen such a thing before, and I doubted that, without that honeyed whisper, I would be able to see it now. The sleeping magic in my blood knew this place and that rift: a door between the High Halls and the Waking World. This must have been Gadr's holy ground, like Oulden's Feet and Eang's Shrine on Mount Thyr.

An owl sat next to the door on a standing stone. She ruffled her feathers and watched me, full-moon eyes reflecting the muted forest light. And, like the door between worlds, for the first time I saw the owl for what she truly was.

She was no owl at all. She was a breath, a piece of golden, rushing life trapped in layers of feathers; a final breath of Geta, sister of Eang and Frir, whom Eang, legends said, had killed in retribution for a grave betrayal.

The owl's gaze seemed to intensify, unblinking and fixed.

Do not let the gods see that you stole their magic.

Estavius's warning rang through my ears – perhaps he and his own amber-tainted blood knew the dangers well. Keeping my expression calm and my steps even, I blinked the amber away, left the steam of the caves and approached the owl.

"I am listening," I said, setting my candle atop a standing stone and taking up stance a few feet away. I dropped my small pack – little more than the blanket I'd salvaged from the herder's hut, affixed with rope and leather strips – and added a habitual, "My goddess."

The owl blinked once and a voice came to me.

"Hessa," I sensed Eang, in and around the owl. "You must listen to me. There is much you must know."

I held still.

"Esach's child is dead, though the goddess lives."

My mouth dried. I thought of the labouring goddess, alone in her pain, and momentarily mourned with her. But my mourning ran deeper than that – that child was the bounty of the harvest, one and the same. Their death meant the deaths of many Eangen in a long, hungry winter.

"She told me you were in the High Halls," Eang's voice held blatant warning. "Why? You are not a High Priestess, Hessa."

"I was drugged by a priest of Lathian," I answered, fighting to keep a flash of exasperation from my face. How could Eang not know what the priest of another god had done to me, let alone think that I'd gone to the Halls willingly?

Then again, I was a reprobate. Perhaps she shouldn't have expected anything better from me. That thought, rather than fill me with guilt as it once had, made my heart feel stony.

"Where is that priest now?"

"I don't know," I replied. "Who attacked Rioux and the Archeress?"

"They fled," Eang said, denying me an answer without admitting that she simply didn't know. "But the gods of Ashaklon's order are everywhere, and Ashaklon himself may soon break free again. The balance of power in the upper realms has tipped too far. You must kill Omaskat quickly."

"Why me?" The question slipped out, charged by two months of suffering and struggle. Catching myself, I added, "Goddess... I need to understand. Please."

I felt her anger, but it was tainted with frustration. "No one else can touch him. Not even I."

I stared at the owl. "What?"

Eang's voice became steadier and more deliberate, rising through me like the beat of a drum. "The Gods of the Old World are awakening, Hessa; some of the greatest forces the world has ever seen... gods I bound millennia ago, with the greatest of them at their head. But there's something else coming, too. Two ancient forces are re-entering the world, head to head, one intent on stopping the other."

I kept my expression flat. This sounded all too familiar.

"The Gods of the Old World are dangerous, Hessa, but they are an enemy I know. I've slain and bound all of them before."

I shifted uncertainly at that. Eang had been able to bind the Gods of the Old World because of the Eangi's worship strengthening her, anchoring her to life, and her alliance with other gods like Oulden. But Oulden and many others were dead now, as were nearly all my kind.

Eang's next words made goosebumps race up my arms. "This other force… it is eating away the High Halls, stealing away our refuge. Did you see it? The white light in the north?"

I remembered the light that danced and swelled and had left the world below it faded. "I did."

"It comes from a white lake, in the north. The Gods of the Old World I can fight," Eang insisted, more to herself than to me. "But the power in this lake, so old it was nearly forgotten… it will obliterate us all. They are Omaskat's god. That is why he must be stopped."

Omaskat's god. So, Omaskat truly did not serve Gadr, and he was bound for a white lake. Just as I'd seen in my vision.

"They're one of the Four." My conclusion came naturally, buoyed by the memory of Shanich's ravings and Omaskat's insistence he served a true god – or at least an older one. "Aren't they? Deities that came before the Gods of the Old World. Thvynder and the Weaver, Eiohe and Imilidese."

For a very, very long moment, Eang did not speak. When she did, she was resigned, sober: "Yes. I believe so. I am too young to remember. The Gods of the Old World did all that they could to extinguish memory of them… a vanity we will all suffer for, now."

A great weight settled in my belly. However terrifying the thought of such an ancient, powerful deity was, at least I had a clearer understanding of what was going on, and why I should seek Omaskat by the white lake.

"But who they are is irrelevant right now," Eang continued. "Fate showed me that you would stand before Omaskat in the Hall, and that you would be the one to take his life. One of my own Eangi. Human enough to pass through his unnatural defenses, yet divine enough to defeat him. That is why I sent the vision to Svala. That is why you must kill Omaskat before he can do whatever he intends to do."

I stood there beneath the pines, mute and contemplative, until a question emerged, "Is that why my Fire dies around him? Your power cannot affect him?"

"Yes." The reply came simply, unashamed.

My heart, already cold, chilled still more. So, Eang had not held back her Fire when I faced Omaskat, back in the Algatt camp. That had been an outright lie.

"Is Omaskat a Vestige of some kind?" I inquired tonelessly.

Even though I could not see her, I felt Eang still. "What do you know of Vestiges?"

"I know I'm yours."

There was a fraction of silence, then Eang's voice lowered. "Who told you that?"

"Rioux and the Archeress," I said.

"Yes." Eang's response was flat. "And it is a blessing, Hessa. Do you not cherish your Eangi Fire? Do you not think it an honor to give your life for your goddess?"

My heart swelled at the same time as my mind took a cautious step back. True, Eang's Fire was powerful, but it was also jealous, submerging the power of the High Halls and all its potential. And perhaps it was an honor to die so a goddess might live, but I knew very clearly that it was not a fate I wanted, not now. There was no gratitude in Eang, no compassion or comprehension of the loss of human life. She would use me and forget I had ever existed.

"Hessa, you must kill Omaskat." Eang's voice was still cold, but it softened somewhat. Perhaps she could see something of my thoughts in my face, for she added, "Do this and the High Halls will be yours. You will have a seat of your own in my Hall, and whenever you choose, you may lay yourself down next to Eidr for the long sleep. Yes, I remember him, Hessa. He was my Eangi, too. I mourn him, too."

Her words struck me like stones, each one more painful than the last. There was regret in her voice, but it was hollow. She did not mourn Eidr, not truly.

"Hessa." When Eang repeated my name, there was pleading in her voice. The sound reached into my heart, searching for the devotion and passion I'd once borne for my goddess. But if it found any, it was lean and wan.

"If you swear that you will acquit me, and that I will have a place with Eidr in the High Halls when I die," I vowed, voice low, "then I will do everything in my power to kill Omaskat."

"Good." There was a change in Eang's tone, as if my solemnity had surprised her. The direction of her voice shifted. "Two days north of here on the road, you will find a village the Arpa overran but did not sack. There are weapons and supplies there. But you must be cautious. Do not invite the attention of Ashaklon's ilk. Where you can, shelter in Gadr's temples. The echo of him will conceal you."

I cocked my head at that. "What? Shelter in Gadr's temples?"

"Use him, do not worship him," Eang warned. "The God of the Mountain is not what he once was, in any case. You understand where Omaskat is going now? To the white lake?"

An eagle called from high overhead, its sharp cry bouncing from one side of the little valley to another. Eang's owl ruffled its feathers, disgruntled by the sound, and the doorway between the worlds glinted and rippled.

I nodded, pulling my eyes from the rift. "I saw him there, in a vision. Svala told me it's where the sky bled into the mountain."

"You saw Svala?" Eang's presence rushed forward, her words accusatory. "How? Where?"

I retreated a step. "In the High Hall. Ogam went to find her."

A long hiss curled through the forest. "My son? My son has returned?"

Abruptly the owl took flight and Eang's presence vanished. The bird plunged through the crack between worlds with a rustle of wings and a rush of heady, honeyed air.

Alone again, a knot formed in my throat. So, Eang had finally given me the answers I craved and assured me of a place in the High Halls.

Yet she had also confirmed that I was her Vestige, her confidence in her ability to subdue the Gods of the Old World felt too blind, and her tone when she'd spoken of Ogam made my skin crawl. Did the goddess not trust him?

For all his faults, Ogam had saved Sixnit and Vistic. He'd shown me the magic of the High Halls and given me the strength to break Quentis's curse. It was his name that had made Rioux and the Archeress hesitate in the High Halls. Not Eang's.

I leant against the rough bark of a tree, trying to sort my thoughts. I was a lone human in a war of the gods, a divine war that I'd never been prepared for and knew almost nothing about. But Eang didn't expect me to think or understand; I had my charge. All I needed to do was accomplish it.

I approached the rift between worlds and eyed it for a long moment. As if in response to my presence, it widened from a crack into a shimmering, sunset divide. My last visit to the High Halls had been in spirit; I'd no idea what would happen if I stepped through it in physical form, like the owl had.

But if I was in a war of the gods, and if my goddess could not be relied upon to protect me – from others, let alone herself – then I needed to protect myself. I needed a weapon to wield when Eang's fire failed.

"Do not let the gods see that you stole their magic."

I waited a few more moments to ensure that the owl would not return, then took up my pack and stepped through the rift.

The world flickered. My stomach wrenched and I stumbled, reaching out to catch myself. My hand met cool stone, rough with lichen – a standing stone, in an identical valley to the one I'd just left, with the same amber crack between worlds. But it was night, and when I looked up towards the valley's roof, I glimpsed the tell-tale division of the High Halls – the violet west, the snow-clouded south, the ominous white of the north and the rich dark of a midnight east.

A temerarious smile snatched at my lips. I'd done it. I'd passed into the High Halls, alive and whole. Now all I needed to do was gather supplies and slip back into the Waking World before anyone knew I was here.

Then I saw the mist. It surged towards me and wrapped around my ankles, rising to my waist and chest, my throat and the crown of my head like an inquisitive snake. I flinched as it pried into my nose and mouth, and down into my lungs. My heartbeat faltered and I held absolutely still, fingers poised to sketch a rune.

The mist seemed to find what it was looking for – a honeyed glow beneath the smolder of Eang's Fire. At once it disentangled from my lungs and mouth and swirled away, broader and broader. I might have sworn I saw a figure there, bowing in concession as the mist faded.

I blinked hard and dragged even breaths until my heartbeat steadied. Then I unslung my pack, shook the tension out of my shoulders, and went to work.

Half an hour later, I darted back into the Waking World. There had been a version of the Algatt village in the High Halls, empty and desolate, but my pack bulged with pine needles and mushrooms, berries and wildflowers. My belly and flask were full of the stolen water, and as I reentered the sunny warmth of the Waking World again, I felt stronger than ever.

Resolute, I wove back through the mountain to the Waking World's Algatt village. There, in the musty shadows of the house I'd explored earlier, I took up the lynx shield. I looked it over and tested its strength, and when I was satisfied, slung it over my back.

Then I turned my feet north.

THIRTY-TWO

My journey to the Algatt village Eang had mentioned was solitary and uneventful, and by the time I saw signs of a settlement, my bleeding was nearly through. Nonetheless, I took a moment to prepare before I went on, stashing my pack in a tree and slipping my hand through the grip of my shield. Then I took Estavius's knife in my right hand and crept towards the settlement.

Ten minutes later I stood in the overgrown center of the village, stomach sick and eyes round with horror. Albor and Iskir had been awful sights, sights that would stay with me forever. But this Algatt village was something else entirely.

Bodies hung from beams like dolls, strung up by nooses, clothing and even their own looping braids. Some had been alive when they were displayed; the veins in their faces were ruptured, their nails torn away and their throats raw from struggling. Their toes – some bare, others booted – brushed the tops of weeds, sprouted up in once well-worn pathways; a tuft of grass here, a winking wildflower there.

I walked past a row of corpses, gawking and gagging all at once. The Algatt were killers, yes, but like the Eangen they struck to kill. Quickly. They did not torture or toy with their opponents.

The Arpa who did this had taken their time. There were men, women and children, old and young, strong and weak. Most of them had been brutalized in some way, yet even that was not the most disconcerting part.

Not one of them had eyes. Every Algatt here had been blinded, forming a sea of blinded bodies that I had seen in my vision, back in Souldern.

And then there were the souls. The weight of them crept into my new senses, seeping up from the earth on which they'd died – where they lay trapped, screaming and begging for a priest to release them. I felt them in my bones, from my toes to my twitching fingertips.

I vomited, stumbled back to my pack, and ran.

I did not stop running until I found a temple. It was not hard to recognize, built deep into a cliff face above the trees. Its triangular mouth had been carved in the same manner as the archway in the Algatt house, depictions of Gadr entwined with the complex Gatti runes for sacredness, shelter and worship.

I steeled myself and ducked inside. It was cool and damp and dominated by a tall, slim standing stone carved with more Algatt runes, but there was plenty of light and, most importantly, it was free of blinded bodies.

I tried to sit but could not. How could I rest on ground sacred to Gadr? How could I be still when I had just seen something so horrific?

I stepped up to the temple mouth and angled my face to the sun. My mind quieted momentarily, but the images raced back in. A blinded man hung by his feet. A blinded little girl, her stiff fingers tangled in a noose of her own braids.

How could the Arpa have been so cruel? I recalled the faces of the legionaries I knew. They were not necessarily good men, but they were ordered, regimented. Strict. I could not see Polinus permitting something like this, nor Commander Athiliu, nor even Castor, who despised we "barbarians" so much.

But Quentis… Quentis I could imagine doing such a thing. He would do it in the sight of his twisted gods and cherish every cry.

Following this line of thought, it struck me that the bodies had to be at least two months old, presuming they'd died just before the Algatt's push into Eangen – timing which the overgrown village paths affirmed.

Yet they were barely decayed and there were no signs of scavengers. There hadn't even been flies.

I shuddered and retreated into the cool of the cave, arms clasped over my chest. Perhaps human Arpa had slaughtered that village, as Eang had told me. But I suspected something more than men had been involved. Was this the will of one of their gods?

I paced the temple until my nerves settled. But with composure came the reality that Eang had sent me to the village to arm and supply myself, a charge which I had abandoned. Again.

I glanced out the cave mouth at the angle of the sun. I had two more hours of daylight, give or take. That was enough to get to the village and back.

Half-heartedly, I took up my shield and knife and returned to the settlement. This time I avoided the corpses, though it was hard not to see their fluttering clothes in the corner of my eye or feel the gut-watering distress of their souls beneath my feet.

I ducked into the first house. Chairs had been overturned but moldering bread, meat and shriveled vegetables still sat on the tabletop. Knowing Algatt homes now, I headed for the cave at the back. There in sealed jars, I found the last of the winter's seeds and nuts, and wrapped bundles of dry meat and hard cheese tucked into a dry shelf in the rock.

Weapons and clothing were just as easy to find. I armed myself with a bearded axe, a brace of hatchets and a broad, practical hunting knife. I found a long mail vest to supplement my padded armor and belted it around my waist. I also found a bow with a draw I could manage and packed it with a quiver of arrows and three extra bowstrings.

I took all the food I could carry and headed back to the temple as the sun began to set – the sustenance I'd taken from the High Halls, after all, were intended to feed my magic, not nourish my travelling body.

I didn't intend to look back, but as I reached the village boundary the weight of the souls slowed me, soundlessly begging and pleading and clawing at my thoughts. I stopped and shut my eyes, unable to stop thinking of Albor.

Was this what I would feel if I returned home, now? Would the souls of Eidr and Yske and Sixnit's husband Vist keen beneath the earth and tear at me, because I'd failed to release them?

All at once my solitude and guilt crashed down upon me, as heavy and as crushing as it had been after Shanich's attack. Distantly, I recalled the warmth of Eidr's arms and Yske's laugh, the songs of the Eangi on a winter night and a thousand small moments, small memories, all poisoned by my failure.

My eyes dragged to the ground. The souls here were Algatt, my enemies; they were none of my concern. But that division did not seem so great just then, with Albor before my eyes and misery beneath my feet.

I wasn't sure I could do anything for them, but I crouched. There in the earth, I sketched the runes for release and peace, but when it came time to infuse them with Eang's Fire, I reached beneath it instead. I pulled at a wisp of stolen amber magic. Eang's Fire immediately arose, burning and forcing me away, but I tried again. Finally, I found a thread of power that Eang could not smother, and I pushed it into the runes.

Under my feet, the souls eased. Their silent cries faded and the sensations of the wider world slid back in: the song of a single, brave bird; the brush of the wind down the crags; and the cool of the coming night.

A strange feeling overtook me as I stood up, guilt merging with resolve and a hollow, aching grief. Unable to bear the sight of the village's empty homes and abandoned corpses any longer, I turned my feet away.

Now armed, recovered and well-supplied, I returned my focus to finding Omaskat. I sipped tea made from High Halls' pine needles each night, and though the supplies I'd brought back from that other world did eventually dwindle, their sleeping power grew in my blood and bones. This boon and its mystery helped take my mind from my loneliness, but only just. My dreams each night were full of Eidr and Yske and Sixnit, memories of Eangi songs and the security of a dozen round shields locked with mine. I even thought of Nisien, of the consolation

I'd found when he rolled his bedroll out next to me, or the kindness in the enigmatic Estavius's eyes as the wind and rain howled around him.

Still, my sense of purpose increased. I might never see Nisien and Estavius again, but every day I grew closer to Omaskat and my redemption. Every day, I grew closer to a reunion with Eidr in the High Halls. Then my questions, my doubts and fears would cease to matter – or so I told myself.

I had no maps to guide me, so I determined that the swiftest way to find the white lake would be to locate the peak it sat below. But the peaks here were gradual, low and largely tree-covered, while the one above the lake in my vision had been jagged and towering.

I had to go deeper into the mountains.

I travelled with the sunrise to my right and the sunset to my left. Villages were not infrequent, nor were herder's huts and temples, so I'd no need to sleep without shelter. But the settlements unnerved me. Over the next four days, I found two more that had been abandoned and slept in their temples – caves, again, as the first one had been. In the third town I came across the remains of a huge pyre. I found fragments of skulls among the ashes and no souls in the earth, and left at a run.

That was the only night I spent out in the open. The mountains were stark and barren here, lending no shelter save one bent pine. I had to climb ten minutes off the path to reach it and when I did, I almost climbed back down. I was incredibly exposed. But light retreated over the western peaks and clouds closed in from the east. I would soon be out of daylight.

I had to make the best of it. The tree smelled of sap and the wind was clean, whisking the heat of the day away up the long, curving valley. I pulled off my boots to air and sat on my bedroll while I ate and watched the light flee from the western sky.

Deep in the night, I awoke to the clatter of hooves. My heart lunged into my throat and, before my eyes were half-open, I'd seized my bow.

It was the Arpa. They passed through the valley in a trail of silver and horseflesh, their armor glinting under a thinly veiled moon.

I dropped onto my belly and searched for Nisien and his bay mount. But every man looked the same from this distance – except for a handful who wore no armor or helmets and rode no horses. They trailed behind, bound to one another by the neck.

The prisoners wore fitted trousers and angular tunics, and one of them – maybe female, by her dress and proportions – had a wild knot of pale red hair. Algatt?

I watched until the last swish of a horse's tail vanished over the next ridge, then sat back into my heels to think. Why would Polinus drag captive Algatt around the mountains?

Unless these were not the legionaries I knew. I cast a long look back up the valley, wondering. There had been around the right number of men for Polinus's group and they had all been mounted. I thought it unlikely that the legionaries responsible for the Algatt slaughter would all be riders, let alone still be so ordered after a year in the north.

No, these Arpa were almost certainly Polinus's. Perhaps he was using the captive Algatt as guides?

I came up into a crouch, watching the spot where the party had vanished with new intensity. If the Arpa could use Algatt to find their goal, so could I.

THIRTY-THREE

The Arpa were easy to follow, even on a rocky stretch of mountain. All I had to do was pick my way along a predictable trail of manure. The horses also required grazing, which meant that as soon as they passed through a green valley, the legionaries stopped to make camp.

I diverted off the road. Evergreen forests folded in around me, murky in the night and pungent with sap. I stashed my pack up into the boughs of one and proceeded with only my weapons.

By now I had spent enough time with the Arpa to know their scouting routines. I crept as close as I dared, avoided two scouts, then proceeded in an awkward belly-crawl.

I scraped spider-silk from my face and peered ahead. The trees thinned here, allowing patches of grass and stalwart alpine flowers, pale in the moonlight. The horses were already at their ease, watched by half of the men. The remainder of the legionaries erected tents or gathered around a quick-flowing creek, and a second pair of scouts circled the valley further west.

The prisoners were with the horses. One by one, the legionaries permitted them to relieve themselves a dozen paces away from me.

I slithered forward, keeping to the heaviest shadows.

They let the red-haired woman go last. As I had hoped, their Arpa sensibilities meant that they gave her privacy behind a thick fir.

I cupped a hand over my mouth and made a low, mournful warble. It was a fair impression of a sunbelly finch, but the song of a sunbelly was out of place at night. Any northerner knew that.

The woman, in the midst of gathering her skirts around her waist, glanced towards me.

I warbled again. The other Algatt looked up too, but surreptitiously. Their guards just scanned their surroundings absently and continued their conversation.

The woman edged deeper into the firs.

I slipped closer. Closer. Then I hooked the cold head of my axe around her throat.

"Algatt," I whispered.

She instantly recognized my accent. "Eangen," she grunted back.

"Eangi," I corrected.

She stiffened. She was perhaps thirty, with deepening lines about the eyes and so much weariness in her that I almost felt compassion.

"If you answer my questions, I'll give you a knife and distract the Arpa so you can escape."

She did not answer for an instant, then gave a tight, "Why?"

"I swear it upon Eang herself."

The woman's breath escaped in a hiss. "Why?"

It was a fair question. I was still asking myself the same thing. Her people had slaughtered Albor. Iskir. Hot Eangi anger smoldered in my gut at the thought. But then I remembered Quentis, the village without eyes and its trapped souls.

"I saw what they did to your villages," I said finally.

She took another two heartbeats to think. "Fine."

"Where is the white lake?"

"The white lake? There are three. All east in high valleys, where the mountains end in the Headwaters."

My heart swelled. "Do you swear it?"

"I swear it on Gadr. Where's the knife?"

I pressed its hilt into her back. "It's here. Why are you still in the mountains?"

"We were sent back to see if it was safe." Her voice faltered. "It's not."

"Are you leading them to the other Arpa?"

I saw her throat contract.

"Woman!" one of the guards called.

"Almost," she replied to him. Lowering her voice, she said to me, "Yes, we're taking them to the last place the Arpa were seen."

"Where?"

"East."

"All right." I had a dozen more questions, but I needed to get away while I could. I eased myself backwards and set the hunting knife on the ground beneath her. "A distraction. Within an hour."

I vanished into the spider-silk and shadows.

I began to climb. I moved across the southern side of the valley, sheltered by the trees and a solid wall of shadow. I had hidden anything that might glint in my pack and carried only my bow, low to my side.

When I reached a safe distance, I slit the ends of my fingers. My hands were not as steady as they might have been, but they quietened as I streaked blood across my eyelids and bottom lip to begin the ritual. No amber glistened in the starlight – Eang's Fire remained dominant.

What I intended to do I had seen just once before.

That day, I had crouched beside Eidr in tall grasses. The sky beyond was pink with dawn and a cool mist pooled in the rocky ravines of northern Eangen. Nearby, Ardam slit the ends of his fingers and touched the blood to his eyelids and lips, murmuring while the laden heads of the grasses rustled over him in an ever-changing pattern of swirls and bends and collisions.

One stalk of grass bowed as a bleary sparrow landed, sending it down in a graceful arc.

Two dozen Eangi and Eangen warriors spun on the bird. It exploded in a flurry of wings and shrieked into the dawn.

Ardam went still. We all did, ears straining for any sign that the Algatt had been alerted.

The blood on Ardam's face was nearly dry by the time he signaled for us to relax. Together, we bellied up to the top of the rise and peered down like a row of well-armed, shield-backed salamanders.

Twenty tents of various shapes hid among a young, autumn forest. There were no herds here, though two dozen horses grazed further south in a haze of mist. Algatt moved between the tents, crouching over pitted fires and beginning the morning's routine.

"Eang, Eang. The Brave, the Vengeful, the Swift and the Watchful." I watched Ardam as he spoke, his eyes focused on the distant horses. "The Wrath and the Fire in our bones."

I saw a disturbance run through the animals. They lifted their heads and shifted on their feet, their muffled whickers carrying through the mist to us, high on our hill.

"Slayer of the Old Gods, Conqueror of the New. The Setting Sun and the Rising Moon."

A horse reared in sudden panic. As soon as it dropped back down, the mass of equine flesh split in a thunder of hooves.

Ardam let out a long breath.

"What did you do?" someone asked.

"Put the Fire in their blood," Ardam replied, settling his shoulders back. His skin had paled against the black streaks of kohl around his eyes, but that didn't stop him from peeling his lips back in a bare-toothed grin. He jerked his chin up to one side. "Now go take care of their masters, my hellions."

Now, as I crouched on the dark mountainside over the Arpa camp, I finished, "Slayer of the Old Gods, Conqueror of the New... The Setting Sun. The Rising Moon."

All at once, I felt dizzy. My cuts and scrapes knit of their own accord and, down in the valley, a horse whinnied. I leant forward and focused harder, running one hand across a forehead slick with sweat.

I couldn't see much from this distance, but it was hard to miss the break when it came. Eighty panicked horses scattered across the valley.

The chaos was glorious. Weak as I felt, I stifled a laugh. My exhilaration was only tempered by the knowledge that my sweet Melid was somewhere among them, frightened by the heat in her veins. I even considered going to find her, but the thought was passing.

It took the Arpa over an hour to recover all their horses. I used the time to finish rounding the valley, but my limbs were slower and weaker than they'd been in days.

A tendril of fear wrapped around my drumming heart. I had not expected this. Ardam had been pale, yes, but he had gone from the ritual into battle with little falter. Yet Ardam had also been a veteran Eangi war chief of forty years, one of the oldest and most experienced. I was not.

A wave of dizziness struck me. I sank down onto an outcropping of rock and bowed my head, willing my fluttering pulse to steady.

Then I felt the cold. It pushed in around me, turning and swirling like a cyclone of autumn leaves.

This was not Ogam's cold. Ogam's cold was sharp and crisp; it brightened the mind and made the teeth ache. This cold, this was heavy and thick, like clammy clay – like a corpse.

Eang's voice reverberated in the recesses of my mind.

Do not invite the attention of Ashaklon's ilk.

"There you are." The voice crept through my mind, invading each corner and cracking it wide. "Ah… I smell the iron upon you, servant of Eang. And… something other. A winter wind? The blessing of thunder?"

Down in the valley, men shouted, and hooves clattered on rock. Each sound came to me muffled, as if the mysterious presence suppressed it.

"What did you do to them?" The voice rippled with amusement.

"I put Fire in their horses' blood."

"Ah." The thing made a hissing, rasping sound – a laugh? Whatever it was, it ended in a contented sigh. "Now, tell me where your mistress is."

"I don't know," I said, not bothering to hide how heavily that truth weighed on me. "Who… who are you?"

"I have been called Styga by some, though your people never had a name for me…" As they spoke, the presence tightened around me.

Time stretched on, marked by the stifled shouts and whinnies from down in the valley. "Hmm… It is as Rioux said. You were there at the fall of Ashaklon."

Lies wedged in my throat. I had no way of knowing how much this creature – possibly god – already knew, and I doubted untruths would go over well.

"Yes," I responded as levelly as I could. "I helped Oulden and Eang destroy him."

"Destroy? No. You bound him anew," the presence reminded me. Their grip undulated and cinched around me, like a coiling snake. "Only one force can destroy a god. There is no High Hall in such a death, no chance of return. It is… as if they never were. That is true destruction."

I knew they were baiting me. I ran my teeth over the inside of my lip. Whoever Styga was, whatever they were, they wanted me to talk.

My hunger for the truth won out. "What could do that? The light in the north? One of the Four?"

The cold solidified in front of me. One by one, it gathered the shadows and robed itself in them, drawing smooth tendrils and draping folds. Then it lifted one hand and leached starlight from the sky. The light dribbled over the featureless orb of their head like water and seeped into the lines of a hairless, genderless face.

A being of starlight and shadow, just like the one Ogam said had attacked Esach over Souldern.

"One of the Four? Hm. Yes," Styga told me. "That power sleeps. Or so it did. So it has. The God-Killer, that is what they are."

"God-Killer? Are they your enemy?"

The being drew down more light from the sky and dappled it across its cheeks, imitating my freckles.

"In a way," Styga said. "While it sleeps, no. When it rises, yes."

"Then let me go." I surprised myself with the strength in my voice. "Your enemy is mine, too."

"Oh no," the being tsked. "A common enemy, yes, but you and I are very much at odds. I am a God of the Old World and your patron is of the New."

A God of the Old World. I was facing down another ancient god, but this time I felt no surprise. Suspicions affirmed, I settled into my heels.

"She and her cohorts killed half of my siblings and bound me with the rest," they said. "Would you forgive such a thing?"

No, I wouldn't. And if they wanted Eang to stay dead, I couldn't be left alive.

"Eang sent me to stop this… God-Killer from rising," I told them. "To stop the man called Omaskat. Think about what you just said, divinity. This power can annihilate you, too. So let me go stop it."

Styga considered me more directly for a long minute. Slowly, they brought their nose up to my cheek and inhaled. "Perhaps you can… A human vessel, a spark of the divine?"

They stepped back and glanced down at the valley. "Go then. Stop Omaskat. You have caused these men chaos, and in that I see a… kindred spirit. But," their voice tipped up in warning, then dropped into a whisper, "I will be watching."

THIRTY-FOUR

I did not see the Arpa or the being of starlight and shadow again, and after a few more days of eastern travel, I found myself on a broad, windy ridgeline. Mountains and high valleys opened all around me except to the south, where Iskir's smooth expanse of rock and marshes hazed under the summer sun.

To the east, the mountains divided into a deep, tiered valley. And there, at its furthest reaches, sunlight glistened off a pristine, milky lake.

The sight of it made all my trepidation evaporate like candle smoke. It was four days away at most.

Excitement spurred me on. I skittered into the valley by a herder's path and jogged until my legs were jittery with fatigue.

In the forest below, I slowed to catch my breath. Birdsong swelled around me and sun glinted through the treetops, where birds flitted branch to branch. And beyond them, above the canopy, the long stream of a narrow waterfall frayed in the wind.

I walked until I found the broad pool at the base of the waterfall. The water spattered into a ledge just above my head, and slid down into the pool in a smooth, seamless sheet; gentle and inviting.

I couldn't pass the opportunity by, not as sweaty and stinking and hopeful as I was. I bundled my weapons and clothing on a rock and plunged into the water with a muffled shriek. I came up sputtering and laughing and dragged my hands over my hot cheeks, relishing the cold water.

I was happy. It was an insidious feeling, terrifying in its own right.

Yes, my doubts about Eang wormed through my soul. Yes, I had no idea when Omaskat would arrive at that distant white lake. But I was so close now. This time, when I met the traveler, I would not allow myself to be disarmed by his kindness, as I had on our first meeting. Nor would I lack the strength as I had on our second. With two months of hardship fortifying my heart and the aid of my magic from the High Halls, I was sure that this time I'd defeat him.

I had no soap, but I floated until my fatigued body cooled and much of my sweat had washed away. Then I clambered back to shore, energized and ready to be on my way.

I heard a clatter. There on the rocks, the hindquarters of a raccoon protruded from my pack.

"Hey!" I snatched up a dripping stone and hurled it through the air. "Get away! Go!"

The raccoon's legs scrabbled. Whatever it had a hold of – the last of my barley cakes, I suspected – it couldn't pull it free of the bag. But it also wasn't willing to let go.

My second stone hit its flank. I came directly after it, naked, cold and angry.

The raccoon's head popped free. It turned its face towards me, not unlike an Eangi with its black-rimmed eyes, and jerked a bundle after it. Before I could intercept, the creature took off at a shambling run, half holding, half biting the packet.

I snatched up a hatchet and hurled it. It thudded into a tree, but the raccoon skittered sideways and leapt for the safety of another high pine. I threw rock after rock, shouting and cursing.

By the time it reached the pine's high spread of branches, I was laughing instead. The animal perched on the branch and began to eat, raining crumbs down towards me.

"I've a soft spot for them, myself," a male voice commented.

My hand shot to the haft of my axe, resting on my pack.

The man stood calmly, a pace away. He wore fitted trousers and a broad leather belt, revealing a muscular chest that sagged with age.

I wanted to bolt for my clothes, but I didn't dare take my eyes off him. I hefted the axe instead. "Who are you?"

The man scrutinized me, impassive to my state of undress. His nose had been broken several times and his hair escaped from a long, single braid around a weather-worn face. "Where are you headed?"

I decided to risk grabbing my tunic. I put half a dozen paces between us and jerked the garment over my head. Feeling less absurd, I snatched up my shield and faced him again at guard, watching him around its edge.

The man laughed at me. "Where are you headed, woman?"

I kept my axe out behind me, its blade – and potential angle of attack – hidden from sight. "You're Algatt."

A smile twitched across his face. Over his shoulder, more crumbs rained down. "Yes. Calm yourself. I'm not going to harm you."

When he smiled, something about his face struck me as familiar. "You're one of the men the Arpa had captive," I accused.

The man pushed out his lower lip, considering. "Maybe. Maybe we've met elsewhere."

I shifted my feet on the rocks, finding a better grip. My legs still dripped, and I could feel my hair soaking my tunic. "Tell me your name."

"You wouldn't believe me."

"I might."

He glanced up as the raccoon chattered. The cloth that had wrapped the cakes floated down onto the pine bed.

I decided to take a different tactic. "Are you human?"

The man burst out laughing and clapped his hands on his tanned belly. "Yes, yes! Good question. Gods below, miscreants above!"

"Yes, you are human?"

He waved a finger at me and sidled towards the pool. He dipped the toe of a gnarled, bare foot into the water. "Ooh, that's cold."

Suspicion crept up my spine. "Are you Gadr?"

"Yes! And you," his voice darkened for the first time, "are an Eangi."

I kept my shield steady. So this, this was Gadr? God of my enemies, god who had let his people loose on my land like rabid dogs?

"What do you want?" I demanded.

"You've been sleeping in my temples." He waded into the water, soaking his trousers up to the knee. He wore no legwraps, and as he moved the fabric stuck to his legs. "Freeing my people. Talking down Gods of the Old World. Even releasing the souls of the dead, according to Frir. Tell me, daughter of Eang, why would you do that? *How* did you do that?"

My throat constricted. "They were trapped. I'm an Eangi."

Gadr peered up at me. "My people should not have responded to Eang's power."

I pressed my lips closed, inwardly berating myself. Now that Gadr knew something was amiss, would his prying eyes notice something about me, some sign of what I'd found in the High Halls?

Gadr advanced two steps. My muscles tensed and I raised the shield another fraction, but the god of the Algatt only scrutinized me for a long minute, then guardedly inquired, "Why are you here?"

I chose my words. "I need to pass through the mountains."

"To the white lakes," he added, considering me from behind a clump of hair sagging out of his braid. "Yes, my people told me. Why would you go there?"

"Eang sent me to do something."

"Elaborate."

"Perhaps you should speak with her," I deflected.

Gadr waved a suggestive hand at the sky. "Then summon her."

I hovered, unsure how to proceed.

"I thought so." He bent to peer through the surface of the water in the posture of an inquisitive toddler, bottom stuck out and palms braced on his knees. Meanwhile, the raccoon finished the last of his meal and scrambled higher up the tree.

"Did you see what they did?" Gadr asked, his eyes flickering after rivulets. "The Arpa?"

I hesitated. "In the villages?"

Gadr continued to stare down into the water, passive at first, then scowled and straightened back up. His gaze met mine, and his humor, his confidence, flaked away to reveal a jagged grief.

"The Gods of the Old World forced me to watch. I heard each of their cries. I felt each of them die."

At the last, he gave bare-toothed grimace and flexed his jaw, locking away some of the grief again. I remained quiet, wondering if Eang had felt anything like this at the death of her people – and knowing she probably hadn't.

"I've been freeing their souls myself, but the task is... heavy." The Algatt god cleared his throat and settled his face into a fresh, narrow-eyed façade. "So, I thank you, Eangi. And in thanks for that, I will not tell your mistress that you drank the waters of the High Halls."

My fingers clenched on my axe and shield. "I did not—"

"Oh, hush," Gadr chided. "How else could you free souls devoted to another god? Our whole world is shattering; I hardly care if one of Eang's chattels has a little too much ichor in her veins, especially if you're using it to free my dead."

"Ichor?" I repeated, as if I didn't recall the amber glistening in my blood.

He surveyed me with marked disapproval. "Why did you think we forbid living humans from feasting in the Halls? It's one of the few things we've always agreed on. Now the dead, a little divine mead and bread won't do a thing to them. But you? Living and breathing?"

I bit the inside of one lip, trying to keep myself quiet. Gadr clearly had information and insight that I did not – and I needed it. If I could keep him talking, who knew what I might inadvertently learn. "What do you mean?"

"I mean, little Eangi," Gadr replied, "that the Halls transform every living being into something more than it once was, as I'm sure you're finding out. Though considering how you reek of Eangi Fire, I take it they haven't mixed well?"

I didn't reply.

"Well," Gadr shrugged, "I'm not your god, why should I care? No more divine secrets for you. Except for… one thing. You should know, I did not order my people to annihilate the Eangi when they fled south. By the time I came to my senses, it was done. I want you to know that. I want your mistress to know that."

I was taken aback. Such transparency, let alone such a confession, seemed out of place for the god who had been sending his people to raid and pillage mine for centuries. Was he toying with me, or had the slaughter of his people made him soft?

Explanation delivered, the God of the Mountain frowned. "Now… you need to go to the white lakes?"

I retreated half a step. "…Yes?"

Gadr straightened and strode towards me, hand outstretched. "Then I will take you."

I kept my axe and shield raised. "Why?"

"You not only freed my people's souls, but you rescued them from the Arpa," he waggled his hand. "I still owe you. Come. I have a… faster road."

The hair on the back of my neck prickled. The raccoon had gone quiet, and in the place of its scrabbling I heard the distant, urgent hoot of an owl.

"I thank you for your kindness," I said carefully, "but I'll continue on foot."

His eyebrows rose. "I will consider my debt to you paid by the offer."

"Perhaps, instead," I suggested, more tightly than I intended, "you might answer a question."

"I might."

"Why did you steal Vistic? The baby?"

Gadr considered me for another long moment, then let out a bark of laughter that held more disgust than humor. The water in his beard fell like rain as he scratched it vigorously with both hands.

"Steal him?" he said around his out-thrust jaw and raking fingers. "Omaskat gave him to me for safekeeping, woman. But Ogam can be rather aggressive. And I'm a poor nursemaid."

With that he wiped off his hands on his bare chest – leaving his beard in disarray – and made for the trees. The raccoon skittered down and leapt onto his shoulders, prattling and clutching at his hair.

I started after him, pale with shock. Omaskat was the one who had stolen Vistic from Sixnit? Anger rushed through me, but confusion was right behind it. The traveler had shown interest in Sixnit in the Hall of Smoke, yes, and he had asked me about the baby. But what did it mean? And why, after stealing him, why would Omaskat give Vistic to Gadr?

"Gadr—" I started after the god.

"My debt is paid." Without looking back, the god of the Algatt flapped a hand at me and strode off into the pines.

"But why did Omaskat—"

"You're the one looking for him – ask him yourself," Gadr retorted. With a final chatter from the raccoon, the two of them vanished.

I was left stunned and confused beside the pool.

THIRTY-FIVE

A t long last, I came to the first white lake. It was small, cradled between sheer cliffs where a bird of prey spun. There was an abandoned village nearby and, since it was late in the day, I slept in the comfort of an Algatt bed. After Gadr's visit, I'd decided to stop seeking shelter in temples, never mind Eang's recommendation. She clearly had not expected Gadr to take notice of my presence, and she had been wrong.

The second lake was half a day further on, long and narrow and capped by a waterfall. The windblown tail of white vanished into a lush evergreen canopy, where it joined a river and snaked away toward a single, familiar peak.

I stepped out onto the rocky shore of the third lake at sunset and tremulously lowered my pack. There before me stretched the landscape from my vision. Lush green meadows crept around huge boulders towards lapping waves. Aspen and birch, pine and spruce flanked me, while in the north-east the great mountain rose.

My heart hammered against my ribs and I battled the urge to run, to scour every corner of the lake in search of Omaskat. I couldn't afford to be rash, not here. I unfastened my shield from my pack and pulled my axe from the leather loop at my belt. Then I settled my shoulders and drew a deep, preparatory breath.

"Eang, Eang," I murmured to the wind, "I'm here."

Leaving my pack behind, I cautiously approached the edge of the lake. Pebbles ground beneath my boots and flowers waved among the soft grasses, transitioning from grey to white the closer I came to the lake. At the shore itself I crouched, keeping one eye on my surroundings as I set down my axe and dipped my fingers in the cool, opaque water.

There was power here. It clung to my fingers and hummed through my bones, even after I shook the water away. It reminded me of what I'd felt in Lathian's temple, radiating from beneath the stone floor, but this was different. Fuller. More whole.

Furthermore, unlike the other two white lakes I'd passed, nothing grew within a pace of this one's perimeter. Instead, the grasses and flowers ended in sunbaked rock. No birds or insects skimmed the surface. The natural world cradled this lake, but it did not dare touch it.

I swept my surroundings with another wary look, then sat back into my heels. I reached out towards the lake again, but this time with the remnant of the High Halls' amber honey. I kept the memory soft, gentle – unobtrusive enough that Eang's Fire did not react.

The air above the lake rippled and faltered. The swelling white light I'd seen in the High Halls, the one that had dominated the north and left it faded, materialized between me, the lake, and the looming, imperious peak of the highest mountain. The light was vague here, visible only to that stretch of my will, but it was undeniably present.

My nerves fluttered. I withdrew to the rim of grass and rustling wildflowers and waited, adjusting my axe and letting the solidity of its haft root me in the real world. Eventually my honeyed sight closed over and the valley returned to its natural, Waking World state. But I knew that there was nothing natural about this lake.

As I processed this, my gaze compulsively swept again for danger. And this time, it found movement.

An Arpa legionnaire inched from the forest to the south. I had one moment to turn, one moment to see the bow in his hands before he drew the string back.

An arrow slammed into my shield, inches from my face. I fell back a step, dropping low and covering as much of my body as possible.

My mind staggered up to speed. My attacker was definitely an

Arpa legionary, though his gear looked battered and worn. But before I could decide if he was Polinus's or not, another arrow struck the stones at my feet, its clatter disconcertingly loud in the peace of the high alpine lake.

Three more archers appeared, with more shadows moving behind them among the trees. My muscles sang with tension. I could take a few of them down with Eang's Fire, but likely not before one of their arrows found its mark. And what if Estavius and Nisien were among their ranks? What if, in my Algatt clothing, they didn't recognize me yet?

"Polinus!" I shouted. "Stand down!"

Another arrow flew past my head and I dropped an inch lower. My eyes darted to my own bow, fastened to my pack a dozen feet away.

I darted forward, crouching over my pack with the shield between me and my assailants. Another arrow slammed into the wood, this one so hard I heard the wood crack. I had to move. But there was little cover between me and the trees. The only destination I had was a boulder, a further ten paces away.

I shoved my axe back through its loop, seized my pack and bolted. Two more arrows whisked past me as I hurled the pack into cover and threw myself after it.

I dropped my shield and snatched at the bindings of my bow. It came free with painstaking slowness, but I'd had the sense to leave it strung. I pulled three arrows from the quiver inside my pack, fanned them between my fingers as I'd been taught, and nocked the first.

I came onto one knee and listened, sheltered behind my boulder with the placid white lake at my back. A warm breeze whisked across my cheeks and I heard the churr of insects, but there was no thrum of bowstrings or clatter of arrows.

A being materialized to my left, dark and abyssal and vaguely human. I drew and loosed my arrow instantly and nocked a second, but my shot went right through them.

I threw Eang's Fire next in a sudden, sharp scream. The being staggered back, leaving me gasping against the boulder. But I'd barely dragged in two breaths before it surged forward again, shreds of ebony coalescing into features of starlight and shadow right in front of me.

Styga, the God of the Old World that I'd met on the mountainside, leant down until my eyes were full of them. The freckles they'd made in imitation of me looked like smears of true night sky, brushed over its nose, cheekbones and up around the curve of its eyes.

"You," they loomed. "How dare you!"

"I'm here to kill Omaskat," I panted. "You do not want to kill me."

"Oh, I very much do," they countered, sinking down into something like a crouch amid the grass and stones. "But that does not seem prudent."

I became aware of the crunch of boots. Legionaries came into sight, legionaries with a feline head on their shields, just like the shield in my vision in Souldern. These men were rugged and worn, their skin darkened by the sun and their gear a mismatched collection of Arpa and Algatt. It was their eyes, however, that caught my attention.

It was a subtle thing, more of a lack than an addition. These men's gazes held none of the blues or greens prevalent among the Arpa I knew. But nor were there browns. Instead, the overly dilated pupils of every Arpa here were rimmed with various shades of grey and black.

Like the flowers back in Souldern, when Ashaklon attacked. And, I realized, with dawning horror, the flowers that fluttered in the grasses around us now. However their condition had come to be, these men must be under the sway of the Old World's gods.

My heart was already pounding, but now the sound of rushing blood became all I could hear. Situations like this were the very reason no infant, no person, was left undevoted to a god. Eang's power would likely still protect me, but the Arpa gods should have protected these men, too. Unless their god was… involved?

My thoughts moved more and more quickly. I scanned their faces of the legionaries, eyes darting from one helmeted face to the next. Nisien was not there. Neither was Estavius, nor anyone else I recognized. These were not Polinus's men.

Only one other party of Arpa was here in these mountains. The ones that had butchered and driven out the Algatt.

My gaze flicked away from them, the horror of this realization wrapping around my throat. These men, these hands, had murdered children and instigated the destruction of Eangen. But at whose bidding? Styga's?

I considered running, using Eang's Fire to scatter Styga and their men. But where would a fight leave me? Injured and running, while I needed to be at this lake. I couldn't afford to leave with more legionaries on my tail, let alone these grey-eyed butchers and a vengeful god.

I didn't risk standing up, but I sat forward and rested my forearms on my knees in feigned nonchalance. I could only hope that Styga didn't hear the blood thundering in my ears. "I'm here to kill Omaskat. Are you and your dogs going to let me do that?"

In answer, Styga gave a breathy, muffled laugh and raised a hand to the Arpa. The men's shields, spears and swords lowered, though the legionaries' grey eyes remained blank and unaffected.

"How like your mistress you sound, Eangi." The god themselves retreated and gave a mocking half-bow. "Yes, we will. Follow me."

Patterns of light and shadow played off worn pathways as I entered the Arpa camp. It was tucked deep into the forest on the southern side of the valley, dozens of tents of Arpa canvas and Algatt hides fanning out around the ruins of an ancient structure. Eight weather-worn stone pillars vanished into the treetops, evenly spaced and smeared with lichen. I eyed these, wondering what they'd been, as Styga led me to the central tent.

A man stood beside its rolled and fastened flap. He wore no armor, but his bearing was one of unquestioned authority. His lean frame was clad in a knee-length tunic of burnt red edged with dark yellow, sleeveless and cinched at the waist by an Algatt belt. An Arpa sword with a round, dark wooden pommel had been affixed, but his shoes were Algatt-made

– simple leather, tied around the ankle. His eyes were grey like his men's, but he considered me with a keen, self-aware gaze as I stopped a few paces away.

Styga went forward to meet him and the two of them conferred in Arpa. I couldn't understand, but I kept one eye on them while I lowered my pack and evaluated the rest of the camp. Legionaries were every-where, moving about their daily business between trees, pillars and tents. I counted at least a hundred – with thirty currently armed and armored – but given the size of the camp there were likely more.

Grey-eyed and silent, they washed and mended clothing, tended cooking pots and sharpened weapons. The steady *clunk-crack-clatter* of someone chopping wood drifted through the air, but there was no singing, no conversation. Not even a cough.

Through the trees I saw several mountain goats being butchered, limp bodies strung up while shirtless, blood-spattered hunters separated skin from meat in precise, measured cuts. Memory of the Algatt's swinging, blinded bodies surged into my mind, and my stomach flipped.

Swallowing bile, I glanced back towards Styga and the singular, self-aware commander.

"Eangi, you are welcome to join us," Styga said, their less than corporeal body turning in a fluid twist. "This is Commander Telios."

The name sunk into my memory, buffeting aside thoughts of butchered Algatt until I found Nisien's voice in an abandoned Eangen village. Had he not called his former commanding officer Telios? The zealot of Lathian who hadn't permitted worship of Oulden?

There was a chance that Telios was a common Arpa name, but recent events hadn't bolstered my faith in coincidence.

Fear for Nisien wedged itself into my chest, vague and insubstantial but present. Polinus and his men were actively searching for the very company I now found myself in. If my instincts proved true, and Telios was who I thought he was, my own reunion with Quentis was only one of my pending concerns. What would happen when Nisien arrived and saw his old commander?

And if Telios was a zealot of Lathian, was it the Arpa's chief god who had stolen the color from these men's eyes?

"Styga tells me that you encountered another group of Arpa in the mountains," the grey-eyed man said, inclining his chin to me. "And that you are an ally. What is your name?"

My skin felt too warm in the afternoon light, my tension turning into a deep, nerve-fraying disquiet. "Hessa, of the Eangi."

Telios nodded and stood aside, gesturing for me to precede him into his tent. I rested a hand on the head of my axe and complied, but Styga did not follow. Glancing back over my shoulder, I saw them evaporate into thin air.

"Sit, if you like." Telios gestured to several stools, positioned around a crude table. Sunlight filled the worn canvas, revealing the rest of the tent to be populated by a cot, a stack of Algatt crates – full of gear and supplies – and a low altar.

The altar, however, was neither Arpa nor Algatt. Like the pillars outside, this was weatherworn and ancient. The tent had been constructed around it, and Telios had placed an idol of Lathian on its pocked stone surface. A bowl lay before it and when I drew closer, I caught the scent of Arpa incense. It invaded my nostrils and crept through my chest, reminding me of Quentis and my visit to Lathian's temple in the High Halls.

"Does your god mind occupying someone else's altar?" I inquired. I wasn't sure who this altar might once have belonged to, but it was certainly not Lathian.

Telios came to stand at my shoulder, one hand clasping the other behind his back. He smelled of the incense too: incense, woodsmoke and mountain air. "Why should he? Lathian belongs on every altar, in every land, even one as old and forgotten as this."

That image, and the placid dogmatism with which he painted it, irked me. "Who did it belong to?"

Telios gave a half-shrug. "The god in the lake. Though they have slept for so long, I doubt the worshipers who built this place even understood what they prayed to. And it was, as you can see, abandoned. This entire valley was, when we discovered it. I tore the vines from this altar myself."

The god in the lake. Omaskat's god.

"Now…" Telios adjusted his stance to consider me. His stance was solid as a hundred-year oak while his knees and shoulders remained loose, bespeaking an enviable agility and grace. But he stood just an inch too close, and the way he kept his hands behind his back made me stiffen. "These other Arpa, who are they and why are they here?"

"Commander Polinus, from the Ilia Gates," I said. There was no point in hiding this, not when Polinus and his men were already on their way. "Searching for you."

Telios's grey eyes narrowed, but at Polinus's name rather than the thought of being sought after. "Athiliu's dog? Well, that is unexpected, but it does not matter. They will find us soon enough, and Polinus and I can… work the matter out."

"What is there to work out?" I tried to bite my tongue, but my indignation came scathing and swift. "You should not be here. This is not your land, and what you've done – you've nearly destroyed the north."

"It is painful to adjust a broken bone, but if it heals badly, what use will it be?" Telios moved towards the table, where he picked up a leather cylinder. He uncapped it and withdrew a scroll like I had seen Quentis carrying at the Ilia Gates. "Come. Let me explain."

I remained where I was as he spread the parchment out, but even from this angle I could see a lattice of careful lines, interrupted by Arpa runes – like the ones Quentis had used in his wards.

"It's a map," the man explained unnecessarily. He turned the scroll towards me and weighted it down with a bronze statuette of an eagle, a whetstone, and two small containers. "This is the Pasidon, and this is the path my men and I took north, through the Headwaters. Do you recognize it?"

So, they had come through the Headwaters rather than Eangen, just as Nisien theorized so long ago in Souldern.

I approached the table. Telios followed the path he and his men had taken with one finger, departing an Arpa fortress east of the Pasidon and heading north through the wilderness, across the Headwaters and into the Algatt Mountains.

If I overlaid the Eangen map I had once seen with the Pasidon as a reference point, the map was familiar. But Eangen was so small, and the area Telios indicated occupied only the top third of the parchment. More lands spread out below, Souldern and other northern provinces merging with entirely new mountains, rivers, marshes, seas and artfully rendered settlements.

"This is the Empire?" I asked, indicating the last two-thirds of the page.

The captain nodded but didn't speak, leaving me to my observations.

I gazed at Eangen, perched between a range of ornate mountains and the bold Arpa wall. Glancing at the mountains again, I noted a small lake marked with indecipherable symbols. "We are... here?"

Again, he nodded.

My eyes roamed further north. Above the mountains, where I expected to find blank space, I instead saw notations in Arpa and several sketched landmarks. They looked to be more recent additions, drawn in a different hand than the rest of the map.

"You crossed the mountains?" I did not intend for the words to come out as an accusation, but they did.

"Yes." The lines around the captain's eyes deepened, though I couldn't tell whether it was in irritation or mirth. He indicated one of the chairs and took the other himself. "Would you like to know what we found?"

I cautiously sat.

"You've met Styga," the commander stated, his fingers resting on the lower half of the map. There, next to his thumb, I saw a depiction of Lathian's domed temple. "And, I hear, Ashaklon. They are Gods of the Old World, as you northerners call them. But just as Eang rose among the Gods of the New World and became their leader, Styga and Ashaklon also bow to one greater than they. The greatest of their generation."

"Who is that?" I prompted.

"Lathian," the man said with reverence.

My stomach dropped. Lathian? Quentis's god, the Arpa's God of Gods – he was the master of the Gods of the Old World?

Telios continued to speak. "Two years ago, I received a vision from him. A divine purpose. Lathian told me to go north, beyond the mountains, and there I would find... him. There I would release him – sever the chains that have bound his physical form for millennia and turn his whisper in the Empire's ears into a roar."

My disembodied visit to the temple in the Arpa capital with Quentis rushed back to me. Even across the tent, the familiar features of the idol on the altar stood out clearly – gravely handsome and kind.

My blood chilled. If Quentis's god was powerful enough to rule the Arpa Pantheon and subdue Ried while supposedly bound, how could Eang and her dwindling allies ever hope to defeat him once he was free?

"So I gathered men – other zealots, like myself – and went north, unofficially," Telios continued. He spoke companionably, if passionately, as if we were old acquaintances. "We slipped through the mountains and there... there in the Hinterlands, we found a tomb, a tomb with many seals. All but seven of those seals were broken, and once we stood there – my men and I – I sensed him."

Telios raised a hand to indicate his eyes, and he smiled a soft, nostalgic smile. "And we changed."

"Lathian did this to you?" I clarified, meeting his grey eyes with what I hoped was a stalwart gaze. "And your men?"

Telios nodded. "It is a natural result, as I understand, of being so near the God of Gods. Those seven seals remained when we left, but we carried Lathian's power with us, into the mountains and to the Algatt. They could not change like us, not while their god lived, but their suffering served our god just as well. Lathian's strength grew. Styga and his cohort took up the hunt. And Lathian's last chains began to break... They're still breaking now."

Dread pooled in my stomach and I wanted to run, to strike this man down and leave the camp as fast as my legs could carry me. But I found the will to ask, "When Polinus and his men arrive, will they... will they become Lathian's, too?"

"Every knee in the Arpa Empire bows to Lathian, ultimately," Telios reminded me. "Polinus and his men have been devoted to him since the day they were born."

All except Nisien. I sent a compulsive prayer to Eang, to Esach, to whoever might listen, asking that Nisien had taken my advice and pledged himself to another northern deity.

Telios continued to speak, his gaze growing more and more distracted. "The Empire has always worshiped Lathian, and he has always spoken to us. We knew that one day he would re-enter our world in power but... never did I think that I would be the instrument of his return."

Telios leant forward with all the earnestness of a man in love. Under the table, my hands clenched with nerves and Eangi Fire churned through my veins, begging to be used, begging to be released.

I dug my fingernails into my palms and pushed it down. We sat as allies, for now. No need to make an untimely enemy.

"The God-Killer, the power in the White Lake, seeks to stop us," Telios continued, "so you will stop them. As, Styga assures me, you are destined to. Until then, you may remain in my camp, unharmed and welcome. A guest."

"And after Lathian is free?" I inquired.

"Then, if you submit, you will live. And your new god, Lathian, God of Gods, will break over this land like water through a dam." Telios's hands rested on the tabletop, fingers splayed, demanding my attention with the timbre of his voice and the fervency of his faith. "He will occupy his temple in the capital, in the flesh, and harness its hidden powers. Then the world, the High Halls and all that is, will bow to the Arpa Empire."

THIRTY-SIX

The next four days passed in hushed, strained solitude. I made my own camp on the northern edge of the forest and requested that Telios keep his men away – I'd no idea what range of human impulse might remain behind their tainted eyes, but I didn't intend to find out.

Telios agreed with surprising ease. I saw only the occasional scout after the first day, when two legionaries arrived with a spare tent, a woodcutter's axe and a day's worth of food. After that I was left to my own devices, and even Styga was nowhere to be seen. Nonetheless, I laid my bedroll in a circle of warding runes each night, written with Eang's Fire and rebellious wisps of honeyed magic, and only then I slept.

I passed the daylight hours in restless anticipation and soul-deep deliberations. I repaired my shield and tended my weapons and armor. I walked the valley, dipped my toes in the lake, and watched its milky surface ripple beneath the wind. By night I surveyed its hidden magic, dancing up into the sky in my subtle, amber-tinged sight. There was a mystery and inevitability to the lake and its power, and though it perturbed me, I found I did not fear it.

In the evenings, I sipped tea made from the pine needles of the High Halls and tugged at the two powers inside of me: Eang's Fire, familiar and loud, and the muzzled magic I'd stolen from the gods. I missed Sixnit and Vistic, and thought of Ogam and Eang. I contemplated Omaskat and Nisien and Telios, Estavius and his blood and the history of the world – what I'd always thought it to be, and what I was beginning to understand now.

It was not until the fourth night, as I stared into my tea and felt the magic of the High Halls warming my lips, that all my ruminations coalesced into two stark conclusions.

I left the warmth of my fireside and picked my way to the edge of the trees. The surface of the lake came into view, silver and docile in the starless night. I touched my sleeping magic, softly so as not to disturb the Fire – a method that was nearly second nature now – and the lake's strange, waxen lights appeared, rippling and shafting into the heavens.

The first realization I'd had was familiar. I still did not want to kill Omaskat. Yes, my personal reasons for obeying Eang's command remained – a place in the High Halls and preventing the God-Killer from obliterating that sacred world – but there was so much more to the situation than I'd originally thought. All Omaskat had said against Eang back in the Algatt camp did not seem so blasphemous now, and it grew heavier by the day.

Secondly, Lathian had to be stopped. I knew that Eang could not quell him, not weakened as she was. And if our goddess could no longer protect us, where did that leave me and my people? Where did that leave the north?

Both Quentis and Telios had told me to submit to Lathian for the good of my people. As difficult as it was for me to admit, they had a point. But what if there was another option?

A dog barked, out in the night. I looked up slowly, my honeyed senses telling me that Omaskat was here long before I saw him.

The light on the surface of the lake rippled and swelled, growing brighter as a man and a hound entered its glow, rounding the flat western shore at a collected pace.

"Are you ready?" Styga coalesced from the shadows at a respectful distance, the starlit outlines of their features stark against the night.

Ready. What a hollow word that was, with my people murdered, the pillars of my faith fracturing and my goddess in flight. Nonetheless, I spoke the truth.

"I am."

A weighty sense of destiny settled over me as I left the trees a few moments later, concealing the glistening head of my axe beneath my lynx-painted shield. The warped Eangi collar I'd found at Lada was secured to my belt. My shield boss was scrubbed with wax and charcoal, and the hatchets at my chest were hooded, leaving me nearly invisible in the night.

Omaskat had stopped at the southern edge of the lake. His silhouette was obscured by the oscillating light, but I could tell that he faced me. The hound sat at his heel, his hand resting on her head in a calming gesture. He knew I was here.

My concentration broke and a spark of fear shot through me. Was Eang here too, on this fateful night? Did she watch me from the trees like I knew Styga did, waiting for me to execute their greatest threat?

But no. I tasted no iron on the air, and the senses the High Hall had gifted me found only Styga, Omaskat, the lake and myself.

I crossed the remaining open ground, shield raised and axe extended loosely behind me, out of sight and ready to strike.

The dog charged. I dropped into a crouch, but the animal only barked and skirted me, her tail waving.

"No," I growled. "Go away."

Pebbles crunched as Omaskat approached my position, fearless and collected. His cloak flowed open, but I couldn't see if he was armed.

At his approach, Eang's Fire predictably waned. But this time, I knew Eang was not holding the Fire back in some twisted form of punishment.

Whatever protected Omaskat was simply more powerful than my goddess.

"How many Arpa are in the forest?" the man asked.

I could not read his face, backed by the lake's light, but my stomach clenched at his voice. I thought of Eang and Svala, of that night when Omaskat had slept in the Hall of Smoke and I'd watched him by firelight. I thought of him snapping my wrist in the Algatt camp, and yet choosing not to kill me.

Old urgency stirred in my bones. I should ignore his question, ignore the riot of doubts in my own head. This was my chance. I should attack now, kill him and run.

"A cohort," I said instead.

"I see." Omaskat looked from the tree line to me. "Who leads them?"

"A commander called Telios, and a God of the Old World. Styga." I began to circle him, the questions I wanted to ask stinging like bile on my tongue. The dog ranged around us in turn, claws clattering on the loose rock, head low and muscles rippling. "But they serve Lathian."

Omaskat nodded, turning to keep me in his sight.

"Who is your god?" I asked.

"They are called Thvynder."

I recognized the name. "One of the Four Pillars."

Omaskat nodded slowly. "You've learned since our last meeting."

"A lot has changed," I replied. "What will your god do, if they rise?"

The man blinked a little, then glanced to the forest over my shoulder. He knew the Arpa were there; did he sense Styga, too? How close would the Old-World god dare to come?

"*When* my god rises, they will set the world to right. Hessa, I've told you before, Eang is no goddess. Neither are Oulden or Gadr – even Lathian. Too long this world has been ruled by those who were never meant to be worshiped."

"Eang is my goddess," I said, though there was little emotion left in those words. It was a statement of practicality, of obligation, rather than inerrant truth. "I belong to her."

"She's using you."

"I know."

The lines of Omaskat's silhouette shifted and, as we turned, the light from the lake broke across his face. The fine muscles beneath his eyes twitched between wariness and a subtle... relief.

"But there's nothing else I can do," I added. "Unless... you give me another choice."

Omaskat smiled, but there was no triumph to it, no malevolence or self-satisfaction. It was a genuine, honest smile.

My own tension eased. But for the sake of the watching Styga, I kept my weapons raised.

"Very well," Omaskat's voice warmed. "Come with me to rescue Vistic, Sixnit and Svala. And you and I will treat. I will answer all your questions, once they're safe, and we can strike a bargain."

I hesitated, my confidence suddenly faltering. "Sixnit and Vistic are with Ogam," I said, pronouncing the words slowly. "And Svala... I don't know where she is, but Six and Vistic are safe."

The man shook his head. "Ogam is a traitor, Hessa. Who hates Eang more than the son she tried to murder at birth? Who has spent more time beyond the mountains, where the banished Gods of the Old World slept in their tombs, than any other?"

My mouth dried and my resolve faltered. Omaskat had to be lying, and if he was, I had made a terrible mistake. Here I stood, negotiating with him, when all the gods and Fate had decreed he should die by my hand.

How could Ogam be a traitor? He had helped me – but then again, I remembered with cold clarity, so had Styga. Styga had helped me because I was destined to kill Omaskat and stop the rise of his forgotten deity, not out of any loyalty or compassion.

Omaskat, a mere two paces away now, reached out his hand. His mismatched eyes were open and unveiled, the most honest gaze I'd seen in months. "Come with me. Rescue your priestess, your friend and the child, and I will tell you everything you want to know."

My thoughts scattered, unable to move past Ogam's betrayal. But so much of what I'd believed had proved false – why not Eang's son, too? And if Sixnit's, Vistic's and Svala's lives hung in the balance, should I not at least investigate?

"You'll answer my every question," I reiterated. "And if I am not satisfied, I may still kill you."

"So be it." Omaskat's hand remained outstretched, though his eyes flicked to the forest. "But the Arpa are on the move. We must run. Now."

For a timeless moment, I hovered there between Omaskat, my questions and the Arpa.

Then my chin dropped, Omaskat whistled to the hound, and we ran.

Down. East and out of the lake's high valley we plunged, over rockfalls and through shallow creeks. Before us our path descended, down the mountainside and towards the distant, flat expanse of the Headwaters. Meanwhile, up the slope to our back, I heard the Arpa shouting, rocks tumbling and the clink of steel.

We descended at least five hundred meters before Styga materialized before us. I stumbled to a halt, just managing to throw my weight back before I skidded off a ledge.

The dog came level with my shoulder on another ledge, a low grumble resonating through her chest. Omaskat drew up to my other side, weaponless and resolute.

Styga barely looked at the man. Instead, they fixed upon me and their face, modeled after my own, contorted in hatred. "You will die for this, Eangi," they spat, and charged.

Omaskat was already between the God of the Old World and I, bearded chin and cloak-clad shoulders level. Styga came up short, the shadow-stuff of their body rippling as if Omaskat had thrown up a solid physical barrier.

Styga howled and charged again. At the same time the hound leapt down to our feet, pressing into the shelter of Omaskat's legs as the god circled and battered, but Omaskat's wards held. Time slowed and my eyes lingered on the man, watching him hold an ancient, spectral deity back as if they were a disgruntled child.

I watched him do what Eang should have had the strength, and the fidelity, to do. And as I did, tendrils of the High Hall's dormant magic trickled up through my sight, amber and gold and sweet. My fingers twitched. Omaskat's and my magic differed, to be sure, but I couldn't help but wonder what those honeyed tendrils would be if Eang's Fire was not in the way. It had resisted Rioux and broken Quentis's curse –

and Quentis's power was sourced from Lathian himself. If it were free, would I, too, be able to hold a creature like Styga at bay?

Beyond Omaskat's invisible defenses, the God of the Old World hissed and cursed in a language I couldn't understand. Omaskat did not respond, and Styga hurtled away up the mountain in a stream of sable.

Omaskat kept his attention on Styga's retreat, but I felt him watch me from the corner of his eye. "You've been stealing from the High Halls. I can see it. Around your eyes."

I blinked the amber magic away and met his gaze over the rim of my shield. Would this realization change his offer?

"I doubt I'd still be alive if I hadn't," I said.

"Eang hasn't noticed?"

"She's not very attentive lately."

Omaskat made an affirming sound. "Do you know what it means?"

I lowered my shield. Anxiety fluttered in my stomach – I didn't know, not in any real sense of the word – but I returned levelly, "Why don't you tell me?"

Something close to amusement etched around Omaskat's eyes. "I will. But for now, let's move."

THIRTY-SEVEN

Dawn over the Headwaters was like nothing I had ever seen. I stood on the end of a peninsula, palms braced against my knees as I fought to catch my breath. Before me, shallow water stretched all the way to the eastern and southern horizons, while in the north mountains encroached like tentative feet into a pond. The reflection of delicate, puffy clouds drifted over the surface, filled with filtered tones of gold and rose.

An instant later, the Headwaters churned. The clouds vanished in a mass of underwater springs, destroying the gentle dawn hues with great belches of cold grey-blue.

"How long until the legionaries catch up?" I asked Omaskat. I still hadn't found my breath, but the question was too urgent to wait.

The dog loped past us, cautiously nosing up to the churning water.

"They won't." Omaskat unclasped his cloak and threw it over a branch. Stepping around the dog, he crouched down on the shore to splash water on his face and drag more through his beard and hair. "They can't touch me, and we have to go back, anyway. They'll just wait."

"We have to go back?" I clarified. "Because Thvynder is in the White Lake?"

Omaskat shook his hands dry and eased himself down onto a rock, gesturing for me to join him. "So you have been paying attention. Yes."

Instead of sitting, I slung my shield down and leant it against a birch tree. Then I angled my axe out of the way and crouched. "Are you a priest?"

Omaskat shook his head. "No."

"A Vestige?"

"No," he said again. He watched as Ayo sniffed the water and took a tentative lap. Deeming it safe, the hound began to drink. "But Vistic is. In a way. Or rather, a Vestige is a faulty imitation of what Vistic is."

I caught myself against the tree. Perhaps sitting was the better option for this conversation. "Vistic? The baby?"

"I need to tell you many things, Hessa." Omaskat measured me, the gold and blue of his eyes filled with intent. "And I will, as I promised, but we need to move on as soon as you've recovered. Shall I start now, or wait?"

My eyes flicked to his brow. Sweat darkened his hairline and tunic, but he did not look as winded as I. I did need to rest. "Start now. Who are you? What are you?"

Omaskat glanced back up the mountains the way we had come. "For you to understand that, I need to start at the beginning."

Slowly, I eased my taxed muscles onto the cool earth and crossed my legs. It felt odd to relax in his presence, but my weapons were close.

"Up there, in that lake," the man began, "sleeps one of the Four Pillars of the World. They are a god, Eangi, and what you have been taught to call a god is not a god at all. They're creations, just as you are. True gods have no beginning. True gods have no end."

Instinct made my spine straighten and my jaw twitch with indignation, but I consciously fought the impulse. "Then what is Eang, if she's not a goddess?"

Omaskat sat forward. "How many days did you spend in the High Halls?"

My eyes narrowed a fraction. "I don't know. Time wasn't... I couldn't really count them. Five days? A week?"

"So you ate and drank?"

I nodded, beginning to sense where he was heading. "And I brought food and water back with me."

At that, Omaskat laughed. "That was cunning of you. But consider,

Hessa, how much a week in the High Halls transformed you, a human. Yet the 'gods'..."

"Yet the gods have spent thousands of years there," I finished for him.

"Precisely. Eang and those like her have been eating and drinking, breathing and conceiving in the Halls for uncounted years. Is it not fitting, then, to wonder what they were like at the beginning of all those ages?"

I found myself nodding, but I pointed out, "That doesn't mean they're not gods, though."

"Well, consider this. The Four created three categories of living things: animals, humans and Miri."

Miri. I recognized the word. Shanich had called both Eang and herself by that name – at the same time as she'd denied being a god.

I suppressed an unsettled breath and refocused on Omaskat's words.

"The Miri are those you call the gods, the Old and the New. The Four created their kind to rule creation as governors... or that was the intention." There was an edge to Omaskat's voice, as if he remembered the event personally. "They had long life and great power, but they were nothing like what they are now. What they became."

"Because of the High Halls?" I prompted.

"Yes," he affirmed. "When humans began to die, as humans are prone to do, their spirits so saturated the earth that another world needed to be created to hold them – the High Halls. One of the Four did this, weaving her power into the grass and the trees, the water and the air to create an afterlife of unparalleled beauty. Some of the Miri were elected to shepherd the dead there and took up residence in the Halls. Then the Four, believing their creation to now be self-sufficient, retreated from the world.

"But the Miri who inhabited the Halls began to change. They discovered the power of the Pillar who created the Halls was soaking into them. They learned how to manipulate their own natural abilities with its aid, to create life themselves and reweave the fabric of creation. The human dead in the Halls could not be altered, being already dead, but their awe inspired the Miri.

"With the Four Pillars' eyes averted, the Miri took advantage of their new power and their long lives to convince humanity that *they* were the gods, and with their worship, the outpouring of human blood-magic and the dedication of souls, they grew stronger than ever. The rest of the Miri, those who hadn't been given governorship of the Halls, were divided. Some tried to steal power their brethren had found – they became the demons. Others resisted the temptation of magic, choosing to make their home in the Waking World instead of going against the created order – like those you know as the rivermen, and some of the woodmaidens."

Disquieted, I thought of the power in my own blood with a new, uncertain anxiety. Pieces of what I'd learned over the last few months began to merge together, more and more cohesive, but I still struggled to believe it was true. "If the Four were so powerful, why didn't they stop it?"

"They were not here," Omaskat said, glancing down at his hands as if they, themselves, had failed the world. "One, she who made the High Halls, sensed the disturbance after a time and returned. She managed to find only two others, Eiohe and Thvynder, my god, while the last, Imilidese, remained elusive. Together, the three strove to reclaim their creation. But the Miri – those who now bore names like Lathian, Styga and Ashaklon – had become too strong, and the magic of the High Halls had grown wild. So she who made the Halls returned to them and wove herself into the frayed ends of time. She is the Weaver, Fate as you know her. She sacrificed her physical presence and bound it to her loom – seeing, influencing, but no longer touching the corporeal world."

I fought to keep my expression still. That aligned with what little I knew of Fate.

"Thvynder and Eiohe took the brunt of the Miri's assault," Omaskat said. "Eiohe faced them down in what is now Apharnum, but with all the petty 'gods' and their armies of enslaved humans against them, they were overwhelmed. They were wounded and bled and fled back into the stars. But Thvynder surrendered, on the advice of Fate. At least then, the two of them could remain in the world and exert some influence on their creation. At least then, they could intervene when the darkness grew too great."

I narrowed my eyes. "And Thvynder was bound beneath the lake."

"Yes."

"But if they were bound, how could they 'intervene'?"

"Vistic," Omaskat replied, unfaltering. "He is a Vestige, or what a Vestige was intended to be, a piece of Thvynder's life transmuted into a human soul. Once he's returned to the lake, my god can rise. A thousand lives of men and women that soul has lived on this earth… watching and waiting, dying and being reborn. Waiting for me to fetch them at the proper time."

"A thousand – what? Vistic is a *baby*," I spluttered. "And what do you mean by return him to the lake?"

"I mean exactly that," Omaskat said, unhelpfully.

"Are you going to kill him?"

The man's brows furrowed. "Only an Eangi would assume that. Vistic will not be harmed – as I said, he is what a Vestige should be, not the faulty mockery that Eang has made in the Eangi. He will not die."

"But I don't understand," I protested, barely consoled. "There's no way Vistic is what you're saying – part of your god. I was there when he was born! I scrubbed his birth-blood off my hands. I grew up with his father."

"You did," Omaskat conceded. "He's a baby, of flesh and blood, but his soul is something vastly other."

Emotion – indignation, confusion, a spark of fear – clogged my throat. "That's mad. Eang would have known. He was born in her Hall. His father was an Eangi."

Omaskat shrugged. "Despite where his soul originates from, he's human, Hessa. There was nothing about him to attract undue attention at this age – not until you brought it upon him. Eang was furious when she realized what he was *and* that she was unable to kill or bind him, because of your vow to protect him."

The words struck me like a lash. "No."

323

"You could ask Gadr," the man offered. "I sent the child north with him. Until Ogam intervened, in any case."

"I already spoke to Gadr," I countered. "I know you stole Vistic from Sixnit and left her enslaved."

Omaskat's eyes bored into mine again. "I'm not finished."

I didn't waver. "Then continue."

The man turned weary eyes back over the Headwaters. The springs had begun to boil again, filling the air with a distant, gulping rush.

"The other way Thvynder retained power was through me. I am the Watchman." Omaskat watched tiny waves skitter against the rocks. "I observe and do what I can to influence the pattern of the world and understand the tapestry Fate weaves. I watched Eang and her generation revolt against their forebears, as their forebears revolted against the Four. I watched the Arpa Empire rise where Eiohe's blood had spilled. And when I sensed the awakening of Lathian and his cohorts, I spent years around the White Lake, beginning the process of waking Thvynder and waiting for the Vestige's – Vistic's – next birth."

"And after all that, you thought giving the baby to Gadr would be a wise idea?" I demanded, partially out of indignation and partially because this event was more tangible than everything else he'd said. "And leaving Sixnit behind?"

"I regret having to leave Sixnit. But Gadr, I met him at the lake, after he lost his people, and we came to an understanding."

"He's on your side?"

"My side?" Omaskat echoed, incredulous. "The side that wants this world to survive an unbound Lathian? Gadr saw what Lathian's zealots did to his people and offered me help."

I took this silently, thoughts darting back to the slaughtered Algatt villages. After having seen the massacre myself, I could hardly blame Gadr for throwing in his lot with Omaskat. He couldn't very well go to Eang for aid.

"Neither of us realized what Ogam had done, back then," Omaskat added. "I believed that Vistic would be safe with Gadr."

"What has Ogam done?" I asked. "He's allied himself with Lathian?"

The traveler held out his hand as Ayo sidled up, sitting at his side and curling her tail around her legs. "Yes, apparently so. At the least, he broke many of the seals on Lathian's tomb and stole Vistic from Gadr."

"But… breaking those seals wasn't enough to release Lathian?"

"No. A binding's strength is more than seals. It relies on the life and power of whoever wrought it, and Eang and Gadr and a few others are still alive."

"Then how close is he to freedom?" I asked, once again weighing which was the greater threat to my world – Lathian or Omaskat's god.

Omaskat made a contemplative sound and settled into a cross-legged position, pulling the dog's head into his lap and beginning to stroke her absently. "He has left his tomb, on the other side of the mountains, and is on his way to the lake. He cannot physically pass through Algatt and Eangen, not with Gadr and Eang still alive. But he's stronger by the day. And now that Ogam has sent more legionaries to feed him, I'm not sure what he will be able to do."

He meant Polinus's men. My heart slammed against my ribs in renewed fear for Nisien and Estavius. "But Thvynder can stop Lathian?"

Omaskat nodded gravely. "Before he's fully released, yes. But once he physically arrives in his temple in Apharnum and gains full power? All will be lost."

"And if… if I let you wake Thvynder, what will happen to my people?" I needed to know. "What will happen to the High Halls? The light from the White Lake is already destroying them."

Omaskat answered without a hint of question in his voice, "Thvynder will rule the north. They will be its god, its protector. The High Halls will be restored – they were made for your kind, Hessa, for your dead, and they will not be withheld." Heat entered his eyes then, sharp and jagged. "And your place there will never again be questioned."

My heart swelled against my ribs. This. This was what I'd desired, this was what I'd fought for.

"And while you live?" Omaskat added, his gold and blue eyes level and candid. "Thvynder will have need of a priesthood, and the Eangen of leaders. The Miri that submit will be permitted to live... but I doubt that Eang will be among them."

My elation faltered into grim agreement. Eang would never submit.

"Do you have any more questions?" Omaskat asked, glancing from the dried sweat on my skin to the Headwaters. "Or will you trust me long enough to save Vistic, your friend, and the High Priestess?"

I was overly conscious of the tarnished Eangi collar fastened to my belt, pressing into my flesh in reminder, warning and condemnation. At the same time as I resisted all Omaskat had told me of history and the gods, I believed him – but the implications were too thick, too complex to sort out now. I had to focus on the task at hand: Sixnit, Svala and Vistic.

"I will," I replied, climbing back to my feet and taking up my shield. "Though I haven't made up my mind."

Omaskat toyed with one of Ayo's ears and the dog shook her head in irritation. He lifted his hand and frowned at the beast as he said, "Very well. You have the day. Now, out there on the Headwaters, Svala and Sixnit and Vistic are trapped in ice. But Ogam will not simply let us retrieve them."

"Why would you be afraid of Ogam?"

"I'm not. But those three – Vistic, Sixnit, your priestess – are going to be weak. While I deal with Ogam, I need you to get them away." His gaze flicked to my hands. "It should not be hard, not with your new skills... whatever they may be."

"About that..." I rested the rim of my shield beside my boots. "I've only been able to fully use the power in the High Halls, when I was cursed by Quentis. Eang's Fire, now... I can't break through it."

Omaskat made a contemplative noise. "Eang's Fire will always seek to dominate, whether that's over your enemies or your own soul. It is a pity, though."

I nodded, considering Quentis's quest to kill Eang's Fire. If he had succeeded, what would I be right now? Would I be a shadow of myself, stripped of the Fire that had carried me through a hundred battles, or would I be… more?

"Will I be punished?" I asked in sudden realization. "Haven't I done exactly what the Miri did, taking the power of the High Halls for myself?"

Omaskat frowned and got to his own feet. "Very little in this world is as it was meant to be, and just because some abused the power you wield doesn't mean that you will. Use what you've gained for good, and I see no fault in you."

My emotions jarred against one another – tentative hope, reckless determination, and no small measure of fear.

If Omaskat's talk of true gods and Miri and Vistic was to be believed, I could still save the north and the High Halls. I could be reunited with Sixnit and Vistic and Svala. I wouldn't be alone anymore, stumbling my way through questions of life and death and deity. The thought made my tentative hope turn desperate and cloying.

But Svala would not listen to any of what Omaskat had just said. She was High Priestess of the Eangi, of all Eangen, and she was as likely to turn on Eang as Eang was to bend the knee to Thvynder.

The thought came with a rush of memory and emotion. I remembered how, as a child, Svala had taken my hands and vowed to protect me. I remembered the Eangi's countless proclamations of Eang's bravery and watchfulness, her power and dedication to the Eangen people. And I recalled Svala joining Eidr's and my hands together, before the altar, before all the Eangi, in the Hall of Smoke.

"Albor," I said distantly.

Omaskat, in the midst of bundling his cloak and stashing it high in a tree, paused.

"You…" I tried to keep my words clear of emotion. "If you're who you say you are, when you came to Albor, did you know what would happen to us?"

Omaskat lowered his arms and settled back into his heels, moving as if I were a skittish horse.

"Did you know?" I repeated. My voice cracked despite my best efforts and my eyes began to burn. "Did you know the Algatt would slaughter them all? That Six and her baby and I would end up with the Algatt?"

The Watchman of Thvynder looked down at me with an unfaltering gaze. "Yes."

I couldn't crack his bones or rupture his mind with Fire. I had my axe, but it never left my hip. I had hands to beat him, nails to claw him, yet my body did not respond. Instead, my knees became butter and my fingers lead.

I raised a trembling hand to my face and tried to control myself, tried to stop the anguish that threatened to collapse my chest, but it only grew.

When I managed to speak, my words were ragged. "You could have saved us."

Omaskat remained where he was, watching me with that same stalwart gaze. "Fate has her own mind, Hessa, and a way of righting herself. Once one's days are written, they can rarely be undone. Even I can't change that, but it is why I came to the Hall of Smoke when I did. I wanted to meet you. To see Sixnit and her husband... before. Perhaps that was selfish of me. Perhaps I should not have done so."

I clamped my eyes shut, careless of my tears, and pressed into a memory of Eidr's strong arms. One more day. Even if Fate could have been evaded for one day more, I...

I felt Omaskat draw closer, but I didn't move. I kept my eyes sealed shut, grasping at the scent of Eidr as if I were drowning.

Omaskat touched my hand. I jerked away but he reached out again, more firmly. Through a fog of tears, I looked down to see him press my three-pronged hairpin from Albor into my palm, engraved with birds and the runes of Eidr's pledge to me: protection, eternal promise and belonging. My thumb twitched over it.

When Omaskat spoke, his words were charged with both empathy and authority. "Come with me, Hessa. Let me, let us, save your people now."

THIRTY-EIGHT

I splashed my face with water and raked my hair into a fresh braid. I wound it into a crown to keep it from the straps of my gear and fastened it with my usual leather wrap, then secured it all with the hairpin Omaskat had returned to me, burrowing it deep so it would not come loose.

I ignored Omaskat's glance at my torn ear and cinched my belt tighter, easing the weight of mail on my tired shoulders.

"Here." Omaskat held out a small pouch.

I took it and looked warily inside. It was packed with dried fruit, last season's nuts and twists of venison. "Do you even need to eat?"

"No, but you do." He took up two long poles. "And take one of these. I don't want to lose you in a well."

A few minutes later, we stepped into the Headwaters. Ayo ranged ahead, water tugging at the fur of her belly as she quested.

"If all else fails, follow her back to shore," Omaskat told me over his shoulder. The arrowhead of rivulets he made rippled towards my own plodding legs. The water only reached his knees, but it was at my hips. "She'll be able to sense any wells or... unpleasant creatures... long before you."

The first of the Headwater's springs were easy to find. Every so often they awoke, interrupting the surface of the water with an arch of lively, ominous bubbles. Ayo skirted them and we followed her path. But when the currents slept, the springs became lurking wells. So, even though both Omaskat and the hound preceded me, I stabbed my staff left and right, making sure I wasn't about to step into unknown depths.

My legs plodded, the water rippled, and I was so focused my steps that I failed to notice danger until Ayo yipped.

I swung my pole just in time to strike a face full of teeth. Omaskat reacted in the same moment and a knife flashed, hurtling through the air before I'd even had a chance to see where he'd had it hidden.

A silvery creature the size of a large otter loosed a horrific shriek and fell away from me, a fine throwing knife protruding from its head.

I sucked in a gasp and staggered, looked back at Omaskat. "What was—"

The solidity of rock vanished beneath my feet and water crashed closed over my head. My back struck stone again, the edge of a hidden well, and I lost my breath in a gargling shout.

I began to sink, clothing and armor and muscle pulling me down. Pain coursed up my leg. My eyes flew wide and I lashed out, but another creature's claws were anchored in my calf.

More claws sunk into my left arm, jerking, dragging me down even further. I tore a hatchet free from the brace across my chest and hacked wildly, legs spasming and one arm desperately searching for grasp on the rim of the well. My fingers found a lip and seized it.

Amid the blood and bubbles, I saw my new attacker. A second sleek creature clung to my arm, vertical eyes – nearly on top of its head – blinking at me as it bit into my flesh. A third clasped my leg with stubby paws, backed by the black depths of the well whose edge I clung to.

Two more creatures approached from the sides, their heads angled down so that their unholy eyes could track me. Almost in unison, their jaws unhinged, widening with every flick of their lithe bodies.

I saw Omaskat's legs plowing towards me, but the creatures would arrive first. Omaskat was too far away to intervene – but he was far enough away for Eang's Fire to burn.

Blood exploded in the water. My wounds started binding as I hauled myself upright with a cry, closing the remaining distance to Omaskat in one frantic, sodden lunge. We fell in back to back, I gasping and dripping and he watching the creatures bleed through his mismatched eyes.

Ayo pounced upon one of the twitching beasts. It was already dead, but that didn't stop the hound from hurtling it away with a vicious toss of the head. It shimmered as it arched through the air and crashed back down into the Headwaters.

Omaskat let out a short breath and looked at me askance. "Now I'm doubly grateful you can't use that Fire on me."

I gave a ragged, panting grunt. "What are those?"

"I've heard them called Silver Seals." He waded towards the nearest body, the one he'd killed with the knife. The creature glistened in the sunlight as he lifted it by the knife haft and suspended it, dripping, between us. "I believe one of the rivermen made them from otters, as pets. But Eang wouldn't permit him to keep them, so he left them out here. They bred."

I grimaced in disgust.

He pried the knife loose with a moist crack and discarded the corpse. "Let's keep moving. There's more out here than one riverman's mischief."

The day lengthened and the Headwaters spread around us in an eerie, windy hush. The springs were less active out here and the sun warmed the shallow water, but my nerves were too raw to find solace. Loose strands of hair tickled my face and I raked them back, squinting towards the shore.

Omaskat waded between me and the peninsula from which we'd come, preceded by his pole. I let my eyes rest on him, then glanced to where the dog roved, ears forward, nose questing after errant scents. They were the only other living things I could see on the Headwaters, the only movement other than the surface of the water and... the mist.

An island of ice came into view, sending thin tendrils of mist out over the water. I saw it at the same time as a strand of winter wind trailed across my cheek, pure and bracing.

"Hessa," the wind whispered.

"Ogam," I replied.

The stillness of the water amplified my voice. Alerted, Omaskat closed the gap between us and took up position at my shoulder.

"Do not do this, Hessa," the disembodied Son of Winter warned.

"Where are you?" I responded, setting my pole on end like a staff. I exchanged a look with Omaskat, trying to determine whether he could hear the immortal's voice too. He gave a silent nod.

The tendril of winter vanished. My companion and I waited briefly before I gave him a significant glance. As one, we began to jog towards the island.

The sunny warmth of the water vanished, replaced by shards of arctic cold. Frazil appeared, twisting through the water in unseen currents. Our going slowed. The dog, lighter and more agile, plowed over the streams of crystals with great, bounding leaps. We followed her trail before it disappeared, avoiding unseen wells.

A sudden crack made me spin. Ice skittered across the Headwaters towards us like lightning, freezing everything in its path and locking the surface in a sheath of frozen water.

"Run!" I dropped my pole and threw myself forward, opening the distance between Omaskat and me until Eang's Fire could flare. Then I bolted for the island, Ayo just ahead and Omaskat barreling along behind.

I followed Ayo's bounding leap onto the ice, landed hard and slid several paces. Omaskat arrived an instant later, his boots having barely left the water before the ice snapped closed. He fell beside me with a convincingly human, "Oof," and rolled.

By the time he struggled to his feet, I was already in a crouch nearby, shield raised and axe resting on one shoulder, waiting.

Then I saw her.

The sight struck me like a midwinter gale. I faltered, unable to pry my eyes from the sight of my High Priestess, my mentor, locked in the ice below my feet.

She was enveloped, every hair on her head frozen in individual movement. Her tawny skin still held the color of life, but a solid foot of ice obscured the details of her condition; I could see closed eyes, an arched neck – divided by Eangi collar – and an open, screaming mouth.

The horror in her face reflected in mine as I stared down at her in growing, overwhelming urgency. I had to get her out. I had to. Now.

But she was not alone. Sixnit rested not far off, curled into a fetal position around a bundle that could only be Vistic. Beyond them, to my further shock, was Cadic. Still saddled, Nisien's horse lay splayed beneath the ice, tail and mane frozen in a frantic bolt for freedom.

"Burn them out," Omaskat panted to me. The dog had fallen in at his side, the thick hair along her spine bristling like a boar's. "I'll hold him back."

My eyes flicked from the empty Headwaters to the ice below my feet. There was no time for indecision. I returned my axe to my belt and crouched again, this time far enough from Omaskat for Eang's Fire to burn.

The instinct to pray hit me and passed. Instead, I tugged at my Fire, pushing it down into my hands in a hot rush. I sketched runes into the ice: one over Svala, one over Sixnit and Vistic, and the last over Cadic.

Omaskat noted my progress, his expression laced with tension. Ogam was still nowhere to be seen, but the hair stood up on the back of my neck. His voice had come to me before over vast distances before – for all we knew he could be in Souldern. But without the burden of humans or Cadic, I had no idea how fast the winds could carry him.

The bones in my arm ached all the way up to my shoulder as I pressed an open palm onto the ice between my runes. Then, gathering every fragment of Fire I could find, I channeled it into the markings.

THIRTY-NINE

S team began to rise in thin, snaking tendrils.

"Keep going," Omaskat urged. "I—"

His voice died at the same time as the light. Clouds locked over the sky; the broad, seamless grey of a winter storm.

"Burn," I hissed to my runes. "Wake."

The symbols flared. I flinched but maintained connection with the ice, which transformed into water around my fingers. The steam began to billow. All the while Omaskat squinted between me and Ogam's oncoming storm, its mass of grey preceded by curls of frigid wind and a portentous hush.

My feet splashed in meltwater as the runes seared deeper into the ice and steam filled my lungs, prickling and constricting. Moisture began to freeze on my lashes, on my hair and clothing. I shook my head and rubbed my face on my arm, but the condensation only returned a moment later.

My breathing thinned. Before long, the miasma was so thick and obscuring that I barely noticed the snowflakes. They fell lazily at first, evaporating on my cheekbones and collecting on Omaskat's shoulders, beard and hair.

"Be ready," I warned Omaskat. "I need a minute longer."

It was so strange to see him standing there, braced and prepared to protect us, to protect me. But there was a rightness to it, a consolation outside simple logic – one that even the thought of Eang could no longer smother.

I pushed these thoughts aside and divided my power further, driving a thread into Cadic's blood. As soon as the others were free, we would need to run.

A blast of midwinter air knocked me backwards. My shield clattered away and I fell on my back, momentarily losing contact with the runes. They froze over.

"No!" I slammed both palms onto the ice as the wind howled around me, tossing my hair and the edges of my clothing into a frenzy. I couldn't see Omaskat anymore. I couldn't even see my own hands, though I could feel them shaking with fatigue. And I felt the heat of my runes, burning down and out from me until a great pit formed in the ice.

The roar of the wind grew so strong that, when Svala's Eangi howl rose, I thought it was part of the storm. Only when it formed into feeble, urgent words did I recognize it.

"Eang, Eang! The Brave, the Vengeful! The Watchful, the—"

I was tired, drained, but I plunged down into the pit. The bottom was smooth rock, worn from millennia of erosion. As it became exposed, the runes had shifted into the walls of the pit around me, each line illuminated by wavering heat.

Svala was on her hands and knees, choking and praying. Nearby, Cadic, awakened early by the Fire in his veins, jerked free from the ice with a clatter of hooves and a terrified whicker. Sixnit still lay on her side on the rocky ground, her body a shield around the tiny child.

I battled the wind to reach Svala first. There was no real thought in my action; years of devotion and admiration pulled me to her, even as the sight of Six and Vistic clotted my throat with emotion.

Svala nearly collapsed when she saw me. Half-upright, her eyes darted over my shoulder, filling themselves with the surreal world of ice and steam and storm.

I was grateful for her distraction. Maybe then she would not notice how the sight of her choked me with guilt, loss – and deep, quiet ire. "High Priestess."

"Hessa, child. Ogam," she croaked. "He—"

"I know." I helped her stand, bolstering the older woman against the wind. "Burn, High Priestess."

She did. She was the strongest Eangi I knew, and within seconds her spine straightened and her eyes began to clear. Still, when I handed her my axe, her fingers shook.

"What is happening?" she asked. Her eyes flicked to the runes, still smoldering. "Did you write those?"

"Yes. There is a…" I hesitated. If Svala realized who Omaskat was, she would likely resist. "Another god above, holding back Ogam. But we need to go. Now."

Svala asked no more questions. She stumbled towards Cadic and I ran for Sixnit.

My friend stirred as I touched her cheek but did not rouse. She was no Eangi; her time in the unnatural ice had brought her near to death.

Vistic's heartbeat, however, was strong beneath my searching fingers. His eyes opened and through a veil of snow and ice-crusted lashes, I saw their color – one was blue, the other gold. The exact reflection of Omaskat's.

He turned those eyes upon me and, for an instant, I forgot the storm. I forgot my fear and my guilt and everything else, lost in the gaze of the uncanny, inscrutable infant. When had his eyes changed? Had they always been this way?

"Hessa!" Omaskat bellowed over the wind. "He's here!"

I tore my attention from Vistic and pushed Eang's Fire into Sixnit's veins. Her eyelids flickered open, but I gave her no time to pull herself together.

"Sixnit, you need to ride."

Sixnit looked down at Vistic, fumbling to ensure he was safe.

"Hessa, now!" Omaskat bellowed. "Take them and go!"

Svala flinched towards him, fingers tight on her weapon. "Hessa, send the girl and the child on. We'll—"

"No," I stopped her. "We have to go with them. We're in the

336

Headwaters. Take Sixnit and the child on the horse; head for the shore, as fast as you can. I'll be right behind."

Svala looked down at me, still holding Cadic by the bit. With the swirling snow behind her, I could almost imagine us back in Albor on a winter's day.

Then the Son of Winter roared. The snow became shards, lashing at our eyes and stealing our breaths away.

"Take them and go!" I screamed to Svala. "I'll be right behind you!"

Something flashed through her eyes. Anger? Questioning. Pride? Then she beckoned Sixnit.

I scrambled back up into the storm, jerking a hatchet from my brace as I went. I saw Omaskat's running form on the other side of the island, obscured by the tempest, and my shield protruding from a growing bank of snow. I took it up at the same time as Cadic, with Svala and Sixnit astride, clattered out of the pit.

"The shore! Which way is the shore?" Svala called to me. One of her hands tangled in Cadic's mane and the other rested on the beast's neck, feeding the wild-eyed steed Eangi strength.

I pointed, Svala spurred Cadic and the maelstrom swallowed them whole. I spun my shield lightly, testing the strength of my tired body, and cast Omaskat one last, hesitant glance. Then I started after them.

A frigid hand dug into my hair and hurled me backwards. I slammed onto the ice and skidded, ending in a frenzied tumble of shield, hatchet, snow and limbs.

I threw my shield up as Ogam fell upon me. I growled in shock and frustration, bracing the shield with both arms. It cracked. His booted foot slipped and, flinching, I momentarily lost sight of him in the snow.

There. A dance of white braids and the blur of pale grey kaftan. I loosed an Eangi battle cry, crackling with Fire, and hurled my hatchet.

Ogam roared again. The sound left no doubt as to whose son he was: it was the crack of ice on a winter lake and thunder of an avalanche in one bone-cracking blast.

His boot came down on my throat this time. I dropped my broken shield and scrabbled, clawing at his foot one instant and my last hatchet the next. I tried to throw more Fire at him, but the boot barely shuddered and black sparked across my vision.

"I should have killed you the day I found you." The Son of Winter bent low, his words piercing through the wind. Blood streamed from his nose, eyes and ears, crusting over with frost – Winter's immortal silver blood, unlike the rest of the gods. The Miri.

My Fire had only angered him. With his impossibly blue eyes boiling, Ogam now looked nothing like the mischievous being I had encountered in Souldern. "Fate and her meddling be damned."

Ayo hurtled out of the snow in a streak of black and grey. Her jaw clamped down on Ogam's head and pulled him sideways, providing just enough of a distraction for me to wriggle away.

Ogam threw the dog back. She hit the ice with a pained yelp and skidded off into a blur of snow.

My mind clacked and stuttered. I struggled onto my hands and knees and tried to stand, but Ogam backhanded me. I crashed down again.

A hand grabbed me under the arm and hauled me upright, but all I could see was a haze of black sparks. I sensed Omaskat more than I recognized him, with his squared shoulders and swirl of hair.

Ogam laughed. His voice was loud, clear, and charged with the power of the storm itself. The fringes of his kaftan rippled around him, silver and red embroidery flashing in the white. "Even if I can't kill that whelp, I can imprison him until the end of time. And with both the last Eangi dead, my mother will fall."

"I will not."

A new voice ruptured the storm. Beyond me, a dozen paces to every side, the wind and snow began to twist and swirl into a tornado. The wind fled from our vicinity, leaving us locked in its heart. Air rushed into my lungs again and what sparks of Eang's Fire remained in my body flared and bucked.

Omaskat released me, hiding his mismatched eyes behind an upthrown arm. Simultaneously, Ogam's head whipped around.

A new figure appeared. The Fire inside me knew her, even if she was disguised by the snow. Her gait was predatory as she circled, her every muscle moving with uncanny grace. Legendary twin axes rested in her hands and bronze armor was cinched over a tunic of pure black.

A blind, ecstatic rush swept over me. My head cleared, a lifetime of prayer, of service, of blood sacrifice and songs beating back my own screaming conscience. This, this magnificent creature, stalking unaffected through the storm, had to be a goddess. The goddess of my people. The goddess who owned my life.

My exhausted muscles eased, strength returning to me in a warm rush.

Go. Eang's voice resonated through my body like a drum. *Help Svala. I will see to my son.*

Blindly, soullessly, I started to step backwards.

Ogam hurled a blade of ice at my throat.

Omaskat's axe knocked it out of the air, and as soon as he neared me again, Eang's hold broke. My own mind rushed back and I staggered into the raging wall of snow, throwing my arms over my head and toppling out into the ice-locked Headwaters on the other side.

Omaskat was a second behind me, stumbling to a halt with his face still concealed. Eang, occupied with her son, naturally did not follow – nor even seem to realize who Omaskat was.

Instead, beyond the stormy wall, I heard Ogam unleash a torrent of hateful curses in a language I did not know. Eang responded, her voice thrumming in my head, as the storm turned in on itself. It streamed in towards its master in a great icy rush, then shot into the sky.

I felt Eang follow the storm. The wall of white disappeared entirely, leaving me alone on the ice with the snow-caked Omaskat and the limping form of Ayo.

An oppressive silence fell between us. The late afternoon sun shafted down through the clouds, glinting off the ice in his hair and beard as his mismatched eyes found mine. I saw caution there, along with a grim question.

Ayo limped over. He reached out a hand and rested it atop her head.

I knew what his look meant. He didn't need to voice it, because the same question clutched at my heart. Now that I had seen my goddess in the flesh, would my mind be changed? Would I throw myself at him, here and now, and bury my hatchet in his chest?

I wiped snow from my face and watched the distant, swirling storm-head that was Ogam and the mother who had tried to murder him at birth, the supposed goddess who hadn't had the strength to save her people, but still believed she could face down Lathian of old. My hand fell to my belt, where the Eangi collar I'd salvaged from the abandoned village was still fastened, warped and glistening in the sunlight.

The tips of my fingers rested on its frigid bronze as the storm raced over the peaks of the mountains to the north, leaving us in sparkling sunlight and disconsolate ice flows. And the more distant it became, the deeper my conviction ran.

I wanted to worship Eang, as my people always had. I wanted her to stand between Styga and me on a mountainside – my blazing Goddess of War, and me, her trusted, valued servant. I wanted to stand in the Hall of Smoke, shoulder to shoulder with a hundred Eangi, as we chanted and sung, united in heart and will and mind. I wanted to rest each night in the security of a goddess's bravery, watchfulness and vengeance.

But I could have none of those things. The Eangi were dead. Eang could not protect us from the threat we now faced, and I had to do what was right for my people, and myself.

I offered Omaskat a humorless, brittle smile. My fingers drifted away from the collar. "Does your offer still stand? The security of the High Halls and the Eangen people, under your god's rule?"

Omaskat nodded, chin still tilted slightly to one side in vigilance.

"Then I agree," I said. I took my hatchet and slit my left palm wide, then held out the hand to him, open and flat so that blood ran down my fingers and trickled onto the ice. Blood that was magic and hinted with the barest breath of sleeping amber ichor, if I looked at it just so. Blood that was sacrifice. Blood, as the gods always demanded.

"Stop Lathian, protect my people, and save our High Halls," I said. I was still so cold that I barely felt the wound, but the weight of the gesture pulled at my bones – down, down through the ice and earth and the fabric of the world. "And I will serve your god."

Omaskat came forward and took my hand, watching blood pool from the livid division of flesh. Then he curled my fingers in on themselves. Blood spilled, dripping down onto the ice between us.

"Not that," he said quietly. "Not ever again. Thvynder does not need your blood, Hessa. That belongs to you."

My jaw flexed, overwhelmed by a dozen darting, incoherent emotions. "Then what must I do?"

Omaskat nodded back towards the shore. "Return to the shores of the White Lake, as everyone expects you to. Fight, if need be – anything to keep Styga, Lathian and Eang from realizing that your loyalties have changed. And when the moment comes, and you and I face one another in the lake, buy me time to complete the ritual."

My chin dropped in slow ascent. "And Vistic?"

"He will return safely to his mother's arms. I promise you."

A second smile touched my lips, still small, but with a hint of genuine hope. No matter what happened now, how the gods clashed or the world shifted, I could cling to the thought of Sixnit and Vistic, together and safe.

My eyes dragged past Omaskat to the peninsula where they and Svala waited for me, and my happiness waned. "Will you take him, then? The baby?"

"Me, no. But Gadr is nearby, on his way to the White Lake with a force of Algatt. I'll send him for the child on his way," Omaskat said. When my eyes widened, he added, "Svala and Sixnit will not be harmed, I promise. But I think it is best if your High Priestess and I do not properly meet and it will give you… a little time together, before what comes next. I'll find Gadr at the lake and take child from there. You'll have an hour together, at most."

I swallowed a lump in my throat. It hurt – Ogam's boot had left its mark – but the pain was secondary. An hour. An hour with my friend, my mentor and the child before we were torn apart again. Unwelcome tears burned in my eyes, and I forcefully squinted them away. They were irrelevant, now.

"Then I need to go." I stepped away from him, clearing my throat. "We'll meet again at the White Lake."

Omaskat stooped to take the whimpering Ayo into his arms, then, straightening, he gave me a nod of farewell. The dog rested her head on his shoulder and let out a weary, whuffling sigh.

"At the White Lake."

FORTY

I hurried back to the peninsula, where a fire winked among the wind-ruffled trees. Svala waited for me on a rock, leaning instead of sitting, and as I separated from the night she wavered upright.

"Where's that man?" she asked, clasping her arms over her chest. The breeze off the lake was cool, but she shivered against a deeper cold.

I slowed, still ankle-deep in the water. In the chaos of snow and supernatural forces, Svala, like Eang, hadn't properly seen or sensed Omaskat. She still didn't realize who he was.

"We were separated," I said simply. My gaze flicked through the forest, searching for any sign of Gadr. Omaskat had said we'd only have an hour, and I could feel the minutes creeping by.

"Who was he?" Svala asked, still on the topic of Omaskat. Her eyes dropped to the Eangi collar at my belt, but she did not rebuke me for carrying it. If anything, her gaze softened. "You called him a god."

"I don't really know." My bruised throat felt tighter than it should as I spoke the lie, my eyes still on the forest. "You know how the gods are."

The other woman nodded. Her eyes left the collar and followed my gaze over her shoulder. "What is it, child?"

I shook my head and stepped up out of the water with a slosh and a tottering step. "Only my nerves."

"I understand." Svala reached out her hand, the network of fine scars across her fingers and palms milky in the twilight. "Come."

I clambered up the rocky shoreline to her outstretched hand. I took

343

it apprehensively, as if she would sense my betrayal through my skin. But all she did was help me up and pull me to a halt.

We looked at each other, older woman to younger, high priestess to priestess, mentor to acolyte. Then she pulled me into her chest. I froze, every muscle springing taut at the long-forgotten feeling of familiar arms around me, of affection flowing from another human being, let alone from Svala.

"I'm sorry." She rasped the words into my ear. "I'm sorry I wasn't there."

Albor. She meant Albor. My resistance crumpled and I sagged into her arms, body trembling in tearless, exhausted grief. Svala held me, letting me hide from the last two months' trials in her firm, if quaking arms, the maternal swell of her breasts, and the scent of sweat, sage and ice.

"Where were you?" I finally managed to ask, forcing myself to pull away. The longer her touch remained, the more my newfound convictions pained me. And the more I feared the approach of Gadr.

"Come to the fire," Svala said, nodding towards the light. "And we can talk."

A few moments later, warm light illuminated the faces of my companions and the shadow of Cadic, off in the trees. I sat close to Sixnit, Vistic sleeping at her breast and her head leant against a tree, red-rimmed eyes closed. She had smiled in greeting, clasped my hand and kissed my cheek, but had yet to speak.

Svala settled in across the fire. I divided my attention between her and the trees, my breath shallow. When would Gadr arrive? How long did the three of us have, here in the quiet night? How long before I had to leave them again and set off alone?

"I left Albor, right after you left for your climb," Svala began with the air of a long-held confession. "I did not know what to do about you, or Omaskat. So I went to pray, deep into the forest. But Eang… was silent."

So I was not the only one whose prayers had gone unheard that day. It was hollow comfort now.

Svala continued, "Then I saw Algatt in the woods. They harried me for days, until I managed to kill them. But by then I was hopelessly lost, far up in Rioki territory. So I drank yifr and visited the Hall, looking for answers."

"You found me," I added.

"Yes, eventually. And soon after that, Ogam found me in turn." Svala evaluated Sixnit, whose eyes were still closed. "That's the last thing I remember."

We both fell quiet and the fire snapped, sending a few sparks whirling up towards the trees above.

"Eang was dead," I said finally. I wasn't sure why I said it – we had so little time before Gadr arrived. But I needed to see Svala's reaction, needed to understand how deep her loyalty to Eang still ran. And how much the High Priestess might be holding back. "That's why she was silent. She died, and she killed an Eangi to pull herself back to life."

I felt, more than saw, Sixnit's eyes snap open. Svala, however, simply paused, lips thinned into a line. "You should not say such things, Hessa."

"I met the gods who killed her."

"But Eang is alive," Sixnit protested. "We saw her!"

"Indeed," Svala affirmed, her voice dropping to a deadly pitch. Her eyes narrowed and I privately mourned the warmth of the embrace we'd shared on the shoreline. "Who told you such a thing? Who 'killed' her?"

I looked at the High Priestess as I replied, my own voice hardening. Svala had to know we were Vestiges – if not she, who would? How dare she deny it?

"I know what we are," I said, willing my spine straight. "I went to the High Halls too, remember. I met two Gods of the Old World, standing over the corpses of Oulden and Riok and Dur – all murdered. They told me they'd killed Eang before, and that once I was dead, she might finally stay down."

Svala's suspicion flickered. "Oulden... Riok and Dur are dead?"

"I'll explain everything," I said, her shock making me bold. "But first, did you know? What we are?"

345

"Yes, I knew. Or rather…" Svala drew a fortifying breath. "I've long suspected. It is why, I believe, Ogam took me – to own the last hope of Eang. He couldn't kill me or any other Eangi outright, not without Frir telling Eang. Then his betrayal would be known."

"Then why didn't he put Hessa in the ice too?" Sixnit asked.

I brushed wind-blown hair from my forehead. "Because I will kill Omaskat, and Ogam wants him dead as much as Eang does. They all do. The Old Gods and the New. It's the only reason I'm alive."

My words seemed to refocus everyone.

"And you'll fulfill that destiny." Svala leaned forward to add wood to the flames. She looked to Sixnit and Vistic, "While you and I and the child wait for Hessa in Iskir."

The ease and simplicity of Svala's trust in me struck like a knife in the gut. She suspected nothing.

The High Priestess continued, "We'll rest here for another hour, then go our separate ways. We need to get the child as far away as possible and you need to finish your task."

I realized I was digging my fingers into my thighs. I pried them loose and nodded, the diligent Eangi to her High Priestess.

"But for now, we rest," Svala said, her eyes softening in some recollection of her earlier embrace. "And I want you, the both of you, to tell me your stories."

So we did. I went first, confessing all that had befallen me since I heard the war horns from Mount Thyr. I told them of Ashaklon and Styga, of Oulden and the Arpa, and Gadr's allegiance with the god beneath the lake. But much of my tale was too raw, too dangerous to divulge. So I concealed it behind genuine emotion and passed the tale on to Sixnit.

Six shifted, preparing to give her half of the tale, and passed me Vistic. Despite weeks in the ice, he was bigger and heavier than I remembered. My body was tired and my arms complained under his weight, but as I took him my discomfort faded.

His eyes remained closed, tiny features at peace and lips slightly parted. He looked so very Eangen, from the black curls on his head to Sixnit's nose, and the angular cut of his sleeping eyes recalled his father.

As Sixnit began to speak, I leant down and took in his sweet infant scent. Whatever else Vistic was, he was the child of a murdered Eangi brother, a baby that I had pledged my protection to and whose mother I loved. And in that moment, all over again, I vowed to never, ever let harm befall him.

Sixnit said, "Ogam came for me in the Algatt camp, after Vistic… vanished. He promised to help me find the baby, so I went with him."

"Why would he take you with him?" Svala voiced the same thought in my own mind. Now that I understood Ogam, his kindness to Sixnit made little sense.

"Because I'm Vistic's mother." Sixnit's smile was sorrowful. "Maybe he assumed there was something special about me, that I had some value. Maybe he thought I should be with my son, since he's still so small."

I recalled Ogam's own story – abandoned as a newborn on a wind-swept mountain. Was it sentimentality, then, that had led him to keep Vistic with Sixnit?

"He told me Vistic wasn't human," my friend added. "I was frightened, so I didn't ask many questions."

"What did he say Vistic was?" I wanted to know.

Sixnit shrugged. Tightness gathered around her eyes and I saw one hand twitch towards her stomach. "His."

I stared at her hand, an odd suspicion trickling into the back of my thoughts, but I did not broach it yet. "What? How?"

Irritation crossed the other woman's face. "Some nonsense about visiting me in the dark of the night."

"If Ogam had entered the Hall of Smoke, I would have known," Svala interjected.

"Well I'm no Eangi," Sixnit replied, her voice cooling. She stared at the baby, adoration and fear conflicting in her expression. "And I did not care what he said, or how untrue it was. I was desperate to find Vistic. When we finally did, when we confronted Gadr… Ogam sounded so cruel, and Gadr was so protective. Something wasn't right. After Gadr fled and I had Vistic in my arms again, I saw his eyes had changed."

At mention of Gadr, my eyes scanned the shadows under the trees again.

Sixnit pried her hand away from her stomach and inched closer to the fire. "But... I felt safe with Ogam. I even lay with him, near the end. I did what I had to do."

That made me pause, recalling Ogam's offers of immortal offspring. "You—"

"Yes," Sixnit said, a little more coldly than before, and she did not meet either of our gazes. "I did. More than once. I've a baby at my breast, Hessa; it's not as though I thought he'd get a child on me. It took Vist and I over a year to become pregnant with Vistic, and you and Eidr never... you know how these things can be."

Eidr's name, and the thought of the family we'd never had, silenced me. That was a side of my loss, a well within my chasm of grief, that I could not risk traversing. Not now. I locked it away and lowered my gaze to the heart of the fire, focusing on its flickers and sparks.

"Ogam has sired a thousand children," Svala corrected. "I do not think his get would care if you were ten years barren."

Sixnit's face turned to scarlet and her eyes to flint. "I did what I had to do," she repeated. "But then I woke one night to him smothering Vistic. I went mad. But Ogam couldn't kill him, so he took us to the ice."

"Was that before or after I came?" Svala wondered, the rest of her thoughts on Sixnit's dalliance with the immortal Son of Winter locked behind her dark eyes.

Sixnit's expression was grim in equal measure. "Before. He formed the island around us and the horse and said he would wake me at the 'proper time.'"

Svala glanced off towards the beast in question. "Why the horse?"

"For me." Sixnit shook her head and drew her knees up, concealing her stomach again, and I suddenly knew the reason why.

I met Svala's eyes and an understanding passed between us. Abruptly, the High Priestess shifted her aching body upright and put out her hand. I saw anger in her expression, frustration and a great, crushing burden. "Give me your waterskin, Hessa."

I handed it over and the priestess moved off, leaving Sixnit and me in silence. The fire hissed, wind rustled the trees and waves lapped the shoreline in tentative slaps and burbles.

"You *are* pregnant with Ogam's child," I murmured. It wasn't a question.

"I think so. But I'm alive," she said. "And I don't care what you or Svala think of me. I did what I had to do. My husband is dead, but I am still alive to raise our son. And this new child, whoever they may be. They're mine, not Ogam's. Mine. Will you abandon me for that?"

"No!" I faltered. Her gaze stabbed into mine, hostile and cold and full of pain. I reached to take her hand, clutching it as firmly as she'd allow, and repeated myself, putting all my hope and honesty into a simple, "No. I'll help you."

Sixnit's eyes filled with tears. Frustrated with herself, she raked them away and reached for Vistic again, her movements taut with love and determination.

I relinquished him. My arms felt suddenly cold as he left and reality swelled in, close and inescapable. Soon, so soon, Gadr would come for that child, Sixnit's grief would break anew, and I would have to leave her again. I would forge off into the night alone, as always.

Vistic awoke in his mother's arms, opening his eyes to reveal their new blue and gold hues. I leant forward to look down at his small face, my shoulder brushing Sixnit's. She nearly flinched away, but then leant into me, warm and familiar. And so we sat there, two women considering the face of the unnatural child we'd bound ourselves to, while yet another, nearly as unnatural infant resided in Sixnit's womb.

"If you survive," Sixnit added quietly, and it took me a moment to realize she was amending my vow. "Don't go after Omaskat, Hessa. Stay with me. Help me get Vistic as far away as we can."

My eyes dropped to the infant. He didn't move, his attention lingering on his mother's face with an uncanny degree of focus.

"Svala will protect you," I consoled her, and myself.

"I don't know Svala."

I looked at the other woman askance. Sixnit knew Svala, of course. We all lived in the same Hall. But simple acquaintance or shared living space was not what she meant.

"You can trust her," I reassured my friend.

Sixnit reached out to grab my hand again. There was no self-pity in her words as she spoke, no more held-back tears. "You and I promised to protect Vistic. Together. What if you don't come back? What will I do? My husband is gone too, Hessa, and who knows if our families in other villages survived. We're all we have left."

The question was too deep, too devouring for me to contemplate. But despite the memories that Svala dug up and Sixnit's pleas, we couldn't be safe, not truly, until Omaskat's god was free.

"I'll find you again," I promised, clutching Sixnit's hand. "All of you. In the High Halls or the Waking World."

Sixnit looked away into the darkness and did not release my grip. When I spoke again, the words felt heavy in my stomach, the simple, immediate truth of them overriding grander thoughts of eternity and gods and fate. "Even if we run, Vistic will still be in danger. So I will remove that danger."

Before Sixnit could gather a response, chattering and scratching came from the tree above us. I looked up, hand flying towards my hatchet at the same time as Sixnit scrambled back.

Armed and on my feet, I peered up into the boughs of a birch tree. Eyes glinted at me from the darkness, followed by a second, scolding chirr. At the same time, Cadic stomped and shuffled off in the trees.

The head of an axe laced around Sixnit's throat. A familiar woman with pale red hair stepped up behind her, her eyes cool and hard as river stones.

To the left and right, more Algatt slipped from the trees.

"Break my warriors' bones," Gadr offered, sidling out of the shadows to lay his own knife across Sixnit's throat. The red-haired woman retreated and Gadr backed Sixnit into a trunk, though he spoke to me. "Curdle their minds. But you cannot stop me, and I doubt you have the strength to get far. Your friend will still die, and I do not want to do that. There has been enough innocent blood spilled on my mountains."

My jaw clenched, stopping an instinctive rush of Eang's Fire. Gadr's theatrics were jarring, but I'd known this was coming. All I could do was hope they were truly theatrics and that Gadr would keep Omaskat's promise not to harm Six and Svala.

But that didn't just mean trusting Omaskat's word. It meant trusting Gadr, ancient enemy of my people, with his fraying braid and bare-toothed snarl – not to mention the Algatt surrounding us.

I met Sixnit's wide, shocked eyes. She clutched Vistic tighter and parted her lips to speak. I knew what she would say, even though she didn't dare say it. *Take Vistic. Run. Leave me.*

I didn't move, heart slamming against my ribs with such force that they threatened to crack.

"Now," Gadr looked back at the red-haired woman, the same woman I'd saved from the Arpa last week. "Take the child."

Sixnit erupted. Heedless of the knife at her throat she screamed and struck out when the Algatt woman tried to pry Vistic from her arms. The knife cut in and blood trickled down my friend's skin.

"Gadr!" I shouted. "Stop this!"

The man wrinkled his nose at me. "Then hand over the child."

Another Algatt lunged for Sixnit.

I'd just enough time to see a flash of metal before I screamed. It was an echoing, wordless clap of power – enough to stagger, but not to kill. Or so I intended. The new attacker reeled, howling, and off in the night I heard an answering scream – Svala's signature Eangi cry, cracking and hissing. More cries followed, branches snapped, and metal struck metal.

I had to stop this. I had to stop it before Svala or Sixnit were killed.

The thought had barely unfolded before an Algatt plucked the screeching Vistic from Sixnit's arms and darted away into the night. Sixnit threw herself after the man, clawing and shrieking like a creature possessed.

Gadr stepped in front of her. He seized her by her clothing and hurled her unceremoniously around the fire, directly into my arms.

We toppled to the ground. My foot struck the fire and sparks exploded up into the canopy. Algatt scattered from the flames and Gadr's voice carried over the rush, "Go, now!"

The Algatt fled in a thunder of footsteps and victorious howls. Each one tore through me, another strike, another blow to my will and conviction. But I did not let Sixnit go, no matter how she howled and flailed, nor did I run after them myself. I held both of us back until the Algatt and Vistic were gone, and we were alone with the scattered remnants of our fire.

"I'll get him back," I vowed, again and again. "I'll get him back. Trust me."

Finally, Svala staggered from the shadows. Her axe – my axe – was bloodied. So were her nails; she'd used her bare hands to claw at her opponents. But her own injuries were superficial. It was her time in the ice, and the fatigue of Eang's Fire, that weighed upon her now.

She leant against a tree across the scattered fire from us and looked at me with the shuttered, taciturn eyes of someone who had long ago experienced the worst life and the gods had to offer.

I watched her over Sixnit's head and wondered if, some day, I would wear the same world-weary expression.

"Take Sixnit south." My voice didn't sound like my own. It was cold and jarring, though I tried to soften it for the sake of my friend, shuddering in my arms. "I know where Gadr will take Vistic. And I know that Omaskat will be there, at the White Lake."

"Where the sky bleeds into the mountain," Svala added. She closed her eyes for a few seconds, gathering herself, then we pulled Sixnit upright, together. My friend had ceased to cry, but her silence was worse.

"We'll meet you in Iskir," Svala offered. "If you haven't come within a week, or if it's not safe, we'll head on to East Meade."

"East Meade?" I repeated the name of my home, only half understanding. "Did…"

"Someone warned them in time," Svala explained. "I saw it in my visions. And West Meade is nearly untouched. We will be safe there, for a time."

I raked at my eyes with a free hand, though I had no tears to shed. My father. My sisters. My cousins. *Alive.* The thought buoyed me and broke me with imaginings of them still living and breathing in this world. I wanted to race to them, to protect them, to hide in them and weep together for all we had lost and all that might have been. But I could not, not yet.

Svala came closer, dropping into the Eangi's sacred tongue so that Sixnit could not understand. "Remember who you serve, child."

My traitor's heart went deathly still.

"And if we do not see you again, we will await you in the High Halls." With that, Svala turned to Sixnit and extended her hands, compassion wheedling into her eyes. "Come, child. We are all in the hands of the gods."

I let Sixnit go. She did not look at me anymore but went to Svala, who put an arm around her shoulders. The space between us opened, wide and suddenly uncrossable – they together, in body and in faith, and I alone in both.

Sixnit looked at me then, her grief and rage and regret fading under the dull mask of a woman who has lost everything.

"Bring him back," she said.

I swallowed my grief, turned my feet towards the mountains and the waiting milk-white lake. And then I began to run.

FORTY-ONE

I dropped low as I entered the forest, ducking branches and traversing loam on soundless feet. I'd passed Gadr and his Algatt horde, some five-hundred strong, an hour ago as they poured into the valley of the White Lake. Though we were allies now – as sickening as that thought was – I'd avoided being seen and had made no attempt to catch sight of the captive Vistic. That would only grieve me more.

Instead, I rounded the valley and made for the Arpa's hidden camp while the crunch of Algatt boots diverted north, making for the eastern shore of the lake beneath the placid, brooding mountain.

As I neared the camp, Styga materialized from the shadows beneath a pine. I threw up my hands and halted.

"I'm here to kill him," I stated. "Nothing more. Then take my life, if you want it. But let me stop him first."

The being of shadow and starlight considered me. Behind them, I could hear the Arpa moving, their uncanny quietness all the starker amid battle preparations.

Styga's star-speckled cheeks were obscure in the night. "Yet yesterday you fled at his side."

"He had information my goddess needed," I returned. The lies came far easier in the face of Styga than they had with Svala and Sixnit. "I serve her, not you."

"Ah yes, lest I forget," Styga unfurled a toothless, abyssal smile. "Then play your part, Eangi, and give me no reason to question you."

We strode into the Arpa camp together. I kept my gaze level as I passed armed ranks of tainted legionaries, forcing my attention not to linger on them. I did not stop walking until I came to Telios himself.

"Give me weapons," I requested.

The zealot smiled.

At the northern edge of the woods, I came to a halt. I tested the Arpa sword and Algatt shield I had commandeered, then set them both aside and unfastened the Eangi collar from my belt. Its metal was cold as I wedged it about my throat, its warped curls of bronze digging into my flesh before they settled atop my collar bones. The weight of it was both foreign and familiar, unsettling and steadying. I told myself that it was a symbol of what I'd left behind, of my people and my place among them. But to everyone else, I hoped it would reinforce my pretense of the devout Eangi, blindly faithful unto death.

Nonetheless, guilt clogged my throat and the collar chafed. But I was not afraid. I kept my thoughts shallow, narrow. I had only three goals today: buy Omaskat time, reclaim Vistic, and escape.

To my right, the Arpa marched out of the trees in ordered, regimented lines. Telios led them, moving with a self-possessed, gratified stride in the pre-dawn light. Two other noteworthy figures joined him: the Archeress and Rioux, who had slain Oulden in the High Halls. I stiffened at the sight of them, but neither approached me.

Styga slipped up to my shoulder. Before us, the first rays of the rising sun struck the solitary peak above the lake and illuminated a scattering of high waterfalls, reminding me of Mount Thyr, of Eang and Albor.

"I cannot help you against the Watchman," Styga said. "But we will keep the battle away from you for as long as we can."

We both looked up as the clatter of hooves sounded out above the march of Telios's men. Mounted Arpa clattered up to the shores of the White Lake from the west, helmets affixed, backs straight and plated armor flashing in the dawn light. Styga's head tilted and Telios turned, his expression unreadable at this distance.

My chest tightened. These were Polinus's men – I saw the commander front and centre, Castor and Quentis to his right, and Estavius to his left. And there, beside Estavius, was Nisien.

I eyed Estavius briefly, thinking again of his amber blood. The sight of Quentis made my nerves flutter, but I was armed and under Styga's protection; I doubted he would try to touch me. In the end it was Nisien, his dark eyes squinting across the Arpa lines from beneath his helmet, that captured my attention. I had to warn him of Lathian and Telios.

Without a second thought, I left the tree line and sprinted toward him.

"Hessa!" At the sight of me, Nisien dropped down from his saddle and pulled his helmet from his head. He stared from me to the distant line of Arpa, then he seemed to forget them entirely. His gaze focused on me, tracing my mail and the wild crown of my hair, and the Arpa sword in my hand. "I wasn't sure you were still... Why are you here?"

I embraced him. It was a strong embrace, a sister's embrace, and I could barely think through the pounding in my ears. "Nisien, you can't be here. You need to—"

"What are you doing here?" He cut me off, repeating his question. His free arm wrapped around me, but it lacked vigor.

I stepped back, the urge to tell him the whole truth burning in my chest. But I couldn't risk it. I pointed my sword across Telios's Arpa to where the Algatt lines gathered, out of sight. "Today I... I kill Omaskat. But Nisien, listen to me. Did you do as I said? Did you devote yourself to a northern god?"

"Omaskat?" Nisien repeated the unfamiliar name. I realized with a pang that I had never told him of my original mission, let alone the pretense I played at now. The confusion in his eyes slipped into wariness. "Who is that? I— No, I didn't."

Just then Estavius dropped down next to us, his head also uncovered.

Our gazes met in momentary acknowledgement and a mutual, knowing kind of appraisal, then he asked Nisien something in rapid Arpa. His gaze flicked from Styga to the other legionaries.

Telios. I had to warn Nisien about Telios.

At that moment Polinus strode out to meet the other commander, who was silhouetted against the rising sun in a fringed helmet. The two men met a dozen paces away from us and began to speak.

I grabbed Nisien's arm just as he heard Telios's voice. His muscles turned to stone beneath my hand.

Estavius followed his gaze and his lips set in a thin line.

"It's Telios," I told Nisien, worry suffusing my voice. "Nisien? I know who he is. He's here at Lathian's bidding, and you are all in grave danger. Nisien?"

The horseman took a compulsive step back, but not at the mention of Lathian. His eyes were locked on Telios, now in heated conference with Polinus. Rapid Arpa passed between them as Styga drifted over, their starlit features a fading glow in the dawn light.

My hand dropped away. "Nisien, listen to me."

The wind picked up, just enough to rustle stray hair across my face. Estavius stepped in front of the other man and blocked his view of the commander. He spoke to him closely, his words low and even. It was not unlike how I'd seen Nisien speak to a frightened horse.

The rest of the legionaries kept their eyes up and ignored the exchange, faces concealed behind their helmets. Except for Quentis. He'd urged his horse out of the line and now stared past us, at the lake, with a revelatory light to his gaze. When I caught his eye, he raised his mixing bowl in greeting and laughed – the laugh of a man who has just discovered a great and unexpected treasure. Whatever he had thought he'd find here, this was not it – and he was overjoyed.

Footsteps signaled the commanders' approach. Estavius pressed his forehead to Nisien's and stood to the side, shoulder to shoulder with the Soulderni. The picture of the Arpa legionary, Estavius adjusted his helmet under his arm and nodded in salute.

Nisien did not. His expression was blank, save a momentary twitch of violent, sickening hatred across his upper lip.

Unexpectedly protective, I turned, placing myself in front of my friend as the commanders drew up.

"Nisien." Telios recognized the horseman. His eyes flashed on either side of his nose guard – malice, satisfaction and hunger.

My hand tightened on my sword.

Polinus either didn't notice the tension between them or didn't care. He turned from Telios and bellowed instructions to his second and third, leaving the other man to cast his gaze appraisingly over the line of cavalry.

Nisien abruptly grabbed my wrist and tugged me close, dropping his voice so the other men couldn't hear. "Do not trust him. Run, Hessa, get out of here as soon as you can."

Before I could reply, he jerked on his helmet and mounted up. Estavius remained in his place a moment longer, exchanging a stare with Telios.

Telios's eyes flicked between the two younger men, a glance so subtle that I might have missed it. Was that… jealousy? Suspicion?

Finally, Telios strode back towards his men, Styga at his side. Polinus mounted up and directed his horse down the line, shouting orders in Arpa that made the men sit up straighter.

I caught Estavius's eye. The legionary murmured in his improved Northman, "Telios is the worst of men. Stay away from him."

"You don't mean to fight with him, do you?" I asked. I wanted to ask who he was, and how he'd found the magic that I had, but souls were on the line. "Lathian has possessed them, all of them, Estavius. You have to leave before he takes you too."

The legionary's expression was grim. "Telios is still Arpa, and Lathian is our god. We fight first and speak of Telios later. I must go, Hessa."

I remained still, my chest full of dread for both Nisien and Estavius. But the weight of the Eangi collar at my throat drew me back to my task; I was here to help Omaskat, save my people and Vistic. Nothing else mattered. Nothing else could matter.

"Look after him," I murmured to Estavius. "Whatever you are."

My last words earned a startled, subtle smile from the legionary, but it was quickly replaced by gravity. He ducked his head, short curls bobbing around his temples, then put his helmet back on. The last thing he looked at was the lake over my shoulder as he swung up into the saddle.

I glanced at the helmeted and silent Nisien once more before I returned to Telios's cohort. With every step, I pushed more and more distractions aside. By the time I drew up to the lines of soldiers, I was single-minded again.

I leapt up onto a boulder. Shafts of dawn bored into the valley, illuminating distant Algatt heads in halos of red and blond.

Light glinted off raised weapons as the Algatt roared and yipped. I could not see Omaskat and Vistic, but Gadr stood chanting before their round, locked shields. He himself had no shield and bore a long, ornate two-handed axe.

Horns sounded, beginning in low, unhurried growls and ending in sharp, jarring cracks. The sound ripped through my ribs and set my teeth on edge, dragging me back up Mount Thyr, back to the shrine where I had knelt and begged for a second chance from a goddess who could not hear me.

If I'd fought beside Eangi today, my people would have responded in kind. Our horns would have wailed and our people raised their eerie, melodic war cry.

But Algatt faced Arpa now, and they were no ordinary men. They did not shout. They stomped no feet and beat no shields. No one prayed. The Arpa remained in their line of rectangular shields, helmets closed, chins dropped, legs poised. The only sound came from the snap of banners in the wind.

I looked from them to the cavalry on the other side of the valley. Distantly, I wondered if Nisien, even Estavius, would have the same dull, charcoal-eyed gaze tomorrow.

And the Algatt who roared for vengeance and hammered their shields, would their corpses swing, eyeless, from the trees?

Another bout of Algatt horns split the air.

I replied this time, blinding myself to everything save my own people and my own goals. I loosed an Eangi howl to the dawn, my lone notes rising up the valley on the shafts of fragile, golden light. In my memory, hundreds of Eangi and Eangen warriors joined me, adding their own tones to the twisting, melodic scream.

As if that were their signal, the battle began.

FORTY-TWO

Lines met with a thunder of shields and Algatt cries. Swords and spears thrust. Axes hooked over Arpa shields and one section of the line faltered, only to snap closed an instant later.

Legs braced and, overhead, arrows began to fly. Arpa archers dropped and loosed, sending a volley over the Algatt front at the same time as the second and third rows of Arpa locked their shields into a roof. An answering rain of Algatt arrows clattered and cracked down onto the barrier, only a handful punching through to do any real damage.

I'd seen this tactic before; it was distraction, not damage, that the Algatt archers aimed for.

As the last Algatt arrow fell, the Miri called Gadr launched himself over the shield wall. He crashed into the Empire's lines, buckling the roof of shields and vanishing beneath them in a glistening ripple of rectangular scales.

I caught my breath, thinking for an instant that he'd been swallowed.

The god of the Algatt reappeared in a circle of scattering, scrambling Arpa. He hacked vengeance for his murdered people in a bloody, glistening arc of axe and muscle, turning and slashing with indomitable strength. He roared and his people roared back, pressing in as their god vanished once more into a forest of spears and shields. Soon, the ripple of chaos his axe left was all I could see of him.

Throughout it all, the Arpa did not speak, not even to shout orders. Even with Gadr in their midst they moved like a flock of ravenous birds, pushing and receding, thrusting and blocking, until the Algatt line began to snake.

My eyes flickered over the battle and shoreline, trying to glimpse Gadr and watching for Omaskat.

The Arpa lines cracked. Gadr unfurled in a scar of butchered Arpa, heaving chest drenched with blood, as his people rushed around him. Their howls reached a fevered pitch and the Arpa began to retreat, leaving dead and dying legionaries in their wake.

But the Arpa retreated too far and too fast, falling into expert formations: shields on all sides, shields overhead. Horns began to blast in warning and Gadr bellowed, but the Algatt force was already too divided.

Polinus and his riders thundered across the empty ground, flowing around the foot soldiers' formations like water around stones.

Omaskat strode into the lake from the east.

I leapt from my boulder and took off at a sprint, sending up a spray of white water as I tore through the shallows toward the Watchman.

An Algatt stumbled in my path and slit the throat of a legionary. As she looked up, her face streaked with blood and her red hair full of the dawn, she paused. She knew me. She was the woman I had freed, who'd threatened Sixnit.

Her eyes rounded, but I had no chance to choose my response. An arrow of white bone slammed into her cheek. She toppled backwards into the water as the Archeress, Goddess of the Old World, fell into step beside me.

"Go, Eangi!" the goddess – the Miri – hissed.

There was no time for shock or qualms – no time for the thought that the Archeress had killed my Eangi brethren in this same way, with these same arrows. Five more Algatt charged into our path.

The attackers faltered as they realized who I was. Eangi instinct still told me to throw myself at them, and I saw the same wild impulse in their eyes. Gadr's alliance with Omaskat could not obliterate centuries of bloodshed.

The Archeress, again, did not wait for me to act. Three bone arrows thudded into the Algatt chests and were buried up to their pale fletching. One collapsed, one stared uncomprehendingly down at the fletching between her breasts, and the last began to keen in a drowning, blood-bubbling shriek.

The remaining two Algatt bolted and my muscles unclenched. Before the Archeress could put arrows into their backs, I pulled Eang's Fire into a scream. It chased them across the surface of the White Lake and they stumbled, crashing down into the water with shrieks of pain.

I sprinted off towards Omaskat, leading the Archeress away before she could see the Algatt get back up.

She followed, her lithe strides easily overtaking me. A hundred paces ahead, Omaskat was knee-deep in the water, a naked Vistic held in his large hands. His eyes bored into the water, lips moving in an inaudible prayer.

"Go!" I yelled to the Archeress. "He's mine!"

She waved an arrow at me in mock salute and turned, facing the shore and settling another fan of arrows between her deft fingers.

"Omaskat!" I yelled, hoping that it sounded more like a threat than a warning. My mind scrambled. What could I do now? I was so close. Styga, the Archeress – they would all expect me to strike him down within moments.

Omaskat, unsurprised by my approach, kept walking. "It will be done soon!"

As he spoke the dawn light faltered; or rather, it narrowed. Over the great peak to the north, thick black clouds loomed. They reached over the shoulders of the mountain in snaking tendrils and began to seep down towards the lake. As they smothered the dawn light, they glowed a distant, eerie red.

The sky was bleeding into the mountain.

I heard a shrill, victorious wail and spun. Quentis stood in the water with his robe floating about his hips, throwing a worshipful face towards the new clouds. He grinned madly and threw out his hands – one clasping a knife, the other his bowl.

"Oh, my lord! Come!" Quentis sang in his deep, crackling voice. "Revel in the death of your enemies!"

Lathian was coming. Blood hammered in my ears and my breath hitched with every inhalation. *Focus.* Quentis didn't matter. Omaskat was almost finished, his god would rise, and Lathian would be destroyed before he reached the lake. I just had to buy him a few more moments.

Then I heard Telios laugh and the crash of someone falling from a horse.

A dozen paces away, Nisien came up out of the lake gasping, Telios's hand dug into his short hair. The older man kept him on his knees, forcing his head back, forcing earthen brown eyes to meet tainted grey.

The horseman stared back. In that horrible moment he was stripped of himself, no longer a man, no longer a soldier; he was a boy on his knees. A boy at the mercy of a man.

Then Nisien bellowed. He jerked at the hand buried in his hair and managed to come to his feet.

Telios's sword flashed toward his legs.

Eang's Fire exploded from me, searing across the surface of the lake towards Telios. It struck him just as his sword thrust. Lathian's zealot staggered and Nisien pried himself free, struck him in the face and seized him by the throat, following his former commander down into the water with a second, hate-filled shout.

For an instant, I thought that my intervention had gone unnoticed. Then I saw Quentis's expression. He glared at me, accusatory and grave, and his eyes had already lost some of their color.

In the north, Lathian stepped down onto the surface of the lake. He was beautiful and devastating, draped in Arpa garb and surrounded by tendrils of midnight fog. He did not look at me. Instead, his gaze fell on Omaskat, still murmuring, still praying, and the wailing form of Vistic, now lifted above his head.

Nearby legionaries began to turn. The Archeress lowered her bow and I felt a hundred, a thousand eyes settle upon me.

It was time. I approached Omaskat slowly, sword and shield in hand.

I'd long forgotten to breathe, long lost linear thought. But Vistic's wails cut me to the bone, and I knew what I had to do.

A handful of paces from Omaskat I turned my back to him, raised my shield, and dropped into a defensive crouch.

With that action, my façade shattered. I heard Styga roar from the shoreline and Rioux laugh in hysterical vindication as the Archeress raised her bow.

An arrow of bone leveled at me. "Finish it, Eangi!"

An owl hooted.

Eang came. She rushed into me as she had in Souldern, but this was far more painful. I spasmed and screamed, railing as Eang blazed through my blood, snapped out into my fingers, and obliterated my mind.

She began to drive me towards Omaskat, though each step was labored, every movement pained. He did not look our way, eyes clenched shut, Vistic wailing, but there was something about him which resisted her, as it had Styga. It was agony, utter agony to the Goddess of War.

And it was not alone in its resistance. Even as my consciousness retreated, I railed against her, battering and clawing. The Fire was hers and that amber sweetness, the honeyed magic that had become my own – it was no match for this, not bound as it was.

Still I felt Eang's horror, her rage and indignation. She knew my mind. She found my stolen power, my traitorous heart, and her hand came down harder than ever. My self, all that was me, sputtered and buckled.

My memory of the next few seconds set in jarring, jagged chunks. My human thoughts – rage against Eang, terror for Vistic and Omaskat and Nisien and dread of Lathian – disintegrated. Water buffeted my chest as my speed increased. My feet found a boulder beneath the surface, I leapt up, and Eang launched me at Omaskat like a stone from a sling.

Omaskat froze, his lips still parted.

Just before impact, the goddess fled in a flurry of vengeful, soul-stripping rage. I was left with a single moment of clarity before my sword came down and the flesh of Omaskat's throat and chest opened like butter. Vistic fell. We collided. The White Lake engulfed us.

By the time I found my footing in the chest-deep water and raked air into my lungs, Omaskat floated on his back. He stared upwards, hands slipping away from the bloody division in his neck. Red turned to brown where it met his tunic and spread out into the water in pinkish tendrils.

"Hessa," Omaskat croaked. "The wind—"

His voice faded. In its place, other voices cried out in chorus: Styga, the Archeress, Rioux, even the distant, unseen strains of Ashaklon. They stabbed me like knives, exultant and victorious as my mind clattered between Omaskat's body, Eang's rage, Lathian and Vistic. Where had Eang gone? Had Omaskat completed the ritual?

No. He was dead. Dead by my hands, as Fate had decreed.

Vistic. Where was he? I focused on this closest, simplest fear. I spun, clutching my chest as if that could somehow keep my ravaged body from falling apart. I searched the surface of the lake for any sign, any bubble or flicker or cry. But there was nothing.

Panic overtook me. I dove back beneath the surface and threw my eyes wide, but the water was too foggy. I could see nothing except the broadening stain of Omaskat's blood.

I jerked upright again and saw Lathian looming over the north shore, Quentis wading out on the south. Telios was in the midst of dragging Nisien onto the rocks not far off and, between the lake and the trees, the Arpa had surrounded the remaining Algatt.

By the time I looked back to Omaskat, he was perfectly still.

"No! How?! How could you let this happen?" The words tore out of my throat, meant far more for myself than for him. Desperate, I grabbed at the dead man's tunic and heaved him upright, trying to shake him back to life, but his sodden weight was too much.

I let Omaskat go, unable to bear the sight of him and my failure, and staggered back to my feet. My bleary eyes found Lathian, under gathering clouds. Styga was with him, and Rioux and the Archeress.

The sight of them was like the smell of decay; it struck me, winded me, and made me gag.

Omaskat was dead. Vistic – I couldn't even think of him. Nisien captured. And me? My betrayal was known to the creature I called my goddess, the goddess of vengeance who, despite my will, still owned me.

And furthermore, my betrayal did not even matter. I'd chosen to break my faith, and Omaskat had still died by my own hand. Fate's word had held true, to the detriment of all.

Eang's recompense would not be long in coming. Perhaps it would not be immediate death, not while I remained her Vestige, but I'd no doubt Eang could devise something equally as dreadful.

A desperate urge to pray came over me, to beg for forgiveness and take back my betrayal now, when it ceased to matter. I closed my throat, physically rebelling against the instinct, but her name still escaped my lips – half belligerent plea, half hateful growl.

"Eang."

"Oh, she's finished with you now, you delightful little traitor." Ogam strode towards me, the lake freezing beneath his feet. "Aren't you, Mother?"

Eang appeared. There was no flash of light, no gathering of smoke. One moment the space between Ogam and me was empty, and the next she was there.

I had never seen Eang outside of a vision or a veil of snow. She was everything I'd been told she was: glorious, staggering, frightful, wrathful. And she was beautiful, captivating in a way that matched even Lathian.

But at the sight of her I felt only dread, and her Fire in my chest seared with true, violent pain. I staggered to the boulder I'd leapt off moments ago, clutching at my ribs and trying vainly to access the sleeping, golden well of power beneath the flame.

Eang's twin axes absently divided the surface of the water as she considered her son, the muscles of her shoulders and biceps standing out and her forearms wrapped in bronze-plated bracers. She was certainly aware of the Old Gods, gathering power on the other side of the lake – her head cocked slightly towards them, and several of her owls circled overhead. I thought that she even glanced at me, at the Eangi collar resting against my throat, and that I saw my death in her dark eyes. But her focus was on the Son of Winter.

"Ogam. My spawn. Explain yourself."

Ogam's grin was wild and wicked. "Look at your Vestige, Mother. Even she saw through you, even she betrayed you. See how piteous she is. See!"

Eang did not turn as I battled to find some scrap of dignity here, at the end of all things.

Ogam spat in disgust. "Perhaps you'll care if I show you this." With that, he held up Svala's severed head.

I vomited into the lake.

"Hessa." Though Eang spoke to me, she did not tear her eyes from Ogam. "Keep back."

"See?" Ogam crowed. "Now you matter, Hessa. Now you're her only anchor, traitorous as you are."

Eang glared at me, her expression written with disdain and crippling fury. But I had seen enough of her mind by this point to recognize the fear, too – hidden in the creases around her eyes and the flutter of her throat.

My eyes dragged to Svala's head, dangling from Ogam's hand, and I swayed.

Eang spun back on her son. "Ogam. If I die, if the binding on Lathian fails – that is no world to live in. I bore you. I nursed you. I—"

"You despised me." Ogam issued the words in a deadly, even tone. As he spoke, he threw aside Svala's head and a spear of ice appeared in his hands. "You loved yourself in me, nothing more. Come now, Mother. It's well time we rid ourselves of one another."

"No." Eang's response took me by surprise. "Ogam—"

"Do it!" Ogam screamed in a winter's gale. "By your own hand! Kill me! Drown me!"

"No!" Eang had raised her weapons, but I heard the pain in her voice. "Stop this!"

Ogam threw himself upon Eang with millennia of hatred in his roar. She retreated under his blows – once, twice – then the anguish in her face locked. The mother faded. The Goddess remained.

The Goddess of War and the Son of Winter hacked at one another with strength and skill that belonged to legend and myth. I stumbled backwards as they burst past me, Ogam chasing his mother a dozen paces up the lake. Eang plowed through the water but Ogam thundered across a sheaf of ice, his steps sure and more water freezing in his path. He slashed with his spear and Eang leapt aside, the distance between them and me widening with every step.

Svala's severed head drifted by my knees, eyes half-open and jaw cracked wide. My world tapered into a stifling, soundless tunnel.

I fled, stumbling into the shallows and toppling onto my hands and knees. Rocks jarred into my shins, knees and palms, but the pain was little more than a flicker on the edge of my mind.

Someone crouched before me. I raised my head and found Quentis's grey-tinted, bloodshot eyes mere inches from mine.

I toppled back, splashing and clattering on the rocks, but he didn't move after me. Instead, he sunk back into a kneel and raised his eyes to the lake, his grey robe darkened and clinging with lake water.

"Look, Eangi," he whispered, voice barely penetrating the silent storm in my skull. "Watch the gods battle. This is our privilege, you and I; priest and priestess."

I didn't want to watch, but my eyes dragged out across the water all the same. Ogam and Eang clashed, broke apart and harried one another. Meanwhile the Gods of the Old World converged on the far side of the water, gathering around the feet of Lathian to watch the conflict unfold.

Quentis followed my gaze. "Lathian gathers," the priest explained, "drawing his strength. Omaskat is dead, and the binding weakens. He will come to us soon. Perhaps by morning?"

Eang's scream tore through the air. Her cry was the pattern of an Eangi's, the original which we echoed on the battlefield. But now it wavered, turning from rage to sorrow and terrible pain.

My eyes snapped back to Eang just as Ogam drove his spear deeper into her chest. She staggered. Ogam jerked the spear free and prepared for another thrust, but Eang did not give him the chance. She screamed again, a cry of vengeance and pain, and vanished into thin air.

I would have been stunned, but I had no room left for such feelings. There was only reality: the reality that Svala was dead and our patron had fled, leaving me, her last Vestige, collapsed beside Quentis.

Had her wound been mortal? And if so, how long would it be before she traded my life for her own? I wondered how it would feel, as Eang pulled herself from the grave. Would the pain be great? Greater than what I felt now, with Eang's Fire blazing in constant, soul-rending wrath, and the image of Svala's bloody head engraved on my eyes?

My fingers came to my throat, where the Eangi collar still lay. Eang's Fire made every movement agony. Beneath it, the magic of the High Halls roiled, begging for release – and with that I found one last, frail hope. It was a sallow thing, senseless and blind, but I couldn't surrender, not after I'd sacrificed so much. Not when Lathian prepared to sweep through my land like a tide.

I pulled the collar off. It dug into my throat as it came free, as if it tried to cling in place, but the discomfort was a shadow compared to the Fire. And, once it was free, my breaths seemed to come a little easier.

With the circlet loose in one hand, I looked at Quentis. My gaze ran from his stained fingers to his bowl, and I pushed myself up onto my knees.

He looked at me, his gaze lightening as if I were an old friend. "What is it?"

"Do you still think you can kill Eang's Fire?"

Quentis looked from me to the lake and laughed softly. Crawling closer to me, he reached out and cupped my cheeks. His hands smelled of musky herbs and something like sour milk, but I forced myself not to pull away.

"Yes," he whispered. "Yes, I can."

FORTY-THREE

I sat before Quentis in a solitary corner of the afternoon forest, hands bound in my lap and my fevered body aching. The priest occupied a patch of muted sunlight in front of me, bowls and scrolls arrayed around him like wards. My collar lay there too, resting on the leaves between us as a reminder and a promise.

Quentis ground herbs and tested their texture between his stained fingers, his eyes narrowed in a wistful, detached intensity.

He didn't flinch as a new bout of screams shattered the forest. We were just out of sight of the camp, where the Algatt prisoners were being held. Telios, unable to bring the Algatt under Lathian's thrall – Gadr had both survived and escaped, it seemed – milked the fear from them while I sat on a cool bed of pine needles, watching Quentis mix his poisons.

My stomach roiled.

"He whispers to me now," Quentis said, absently. He blew his mortar free of powder from the last ingredient in a heady swirl and sprinkled a new one in. Pods cracked beneath his pestle as he went to work, raising his eyes to mine. They were greyer than they'd been that morning, remnants of his former blue barely visible around the pupils. "Lathian. He tells me secrets."

Goosebumps prickled up my flesh. The grey of his eyes was the only thing that made me fear my choice. Once Eang's Fire was gone, would Lathian's influence wash over me, too? Eang would certainly not protect me – if she even lived out the night.

Still, honeyed power whispered beneath my skin, and with it, potential. I plucked at its threads, cool and full of promise, and met Quentis's eyes. He smiled, oblivious, and lifted a pinch of the latest powder he'd ground to his nose. He inhaled, and his grin broadened.

"The lake itself is the key," he said, putting another few pinches into his mixing bowl. As he spoke, he took up a flask and uncapped it, holding it out as if I could see the water inside, though the neck was too narrow. "The lake where the God-Killer sleeps, where their essence resides."

My throat tightened and, in my lap, my knuckles grew white. "Is that the last ingredient, then?"

"It is." Quentis poured a stream of milky lake water into his bowl, mixing it with two fingers. It turned to an orange paste, then a viscous liquid the color of old blood. He sniffed at the concoction and, apparently satisfied, held out the bowl.

I took it carefully into my bound hands and rested it in my lap, trying to stifle a surge of anxiety. "It will work?"

Quentis's voice was candid, without malice. "Lathian believes it will. But if it should fail, or you should still resist my god... I will have to kill you, Hessa. You can die with the Algatt and the Soulderni, in the morning."

My eyes flicked up to his face. "Nisien?"

The Arpa began to gather his things into a basket, which he clasped to his belly as he stood. "Yes."

"Lathian hasn't taken him yet?"

Quentis tsked his tongue in displeasure. "Hush. The drug may take time, Eangi, so drink now. I will return for you in the morning."

I glanced at the forest around us, dim and empty. His departure would give me opportunity – perhaps even to save Nisien, if he was still untainted – but I was vulnerable. "You're going to leave me out here alone?"

"I doubt you will be in any condition to wander away," Quentis said, as if this should reassure me. "And Estavius has volunteered to keep watch over you while you... while this works. He'll be here soon."

Estavius, kind Estavius with secrets in his blood. That was some consolation, at least.

"There's nothing more to fear, my sister," Quentis added.

The familial term crawled into my ear like an insect. I hid my revulsion until he looked away, stooping to pick up one final pouch of herbs. Then I clenched my eyes shut and steeled my nerves.

Before he'd straightened again, I put the bowl to my lips. It smelled disarmingly sweet, husky and warm, like autumn earth and summer rain on hot stone. Even Eang's Fire did not respond to the scent, maintaining the steady, punishing burn it had since my betrayal.

I paused then, with the stained wooden brim on my lips. There would be no going back from this decision, no second chances. If this drug worked, when its throes had passed, I would no longer be an Eangi. My screams would not turn my enemies' bones to dust or boil their blood. My wounds would not knit and my soul would no longer be tied to Eang, she who had given my people their very name.

She who had not been able to save them. She who, I now accepted, was no true goddess.

I drank, deep and full. Grit clung to my teeth and scraped my throat, but I took it down, slow and steady, until it was drained.

I felt Quentis take the bowl from my hands. I was already sagging back onto the earth, watching leaves flutter against a sky muffled by swirls of slate-grey cloud. With every dance of the leaves, my body grew heavier. I felt the hairpin Eidr had given me, tangled beneath my tattered braids, dig into my scalp. I felt leaves tickle my melting skin and roots arch into my back, but there was no pain to any of it. No pain at all.

Then the Fire burst. My body bucked and I screamed into the forest's muted light; a crackling, twisted memory of an Eangi howl and a human wail of pain.

The world furled into blackness. I writhed and sank out of the world itself, until time and space became irrelevant. There was only agony, heat and the fever-haze of mortal illness.

Eventually, I eased into a body that no longer hurt. My lungs contracted, my jaw cracked, and I drew a shuddering breath of smoke, dense warmth and smoldering sage.

I turned my head. My eyes dragged through the world before me, like a finger through honey, and settled on pillars of ancient wood.

I lay in a shadowed corner of the High Hall itself, with its dark wooden beams and circle of thrones. The bodies of Oulden, Riok and Dur were gone. Nothing moved save smoke, rising from the low-burning fireplace between the thrones, and I heard only the rattle of my breath.

I coughed. The sound was loud in the quiet space, but I didn't care. I was alone, after all, and my mouth was full of grit. It was all I could feel; there was no conscious thought in my mind yet, no comprehension of my state – dead or alive, Eangi or other. Just the grit of Quentis's poison.

I rolled over, coughing and spitting, until I made my way onto my hands and knees. My hand collided with something hard and cool. It made a deep, full-bellied clink.

I blinked, swallowing another wave of coughing. There, on the floor before me, sat a full clay pitcher. I glanced around, wondering who had brought it, but I was still alone. Cautiously, I bent down and sniffed at its dark contents. It smelled of honey, fermented and full. Mead. The Mead of the Gods.

I wanted to laugh, but I'd forgotten how. Palms braced on the floor, I stared down into the pitcher with a bleary comprehension. Had my thirst conjured this, or had the High Halls sensed my need?

Either way, I did not pick it up. My memory was returning to me like waves of a waxing tide, each moment bringing me closer and closer to full awareness.

Kneeling, I sank down onto my heels and lifted my hands, staring at them in the Hall's half-light. My scars were still there and my flesh looked just as it had on every other visit to the High Halls – vital and real.

I wasn't dead. I was sure of that – if Quentis's poison had killed me, I would not be in the High Halls. But I was not myself, either. I felt cool and subdued, like a bed of coals after the rain. I turned my hands again, brushing one scarred fingertip against another, comforted by their normality.

Gradually, cautiously, I reached for Eang's Fire. Silence met my touch, but not the yawning emptiness I'd anticipated. In the space where the shard of Eang had once resided, I found only more of myself, entwined with honeyed, golden threads.

I closed my eyes. The more I prodded at those threads the more vibrant they became, warming me and pulling all tension, all strain, from my muscles. I drew it into my lungs and felt it disperse in my blood with each beat of my heart.

My throat was still full of grit, however. I sat back against a pillar, took up the pitcher up with both hands and drank. For every gulp I swallowed, there was always more, full and rich. It was too sweet, but I didn't mind. It passed from my lips into my veins and my skull, until my vision blurred with amber magic.

At some point I set the pitcher on the floor at my side and extended my legs, wondering how long it would be before someone discovered me or Quentis dragged me back into the Waking World. Did the Archeress and Rioux stalk these halls, or did they still curl at Lathian's feet like dogs? Would Eang come to exact her vengeance upon me, in the darkness between these pillars? What would she think, now, of what she found?

As if in answer to my thoughts, the gods – the Miri – took shape before me. One by one they appeared among the thrones and the low-burning fire. Stormy Esach. A woman in a broad-necked gown the color of chicory blossoms, with piles of blond hair – Aita. Gadr was there too, blank-eyed, sunken into one of the thrones while Aita attended his wounds.

"You should have come," Gadr's said through his teeth. Neither he nor the women appeared to see me.

"Resurrecting the God Under the Lake was never the answer." Aita continued to brush a salve onto a horrible wound in his chest. As she did, I watched amber magic dance around her fingertips, and her voice was the essence of solace, low and gentle. "I still believe that Lathian—"

Gadr's face snapped up. "Gods below, Aita, stop. After what happened today—"

"I think we'd best stop swearing on the gods below," Esach interjected, glaring at an empty space across the room. "Considering we may soon trade places with them."

"You must both return with me." Gadr shooed Aita with an angry hand. "The ritual was nearly finished. The lake took the child, and Omaskat's body and blood. If only one of us can reach the water, we can still finish it."

My chin drifted to one side, my right hand poised on the pitcher of mead. The ritual could still be finished?

"How?" Esach retorted. "Ashaklon's ilk gather like flies. Ashaklon himself is free again and he'll join them soon."

"Can we not treat with Lathian?" Aita inquired.

"No!" Gadr bellowed and the foundations of the Hall shook. "Where is Eang, Aita, where did she go after you healed her? Eang, you traitorous witch! Show your face!"

I pressed myself back into my pillar and retracted my legs. So, the Great Healer had seen to Eang? I doubted a wound as grievous as Eang's could be completely healed so fast, but even injured she was dangerous.

"There are some who might call you the traitor in this circle," Aita said. Her weight rested in one hip and she appeared unperturbed by Gadr's rage, now that she was out of range.

"I tried to convince you," the god of the Algatt loomed, the stomach-dropping gash on his chest oozing amber-red. "If you'd come, any of you, Omaskat would have lived long enough to complete the ritual himself. My people would have lived – or at least died for something."

Aita spoke again, her voice even lower than before, "If you'd killed the Eangi girl when you had her, things would certainly be different."

My blood cooled. I knew I should leave, before I was spotted and Gadr's rage turned on me. But I was loath to return to my body, forsaken in the forest, and whatever the Miri said next would likely be important.

"Omaskat himself insisted she had a part to play," Gadr retorted. "Besides, how could I kill one of Eang's last Vestiges? I'm not that foolish."

My throat tightened. None of the gods here realized what I'd had Quentis do, that my Fire was gone. Eang's next death would be final. That had hardly mattered a few minutes ago, when I thought all hope was already lost. But if the ritual could still be finished, if the Miri might still intervene...

But no. I couldn't regret what I'd done. Perhaps that was selfish. Perhaps it was cold. But I could not regret breaking free of Eang's lies and machinations.

"And now look where we are," Aita snapped. "You should have killed her."

Gadr spun away from her, his face twitching in rage. "Eang! Come!"

"She's gone to fetch the immortal's sire," Esach spoke over the end of Gadr's echoing shout.

"As she well should," Aita mused. "She should stay as far away as possible. If she dies, if we die, the binding fails completely. And the world belongs to Lathian once more."

"He will be able to break it anyway," Esach said. "Once he gathers enough followers. It's a matter of days, now."

Gadr cut back in, "I will not hide."

"Agreed." Esach's hand drifted to her stomach. She covered the movement by clasping her opposite wrist and inclined her head to Gadr. "I'll return with you. This is our best chance. If I must bow to Thvynder, so be it, but I will not grovel before those who killed my child."

"Eang will never bow with us," Gadr interjected.

Aita was quick to reply, "Then we do not tell her we've completed the ritual, until it is too late."

The gods descended into rapid negotiations. I rested back against my pillar, letting the scent of mead and sage fill my nostrils. If the gods intervened at the White Lake, I might be able to escape. I might even be able to rescue Nisien and... what? Where would we go?

Aita's voice rose over the prattle. "Ah, Aliastros. Welcome. Where do you stand?"

Startled, I peered around the pillar. Aliastros? Why would the northern gods welcome an Arpa one? Shouldn't he be attending Lathian?

No. I remembered in a flash that Aliastros had an alliance with Oulden. Iosas had been free to worship the Arpa God of Wind on Oulden's land. Estavius, amber-blooded son of his High Priest, had aided me. In the High Hall, when Rioux and the Archeress had attacked me, whoever intervened had come with a gale. And Omaskat's last words had been...

A new voice, a familiar voice, rushed through the High Hall, and I saw him, striding out from the pillars in the armor of an Arpa legionary. He spoke Northman – at least to my ears – with only the lightest of accents, high on his tongue. "On the shores of the White Lake, my sisters. My brother."

It was Estavius himself. He looked my way and, through the pillars and smoke of the Hall, met my gaze. I saw nothing out of the ordinary in his wide-set blue eyes, besides the acknowledgement that he knew I was there. There was no aura of divinity about him like Ogam exuded, no visible magic like Aita's, no marrow-crackling presence like Eang. Even my newly freed golden sight saw him as a simple, innocuous man.

But that couldn't be, not with the way the Miri looked at him now. And they had called him Aliastros. Could Estavius be possessed by his patron, as I had been, and gifted with the magic of the High Halls? Or was Estavius no man at all?

I heard Ogam's voice in my mind, all the way back in Souldern. *Are you sure he's human?*

"What are you looking at?" Esach asked, her tone mild.

"Nothing at all." Estavius looked back at the thrones. "But I haven't much time. Tomorrow, when the sun rises, all the prisoners here will be sacrificed to Lathian, and I have little doubt that his binding will break. Between now and then, I will finish what Omaskat began. But Thvynder's rising will not be instantaneous."

At this, his eyes drifted back to me, drawing me in, giving the words to me, too. "There will be a battle tomorrow, and a chance for all of us to claim our places in the new order of the world. So run, if you choose. I will not blame you. But I would be honored to fight by your side."

FORTY-FOUR

I awoke gradually, my mind vacillating between the sage-scented air of the High Halls, the echoes of Estavius's voice and the close air of a tent. Eventually I settled into the last, reawakening to limbs of weary muscle, a mouth full of grit and the sensation of a hand resting on my back.

I lay on my side. The hand was large and gentle, unthreatening and protective. It came with a shadow, just visible out of the corner of my eye, and the warmth of a nearby body.

My heart fluttered against my ribs, memories of the Halls and Estavius's words flaking away at this immediate threat.

"Nisien?" I whispered, fervently hoping I'd guessed correctly. And hoping that he was still himself.

"Hessa." The hand immediately withdrew. I sat up, inching far enough away to make him out. It was difficult to read his expression in the dark, but his posture was sore, closed, and he smelled of sweat, horse and blood. The sight was grim, but also comforting – he acted nothing like Telios's tainted legionaries. He hadn't succumbed to Lathian yet.

I shifted onto my knees, taking a moment to measure my own strength. The headiness of the mead I'd consumed in the High Halls had not transmitted back to the Waking World, but the power of that place remained. It slipped through my blood and bone in a way Fang's Fire never had, promising and constant in its flow.

Still, the absence of the Fire jarred and unsettled me. I caught hold

381

of those feelings before they could grow and pushed them aside for later contemplation. If Estavius's words held true, my fight was not yet over.

As I knelt, something dug into my leg. My hand dropped to my calf and there, hidden inside my legwraps, I felt the shape of a small, sheathed knife.

"Did Estavius bring me here?" I asked, though I already suspected the answer.

"Yes. Are you all right?" Nisien asked. He held his tone steady, but I heard the falter beneath its calculated edges. "You've been unconscious for hours."

"Yes," the word came with a laugh, soft and a little unhinged.

Nisien shot me a look between reproach and despondency, and my elation faltered. A pregnant silence opened between us and the man shifted, stretching his long legs and holding up his unbound hands. He waved his fingers. "Estavius is doing what he can for us."

Judging by the fact that Nisien had yet succumb to Lathian's thrall, the anomaly that was Estavius – and his supposed god – might be doing far more than the horseman realized.

"At least," he added, "you and I… we won't have to wait to die alone."

I let this sentiment sit between us for a moment, melancholic and strained, before I nodded gently. I indicated his hands. "Did you try to escape yet?"

Real, raw hopelessness cracked through his façade. "There's no point, Hessa. Where would I go? How would I live with myself? I can't go back to my mother, even if the world wasn't burning. And what I let Quentis do… I'm sorry. I'm so sorry. Estavius told me what he did, letting you go. I should have been the one… I'm so sorry."

My hand reached out of its own accord, grabbing one of his in the darkness and holding it tight. I opened my mouth to protest, to forgive him – because how could I not on this of all nights, with his voice cracking and my own failures piled around me. I wanted to tell him that, tell him what Estavius might be – empowered vessel or even Miri – and that within a few short hours, he and I would have one last chance to save ourselves and our world.

Nisien, it seemed, did not want my forgiveness. He spoke again, cutting me off before my dry throat could put a sentence together. But he left his loose-fingered hand in mine, rough and scabbed and inept.

"Telios stopped them from executing me."

Another hush fell between us. The conversation of Polinus's men drifted through the night, merging with the rustle of the trees and interrupted by the rasp of a sword being sharpened. Telios's men did not converse, but I sensed them around us – brushes of unnatural life against my new, golden senses.

"Why?"

The Soulderni held my gaze, though neither of us could really see the other's eyes in the shadows.

"I'll listen, if you want to tell me," I said at last, echoing his own words to me by the lake in Gilda.

"It won't make tonight any easier."

I shrugged. "It might."

Nisien took another minute to make up his mind, then his fingers pulled free of mine and spoke again. "He was my mentor."

I curled my hands back in my lap and sat poised, fearing that any more movement might stop his flow of words.

"I was young. I idolized him. When he took me under his wing, there was nothing I wouldn't do for him." Nisien paused. "Fight for him. Die for him. Lie with him. Bear his abuse. I was a thousand miles from home, and he offered me protection. Influence. He kept me alive, and for that I thought I loved him."

I held his gaze.

"Those years were... They ended. I realized the type of man Telios was, and I pulled away. He made a play for power in the army. I had to choose a side and I put a knife in his back. But Telios had so much influence with the priests of Lathian... he went unpunished, publicly. My general, who I'd sided with against Telios, sent me home to Souldern, half in thanks and half to keep me safe. I never expected to see Telios again."

I let him sit mutely for a time, ensuring he had nothing more to say and letting myself digest this information.

Euweth's face drifted up through the gloom of Nisien's tale. I recalled the laughing Soulderni horsewoman, her shield of mirth splintered on the night she had banished me. I had never truly resented her for sending me away, even before I understood why she had been so desperate to keep her son away from the Arpa. From the shadow of Telios.

I crawled over to sit beside Nisien, lending my friend the bulwark of my presence without touching him. I couldn't offer any comforting words. What was there to say? I had sat with enough warriors after battle, enough friends after the death of a loved one, to know what little use words were.

But I could bare my own soul in return.

I cleared my throat, conscious of the absence of an Eangi collar at my throat – I'd left the battered one on the forest floor, and I had a feeling I would never see it again. But my hairpin was still tucked into my hair, tangled and innocuous – my last talisman of Albor and my husband.

"Will you still listen, if I tell you why I'm here?" I asked.

Nisien opened his hands in an inviting gesture, without looking up. "Of course."

"And what Estavius and I have planned for tomorrow?"

At that, Nisien raised his head.

I told him. I told him everything and, in the end, I edged the knife out from my legwrap and put it in his hands.

Nisien's eyes darted from the weapon to me. "Where did you get this?"

"Estavius." I crooked him a wan smile. "I assume."

"Estavius…" Nisien shook his head, turning the knife over in his hands. "What is he? Aliastros, or… is he like you?"

"I don't know," I answered truthfully. "And as long as he plays his part, it doesn't matter. Do you want vengeance, Soulderni? Do you want to bring down Telios and his god?"

He gave a short exhale. "Gods above and below, Hessa."

"Those gods are coming, and after tomorrow they will be gods no more." I leant forward, putting one warm hand on his forearm. "I have a knife, and a hairpin. I have no Fire, but I have something better. And if we stand together, perhaps we can end Telios, and Quentis. Perhaps we can even survive. At least, Nisien, we can die a decent death."

Nisien watched, still dumbstruck, as I took the knife back from him and tucked it into my legwrap. I disentangled my hairpin and hid it there, too; two small weapons in a war of the gods.

Then, softly, Nisien began to laugh.

My knees hit damp stone and trampled grass in the light of dawn. More prisoners dropped in rows to either side of me along the lakeshore – Algatt warriors, most of them barely conscious after the night's horrors.

I squinted out towards the twilit water, hands bound behind my back. Black clouds still girded Lathian's beautiful form and his aura saturated the air like an approaching storm. Ogam was with him. I saw the Son of Winter's impossibly pale skin and white hair, pacing through fog atop an island of ice. And with them, newly arrived in the night, was the shadow that was Ashaklon, free and roiling around the other Old-World gods.

A shadow fell across me and I looked up into Quentis's slate-grey eyes. There was nothing human left inside them, no threads of blue or human expression.

"I told him you would not bow." When Quentis spoke, his voice had changed too. It was broader somehow, vast and shallow and detached.

Nisien thudded down on my left. When I glanced at him, his gaunt face produced a smile. It was a feeble thing and, given our circumstances, it was absurd. But it strengthened me.

"I will offer you only one more chance," Quentis said, ignoring my companion.

I did not reply. The Arpa reached out, once, and touched the top of my head. Then his gaze drifted away and he left, the tips of his fingers trailing across my scalp in abstract farewell. I suppressed a shiver.

Nisien leant into my shoulder, voice low. "I'm ready."

His words wrapped around the knot of determination in my chest and cinched it tight. I pushed aside the thought of Quentis and nodded back, hard and grim. "Then let's begin."

I leant towards the Algatt on my other side. I thought she was a few years my senior, but her face was so bruised and swollen that it was hard to tell. "I can free you. Will you fight with me?"

A ripple passed down the line. I looked up cautiously, concerned that the Arpa might notice, but most of the soldiers were Telios's. Their focus was on Lathian.

"What do you mean, Eangi?" the woman hissed.

"I mean, we can escape together."

She gave a derisive snort, but any other reply died as black clouds began to advance across the lake. Lathian strode in the midst of them with his court – Styga, Ogam, Rioux, the Archeress, Ashaklon and a dozen others I didn't recognize.

The Arpa snapped to attention. A glance over my shoulder found Polinus's men filtering from the trees, some of their strides marked with caution. I could not make out Castor among the ranks but Estavius was there, striding behind Polinus with the cheekplates of his helmet fastened. There was nothing to betray him as anything other than human, save the fact that his eyes, among a handful of others, were not yet grey.

"Is Lathian free?" Nisien hissed, watching the god progress across the lake.

"Not fully," I replied, my words quick and quiet.

Quentis stepped into the shallows, dragging an Algatt prisoner by the hair. The prisoner was so far gone that he could barely kneel, let alone resist.

"Behold, my lord, the death of your enemies!" Quentis crowed, echoing his own words from the day before. "Feast upon their fear and break the last of your chains!"

I leant into the Algatt woman again, who stared at the scene in bleak, watery-eyed horror. "Hurry. Move your arms. I'll cut your bindings. Hide the ends and wait for my signal."

She tore her eyes from Quentis and his victim and met my gaze for another, helpless instant. Then she seemed to find a scrap of courage and nodded slightly.

"Be ready to free your people."

Both our heads jerked up as Quentis threw out one hand, a long knife poised, while the other still grasped his prisoner. He began to chant.

I slit the Algatt woman's bonds, then Nisien's. He loosed mine before hiding the blade up his own sleeve and I slipped my hairpin between my palms.

The first Algatt died. As his body was dragged away, the soldiers shoved a woman forward. She was younger than me, barely older than sixteen. She looked like my sister Hulda, her face a mask of determination and angry tears.

"Quentis," I called with only a slight hitch in my voice, "take me next."

The priest turned. A flicker of his old interest passed behind his charcoal eyes and he nodded for the soldiers to fetch me. The girl was shoved back into line.

I stood before the Arpa priest. The water of the White Lake was as cool around my ankles as the hairpin resting against my forearm; Eidr's runes of protection, belonging and promise pressed against my skin above deadly silver prongs.

"I offer you this last chance, Eangi," Quentis said. He gestured towards the Old Gods with his scarlet knife and stained fingers. "I see you. I see what you could be. Worship. Join us. Lead your people into the coming age. High Priestess of the North. High Priestess of Lathian."

His words had a latent power to them. I recognized that power; it was the same one that had tried to arrest me in the vision of the Arpa temple. Now it pulsed through Quentis, attempting to draw my desires towards him like the pull of a tide.

But it had no effect. Amber pricked at the corners of my eyes and I slipped the pin between my fingers.

"No."

I stabbed Quentis in the throat. Briefly, the delicate skin beneath his jaw held against the silver prongs. Then they punched through, right up to its decorative runes and my curling fingers.

Quentis crashed into the water. I grabbed his own knife before it could disappear and slit his throat wide. Quentis thrashed. Telios shouted. The legionaries charged.

I threw Quentis's knife to the Algatt woman. Her free hands snatched it from the air and she scrambled toward the next person in line.

Telios's armored form charged at me. I dodged a stabbing, horizontal blow from his shield and skittered backwards.

Nisien leapt upon his commander in a blur of muscle and plunging knife. I spun on another soldier and caught his forearm as he hacked at me. Throwing my weight forward, I jerked his arm behind his back and snapped it.

I had his sword now.

"Eang," I said. Each word I spoke became a pledge, a memorial to the life I had once led; a pledge of the person I would become today instead. "The Brave and the Vengeful."

I ran an Arpa through, wrenched my sword free and seized his Algatt shield. Out of the corner of my eye, I saw Nisien retreating, avoiding strike after strike from Telios. He still wielded the knife, but even from this distance, I saw the young man's resolve falter.

"The Watchful."

I dropped another blank-eyed Arpa. Down the shoreline, Telios landed a blow on Nisien's chest with the side of his shield. The horseman went down.

"The Swift."

Telios raised his sword for a killing thrust. I broke into a sprint.

Estavius leapt between Nisien and Telios. The commander's sword met his shield with a jarring clang and crack, followed by the commander's full-shouldered impact.

Estavius braced, taking the blow, but Telios's hit had been calculated. The young Arpa's shield tilted left and Telios went with it, rounding him and driving his sword up into Estavius's exposed back. I didn't see it connect, but I saw the shock in Estavius's face. He – man, Miri, combination of the two – staggered.

I closed in. For the space of one labored heartbeat, Nisien watched his friend struggle to stand. Then Telios was in front of him, sword extended. Unable to get any closer, Nisien snapped. He hurled his knife at the commander's throat in one last, desperate play. Telios barely deflected it with a flash of steel and it sliced into the water twenty feet away.

"Nisien!" I screamed.

His face lifted. I caught his eye, just the barest of glances, and threw my sword the remaining distance.

Nisien darted right. The hilt dropped into his hand and the blade arched in one silent, deft swing.

Telios's head left his shoulders.

The Soulderni should have had a moment then, to reflect on the death of his tormentor. But this was battle. Panting, he hauled Estavius back to his feet and I shoved my arm under his other shoulder. Behind us, Telios's body collapsed, headless and unmourned.

"Bow."

It was not a word. It was a… pulse. That pulse radiated over the water and drove everyone, Arpa, Algatt, Nisien, Estavius and I, to our knees in a clattering, splashing thud.

Only one person got back up. Estavius. The Arpa extricated himself from Nisien's and my grasp and, grimacing through what should have been a mortal wound, faced the Gods of the Old World. The blood streaming down his back and legs waned, vanishing into the water around him.

His blood glistened with amber. At first the color was subtle and wavering, as if I saw it though a fluttering veil. But as Estavius spoke, that veil began to lift. The amber glint intensified, the bleeding slowed still more, and Estavius began to change.

"Go back to sleep, Lathian." The legionary's voice shook out over the water. He did not speak in Northman, but somehow I understood him. "Your chains will remain."

I'd known something like this was coming, but my mouth still fell open. The features of Estavius's face remained the same, but I felt as though I'd only ever seen him in shadow, and now saw him in the unfiltered light of day. His eyes were pale, pale as mist, and his skin itself seemed to move – the subtle, nearly imperceptible swirls and alterations of a cloudy summer sky.

Once more, amber power rushed around him like the wind itself, ethereal and alive and laden with dust of gold.

Are you sure he's human?

This was no matter of possession, as Eang had done to me. Estavius was not human, I did not doubt that now. He *was* Aliastros.

Lathian was over the center of the lake now, billows of tainted cloud ensconcing almost the entire surface.

"Aliastros," he rumbled, "what are you doing?"

Estavius – Aliastros – strode out into the lake until the water reached his hip. The farthest of the black tendrils began to skirt him in a broad, cautious swirl. "Throwing in my lot."

FORTY-FIVE

Lathian's court spread out around him, arraying themselves for true battle. Perhaps Lathian's full power had not yet been unleashed, but these lesser beings were free, from Ashaklon's murk to the Archeress with her bow and arrows of bone. Estavius faced them all, unaided.

I saw the way Lathian beheld him: hard, cold and… cautious. "You cannot stop me alone. Bow, God of Wind. You have eluded me long enough."

Estavius – for I still couldn't help but think of him by that name – watched him coolly. "I finished the ritual last night, Lathian, while your servants cavorted. The God Under the Lake rises as we speak."

Lathian paused. Down the line, I saw the Archeress shift her bow and Rioux snarl, both their expressions darkening as they realized that this was the god who had attacked them in the storm and darkness of the High Hall.

Ogam slipped forward one slight step.

"And besides," Estavius added, his voice filled with the billowing, soul-cracking weight of power, "I am not alone."

Thunder rolled. Clouds gathered in the south and the unmistakable crackle of Esach's fury echoed through the valley. I tasted a fresh, clear wind.

The wind rushed towards Aliastros, tossing his curls about his head. Gadr strode up to his shoulder. Esach appeared with a crack, her belly flat and her eyes filled with deadly intent. Aita came too, sweet and regal and smelling of lavender and pine.

Out across the water, the Miri converged; the remaining Gods of the New World, facing down the Gods of the Old.

I did not feel Eang when she came. She appeared next to Esach, healed – or at least mended enough to fight – with her bearded axes loose in hand.

My heart slammed into my throat. Eang. Eang had come? I stared at my former goddess, snared in a web of emotions so thick I could barely claw my way out. My instincts still screamed to run to her, to bow to her. I thought of myself begging for her forgiveness in a mountain meadow, trembling in the rain for fear of her vengeance.

Vengeance that today, I might finally meet.

I gripped my shield and pulled my magic in close – amber and free. The pressure driving me to my knees eased, but I did not reveal my advantage yet. I might not be a Miri myself, but a whisper of their power ran in my veins. Perhaps Eang would not find me so easy to punish.

A moment after my former goddess arrived, the winter wind came. It gusted around her and took on the form of a great, muscular man: Winter himself. Ogam's father.

Out on the water, I saw Ogam throw out one hand. His ice-spear appeared, tall and glistening. To his left and right more gods assembled, Arpa gods I recognized from statues and figurines – all answering the summons of their God of Gods.

Without warning, Lathian released his hold on the Arpa soldiers. They surged to their feet and slaughtered half a dozen Algatt before the northerners realized what was happening.

The wind struck. It was Aliastros's and Winter's all at once, cold and strident and wild. It rushed up our bodies from foot to head and poured into our lungs, cleansing and freeing. I gasped, blinded by the swirl of my own fraying hair as the force that kept Nisien and the Algatt on their knees broke.

Nisien, still at my side, staggered to his feet shouting, "Run!"

I couldn't remember how I found an axe in the chaos that ensued. I blocked and hacked and stumbled, coming back to back with an

Algatt. If the man noticed I was Eangen, he gave no sign. We simply defended.

Nisien had been right beside me, but within seconds I lost sight of him. Block. Dodge. My Algatt companion died and I sprinted again, stumbling up the shoreline. An Arpa charged me. I raised a commandeered Algatt shield and hurled it, taking him full across the face.

Out across the water, the gods collided – wind and lightning raged while snow and thunder clashed, all of it obscured by Lathian's smoke. I caught only glimpses – Gadr chasing down Ashaklon, the Archeress's arrows flying, Esach driving a bolt of lightning into Styga's chest. Styga exploded into a burst of starlight and shadow before regathering, sweeping themselves into the bands of black that encircled Lathian.

Ogam dropped down in front of me and drove his spear into my shoulder. I screamed so wildly that I thought my head might rupture. But the cold was worse. It spread through my body in a great rush, dulling all pain, freezing my lungs and threatening to crack my bones.

"I gave you the secret of the gods," Ogam hissed, shoving his face into mine. His spear cut deeper, separating skin and muscle like a lever. My feet slipped and he slammed me down onto the ice.

The air was knocked from my body. For a heart-pounding, muffled instant, all I could do was lay there. Blood brimmed and overflowed from the wound beneath his spear, languid and dark with the cold. But neither he, nor I, missed that it glistened with amber.

The sight enraged him even more. "And what have you done? You squandered it. You turned against *me!*"

Words were not something I could muster – cold and shock left my mind blank and my lungs shuddering – but there was something far greater, far more powerful, beneath it.

Defiance. For his own selfishness, for his bitterness against his mother, he had handed Lathian the world. My world. My people. Yet he would remain, immortal and untouchable?

I began to amass the magic of the High Halls – the magic that he had led me to, the magic that had enabled his mother and those like her to masquerade as divine. Power that they, long before I, had stolen.

Ogam's spear crackled with amber light, lancing up from my shoulder towards his hand, and shattered. Fine shards and dust like powdered glass burst left and right, separating the Son of Winter and me for a timeless, glistening instant.

He lurched back, stunned and unexpectedly weaponless. Then, as the dust fell, I forced my numb body to its feet.

Another spear materialized in Ogam's hand, flashing in the smothered pastel hues of dawn. I shattered it with a flash of will and threw the full force of my rebellion into his chest. This was no subtle magic, nor was it the invisible burn of Eang's Fire. This left my scarred hands in cords of rippling amber, fast as whips and thick as snakes. They slammed into Ogam's chest and punctured his flesh, seizing his bones and jerking him down.

The Son of Winter crashed onto his knees. The ice beneath him groaned and began to fall away, separating into floes to either side of our own drifting island. Ogam's eyes bulged, gawking and gasping with dull shock. Silver-scarlet blood welled, soaking the fine, punctured cloth of his kaftan in a dozen widening stains.

Then, from one rapid blink to the next, Eang was there. She stood behind Ogam, chest heaving with exertion, blood clinging to her disheveled black braids. Below a windblown tangle of hair, her gaze leveled with mine, hard and flinty as a raven's. She raised one of her twin axes, her upper body turning and knotted muscles coiling beneath her black tunic.

I jerked my magic back into my veins in one frantic tug and retreated across the ice, regathering my strength for a defense. But the axe was not meant for me.

The weapon buried itself in Ogam's back. I made a sound – a scream, a choke – as Eang spun her son around, hauled him off the ice and drove him under the surface of the lake.

Face down in the water, Ogam bucked and flailed. Bubbles surged around him like the Headwater's springs, but Eang did not release him. She held her son under the surface of the White Lake until his protests slowly, slowly faded.

Far out across the water, the ice floats Ogam had made ruptured with resounding cracks, scattering those who battled atop them. But no one cried out for the fall of Ogam. No one rushed to his defense. Lathian himself, wrapped in black cloud, did not even falter in his progress across the lake.

The wind lessened and a spattering of snowflakes caught in Eang's braids. Kneeling in the water, she released her son's motionless body. The axe remained in his back, while the other had fallen on the ice close to me, dormant and forgotten.

Together, Eang and I watched Ogam drift; I with the stunned certainty that he would stand up again, and she with a numb, frigid kind of wistfulness.

"The lake of the God-Killer," she who had been my goddess said, letting droplets of lake water fall from her fingers. The sky had grown darker now, but she did not seem to notice. Nor did she look to where humans cut one another down and Miri clashed in a chaos of wrath and elements. "The one place on earth where an immortal can die."

The water. I understood its significance, even as my eyes filled with the sight of Eang and Ogam's drifting body. The water of this lake had killed Eang's Fire, and finally extinguished the immortal Son of Winter.

"Did he tell you, Hessa, how I left him to die when he was a child?" Eang rose as she spoke and, without looking at her son again, hinged her axe free from his back. Then she stepped back up on to the ice where I crouched, water dripping from her sodden clothes and Ogam's silvered blood from her murderous axe. "I did it on the word of Fate, you see – the promise that my son, one day, would be my downfall. Perhaps if I'd tried harder to destroy him, perhaps if I'd had the will to bring him here... But even I am not without feeling. Even I was not without hope."

My eyes darted to her other axe, lying on the ice a pace away. The shoulder Ogam had pierced, my left, was nearly crippled. But my right was whole.

"This is what happens, Hessa, when we try to evade Fate." Eang moved closer now. Amber flickered through my eyes and I sensed the Fire in her, liquid and brutal, harsh and building – the well from which all Eangi power had flowed. It was a wave which, in moments, would crash over me.

"And that?" She indicated Ogam's corpse with her silvered blade. "That is the fate of traitors."

I lunged for the fallen axe.

Eang screamed. As her Fire had been the source of ours, so her scream was the pattern after which our own were formed. It filled the mountain valley like a clap of melodic thunder, undulating and crackling and reverberating. It turned my stomach to water and burst through my head, howling in my ears.

But I did not collapse. My bones did not break, nor my senses yield to the force of her wrath. Instead I rose to my feet, Eang's own axe in my good hand and amber power twining my body like a second skin.

There was an instant of quiet in the wake of her cry. As its last echoes drifted up the sides of the mountains I felt eyes upon us, felt even Lathian cock his head and cast an indifferent glance as a lone human woman faced down the Goddess of War. Somewhere nearby, Nisien stood at Estavius's shoulder, and Esach pulled Gadr to his feet and the Archeress lowered her bow.

We mirrored one another, Eang and I – our postures, our axes and the black of our hair. She had shaped me in her image, after all. I was the product of her Fire and rage and hunger for vengeance, the last of the priesthood who had served her and anchored her for a hundred generations. The priesthood that she had used, and abandoned.

How many Eangi's spirits surged through her veins, Vestiges depleted and forgotten? How many lives had she snuffed for her own, and how many Eangen had she left to perish while she hid from Rioux and the

Archeress? How many promises had she broken?

There was nothing just in Eang, nothing righteous. And with that understanding in my veins, I screamed back.

It was less a scream than a roar, backed by a tide of smothering, quenching magic. It struck Eang like a hurricane wind and bent her double. Her heel slipped back and one hand clawed at the ice, catching herself before she could fall, but the constant heat of her Fire rippled and extinguished for one brief instant.

In that same moment, the water of the lake began to glow. I felt power there, power beyond mine or Eang's or even Lathian's. Power that grew and mounted and made Lathian himself screech in sudden, dreadful understanding.

Thvynder, Omaskat's god, was rising.

Eang looked up at the same time as I did. Our eyes locked, and I attacked. I launched myself across the ice and drove into her, hooking her axe beneath mine and hurling it down. Eang howled, her Fire whipping out in renewed and savage force, but my blade had already swung again and found its mark. Her collarbone shattered, skin and bone and vein divided, and my magic poured into her blood.

The Goddess of War fell. I stepped back, blinded by both the spray of warm ichor and the light shafting out of the lake. The ice barely diffused it, leaving me sightless to everything except the ferocity of my own magic and the crumpling, ragged form of Eang.

Somewhere in the back of my mind, the corner of my soul, I realized what I had done. But there was no rejoicing, no thrill of bloody vengeance. There was only serenity, and a stolid, sober vindication. Eang would never manipulate or threaten me, or my people, again.

A dog barked, and the light of the lake waned. Eang still lay spluttering on the ice as I stooped to pick up her own fallen axe and retreated, carefully cradling both weapons as my shoulder bled and my vision greyed.

The dog barked again. I turned my head and squinted as Ayo streaked down the shoreline in a limping run. She made for a man who looked like Omaskat, wore a blue tunic like Omaskat, but was wholly alive. And when I glimpsed his face, both of his eyes were gold.

Without a word, the man lifted one arm. The other, I saw, held an infant to his chest. Vistic.

Lathian screamed. Old Gods and New fell to their knees or scattered to the wind – submitting. Fleeing.

But there was no escape. A second pulse of light burst out of the center of the lake with the force of a breaking dam and a great cloud of shimmering steam filled the valley.

I saw it billow towards me, enveloping the gods as it came. Aita bowed and the wave passed her, ruffling her hair and skirts but leaving her unharmed. It rushed past Esach, Aliastros, and Gadr too, each falling to one knee or bowing as the light touched them.

Only when the light reached Lathian did it falter. For the barest second the Arpa's God of Gods held against the blazing tide, braced, howling in fury and contempt. Then, with one last scream, he was extinguished.

By the time it reached Eang she was still, and Ogam's body had long ceased to twitch. But Ashaklon, Rioux and the Archeress were not so fortunate. They vanished in a screaming swirl of smoke, along with what remained of Styga and a dozen others. One by one, the wave took them.

Then the wave struck me, and my world buckled into silence.

EPILOGUE

The last of the winter snow melts beneath my palms as I press them into Albor's frigid earth. The white-crusted beams of the Hall of Smoke stand out against the sky, stark and devoid of life.

Beneath the snow, bones lie cold and silent. Below them, in the blood-saturated dirt, the souls of my people twist and ache and yearn. Eidr. Yske. Vist. I can sense them, but they are lost in the horde of restless spirits.

The rest of my traveling companions remain outside the walls. I am the only living thing in town save Omaskat's dog, who noses around the ruins. At the traveler's bidding, the animal has not left my side since the aftermath of the White Lake, guarding me over a long winter of negotiation with the Algatt and the journey south, after the last of the winter storms.

"Forgive me for not coming to you sooner…" I whisper to the earth.

Wind whisks through the empty homes, hollow and forlorn, and under my palms, the spirits of my people roil. Their distress fills my ears and it is all I can do not to flee. Sweat breaks out across my back and tears run down my cheeks. I am grateful now that I cannot pick out Eidr and Yske among them. I could not bear to hear the suffering in their voices.

"I release you now," I say and begin to draw runes in the snow, laced with a steady, amber magic. "I release your reward and the Long Sleep. Thvynder has granted us our High Halls, and I will join you there when my days are at an end."

One by one, the keens of the dead fade, and I sing them from the Waking World with a soft, mournful song. The tension in the earth eases beneath my hands but I continue to kneel, quelling an old, familiar sorrow. At last, I reach out and draw one more symbol in the snow. The rune for closure and finality.

A head butts my shoulder – my right, thankfully, as my left still aches in the cold from Ogam's spear. I drop back into my heels as Ayo burrows her way under my arm and sits, lending me her warm, solid bulk. Comforting position thus assumed, she casts her gaze back out across the village, ears twitching.

"I'm sorry," I murmur to the earth.

Once, Ogam accused me of insincerity. But now I know my weakness and my place in the world. I understand it. So I issue my apology to my people for their suffering, and for Eang, who failed them so thoroughly.

Thvynder, through Omaskat, has made peace with the New Gods, annihilated the Old and thrust the Arpa threat back beyond our borders. They have kept their word, and our High Halls await the arrival of these souls – and mine. Yet as I kneel here, memories of my old life overwhelm me. I marvel at how the pain can be so fresh, so stark even after nearly a year. I ache for Eidr's arms, to bury my face beneath his beard and take in the scent of him. I long for Yske, for how we would lean against one another on cold winter nights, for the sound of her voice rising into the rafters of the Hall of Smoke.

Now Sixnit crouches before me, her face lined with compassion. As I squint through my tears, my eyes snag on the baby strapped across her chest. This is not Vistic – no, Sixnit's growing son remains, for now, with Omaskat on the shores of the White Lake. This infant is entirely other, her eyes closed beneath a fan of snow-white lashes. Ogam's lashes.

Nisien is not far behind Sixnit, one hand holding Cadic's bridle as he scans the empty village.

The other woman takes my hands. "Come, Hessa. It's time to go home."

Another summer passes. Another autumn.

The fire burns low. I take a handful of sage from the bowl at my side and toss it into the flames, where it curls and blackens. Smoke lifts the heady scent over the assembled inhabitants of East Meade and on into the high, dark rafters.

The Eangen watch, their hush disturbed only by the crackle of the fire, the howl of winter wind and the brush of heavy clothing. They are a rugged lot, these survivors, and so many faces are missing. But the meeting hall of East Meade is still full, bolstered by Soulderni refugees. Lathian and his court may be gone, but their absence has sent the Arpa Empire into turmoil. Danger continues to roam beyond the north.

My eyes linger on one Soulderni man. The dark curls of his beard and the smooth planes of his cheekbones are familiar, beginning to fill the gap in my soul where Eangi sisters and brothers once were. He is my friend, he is my confidant, and his presence strengthens me.

Nisien meets my gaze and smiles.

The child sleeping in my lap does not stir as I lean around her, her tiny forehead tucked into my stomach. Sixnit, next to me, brushes at the little girl's milky curls. Both anxiety and hope are written across my friend's face, but undergirding it all is love.

"Headwaters of Life, Weaver of the Stars. Pillar of the Four, Eternal, Unfaltering." My voice carries throughout East Meade's Meeting Hall, like Svala's once did through the Hall of Smoke, though now I pray to a different and true god. "We dedicate this child to you; a daughter wrought in the darkness of the Old World and born into the clarity of the New. Write her name upon your hands and prepare a place for her at your feet."

The crowd ripples as the doors of the hall open. A gust of winter breeze laces through the air and rustles the baby's hair.

The crowd parts for Omaskat, the Watchman of Thvynder. Eangen murmur and touch their foreheads in respect, eyes downcast. Others mutter their displeasure and retreat to the periphery of the Hall. The former gods now known as the Miri may have fallen or submitted, but millennia of worship have not faded overnight. The New Age comes gradually.

Ayo, who has been lying near my feet, rushes to her former master. Omaskat releases the hand of the small boy at his side and drops down to scratch Ayo between the ears. The boy's two golden eyes light upon the dog and he laughs a delighted, mortal sound that makes Sixnit's expression slacken with sorrow and... relief.

My friend leans forward and, in a voice that trembles with hope, she calls, "Vistic?"

The boy looks up. For a moment, I think he doesn't know Sixnit, and my heart aches for my friend. How could he remember? He was not even a year old when we left him with Omaskat at the White Lake.

But Vistic is no ordinary child. My breath hitches as he runs to Sixnit, toppling into her arms as she laughs and cries and strokes his Eangen black curls.

I stand and lift Sixnit's daughter up to my shoulder. She stirs, eyelids fluttering. As pale as her lashes are, her eyes are her mother's: green, twined with violet. Her gaze drifts up to my face, then her lashes close again.

Omaskat comes to a halt across the fire. His shoulders are level beneath a bearskin cloak, his stance easy. His golden eyes soften as he looks at us and, not for the first time, I wonder what he sees. The two women who loved and protected newborn Vistic? The Eangi who slew him, once, in the thrall of a usurper god?

Ayo sits against the Watchman's leg and, in Sixnit's arms, Vistic leans back to pat at her cheeks. "Mama," he pronounces.

Sixnit closes her over-bright eyes and, at her side, I swallow a great knot of happiness.

"Will you take him for a time?" Omaskat asks the other woman, drawing a few steps closer. "Our work in the north is finished and, for all that he is part of Thvynder, I would have Vistic know a normal life."

Sixnit gives a wordless, eager nod and Omaskat turns to face the assembly. As he does his eyes catch mine and he smiles, a private, knowing look that makes my heart swell. I smile back.

"Now," Omaskat raises his voice to carry across the Hall. "Thvynder accepts the dedication of the Daughter of Ogam, the Last Daughter of Winter. Hessa?"

I round the fire and hand the girl over. Omaskat holds her with the ease of a veteran father and passes his thumb gently over her tiny, bowed lips.

"With this daughter, the first generation of a new order will rise." Omaskat lifts his eyes towards me, weighing each word with meaning. "A new breed of warrior-priestesses, and priests, to protect you."

The occupants of the Hall are quiet, save for the whispers of a few curious children. Out of the corner of my eye, I see my sister Hulda sit forward in her woven chair. Her calculating eyes, so like our mother's, wander between Omaskat, Ogam's daughter and me.

Omaskat continues to speak to the assembly, but my vision fades and his voice grows distant. East Meade is gone, and I drift back to a high mountain meadow, where poppies sway under a gathering sky, a shrine lies forgotten, and a man with red hair waits patiently in the forest.

Back in the Hall, I hear Sixnit raise her voice in the first notes of a song. It draws me back into the Waking World, a mixture of old tune and new words, but it sounds right; as if our melodies have finally found the right lyrics. The people join in and eventually, Omaskat does too. His voice is deep and warm, rumbling through my bones. He stands in the midst of us, cradling Sixnit's daughter, as Sixnit cradles Vistic.

My hand drifts up to my naked throat. My skin is smooth under my fingers and, I find, I do not miss my Eangi collar.

I part my lips and begin to sing.

THE END

GLOSSARY OF NAMES

A

Addack – The Eangen province on the western coast.

Aegr (*Ahy-ger*) – The eternally wounded bear healed by Liv, daughter of Risix.

Aita (*Ahy-tah*) – A God of the New World. The Great Healer.

Albor – The town in which the Hall of Smoke is built. Albor, with Iskir, is one of the main centers of Eangi activity.

Algatt – The land, and the people, of Gadr, the God of the Mountain. Raiders, they reside in the mountains north of Eangen.

Aliastros (*Al-ee-ah-stros*) – A member of the Arpa Pantheon. A god of wind.

Ama – An Eangen woman of Albor.

Amdur – The people of Dur, a subordinate god to Eang. A central Eangen people.

Apharnum – The capital of the Arpa Empire, where the Temple of Lathian and its hidden well of power resides.

Archeress, the – A God of the Old World.

Ardam – High Priest of Eang and the Eangi priesthood, War Chief of the Eangi, residing in the Hall of Smoke in Albor.

Arpa – The land and people of the great Arpa Empire, who control much of the known world.

Ashaklon (*Asha-klon*) – A God of the Old World.

Athiliu (*A-thil-ee-oo*) – Commander of the Ilia Gates, 1st General of the Outer Territories of the Arpa Empire.

Ayo (*Ey-oh*) – Omaskat's dog.

B–C

Berin – Hessa's father.

Binding tree – A tree in which an unnatural beast, being, or a god is imprisoned.

Boilingbrook – A location south of Mount Thyr, right on the Arpa border.

Cadic – Nisien's mare.

Castor – An Arpa legionary, son of a senator.

Ceydr (*Kee-der*) – A Soulderni man. Husband of Silgi, relative of the horseman Nisien.

Climb of Atonement – A pilgrimage to Eang's holy ground which an Eangi must undertake after breaking a sacred law or displeasing the goddess.

D–E

Dur – God of the Amdur people, a central Eangen clan.

Eang (*Eeng*) – A God of the New World who rose to be the strongest and most influential of the New Gods. Goddess of War and patron of the Eangen people.

Eangen (*Een-gehn*) – The people and land devoted to Eang.

Eangi (*Een-gee*) – The order of warrior-priests who serve Eang and protect the Eangen people.

Eangi Fire – The power that Eang blesses an Eangi priest or priestess with via a shard of her own life-force, tied to the blood of the Eangen people.

East Meade – A town on the western foot of Mount Thyr. The birthplace of Hessa.

Eidr (*Ee-der*) – Hessa's husband, an Eangi warrior-priest.

Eiohe (*Eye-oh-heh*) – An ancient, forgotten deity.

Erd (*Air-d*) – Albor's village blacksmith.

Esach (*Ee-sak*) – Goddess of Storms and Harvest.

Estavius – An Arpa legionary, son of the High Priest of Aliastros and a devotee of that god.

Etha – (*Ee-tha*) – Hessa's youngest sister.

Euweth (*Yew-weth*) – A Soulderni woman of the Ridings. Mother of the horseman Nisien, cousin to Ceydr.

F–G

Fate – Also called the Weaver, Fate was once a deity and now exists in a non-corporeal state, weaving the patterns of time and destiny for all.

Frir (*Fr-eer*) – Goddess of Death, sister of Eang. Aunt to Ogam.

Gadr (*Gad-derr*) – God of the Mountain, god of the Algatt people and land. A God of the New World, peer to Eang.

Galger – One of Eang's set of legendary axes, Galger and Gammler.

Gammler – One of Eang's set of legendary axes, Galger and Gammler.

Geda (*Gee-dah*) – A sister of Eang, executed for a grave betrayal. Her final breaths were used to give life to Eang's owl messengers.

Gilda – An eastern province of Eangen and a town.

Gods of the New World – Begotten by the Gods of the Old World, the Gods of the New bound or slew their predecessors and reshaped the world for themselves.

Gods of the Old World – The original gods, who begot the Gods of the New World and all other beings in creation.

H

Hall of Smoke – The foremost hall of the Eangi priesthood, located in Albor in the south of Eangen.

Hall of Vision – The secondary hall of the Eangi priesthood, located in Iskir in the north of Eangen.

Headwaters – The source of the river Pasidon.

Hessa – An Eangi warrior-priestess, born to Berin in East Meade, raised in the Hall of Smoke in Albor.

High Halls, the – The upper realms in which the Gods of the New World, the rivermen, the woodmaidens and various other beings dwell. In death, humans travel to the High Halls to tell of their living days and await the passing of loved ones. Then, they may lie down together for the Long Sleep in Frir's Realm of Death.

Hinterlands – The wasteland north of the Algatt Mountains.

Hulda (*Hull-dah*) – Hessa's eldest sister.

I

Iosas (*Ee-oh-sas*) – The half-Arpa son of Silgi, a devotee of Aliastros.

Ilia Gates – Lying south of Urgi, these gates form the northernmost outpost of the Arpa Empire. Commanded by Athiliu.

Iskir (*Isk-eer*) – A town and region in north-eastern Eangen.

Iskiri (*Iss-keer-ee*) – The people of Iskir. An Eangen clan.

J–L

Lathian – The Arpa Empire's God of Gods.

M–N

Melid – Hessa's mare.

Miri – The Gods of the Old World and the Gods of the New World.

Nisien (*Niss-ee-en*) – A Soulderni horseman, member of the mounted Arpa auxiliary.

O

Ogam (*Oh-gam*) – Immortal son of Eang and the elemental being Winter.

Omaskat (*Oh-ma-skat*) – A supposed Eangen traveler.

Orthskar (*Or-th-skar*) – A region, people, and large settlement in Northern Eangen.

Oulden (*Old-en*) – A God of the New World, God of the Soulderni people.

Oulden's Feet – The central place of worship for the Soulderni people.

P

Pasidon – The great river that flows from the Headwaters, down through Eangen and into the Arpa Empire.

Polinus (*Poe-lie-nus*) – An Arpa commander.

Q–R

Quentis – An Arpa priest of Lathian.

Ridings, the – The northern half of Soulderni, occupied by extensive grasslands and pastures.

Ried (*Ree-ed*) – A God of the New World who rebelled against Eang. He was slain and buried under the Hall of Vision.

Riok (*Ree-oak*) – Woodmaiden goddess of the Rioki people. One of Eang's court.

Rioki (*Ree-oak-kee*) – The central-most province and people of Eangen.

Rioux (*Ree-oo*) – A God of the Old World.

Risix (*Rih-six*) – A semi-deified descendant of woodmaidens.

Rivermen – A subclass of male, river-dwelling demi-gods begotten by the Gods of the Old World.

S

Shanich (*Shah-nick*) – A daughter of an Old-World goddess, bound originally by her own kin and rebound by Eang during the Eangen age.

Silgi (*Sill-gee*) – An Algatt woman, wife of Ceydr and a relative of the horseman Nisien.

Silver Seals – Creations of the rivermen.

Sixnit – An Eangi woman of Albor, wife of Vist.

Skay – Hessa's second-eldest sister.

Souldern (*Sol-dern*) – The land of the Soulderni people, occupied by the Arpa Empire.

Soulderni – The people of Souldern, devoted to the God of the New World called Oulden. Occupied by the Arpa Empire.

Spines, the – A natural border of rock formations between Eangen and Arpa-occupied Souldern.

Styga – A God of the Old World.

Svala – High Priestess of Eang and the Eangi priesthood, residing in the Hall of Smoke in Albor.

T

Telios – One of Nisien's superiors and patrons during the Southern Campaigns.

Thvynder (*Th-vin-der*) – An ancient deity.

Thyr, Mount – A mountain in south Eangen that looks over Albor and East Meade.

U

Unmaking of the World – The end of an era, when all that exists is unmade and the next era begins from smoke and ashes.

Urgi (*Er-gee*) – A town in southern Eangen, close to the Arpa border.

Uwi (*Yew-wee*) – A Soulderni girl, a second cousin to Nisien.

V

Vestige – A physical object or living being to which a god anchors their life in the Waking World.

Vist – An Eangi man, husband of Sixnit.

Vistic – Son of Sixnit and Vist.

W

Waking World – The material world in which human beings live and die.

Waystone – Markers which indicate villages, temples, and other landmarks on Eangen roads.

Winter – A reclusive, elemental god, father of Ogam and lover of Eang.

Woodmaidens – A subclass of female, forest-dwelling demi-goddesses begotten by the Gods of the Old World.

X–Z

Yifr (*Yif-fer*) – The drink with which elder Eangi travel spiritually to the High Halls.

Yske (*Yih-skah*) – Hessa's cousin and stepsister. An Eangi.

ACKNOWLEDGEMENTS

A few years ago, when I finished drafting *Hall of Smoke*, I'd no idea how many people would be involved in getting it to print. Even before this book came into being, I was blessed by a huge network of friends and family who supported my love of writing. As I put these acknowledgements on paper, I'm all the more grateful for them, for every single person who encouraged an eight-year-old to write down her stories, a teenager not to burn them, and a woman to push through another phase of editing.

First, I need to thank my wonderful agent, Naomi Davis for passionately representing me and *Hall of Smoke*, for your patience and guidance in every area of my career.

This book would be a shadow of what it is now without my editors George Sandison and Joanna Harwood, whose insight and suggestions took *Hall of Smoke* to an entirely new level. Thank you.

I'm so grateful for my copyeditor Hayley Shepherd, for helping me patch all the little holes in the manuscript, for Julia Lloyd, for creating *Hall of Smoke*'s truly epic cover, and for Adrian McLaughlin, who typeset the manuscript and made it beautiful. My publicity team, Lydia Gittins, Katharine Carroll, Polly Grice, and Julia Bradley, thank you so much for everything you've done and are doing to get *Hall of Smoke* out into the world.

To my dear friend Cheryl Bowman, reader of the most wretched drafts and encourager through the darkest times, nothing I write would be half what it is without you. Thank you for all the work you put into the runes and the languages of this book (much of it behind the scenes) and for hand-drawing the map in the back of the book.

To my beta readers, Loie Dunn, Jenny Anderson, Jean Malone, Milo Nelakho and Audrey Henley, thank you for slogging through my early drafts of your own free will, for your insightful criticism, for celebrating my wins and helping me believe in this book through the query trenches.

To Genevieve Gornichec, Mallory Kuhn and all the talented debut authors of my 2020 and 2021 author groups, thank you so much for sharing your wisdom and for being there throughout all the highs and lows of the debut journey.

Now, my family. When I tried to write out all you've done it took up far too many pages, so I hope you feel the weight of the simpler words I've chosen here.

Mum and Dad, thank you for always encouraging and nudging my career forward, for reading to me, for the audiobooks and trips to the library that sparked my love of reading and taught me how to write.

Eric, thank you for teaching me to take my writing and my dreams seriously, for listening to my rambles about plot, for editing and proof-reading, and never letting me give up.

To my grandparents, Ian and Janet, Ruth and Bill: Thank you for always showing an interest in my writing, for reading my stories and encouraging me, for loving me and always being such a constant, stable source of support.

Lastly, my brilliant, nerdy husband Marco. Thank you for giving me the opportunity and the security to seriously write, for celebrating me, helping me through every challenge, and being the cheerful victim in the choreography of so many fight scenes. I love you.

ABOUT THE AUTHOR

H. M. Long is a Canadian writer who loves history, hiking, and exploring the world. She lives in Ontario, but can often be spotted snooping about European museums or wandering the Alps with her German husband. *Hall of Smoke* is her first novel.

For more fantastic fiction, author events, exclusive excerpts,
competitions, limited editions and more

VISIT OUR WEBSITE
titanbooks.com

LIKE US ON FACEBOOK
facebook.com/titanbooks

FOLLOW US ON TWITTER
@TitanBooks

EMAIL US
readerfeedback@titanemail.com